Queen of the Universe

A NOVEL BY
Pia Wurtzbach

T0026305

TUTTLE Publishing
Tokyo | Rutland, Vermont | Singapore

Contents

Media Noche

It's a couple of hours before midnight, and we're giving you the top hit songs that made it to billboard this year!

We are live here at the seaside boulevard with the famous band Ace of Spades! As you can see behind me, people crowd the area as we count down the hours to midnight. Back to you, Jing.

As an actress, I'm looking forward to the coming year. I've got so many plans in store for all of you! So, you guys should watch out for them!

The 2020 Pantone color of the year is classic blue. It's calming and has a sense of familiarity. It's a timeless shade of blue.

"**Y**ou believe that?"

Cleo raises an eyebrow at her sister, Anne, whose mouth is stuffed with *lumpiang shanghai*. Bits of the spring roll's ground pork are stuck on her chin. Just the thought of *lumpiang shanghai* has Cleo drooling over it, and now she's tempted to get one, too. Imagining it, she can already taste its yummy sweet goodness, especially when dipped in ketchup.

"What?" Anne asks, fixing her full bangs on display and acting innocent because she's not supposed to eat anything until the clock strikes twelve.

Cleo touches her chin. "You have something on your chin."

Anne takes a tissue and wipes her chin clean. "We should just eat, instead of watching this *feng shui* expert tell you your whole life."

"There's no harm in believing," Cleo replies. Besides, she's already wearing a classic blue polka dot dress. And she also likes the color, a sea of tranquility, a canvas of serenity. It makes her wonder if this classic blue can bring her good luck in the coming year.

"Classic blue," Anne muses as she flops down on the couch next to Cleo, taking Candy, their Shih Tzu, onto her lap. "That's something we can agree on. I think it suits you, but really, you should stop watching someone decide what's good or what's bad for you. You're the only one who can determine your fate."

Oh, if only life had Anne's positive outlook and youthful appearance. Instead, life had Cleo's lousy luck. Should she toss a coin right now, no matter what she chooses—tails or heads—the coin has a higher probability of spinning mid-air than landing on the floor and showing her the result.

"Let's just watch this part. I've got a good feeling about this coming year," Cleo says without looking at Anne. Their eyes are both glued to the TV as some *feng shui* expert keeps talking about the year of the metal rat. Candy wags her tail as she listens too.

"The year of the metal rat is deemed to be a year of new beginnings and renewals. It will be good for those taking advantage of the opportunities happening this year, but it will also be a challenging year ahead. Some may notice slow progress in their plans and projects, but it's only a call for everyone to cultivate enough confidence and strength to bring a successful result."

Cleo listens intently to the T.V., mentally nodding in agreement with the Chinese Astrology Prediction this year. It's become her ritual, listening to predictions at the end of the year, so she has something to look forward to in the coming one.

"Geez, Leo. You might end up replacing that *feng shui* expert," Anne warns.

If Cleo were to be a *feng shui* expert, she'd give everyone a good year ahead. A few bumps here and there, but other than that, they'll get everything they want. Want to win in the lottery? No problem, she'll give random numbers. Are they praying for good grades? She'll give you a memory retainer medicine. Are they dreaming of being rich? Then, she can look for a *team* of skilled robbers to steal from the bank. Predictions are such life scams, but people will believe them anyway because they love gambling against the invisible force of fate.

And Cleo? She's one of the most scammed beings on God's green earth. She's beginning to think she's gambling against the devil—whoever stops betting loses.

"They're coming," Anne says, switching the channel to the top hits music countdown.

Cleo sighs. Of course, they are. There's no New Year's Eve without family gatherings in the Philippines. It's a known fact that all Filipinos love family gatherings, except for Cleo. Don't get her wrong. She loves her relatives, but there are times when they're overbearingly intrusive. And when they're not, they can make her feel ordinary and insignificant. There's no middle ground when it comes to them, she's either well-praised for her efforts, or she just doesn't know what she's doing in her life.

It's New Year's Eve, Cleo reminds herself. Surely her relatives will be more pleasant this time around. Cleo stands up and helps her mom, Thea, prepares the *Media Noche*, or as she likes to call it: Midnight Snacks.

"*Ma*, at around what time will they be here?" Cleo asks as she looks over their black smoked glass dining table, spotting sticky rice cakes like *biko* and *suman*. "Isn't this too much?"

Thea, Cleo's mother, crosses her arms. "Nothing is ever too much in family gatherings. Sticky rice cakes will improve the bonds and relationships of the family. *Pahalagahan mo ang* "

"*Pamilyang meron ka*," Cleo finishes for Thea. "Yes, *Ma*. I know. Family should be given importance and not be taken for granted, but they're not even going to clean the plates afterward."

At the end of the party, Cleo also expects that there will be leftover food for three days' worth of eating. She doesn't eat any new food until the leftovers have been consumed. It's re-heat, repeat, and eat. That's just how celebrations are. Festivities have always been so big and grand in the country that Christmas begins on *Ber* months, overlapping with New Year's Eve and lasting almost until the Feast of the Three Kings.

"They should arrive at any time now. They're just around—" Thea quickly drops the banana leaves on the table when they all hear the loud yelling of none other than Cleo's loud uncle: *Tito Allan.* "They're here."

Cleo turns to Thea and sees how delicately motherish she is even with her cake-flour-covered apron, messy bun jet-black hair, and panicked look. Both Thea and Anne are a ray of sunshine, but her mom's softer and more affectionate, save for the times when she's really up for giving a good scolding like when the kids forgot to bring the Tupperware back home from school when they were young. On the other hand, Anne's heart-shaped face and happy-go-lucky personality make everything about her sweet instead of Cleo's calm, restful face and spontaneity.

Cleo just can't make up her mind most of the time, but when she finally decides on something, there's no changing her mind. She also comes off as too strong, which, to some people, might be a bad thing.

When she was in grade school, there was this boy she liked a lot, so she did everything to be just like the other pretty girls in the class. That boy told her she was pretty, but she didn't have fair skin like the others, so she did everything to make herself even more appealing. One morning, she came in with full makeup on—courtesy of her mom's makeup kit—but he ended up avoiding her. It turned out she looked like a clown, and ever since then, her confidence tended to vacillate. It was her first heartbreak. She envied the naturally sweet girls and, at one point, she even envied Anne. But then she realized that wasn't her. She wasn't going to greet everyone like Anne. She enjoyed her quietness and spur-of-the-moment-ness. And although the two sisters are opposites, they complement each other—Cleo weathers the storm while Anne navigates the way.

"*Ma!*" Anne calls out. "We'll get them!"

Cleo nods in agreement.

"Okay. Thank you, *mga anak.*" Thea smiles at her daughters.

"Don't sweat it, *Ma.* And no rush. New Year isn't going anywhere," Cleo responds, following Anne, who's already out on the porch and opening their rusting metal gate.

As soon as Cleo's out in the open area, she hears the loud uproar of *torotots.* She sees the colorful sparks of *lusis,* and the handheld fireworks lit by the children on the streets. Two houses away, she can already hear the drunken songs. A couple of guys at the karaoke are singing rather badly about giving their heart away last Christmas. Across from their two-story home, two Civic cars are already parked one behind the other, but Cleo's relatives, having no parking space, have decided to double-park.

"*Tito* Allan, I don't think—" Cleo begins.

Tito Allan wipes his eyeglasses with his shirt and places them on the bridge of his nose. "Is that you, Cleo? Why you're all grown up!"

She's all grown up to him because the last time they met each other was five years ago in the province of Pampanga, the hometown of her *Tito* Allan. He used to be an overseas Filipino worker—an OFW—so naturally, he missed a lot of celebrations, like the feast in his province every twelfth of May. It's the feast that honors the patron saint Sta. Maria of *Balen Bayu,* which translates to "New Town." The locals are called Kapampangan, a large ethnolinguistic group residing mainly in the central plain of Luzon, and they speak Kapampangan, one of the major dialects in the country. And although she can't understand the dialect, Cleo likes to listen to them. After all, the Philippines is home to so many unique and distinctive languages and dialects.

Feasts in provinces are not to be missed. Cleo remembered watching the marching bands parade on the streets and having boodle fights in the afternoon with everyone as they visited one home after another. It's great because she can also see the ancestral houses like the *Bahay Kubo* or Nipa Hut and the brick-tile roofing and wooden walls that used to house the Spaniards during their occupation of the country. And then, at night, she and her cousins would go to the *perya*, a fair teeming with games and rides. Sadly, she got busier with work, so she didn't have that much time to travel to Pampanga. But fortunately for her, when *Tito* Allan went on retirement last year, he promised everyone he'd be there for every occasion. She barely knows the man, but she knows he misses home, so she really can't blame this overly-excited lively character when he visits any of them.

Cleo puts the double parking aside. She'll just talk to their neighbor and let *Tito* Allan know if the car needs to be moved somewhere. Then, one by one, her relatives come out of the car. There's her godmother: *Ninang* Erlina; her godfathers: *Ninong* Arjun and *Ninong* Ray; her aunts: *Tita* April, *Tita* Angela, and *Tita* Jennie; her younger cousins: Juan, Carlo, Ashley, and Amber.

🐜 🐜 🐜

Cleo does the *pagmamano* as a sign of respect and honor, making this traditional greeting to her aunts and uncles. She takes the hand of *Ninang* Erlina, her godmother, and presses it to her forehead.

"*Mano Po*," Cleo says.

Ninang Erlina replies, "God bless you."

Cleo gives the greeting to all her aunts, uncles, godmothers, and godfathers—anyone who's older than she is—well, except for *Tita* April. Her aunt refuses the *pagmamano* because she thinks it'll make her older. Though *Tita* April is in her late thirties, she looks like she's still in her late twenties, with all the whitening and anti-aging creams she slathers on her face every morning.

"You know me, Cleo. I'm forever young," *Tita* April says in high spirits, tucking a strand of her bronze-highlighted hair behind her ear. "Is that Candy? Come here, girl!"

Candy, always playful with everyone, goes to *Tita* April, licking her face. Cleo considers her *Tita* April a millennial *Tita*. She's the kind of aunt who'll invite you to parties and make you chug down a huge bottle of beer. But she tries not to drink so much now. Her beer belly's showing, and it's making her self-conscious whenever she goes to the beach with her friends.

"We brought round fruits!" *Tita* Jennie announces the basket of oranges, grapes, and apples in her arms. "It's a *kiat kiat*."

Juan, Cleo's seven-year-old cousin, quickly takes one *kiat kiat* from *Ninang* Erlina. "Yay, small orange!"

Juan has always loved anything small. Cleo thinks it's probably because he's so small, himself. He's really cute, with his button nose. Anne takes him along with the rest of their younger cousins inside. She's always been good with kids. It comes instinctively to her since she's a preschool teacher. She handles the kids while Cleo handles the adults. And with so many people in the house, their hands can hold only some of them at a time.

Inside the house, Cleo gives their guests home slippers to change into. Once they're all settled, she neatly arranges their shoes in the shoe rack. Back in the living room, her aunt and godmothers are talking about the latest love teams in show business, or as they like to call it: showbiz. She likes to call them the *Titas* of Manila.

"I heard Jerrie broke up!" *Tita* April starts, disappointed that her favorite love team of three years has just broken up. "JerLie's supposed to get married soon. I saw it on Nellie's Instashot story!"

Tita Jennie butts in, pulling her brand-new designer bag onto her lap. Her newly manicured nails are lustrous and popping. The golden hoops in her ears must have been costly. She's always been the high-end *tita*. "I think it's her mom who's getting married and not her."

"Why are you so surprised? Celebrities break up all the time.

Don't you have anything else to talk about besides their love lives?" *Tita* Angela says bitterly, her graying hair tied in a bun. And unlike *Tita* April and *Tita* Jennie, who are fashionably dressed in a maxi and a wrap dress, she's clad in a duster, a long and loose-fitting home dress.

Cleo knows her *Tita* Angela won't admit to it, but the reason why she's always bitter when it comes to love stories is that she's an old maid. Cleo bets that's why she's always frowning and scolding the children too.

"It's just that they started in a reality show! And now they're here," *Tita* April responds, obviously saddened by the news.

"And now they're not," *Ninang* Erlina adds. "There's still Selene and Jake—the dazzling golden couple!"

Cleo doesn't listen much. She lets their conversation drone along, Lil Nas' "Old Town Road" blasting on the TV. It's not even five minutes since Cleo helped *Tito* Allan set up the drinks table before *Tita* Angela comes out with, "Why, you're too skinny, *hija*."

Cleo knows her godmother is referring to her because Anne has already quietly retreated upstairs with the kids, murmuring, "And that's my cue."

Anne doesn't want anyone to comment on her figure. She's said it many times before: she's getting a bit rounder than she used to be. But if anyone's allowed to comment on her physique, it can only be Anne herself. Without Anne around, Cleo's the one to be subjected to her aunts' and godmother's scrutiny.

"And too brown, too dark," *Tita* Jennie adds, touching Cleo's skin with her index finger. "I mean, Thea has great skin. She does, but everyone wants whiter skin now."

Candy barks at *Tita* Jennie as if she can understand her and is defending Cleo.

"Maybe that's why you don't get so far in life, *hija*," *Tita* Angela suggests.

"Yes, yes! Oh, if only she had her father's white skin," *Tita* Jennie agrees.

Tita April cuts them off. "Give her a break! She's pretty even without some of her father's American features."

Nobody even bothers to ask Cleo what she likes. They always assume what looks good on her. But the thing is, what looks good on her may not be what she likes at all. She loves her brown skin, as earthy as it is. And she's always been comfortable in it. Her skin has been her income and her familiy's for a decade and more, with her modeling jobs. She hustles hard for the family.

It's New Year's Eve, Cleo chants in her mind, trying not to talk back. Talking back is considered disrespectful, so she'll just be the bigger person. It just happens that long ago, someone invented family reunions so relatives can insult young women's bodies and complexions and talk about their failures. Who cares? She can let it slide. She's good at ignoring their jabs. But her mother? Not so much. Thea's bothered by all of this.

After hearing all this picking, Thea stands up and heads for the kitchen. Cleo follows her mother and helps her out instead of staying with the guests. No words are spoken between them. It's just Cleo helping Thea set the *embutido*, meatloaf stuffed with eggs, vegetables, and other meat inside, on platters. The TV's ringing out loud with party music, and she's still thinking about her skin and her father. She takes a glance out the door and sees the V.J. of the music channel happily chatting with the rising Original Pinoy Music (OPM) artists.

"Can you take the *embutido* to the dining table, please?" Thea asks, now washing the dishes.

Cleo can offer to wash the dishes, and she should, but a part of her knows her mom is just using it as an excuse to not be in the same room as her siblings, who only talk about the past.

"Sure, *Ma*." Cleo takes the *embutido* on the table and stares at the TV screen again. In the bottom right corner screen: a digital timer, counting down from 60. It's three hours before midnight, and she's hungry. But she can't eat until the clock strikes midnight.

So, Cleo sits down with her relatives and pretends she's interested. Partly, she is, but only because she'd rather listen to them talk about other celebrities than about her and her mother. And half an hour later? They're still chattering about it. They're relentless, and she's bored. She feels like her ears are about to fall off.

Thankfully, a call from Cleo's talent agency gives her an excuse to leave the room. Going outside where her drinking uncle and godfathers are talking, she takes the call.

"Hello?"

"Happy New Year! Guess what? Your flip-flop commercial will air a few minutes before midnight on ABS!".

Is Cleo hearing her right?

Minutes before midnight? It's fantastic. Her usual New Year's Eve has just become interesting. Suddenly, she doesn't mind her relatives and their tactless comments. It's perfect that they're here to witness her stardom. She's not just a model in print ads—she's now a brand ambassador of the national flip-flops! Her cup's running over with excitement and joy.

"Happy New Year to you too, Ms. Aika!" Cleo practically squeals at her agent. "Oh, wow!! This is the *best news*! Thank you!"

What a way to welcome the New Year! Cleo hangs up, grabs the remote and clicks through the channels. Her relatives don't mind. They're busy talking about celebrities. Quickly, she slides through her phone contacts and starts texting Owen.

TsineLAST—Flip-Flops That Last (And Hopefully Cleo's Career Will Too)

O wen Velazco is mindlessly drinking wine as the night drags on. He's bored to death, and his necktie feels too tight. Tugging it loose, Owen looks around and sees endless and nonsensical chatterers. He's celebrating New Year's Eve in a posh five-star hotel again. Just like last year. And the years before that. Dinner's about to come out, but his mother, Reyna, is complaining to the server about the bland chicken paella she had last time she was here, which was only two days ago.

"Tell me the main course won't be that dry and bland," Reyna says, pulling out a compact mirror and sliding her hand through her glitzy hair. She is a force to be reckoned with in a white sheath dress and diamond-studded earrings and necklace.

"I assure you, madam, our food is of the highest quality. Let us know if there's anything else we can do for you," the server replies, giving Reyna a new table napkin.

Owen smiles at the server. "Thank you."

"So, Reyna, this is Kate, my eldest daughter. She just came back from the States after taking her Master's degree in Business Administration," Vina boasts. Vina is of their family's elite. She has a lot of retail shoe stores in the metro, but that's only because took the business over from—or more like away from—her former partner, also her former best friend. Elaiza did all the work, but since Vina's the high-profile one, she rebranded the business with her name and image. Now, Elaiza works under her instead of working *with* her.

Nobody talks about Vina's underhandedness. If it ever comes up in conversation, she simply covers up or glosses over the truth. It's what she's good at, and it's what Owen, his family, and everyone in this party is good at—pretending that lies are as good as the truth because it makes them great and powerful. They're the masters of smoke and mirrors. But the truth is the truth. So, while everyone applauds Vina as a shrewd businesswoman, what she did to her former partner still makes her a dishonest one.

Owen knows this because Reyna persevered to take her own business to the elite level that has made her as proud as she is. She started her real estate business from scratch and trusted no one but herself. So, Reyna justifies her lavish spending with her truth: she started from the bottom, and now she's here. She got even richer when she married Luis, the CEO of Sta. Isabel Land Inc., one of the country's top ten real estate companies. The couple eventually merged their companies, forming the world-class agency Time Properties. And now Owen's brother, Mark and sister Sheila, are groomed for it—to sit in the same conference room as their father, to build an empire.

"Hello, dear," Reyna greets Kate. Kate looks shy and anxious. "Have you met my youngest son, Owen?"

While Owen doesn't like this maneuver, he has no choice but to play along. Reyna knows he has a girlfriend, but that doesn't stop her from urging him to try "better options," as she calls it.

"Nice to meet you, Kate," Owen says, smiling at Kate.

"He's dashing, isn't he?" Reyna teases Kate.

Kate blushes, and Owen offers her a seat. "He is."

Owen doesn't have a clue as to why he's so dashing in this suit and tie. Standard. Repetitive. Or maybe because he's always at the same party.

"Well, I'm sure what's even more dashing right now is your booming business, Reyna," Vina comments.

Reyna nods, obviously in agreement with Vina's assumption. "Mark and Sheila are learning the ropes. We want them to take on the role of V.P. or director. We also want them to take over in the future, of course. But right now, my husband and I are still thriving, and retirement is still far off the plan."

Reyna's always been proud of Mark and Sheila. Their parents' golden children. And Owen? Well, he's Owen.

"Wow! They're such a great duo! Are you sure they're not twins?" Vina takes a sip of her wine, smiling a fake smile with her poison-apple-painted lips. She's always been envious of how successful Mark and Sheila are. Deep down, Vina wants Kate to be just like Sheila. But Owen has a feeling she's starting to rethink her plans. It'd be financially better for her if Kate were to marry someone in the Velazco family.

"They're not." Reyna rolls her eyes like she's tired of answering the question over and over again. "They're unique individuals. No shared anything but our genes."

Vina pretends to ignore the swagger and quickly turns her eyes to Owen. "How about Owen?"

Owen can tell Kate's interested, too. She's looking at him after staring at her empty plate for five minutes. She's curious about him but is too shy to ask him, so she lets her mother do the talking. Too bad he's not interested. It's not that she's not pretty—she is, but no one compares to his girlfriend, Cleo.

"I think Kate wants to get to know him a little," Vina adds, knowing all too well that the family's weak link is Owen.

"Oh, Owen!" Reyna gushes. "He's doing *wonderfully*. In his last year of architecture school, working almost around the clock. Going to be able to design the projects we build!"

Just then, Mark and Sheila arrive at the table, dressed for the occasion. Mark rolls his sleeves and checks his watch. "We're just in time for dinner. Sorry, we're late, mom. We just got back from a last-minute meeting with a client overseas."

"What great kids! We're just talking about Owen and his dream of being an . . . what do you call it?" Vina asks.

Vina likes to play dumb.

"An architect," Sheila answers, winking at Vina. "He'll be an architect soon. He's reviewing for his board exams. We're proud of him. It's his own thing."

"Yes, it's a good job, isn't it? He'll design houses, and we'll work on them," Mark confirms.

All this gushing alienates Owen It would be great to hear, if it were true. It's family propaganda. But he keeps his cool. He smiles, letting them do the talking as he keeps Kate company. Even then, it's not just Kate he has to entertain, but other daughters of this and that friend. He knows these people are only interested in him because of his family, but he respects their daughters, so he just nods at whatever they're saying, spacing out during conversation. He gazes across the banquet room to the long buffet and watches the server arrange their New Year's five-course meal. Midnight's not far off.

Needing a break, Owen stands up and says, "Let me get you a drink, Kate."

"Sure." Kate smiles at him, her confidence deflated as she has noticed the many other eligible young ladies vying for his attention.

Owen pulls out his phone and reads Cleo's text on his way to the servers. her commercial will air minutes before midnight! He's genuinely happy for her. It quickly pulls him out of his dark mood. He eagerly replies.

🪶　🪶　🪶

Minutes later, Cleo gets a response from Owen.

Owen Velazco (9:45 p.m.)
"Maligayang Bagong Taon! *Wow, I'll stay tuned to it. I love you.
P.S. I knew you could do it. You always do.*

Cleo smiles, humming a song to herself; she turns around and calls for everyone's attention. "The commercial I'm starring in . . . will air tonight!"

Everyone in the living room falls silent. Cleo knows disbelief when she sees it. They can talk on and on about celebrities and their friends, but they think Cleo's just riding on her father's fame. Everett Walter, an acclaimed director around the world. After all, that last name is the reason why Cleo's sort of famous. They probably think she has no pride at all in actually being on the same path as her father.

Cleo can do things on her own. She's a girl who works hard, and soon, they won't be talking about Selene and Jake or JerLie. Soon, she'll be the talk of the town—a star.

After the brief silence, Cleo's aunts and godmother pull her into the middle, crowding her and asking her questions and probing for information. They're loud and persistent, and for the first time, she doesn't mind their booming voices. Being huddled over feels terrific. To be bombarded with requests.

"So, Cleo, how'd you get this opportunity?" *Tita* Jennie asks, now curious about her career.

"Let me show you something. Just a sec." Cleo opens her phone and skims through her photos and videos. Eventually, she finds her audition reel. She shows it to them as they pass the phone from one person to another to get a better look at it.

The reel features Cleo showing off every bit and part of her skin. She looks daring, bold, and confident and everyone admires the sight except for *Tita* Angela. *Tita* Angela scolds her, "You should cover up your skin! Are you sure this commercial of yours isn't for a condom brand?"

Just in time, Anne, with all the kids in tow, has just come down to get some drinks. When they heard the commotion, they all settled in the living room to hear about Cleo's commercial. Anne tries to pacify their aunt while Cleo laughs and continues her story. "It all started in November last year . . . ."

Getting a call back was like winning the lottery, and Cleo Walter might have just won her lucky number combination. But it wasn't just any game of luck; it was an effort in every possible way. It was almost like buying three-in-one t coffee sachets in the supermarket every chance you got in hopes of getting the winning scratch card—well, you know what they say: more entries, more chances of winning, that was what Cleo did. She didn't stop auditioning, and she finally got the winning scratch card!

Some people might say, *oh, big deal. It's just a callback*. If Cleo could poll the cast of every film, TV, and play about that little remark, there would be a massive revolution against people who think casting calls are beneath them. The audition was a demanding process—both for the hopeful actors vying for a part and for those whose job it was to screen and filter them. It was this laborious task that moved the entire show and ensured that the character was genuinely alive on the screen or the stage. Cleo thought about what it must have been like to audition to play the revered *Darna*, that Filipino superhero whose earthly name was *Narda*. She represented the diversity of Filipino women, the power of a woman to be both soft and firm. An ordinary person and a superhero. An icon.

And that was what Cleo wanted to be—an icon. A brand in her own right. Rain or shine, she went through countless auditions, waiting in long lines at the mall and befriending talents so she could get a second or two of screen time. Some *auditioners* from the remote provinces even slept outside the mall to save time and money. But, just like Cleo, they came because they all wanted fame, the name, and the spotlight. It was a promising dream.

Cleo could already imagine a dazzling future for herself. She would be in gossip magazines and on billboards as she starred in rom-com *teleseryes*. Going to shoots every day without commuting in *EDSA*, the highway around Manila that was constantly jammed with hellish traffic, would also be a blessing and a privilege that only the rich could afford. And rich she wasn't. Yet.

"I will have this," Cleo whispered under her breath as she sat on the green plastic chair along with four others who also got the callback. Okay, maybe it wasn't the lottery jackpot yet, but it was close enough. It was getting four numbers right out of six.

"Hey, have you heard?" said one girl in a flimsy outfit who was calling out to a woman with newly-made French tips. "We're the last-minute callbacks. The original girl has decided to back out because she got accepted into Elle's elite beauty camp!"

Cleo didn't care. Whoever the original girl was, Cleo wanted to thank her. The original girl gave five others a chance to be in her position. Cleo would try her hardest to be the right person for the upcoming *teleserye* about a high-powered woman in a criminal family.

Just then, the talent coordinator came out and called her name, "Cleo Walter. Please proceed inside."

Cleo had no idea if luck was with her that day, but she would give it all she had. Inside the room she was greeted, sort of, by two men in suits. Both had their faces in their phones. They didn't bother to check her name or where she came from; they just told her to act like a strong woman. Cleo did her best to appear strong as she read her lines. She delivered with what she hoped sounded like conviction and a hint of vindictiveness.

"We want this strong woman to look like she's the alpha of the pack—ruthless and fierce," said one of the guys as he scrutinized her face.

Minutes ticked by, but Cleo still couldn't get a grasp on what they wanted her to be. She had the face, but they said she was too stoic. She had to be extreme: too angry, too sad, too powerful. But all she could show was a flat emotion, cold and unfeeling. She really was trying. Her face was made for this kind of character, so why couldn't she get it right?

"That's terrible! So, what happened?" *Tita* Erlina gasps.

Cleo shrugs it off and says, "Rejection, and I go way back. But you know what they say. Keep going no matter what. Onward and upward. One thing I know for sure is this year will be life-changing for me."

Tita April gets a beer, raises it, and shouts, "Claim it, Cleo! You are a star in the making!"

Candy barks in agreement while Cleo accepts a beer from *Tita* April, who is pushing for more of the story. She smiles wryly at the memory of that audition. But before she can get any further with her tale, Cleo hears a rasping bang on their gates. She goes out and finds Owen outside, surrounded by the children with their *torotots*.

"Owen?"

Cleo's heart swells as she looks at her longtime boyfriend, even after years together, and finds herself yearning for him. Maybe it's his dark eyes—the night before Christmas that always keeps her on her toes with anticipation. Almost as if he knows what she's thinking about, he smiles goofily, looking all sorts of shy but also happy. He stands tall and proud of her from his suit and tie and stylized undercut hair. He kisses her cheek, and she sniffs to catch a whiff of his sweet mint scent.

"Why do you always do that?" Owen laughs at her, clasping her hand and lacing his fingers through hers.

"Force of habit."

Suddenly, *Tita* Angela breaks up the romantic scene. "Why is that boy here? Doesn't he have anywhere else to be right now? On New Year's Eve?"

Tita Angela's the kind of person who always assumes the worst of everyone. Owen has been a hot topic for her aunt for a long time now. She thinks Owen is just a snobby rich kid, selfish and frivolous. She doesn't know him, and that matters not at all. Because Cleo does know him.

Owen, ever the gentleman, does the *pagmamano* to Cleo's relatives who are coming out to greet him. When he reaches *Tita* Angela, he smiles sheepishly at her. He's always been like that—the good, soft boy vibe. He's the kind of person who can't seem to do anything wrong. Disarming. When she met him in college, Cleo was kind of surprised that he turned out to be different from his background. He was just . . . him—rich, famous, on good terms with everyone. But he wasn't friends with the wealthy students. He thought of them as his family's acquaintances. His *real* friends came from different walks of life: the janitor, the street vendor, and the *jeepney* driver. In the college, he was best friends with the students on scholarship. At first, Cleo thought he was just using them, and even felt a little hostile toward him because she was also riding on a scholarship. But she came to realize that she was wrong.

Owen is so much more than just his family's wealth and status. Cleo sees that. Everyone in her family except *Tita* Angela sees that.

Tita Angela has always warned Cleo to be wary of people who have all the good things in life because chances are, they're hiding something. But Cleo doesn't think about Owen's secrets, if he has any . . . . Whatever they are, she believes that love can always conquer any darkness.

"I've got my eyes on you, *hijo*," *Tita* Angela warns, her fierce eyes following Owen's figure as he respectfully retreats from her and proceeds to Cleo's uncles.

"It's okay, Angela. Owen's welcome here anytime," Thea says from the doorstep. "Come in, Owen."

Cleo knows that Owen considers Thea his second mother; he feels much more at home with her family than with his, so all is well.

"Don't mind, Angela. She's an old maid," *Tita* April teases. "Come celebrate with us."

"Sorry I turned up out of the blue. I just couldn't resist coming." Owen gave Cleo a look full of admiration, and smiled softly at the chorus of "Awwww" that came from her family. "And I've done my part at the hotel," he added, "so it's fine."

Cleo doesn't care why he came. He's here.

"He's a keeper!" *Tita* Jennie giggles, looking at her amethyst ring, a present from her last boyfriend, the closest one she'd had to a keeper.

"Anyway," Cleo cuts their chatter, pulling Owen into the living room. "I was just telling them how I got this commercial job."

"Yes, yes! So, what happened next?" *Ninang* Erlina asks impatiently, making Owen sit so Cleo can go on with the story.

Cleo then began to tell what happened next: on the way home, she thought she hadn't been so lucky, after all. But that was okay. Maybe she had assumed too much. But just as she was putting away her disappointment, she got a call from her talent agency.

"Cleo Walter, are you busy right now?" came the question from the other line.

Cleo hailed a tricycle outside the compound audition and paid twenty pesos to get to Quezon Avenue train station. She'd wanted to go to the nearest mall to do a grocery run before she went home, but apparently, her day was far from over. Inside the tricycle, trying to muffle the sound of whipping wind, she pressed her phone tightly against her ear.

"Not really, but I'm outside."

"Oh, okay. Well, I'd just like to check on your schedule for the first week of December. I sent your audition reel to this local brand called *TsineLast*—slippers that last—and they love it. Next year, they want to release a commercial. They want to launch their new campaign with a blast, and they want you. I know December is a busy month, but—"

"Of course!" Cleo exclaimed. She'd make herself free for any opportunity that came her way. And this was a local brand hoping to become an international one. Kind of like Cleo's hopes for herself. It felt like a match made in heaven.

"Great!" the agent said. "I'll let them know so they can schedule you for that week. Thanks, Cleo!"

Cleo was over the moon. She would star in a commercial for a local flip-flop brand—she would be the brand's ambassador! Sure, she'd had commercials before, but nothing like this, for a rising brand. An outstanding personal achievement because the general public always saw her as just an extra, a model—and the daughter of *Direk* Everett, the great German film director who'd made major films in the Philippines and all over the world. But she didn't want to be known as the great director's daughter. She wanted to be famous for herself alone, and not because of anyone else. Thrilled, she texted Owen.

Two weeks later, Cleo went to La Union, a province in the Ilo-cos region and a five-hour drive from Manila, for the commercial beach shoot. She'd thought of La Union as just a place to pass through on the way to Baguio City, the summer capital of the Philippines, but having visited the place, she realized it deserved more than a passing glance. In that province, the town of San Juan, well-known surfing capital of the Northern Philippines, was arresting, even under the cold December sky. The huge glittering waves were a breathtaking sight to see.

And the shoot? It went perfectly smoothly.

"Wow," *Tita* April says.

"The shoot was amazing," Cleo continues. "So—"

"It's almost time, isn't it?" Owen interrupts, and everyone swiftly finds a place to sit. Even Cleo's uncles and godfather have pulled their chairs inside so they can watch. *Tita* April puts Amber on her lap while she tells Juan, Carlo, and Ashley that Cleo will appear on the television; they're ecstatic, saying that, for sure, she'll be the next big star.

Everyone's treating Cleo like a queen. They think she'll make all their lives better. The aunts are planning the next reunion already—somewhere far and maybe out of the country. It'll be a good summer getaway, they say.

"We are so proud of you, *hija*," *Tita* Angela says, sounding pleased like she's never sounded before. "It's good that you're finally making something of yourself. I thought we'd never see you on the screen as the lead. Not that your premiere this week doesn't count."

"Come with me to Europe this year, Cleo! I'm sure my friends would like to get to know you," *Tita* Jennie offers, group-chatting with her foreign friends to let them know that she has a niece who's about to become a starlet.

Cleo feels pressured but, at the same time, accepts. This attention doesn't happen so often, so she basks in it, celebrates with them, and says yes, she'll be their star. Yes, she wants to go to Europe this year with her *Tita* Jennie. Yes, there will be more offers to come. And yes, she's also telling her previous co-talents that the commercial she featured in will air in a few minutes. She's a brand ambassador, and she likes it. Loves it.

Anne quiets everyone. "Shh!"

They keep their attention on the TV Everyone's phones are ready to capture the moment, so they can post it on social media and send it to their friends.

Fifteen minutes later, the commercial airs. It's five minutes before midnight. It's just in time. The commercial features the beach at sunset, silhouettes of the palm trees, and a woman walks on the beach. She has a great slim and toned figure.

Everyone's babbling and saying, "OMG! It's Cleo!"

"It's Cleo, isn't it?"

"Hi, guys! So that's my niece! She's Cleo Walter!"

And then on the TV: tight close-up—but not of Cleo, exactly. Of her feet. Barefoot on the sand. Then, magically, in the flip-flops. They're nice flip-flops. And a beautiful, shapely pair of feet, no question, but they could be anybody's—the commercial ends.

Total silence in the room. Nobody's speaking. Cleo feels like throwing up, but she tries not to. She got the role because they liked her for her great body and feet, but it's a flip-flops brand with beautiful decorative patterns. What did she expect? A close-up of her face? Now, she just feels ridiculous and stupid. Disappointment fills her, leaving nothing but a hopeless feeling.

Somebody switches the channel, and the reporter counts down to 10. "10 . . . 9 . . . 8 . . ."

It's okay. It's just a commercial, Cleo tells herself.

"7 . . . 6 . . . 5 . . . 4 . . ."

It really is okay; this will never bring her down. The thing about emotions is that they're not permanent; she might be sad now, but she's not going to be miserable for the rest of her life, and there are other things to look forward to in life.

"3 . . . 2 . . . 1 . . . *Maligayang Bagong Taon!*"

Tita April hands Cleo a beer and says, "Happy New Year, Cleo. Cheers!"

Cleo smiles as Owen squeezes her hand. She looks at him with renewed faith. "Cheers!"

"Cheers!" Owen has also taken a beer, drinking a toast to her. Everyone follows, quietly trying to forget what just happened.

CHAPTER 3

Check the Guest List, There's Always a Party Crasher

*e*verything is looking good so far. Better than that New Year's Eve, at least. Cleo feels like she's just warming up to the New Year. It can't be that bad, right? She still has an indie movie releasing this week. It might not be mainstream, but the story and concept are great.

Cleo got this lead because Owen had connections with some filmmakers—an indie production company called Out Of Club. They were young and new, but they had won international awards before. When they were ready to hold auditions, Cleo tried her luck. And they liked her, thinking the role would fit her because of the mystique that came with her so-called glacial face. She worked hard for it because she wanted to try indie films, thinking it might be the first step toward getting herself out there; on her own, with a production company that was also still starting. But then, she realized that maybe she needed to start somewhere else.

The indie film is called *Doll*. It's a horror- thriller film about a psychiatrist who has befriended a family with mental disorders in the asylum where she works. It's crazy and deep, which is what attracted Cleo to it.

So now Cleo's in the movie distributor's office, preparing invitations and doing last-minute posters. It's not all bad. Owen's picking her up for dinner later. Just as he always does—except he's much busier now because he's studying for his board exams. She feels sure he'll ace them and can't wait to celebrate with him.

"Hey, Cleo, should we invite your father?" one of the staff asks, holding out the invitation to her.

Cleo stops for a moment. She glances at the invitation before looking back at the young guy. "Well, of course, Patrick. Don't you invite the biggest director in the country?"

They know Cleo's story. Almost everyone knows her story. She's the daughter who didn't make the cut. She's not as good as her father. But she's used to that delicate question. She has to get used to it because they work in the same industry. Her father's circles may be different from hers, but their mutual acquaintances know about their relationship—if there actually is a relationship between the two of them. Because Cleo's afraid that there isn't.

Cleo thinks it's professional of her to invite her father, even if it some people think she's crazy for doing it. But really, she's asking him as a director. Her father is the most professional man in the world. He didn't involve her in his projects, especially not when he was still at home. He was a man she never really got to know. The man's a rock and as cold as an iceberg. He never once showed up during any of her ongoing *teleseryes* as extras, but she understood that. Why would he watch his daughter as an extra? That would ding his image, make him look soft, make him look like he has time to waste.

Overthinking this brings nothing but anxiety, so Cleo calls home. Anne picks up the second ring. "Hi, Anne."

"Hey, Leo!" Anne's the only one who calls Cleo. When they were young, they were told that their "auras" resemble a lion and a sheep—yes, Anne's the sheep. Their mother used to tell them that Cleo was always doing something every day, perfecting things that she couldn't do in the first place. She always tries, and when she tries, her cute little face becomes ferocious, which is adorable, according to Thea, who's obviously biased.

"You're free to talk right now?"

"Yes, sure. Still at school, but the kids are at recess. What's up?"

"Remember the indie movie I talked about before?" Cleo brings up the topic. "The one I'm starring in?"

"What kind of question is that?" Anne exclaims. "How could I forget, Leo? What about it?"

"It's premiering this Wednesday. I want you and *Ma* to come— if you're not busy."

"We'll come! Of course, we'll come! We'll always be there, for anything you do!" It's nice to hear Anne's excitement. Cleo can also hear a little girl crying.

"Oops, gotta go, Leo! Kids are at it again. Talk to you later!" Anne hangs up the phone, and Cleo goes back to check the invitations. It's a long day ahead, but it'll be worth it in the end.

🐝   🐝   🐝

Standing in his Manila office, Everett Walter looks over the commanding view of Manila. Twenty-five years ago, these high-rise buildings didn't exist. Looking out over the city from this height is as good as a trip to the park Makati. From where he watches, he can see a city in its own right, a city within a city, and thriving like crazy since it officially became urbanized in 1995. These days, hardly anyone gives a thought about what it was like before. They only know it as the city it is today.

Everett has kept pace with the city's rapid development pretty well. He came here when he was an aspiring director because it seemed like the only viable option, and it didn't fail him. It was a significant risk, and quite a learning curve. Looking down, he finds this city to be out of place in this country—the tallest skyscrapers built from the ground up, and the money it took to put them there. Yet, people pass through it like it's always been this way—this glittery, this fast-paced.

These musings are a stolen moment for Everett. Time is of the essence, as he always tells himself. If he wastes even a minute, he loses an hour's worth of productivity. But in his office, where no one else is around—no cameras, no reporters—he can finally loosen up.

Everett sits in his desk chair and closes his eyes. Finally, he's where he wants to be. Not much to do except to keep his reputation and image as good as always, if not better. Everett couldn't have achieved this success if it weren't for that determination. He is his own role model. He doesn't mean to sound arrogant, but his belief in his decisions and his confidence in himself have brought about the best possible outcomes in his work.

Now he's wondering what he'll be doing next. A new *teleserye*? That's one good possibility. He's already in the pre-production phase of his new movie in Alaska, and he hopes to enter it in the Colourette Film Festival in France. His life last year was one festival after another, so he's making this the last one for now. That'll give him some space to try different TV formats. In the past year, seemed to evolve a new approach that could work for a few different genres. Now he wants to put it to the test. It might fail, but it might also be his legacy.

A knock on the door interrupts his thoughts.

"Come in," Everett calls out.

Everett's assistant, Nicole, appears at the door looking as stressed as usual. She's got two phones in her hands, AirPods plugged in her ears as she talks to several people at once. People who need to get in touch with him. It's always him—*Direk* Everett. If he attends a premiere or a charity event, the producers get the boost they want. It's the kind of power and influence he enjoys and one he does not intend to lose.

"*Direk*, I have this week's invitations for you," Nicole hands the stack of invitations to Everett.

Everett looks at the invites: charity benefits, museum openings, and movie premieres. He sifts through until he stops at the still shot of his daughter—Cleo. She looks just as she always does: fierce and beautiful. With thick, lustrous coal-black hair and creamy almond skin, she's a sight to behold. She's always resembled her mother more than she does him. The only thing she inherited from him is height, a key asset to a model. But if she didn't get many of his physical features, she got his drive and ambitions. Otherwise, she wouldn't have made it this far.

It is and isn't a surprise to Everett to be receiving an invite from his very own daughter. He's never really been a father for her. He tried. He did. But she always needed a real, physical presence, and he's never been that. He admits he's been deficient that way, so now he's wondering about this invitation.

"This invitation to *Doll* here, are you sure it's for me?" Everett asks Nicole.

"Absolutely, *Direk*."

It was *for* Everett.

What was going on through his daughter's mind when she sent this? He stands there, turning it over and over in his head. If it came from Cleo, and not from the production company, who did she send it to? The director? Or her father?

🦋　🦋　🦋

It's almost midnight by the time Cleo is finished sending out invitations. Some have already confirmed attendance, but more than half haven't replied, probably don't even know if their schedules will allow them to come. It's killing her to send out those invites. She's a nobody with no awards to show. She's asking the starlets and directors to come to her premiere and hoping they'll come even if it's just because she's the daughter of *Direk* Everett. Because she just wants to be given a chance. And she won't ever have a chance if no one sees her.

Stretching out her arms, Cleo plunks herself down on the office chair, distraught by what she sent to her father. She tells herself for the nth time that it's about the movie. They're in the same line of work. Premiers, even for movies this small, common in this business, they're part of the job.

So why wouldn't she invite him? Whether he comes or not is up to him. At least she's done her part as an actress, and maybe, just maybe, she can even say as a daughter.

"Hey, Jay?" Cleo calls out.

Jay's the only one left in the office, and without him, all this sending of invitations would have been unbearable, impossible. Cleo wants to thank him with a coffee.

"Yes?" Jay replies as he types on the keyboard with his eyes focused on the monitor.

"Care for coffee?"

Jay leans back in his chair and turns it to face her. "You look beat, Cleo. You should go home. I can hold the fort until tomorrow."

Cleo clasps her hands together and smiles at him. "Let me at least buy you a coffee. You've been a lifesaver this whole day. I know what you're working on now is not as big as the other stuff you have going on, but I like this little film of mine."

"Don't worry about it, Cleo." He ties his long hair with the rubber band on his hand before smiling back at her. "It doesn't matter how big a movie is—what matters is how passionately you've played the role. I think everyone starts with something small. That's why I work here. That's why I'm working on your film. I want to see you start small."

There are still kind people in the world. Cleo has to stop beating herself up. She'll do great. If she doesn't, then it's okay. Little steps are still steps. She doesn't know what the future will bring, but she can always hope.

"Thanks so much for that, Jay." Cleo means it. She's grateful to passing strangers, co-workers, and colleagues who think she's worth something even though they don't know each other.

"Anytime, Cleo. So, here's the list of the attendees: Guinevere, a beauty queen and daughter of *Direk* Gary—he's almost as big as

Everett though not international; Jake, leading male TV star, son of *Direk* Gary and twin brother of Guinevere; Selene, Jake's leading lady in a movie Gary is about to shoot; Yeah and . . . ."

The list goes on, but Cleo's only half-listening. She knows they're big people, but she's waiting for another guest's confirmation.

"And Everett Walter."

Oh.

This is good, Cleo convinces herself. It'll benefit the launch, and get it some press. But now, it means she needs to tell her mother and sister about it. Anyway, *Direk* Everett can be professional; like any other director, he can come to the premiere and congratulate the movie's lead. She just never really expected him to attend. After all those years of keeping her hopes up, it seems like this year is her lucky year. For a moment there, there's excitement, and then comes the pressure. What would he think of the movie?

"Do you think the indie movie is good?" Cleo asks Jay even though he hasn't watched it yet. "I mean, what are your predictions?"

Cleo's quietly panicking inside. She can't bear to fail her father, but she knows she's tried her best. She doesn't want to show anyone this side of her—weak in the knees, hoping for an ounce of attention.

"What did I just say, Cleo?" Jay shakes his head. "Don't look at the smallness of it. You're bigger than that."

Cleo smiles earnestly at Jay. "It's so easy to forget about yourself when you're trying to achieve something."

"But?" Jay asks, knowing there's more to come.

"But believing in yourself puts you on the right path. Thanks for today, Jay."

Cleo's about to show everyone what she can do, and no one, not even her father, can stop her. Because she doesn't leave anyone behind, unlike him. She's doing this not just for herself but for her family. She's strong because the most challenging choices in life molded her to be. She can do it. She's been through worse. She'll be the star of the night—the hidden gem among the celebrities. If she can't have a spotlight, then she'll make one.

"Anytime, Cleo," Jay said again. "Get some rest. We still have work to do tomorrow." Then he says, "It's also nice of you, as an actress, to be involved with this stuff too."

Cleo shrugs. "I'm just helping."

She is helping the production team, the film, and herself. It's not like they have a lot of stuff anyway. Suddenly Cleo can't wait for the premiere. She will make it memorable for everyone, including her father.

Congratulations! You've Won the No Critic Award

G ritting her teeth, Cleo takes one piece of *Kwek-Kwek, the to-die-for* boiled quailed egg coated with an orange batter, deep-fried until it was crispy enough to eat from the stick. She adds sweet sauce and vinegar to give it a little extra flavor, and it just tastes good. Anne orders a *gulaman*, a cold refreshment, and drinks.

"Ah, now, that's sweet and refreshing!" Anne exclaims, happy that school is over for the day. "We should look for your perfect dress, Leo."

Cleo thinks that's a good idea. She should look perfect tomorrow for her premiere night. She has to appear in her best form so she can show everyone she's doing exceptionally well. But she needs to broach the topic of *Direk* Everett attending her premiere.

Cleo doesn't want her family to think she's chasing after her father. She's just being courteous and professional—the way *Direk* Everett is. She's making her path by trying out every single opportunity that comes her way. If it doesn't work out, then she can always just jump into another show and be . . . a talent. Thinking about it ruins her mood. The roles shouldn't bother her. It's good she's got a job she likes. So, she lets herself have a *merienda*, unaffected by her image in the world of showbiz. Right now, she's eating the best street foods: *Kwek-Kwek*, chicken balls, and *kikiam*. And loving it.

"The mall's just that way," she points. "Will you help me?"

When a little boy comes near the food cart, the vendor shoos the kid away. Cleo hates seeing people hungry, no one should be hungry, just as no parent should ever let their kids out alone on the streets. But life is terribly hard for so many. The twenty pesos she paid the vendor is a luxury to the very poor.

"*Manong*, another *Kwek-Kwek*, please." Cleo takes coins from her pocket and pays the vendor twelve pesos. She hands the *Kwek-Kwek* to the boy with a smile. "Here you go—have some snacks."

"*Maraming Salamat, Ate*," the boy happily replies, grateful for the treat. He grins from ear to ear and gives some of the food to his sister.

"It's sad, isn't it?" Anne says, watching the boy and the girl share the *Kwek-Kwek* with other homeless kids. "Thank you for always putting food on the table, Leo."

"Hey!" Cleo bursts into a smile. She hates seeing people sad, especially Anne.

"Sorry!" Anne apologizes, shooting her an apologetic look. "Didn't mean to burst your bubble, but yes! You need a spectacular dress. Let's go shopping?"

Cleo can't even remember when she last shopped with Anne. They're both tired and stressed, and this could be their chance to unwind. She hates not saying anything about a specific premiere guest, but she doesn't want to ruin this day. She's decided not to talk about *Direk* Everett until after the premiere. That way, it'll be over.

"G!" Cleo giddily agrees, feeling like she and her sister are young princesses. Cleo and Anne hop from one store to another to give in to their childhood fantasy, not worrying about the price tags. They know what expensive feels like—smooth and carefully threaded with intricate designs, but they don't care; they're there to have some fun.

Back then, they didn't have many toys or dresses because their mother had to work her butt off day and night as a nanny so that they'd have something to eat. And when Cleo saw her mother's weariness whenever she came home, she knew she had to take over.

  🐜 🐜 🐜

On the way home, Cleo gets a text from Owen.
Owen Velazco (9:10 p.m.)
How's your day, My Miss Starlet? Got your eyes
set on a particular outfit yet? Let me know.

"That Owen?" Anne asks.
"Yeah, he's asking if I've got a dress for tomorrow."
Cleo and Anne have managed to carry three shopping bags and one grocery bag in a taxi. Lately, Thea's been experiencing migraine, so they've decided to do the grocery run for her, and they might as well clean the house this weekend if nothing gets in the way.
"He'll come tomorrow, right?"
"Yup," Cleo confirms, replying to Owen's text.

Cleo Walter (9:12 p.m.)
I went shopping with Anne. I will drop by the distribu-
tion office to check on the final details for the premiere. I
don't want anything to go wrong. As for the outfit, you'll
see it tomorrow ;) Love you. Talk to you later x.

Owen will have his two-day exam on Thursday and Friday this week, yet he will attend tomorrow's movie premiere with Cleo. He told her it's not a bother at all and he'd like to get a good night's break before the day of the exams. He is stuck in his room, studying all day and all night, and he says a night out with her will do him good. He makes her happy. Genuinely and truly happy, she hopes he does well. He's been dreaming of becoming an architect forever.

She knows he'll design the world's most remarkable building some-day! And she'll be proud to say, "My boyfriend designed that."

Cleo smiles to herself. The future's looking great so far, and she hopes nothing ever stops them both from achieving their dreams—no matter what others say. They deserve recognition for their talent and hard work. And then a nagging thought bothers her: *Direk* Everett.

"Anne, *Direk* Everett's coming to my premiere," Cleo admits to Anne.

Anne's eyes widened. "He is? Oh, wow, that's new."

"I'm sorry. I—"

Anne shushes Cleo. "Hey! It's okay, but I don't think *Ma* and I will come. Maybe we can watch it after the premiere, or if we can get a copy of it later on? That good?"

Cleo's relieved. She knows the premiere will already be awkward enough. "Yeah, it's more than okay. I'm sorry, and thank you."

"It's okay! You'll do great, Leo," Anne says, understanding Cleo's mind as always. "Show him what you've got, okay?"

Cleo nods and turns to the driver. "Near the next streetlight is fine."

"You take care and get a taxi once you're done, and send me the plate number once you're on the way home, yeah?" Anne tells Cleo.

"Yes, ma'am."

"Okay?" Anne asks again.

Cleo laughs, gets out of the car, and gives Anne a thumbs-up. "Got it, boss! Later!"

Cleo goes inside the building, signing the log sheet at the secu-rity guard's entrance. Then she gets in the elevator and presses five. Only around four people on the fifth floor are still working on their computer screens, but she can see they're all packed up and ready to call it a night. She scoots around the corner and finds Jay holding the guest checklist.

"Oh, hey, Cleo! What brings you to the—" Jay cuts the conver-sation short when his phone rings. He answers, and shock registers on his face. "Oh, that's too terrible. I hope she'll be okay."

Cleo has an ominous feeling that the news is devastating.

"It's Selene's manager. She's been in a car accident, and they're keeping it quiet for now. So that's one guest off the list," Jay explains, now searching on the internet for any details about Selene's accident.

The browser shows various hot topics about Selene: her net worth, previous lovers, and award-winning actress awards. They all fill the web pages with her pictures. She's got all the curves that everyone loves, but it's her lily-white skin that makes her stand out. She's half Australian and half Filipino, so it makes sense. Everyone loves making an actor out of someone whose roots are half elsewhere. It seems like an essential ingredient of being an actor is having fair skin—something Cleo doesn't have. It's easy for some talent agencies to recruit Westernized actors because it's easy to look a part if you have the requisite equipment. That doesn't mean you can act.

Thinking about it, Cleo remembers something her agent once said to her. "Cleo, as an actress, you sell your image, so everything has to be perfect from the shortest strand of your hair to your little toenail."

Well, that certainly seems to be true. It's the picture-perfect actors who seem to have the following. People are drawn primarily to their looks, and there's a certain amount of logic to that. First impressions are usually through the eyes. Talent seems secondary, and you have to work hard to cultivate that, especially if you're not half something else, and have brown skin. But that's what sponsors are for—they can easily arrange the products and treatments that transform skin, and make you someone you're not.

Cleo doesn't mind what actors do to their faces or bodies, but she wants to be famous for what she does. Even if she has chocolate brown skin, she likes it that way. If she had more of her father's features, she might look too much like the over-driven, hiding-in-work Everett.

"There's no news about the accident yet," Cleo comments.

"Hm . . . yes, but that's not gonna last long for someone like Selene Montenegro."

Someone like Selene Montenegro.

Cleo opens her Chirp account to check on Selene's handle. Right, Selene has ten million followers and counting. Her profile picture is a close-up photo of her with sunglasses, while her cover photo shows her with Jake on the beach. Jake, as usual, looks good. He's grinning and his muscles are flexed, which is typical of him. But, oh jeez, while he's famous and together with Selene, Cleo never imagined her childhood friend looking like that.

Anyway, Selene Montenegro. She started acting when she was, like, seven, and then at age ten, she got a lead role, which ultimately led to more *teleseryes* and movies. At sixteen, she was paired off with Jake because they looked good together. They had sizzling chemistry, and everyone rode on that wave. The fans named the couple JaLene. To be fair to Selene, she's not entirely superficial. After training for years and getting challenging roles, she'd grown as an actress—a chance Cleo didn't get. She'll always be the extra friend in a *teleserye*, but at least she's succeeding as a model. It's just that she just wants to be more than that.

"So, anyway, we're still good even without Selene. I'm sure they can't keep that accident a secret. I give it less than twenty-four hours," Jay wagers. He crosses Selene's name off the list and informs Cleo of the latest additional guests for tomorrow. "By the way, why are you here?"

"Just wanted to check in before I go home. I also left some folders on your desk yesterday."

"Here." Jay hands over the folders. "Everything's going perfectly fine. We're all cleared for tomorrow."

Just then, Jay gets another call.

"Good evening. Yes, speaking." Jay frowns. "Oh, I see. We understand. Thank you."

"What is it?" Cleo asks.

Jay stares at her for a moment before finally breaking the news to her. "*Direk* Everett can't come after all. His assistant sends his apologies. He's way wrapped up in pre-prod on a movie set to take place in Alaska. Sorry, Cleo."

Cleo gets Jay's reaction. He probably knows Cleo's expecting Everett in some way or another. "It's fine. Thanks for the work today, Jay."

"Get a good night's sleep, Cleo." Jay smiles. "You're still the star of tomorrow's premiere."

The movie premiere is not going anywhere. Cleo will stand there and be proud of her movie. Anyway, *Direk* Everett can make up as many excuses as he wants, but she knows the truth. She gets it: her father, no surprise, chickened out. Again. He can command a crew of sixty and a cast of fifty, but he can't face down an uncomfortable house even with a glass of champagne. He's everything she'll never be.

*   *   *

On the night of the premiere, Cleo stuns everyone with her royal blue strapless split wide-leg jumpsuit. Her discreetly made-up face looks natural with her glowing skin and flushed red cheeks. She looks divine next to Owen, who's in a suit and bowtie. She gazes at him and then back at the flashing cameras with her lips pursed. Together, they're the perfect pair, and in another lifetime, they can be the love team that everyone adores.

"Thank you for coming," Cleo murmurs to Owen. She knows he doesn't like this kind of event. He's had enough publicity to last a lifetime. He hates the spotlight and attention, but for her, he's more than willing to endure the public eye.

Owen takes Cleo's bouquet so she can walk with ease. "Anything for you, babe. You ready for it?"

"Yeah," Cleo says, smiling from one camera to another with Owen's arm around her waist. "I forgot to tell you, but *Direk* Everett almost came tonight."

Owen looks at Cleo. "What happened?"

Cleo shrugs, pulling him to the side to avoid any reporters or guests. There are still people milling around the mall, crowding the red carpet, and going gaga over their favorite actors. She knows that those mall-goers are simply after their favorite love teams and not her, but they add excellent volume at the cinema. They also say they can't wait to watch the movie soon in theaters nationwide. But Cleo knows the film won't be distributed nationwide. She's not even sure if it'll last three weeks.

"He says he's busy," Cleo replies. Inside the cinema, she and Owen walk to their reserved seats. He takes her hand, squeezing it to comfort and assure her everything will be fine. And it will. She's got engagements, and her movie's making a lot of buzz. She's done fine without *Direk* Everett. So how is tonight any different?

The emcee stands in front of all the seats, microphone in hand as the production team enters the cinema. "Let's all welcome, Out of the Club production house!"

Celebrities, directors, writers, executive producers, and researchers are all in their seats, giving the Out of the Club a round of applause. Cleo and Owen applaud enthusiastically. The production house is a great group of young people with bright ideas, and in Cleo's eyes, they deserve this recognition even more than she does.

The emcee hands the mic to the director, Bryan. He takes it and breathes a sigh of relief. "Ah, finally, after more than a year of trying to produce this film, it's come to fruition. It's been constant push and pull. There's not enough budget, the script needs to be re-written—it's challenge after challenge. But we made it! And that's all that matters. May I now welcome our ever-beautiful lead star, Cleo Walter!"

"Go for it," Owen whispers encouragingly, and it honestly just gives Cleo the confidence to stand up and face the celebrities who are all just probably doing this out of politeness. Their managers probably think it's also good publicity for them, but she doesn't mind. They can be big stars outside, but no one can take the spot-light from her inside this cinema.

Cleo stands in front of everyone and says, "I went for this role because I wanted to be part of a story that speaks to me. It felt like a role that I could give myself to. It's everything I thought it would be and more. I'm also forever grateful to this production team for being so kind to me. Thank you, and I hope everyone enjoys the show!"

There is loud applause and cheers from everyone. Cleo can't honestly believe she just said that, but she means that. She trusts the production team and herself. All that's left to do is to watch it. Soon, when everyone's settled down, the film starts rolling. She isn't watching it—thousand things are going on in her head. She's questioning whether it's good enough for this audience. Why is she not hearing their reactions? Did they fall asleep? Question after question comes to mind, her heart beats loudly in her chest, a drumroll to the beginning of a good show. This is probably the longest-running event of her life, and she just can't wait for it to be over.

After what seems like forever, there is applause. Cleo thinks they appreciate how the film speaks so much of what it must be like to live with a mental disorder and how difficult it can be for patients whose family hardly ever visit.

This is great! Everyone's left speechless, and that's precisely what Cleo's aiming for; she wants them to think about it, to feel as the characters feel, to see themselves in the story.

The after-party takes place in some fancy restaurant. Like any other premiere after-parties, the lead role gets a slew of congratula-tions. The funny thing about it is that when Cleo asks them what part of the movie they liked, they all have the same answer. Their remarks are so generic that none of their congratulations felt genu-ine to her. At this point, she'd rather hear a criticism than a compli-ment. But she smiles at them anyway and is grateful they even took the time to adjust their schedule for this.

"See? I told you they'd love it," Owen says, drinking his wine.

Sometimes, Cleo forgets how this place is so much more his world. He could be an actor, himself, for all the times he masks his face to others.

"Yeah, for sure," Cleo says, a smile plastered on her face.

"Congrats, Cleo!" Guinevere, the beauty queen, and Jake's twin sister says. "You deserve it."

And that's it. No, *oh, your acting skills are on point!* It's always just "Congratulations!". She's waiting for someone to say anything about the movie and her acting. She waits and drinks and eats with everyone. She gets none of it, and yet she celebrates it. The premiere is a success, and while the viewers' reactions don't fully satisfy her, she enjoys her time with them. She should just use this party to her advantage and make connections. It's time to look for a new project. Again.

"Congratulations, Cleo. It's brave of you to try an indie film," says Carol, one of the celebrities in dark red lipstick. She's been friends with Selene as far back as Cleo can remember.

"It's not brave, but I wanted to try. It's nice to be part of different things, and I like working with this company. Have you been in an indie movie ever?" Cleo replies.

Carol shakes her head. "I wouldn't earn much from it. Anyway, you should take on another modeling project to recover from this film's expenses. I'm sure you also contributed to the production given the limited budget."

Cleo didn't chip in any money. The production house took care of her. They'd arranged their budget the best they could to produce a film as good as that. But who's she kidding? Some of these celebrities think she also produced the movie to make people notice her.

"This production team is the best. I didn't do anything but act. Thank you for your suggestion, but I still have enough money."

That's true. Cleo did save a lot ever since she started working; magazines pay her a fair amount for being so good at the job. There were others who hinted she should stick to modeling, but she wanted more.

Carol shrugs. "If you need any modeling projects, let me know. I can connect you to the right people."

"Sure, thank you," Cleo says politely, not wanting to have a row with anyone.

"Thank you for the invite, but I have to go now. Taping day tomorrow and all that." Carol winks at Cleo. "Love the movie!"

As time passes by, Cleo can feel her energy draining. These celebrities are, like, sucking the life out of her, but it's part of the after-party. It's a good thing Owen came with her even though he has his first exams tomorrow. He's much more relaxed than she is, drinking his wine like he always does.

"Tell me if you want to go home and study or have an early night," Cleo says, worried about Owen. "I want you to be rested for your exams."

Owen smiles lazily at her. "I'm fine, babe. Let's just enjoy the night. I've studied enough and this night is for you. It's on my schedule, okay? Also, I've got us booked for this weekend in Hong Kong. I think we both deserve it after this week. Is that okay with you? It's supposed to be a surprise, but I can't bear to see you looking so anxious."

"Of course!" Cleo smiles at him, finally relaxing a bit, until Owen's pocket rings. "That my phone?"

"Yeah, I think so. Hold on." Owen pulls up Cleo's phone from his pocket. He's always her carrier at parties. "Here."

They both look at her phone screen; it's an unknown number. Cleo hesitates then answers the ring. "Hello?"

"I'm sorry I couldn't come." It's Everett. "You know how it is in production, but my spies tell me it's good. Congratulations."

Cleo's waiting for the *I'm proud of you*, but when nothing comes, she says, "Thank you. I appreciate that."

And Cleo does. She knows it's the only thing her father can do. Talk to her over the phone and get the congratulations out of his mouth. Silence reigns looming and heavy, almost like the coming of a storm on a sunny day.

"We know how premieres are. I won't really believe it until I see the movie with a real audience, but thank you," Cleo says again, and then they hang up. It's over, just like that. She heaves a sigh of relief. She took the call as if it had been from a director and not her father.

Cleo looks across the room and finds *Direk* Gary, her father's longtime associate and some would say best friend—if Everett has friends. He's looking at her. As soon as her eyes meet his, he looks away. He's dressed for work, but his wife is well glammed up. for the premiere. Cleo doubts Gary thought the movie was good, but it's nice of him to say so to Everett. She knows he's the spy responsible for her father's call.

As Cleo continues to watch him, *Direk* Gary gets a call. He answers. And as soon as he starts talking, he's looking at her again.

CHAPTER 5

I'm Sorry, Say What Now?

When Cleo wants to know a thing, she goes straight to the source. She can't always trust what people tell her because everyone has their own version of everything, including the truth. And in showbiz, rumors travel faster than the truth. So, the day after the premiere, she's already decided to watch it in the nearest mall, a cinema in a middle-class neighborhood. She needs to watch it in the real world to see how it fares.

"One ticket for *Doll*," Cleo says at the counter.

"What time?" the woman asks, as if Cleo's just one of the many moviegoers. But, of course, Cleo won't be familiar; she's not a big star.

"The 6:45., please."

Ticket in her bag, Cleo goes around the mall, window shopping. She wonders what it'll feel like to be recognized by anyone at any mall. Still, there are posters of her on some of the windows of the boutiques and stores. People might recognize her from those, but most people probably won't be able to place her.

At the mall's activity center, Cleo hears loud jeers and cheers from a crowd. People from every floor gather around to look down into the center. Curious, she follows the uproar and squeezes herself in between them, hoping to see what's all the fuss about. When she's finally able to get a look, she sees it's a movie promotional tour. Usually, the lead stars of upcoming movies promote the movie by going from one city or province to another. They share everything they can about the film, take pictures with fans, and invite lucky people to the block screening. This sort of promo also happens when a *teleserye* is winding down. They call it the Grand Finale Mall Show. The cast talks about the show and how much it's been a home for them. The fans want to see the stars they've been watching week after week and be with other fans as their favorite show comes to an end. A big part of their lives should go out with a big farewell.

In the center of the activity, love team Jerome and Nellie a.k.a. JerLie, are holding hands and singing to the crowd. Too bad Cleo's aunts aren't here. She's sure they'll be the kind who'll run down the escalator and wedge themselves into the jam-packed crowd. It's amazing what love teams can do. They draw fans in by acting sweet and lovey-dovey, but then the fans want more and more from them over time. They want it to be reel to real because it's so much *kilig* that way. *Kilig*—that wonderful butterflies feeling you get in your stomach.

"Yes, Jerome and Nellie! Now, everyone wants to know: what's the real score between the two of you?" the host asks, and everyone screams.

Jerome smiles shyly at Nellie before pulling her close. "We're almost there."

Cleo swears the entire mall is fangirled. They all swoon to Jerome and Nellie, and she might have too if only it were true. But she knows it's all for show. Jerome is secretly dating a non-showbiz person. But, of course, they can't tell the fans. It'll disappoint them. It's how ratings work sometimes, but she hopes that when the time comes, and they want to go their separate ways, the fans can be happy for them.

An hour later, Cleo goes back to the cinema, buying popcorn and cola. She doesn't mind going alone to the mall or watching a movie alone. She enjoys dating herself. She doesn't care what anybody thinks of it. She's her own person, and no one can change her mind.

Inside the cinema, the dim lights show Cleo that there are only, like, three people in there; a man who's dozing off and a couple who are not at all shy with their public display of affection. She shrugs it off, thinking it's probably because she's ten minutes early. Most people go inside five minutes before or so before the start time. Anyway, at least she has time to relax. She can't believe she's doing this, but she has to know what ordinary moviegoers think. Only then will she be convinced that the film is really good.

Minutes later, as the film is about to begin, Cleo stands and looks around and sees if there's anyone else there. There are only four of them, much to her disappointment, but then maybe they'll show up. The love team at the activity center is probably holding them up. It's okay. They'll come in later. But as she watches herself unfold on the big screen, anxiety works through her nerves. She can't help looking around at the empty seats now and then. When a shadow passes by, she thinks she was right. People were tricking in now. But as the owner of the shadow comes closer, she sees it's the security guard.

"This is crazy," Cleo tells herself, laughing, though she's not quite sure why. It's crazy because her feelings are all over the place.

The screenplay and production are good, even if it's an indie film. Watching this movie again feels like the first time. It is beautiful and enchanting. The story, characters, cinematography, and musical scoring are perfect. The film takes the audience straight into *Doll's* life, into what's happening inside her head. She's a psychiatrist who hopes to help a mentally challenged family, but each time she talks with them, she feels less and less safe. Finally, she realizes she's not safe at all. In the end, a revelation of her true identity: she's not a psychiatrist but a patient in the ward.

The editing is phenomenal. They didn't have a big budget, but it was worth every moment of her time. She doesn't regret doing any of this, not even if there is a squeezing pain in her heart telling her she isn't good enough to be watched. It's agonizing to watch it with a sleeping person and a couple who can't get over themselves, but it's even more excruciating for her if she doesn't keep trying.

Thankfully, when the end credits roll, sleepy man and amorous couple get up and leave. Meanwhile, Cleo stands up like a newly resurrected phoenix in front of the cinema The story is good, but maybe her acting just didn't make the grade. She'd thought her trailers were good, but . . . . Oh, well. Maybe this is just a sign that it's time to find something that's really for her. And it's okay. She's game to try other things. She can even produce a movie or TV series. Sometimes, she needs to be her number one fan because if she isn't, how will she survive in showbiz? Armed with this determination, she can say she walked out of the cinema with her head held high. She's jolted out of her reverie by slow clapping. Not so slow as to be insulting. But not so fast that anyone can confuse that sound for enthusiasm.

The lights haven't come up yet. She can't see much as she walks up the aisle. Eventually, she sees *Direk* Gary in the middle of the back row.

"*Direk* Gary."

Director Gary Hillaro had been kind of a fixture in Cleo's life. Her dad would come home with Director Gary to tell their family everything about their day. Director Gary's son Jake was the industry's hottest male star. His daughter Guinevere, Jake's twin, was in some sort of beauty camp for pageantry. Cleo's dad loved Director Gary's family so much that she usually had to scramble crumbs of his attention whenever their families had Sunday dinner nights.

Cleo remembers being close with Jake and Guinevere, and to whom opportunities usually came on a silver platter. Jake had been charming and charismatic, so it was easy for him to become king of the TV screen. For her part, Guinevere had her mother's fierce beauty and was an alpha just like her brother. Their family had always been on the magazines and billboards, practically the industry's royal family. And all Cleo can say is, "*Sana all*," an expression of hope that everyone would have the same chance to reach those heights

Direk Everett's attention had always been on *Direk* Gary's family, so when Guinevere and Jake were on their chosen paths, they kind of forgot about Cleo, the rookie of all time. She used to play house with them until they focused on their workshops and runways. *Direk* Everett forgot he had his own family when the Hillaro clan became even more prominent, more than firmly established in a life full of lights, camera, action.

"I didn't know you were here," Cleo says. "Thank you for letting *Direk* Everett know about the movie."

Direk Gary crosses his legs. "I didn't come here for the movie. I came for you."

"What?"

"I called your house, and Thea told me I could find you here. Sure enough, you're here," *Direk* Gary says, looking at the end credits. "I'll be honest, Cleo. This indie film of yours is a flop."

"It isn't a flop," Cleo assures *Direk* Gary. But even now she's not sure who she's trying to convince—him, or her.

"Whatever. Don't you get it, Cleo?"

"Don't get what?" Cleo asks. She wants to ask what he wants from her, and why did he come all the way here to tell her the movie was already a flop?

That's what she wants—someone to tell her the truth, but she wasn't prepared for it to come from someone close to her father.

"Where you went wrong."

Cleo lets out a nervous laugh. There are a few reasons the movie might have gone wrong, but those same reasons might also explain why the production company decided to take a riskier path. Their aim was to make the story come through, nothing more or less.

"What do you want to say, *Direk* Gary? Did *Direk* Everett send you here?" Cleo asks, tired of going around in circles. If he wants to say something, she wished he'd just say it already.

Direk Gary smiles at Cleo. "Now, not everything has to be

about you and your father. That's not really what you want, is it?"

Cleo doesn't say anything.

"I thought so. I came here because I wanted to see how you're doing. You're a smart girl, Cleo. You don't settle with just a premiere. If there's one way in which you and your father are most alike, it's that you make things happen."

Cleo shrugs. "I don't. I just try."

"Listen. You've spent years on the runway. You're a veteran. You have stage presence, which is great, but it's not the same as a screen presence. Look at how they edited that flip-flop commercial."

This feels like what Cleo needs to hear: the unabridged version of the truth. "Go on."

Direk Gary stands in front of her. "You're twenty-four, Cleo. To be a leading lady by this point in your life, you need to start younger."

"There's more to being an actress than being a leading lady," Cleo retorts. But for once, she wants to be what *Direk* Gary's kids are—famous, loved by everyone.

Direk Gary looks skeptical, though. "Maybe. For some actresses."

"I'll think about what you said. Thank you," Cleo responds. She appreciates his thoughts. At least someone finally gave their honest two cents. Of course, it's better than nothing, but her mind's made up. Cleo is moving on. She will stop chasing ticket sales or fantasies of being the next big star. But perhaps she should try being a producer or director. She is, after all, Everett's daughter.

It's about time Cleo does something different. She's been chasing this dream for so long it might not even be real for her anymore, and she can't just continually self-destruct. She has to help herself rediscover what she's meant for, and it's not acting.

"I'll see you around, Cleo Walter," *Direk* Gary bids his goodbye, leaving Cleo alone in the cinema. She brings out her cinema ticket and stares at it, thinking that the film's title fits her perfectly. She's a doll, only for display and never for action. She can be played and tossed around, but in the end, she'll still be stationary—only moving when others tell her to. She refuses to be just a doll—a pretty thing to look at. She wants to be the mountain, the one that takes their breath away.

Cleo reaches home later that evening with a heavy heart. She feels lost and trapped like she's forever in the bottom part of the broken Ferris wheel. She can't go up, nor does she want to get out of it. She wants to look at the view, but then she sees a solution: other ways to see the incredible view. She doesn't need to wait for the Ferris wheel to be fixed. And believe it, she did her best to fix it, too, even if she isn't a ride operator.

Candy greets Cleo at the door, wagging her tail and jumping up and down, excited and so full of life. She wonders if dogs can feel what people are feeling because Candy just bowed her head, making a whimpering sound as if she's also sad for her.

"It's okay, girl." Cleo caresses Candy's head before rubbing her belly. "Thank you."

"*Anak?*" Thea calls out. Cleo's heart always melts when her mom calls her *anak*—her child—because it makes her feel safe. "Did you meet Gary? He called earlier, asking for you. I told him where you were."

"Yeah, I did," Cleo says, taking a mug out of the fridge. "Just gave some advice, is all."

"How'd your date with yourself go?" Thea sits in a dining chair, offering Cleo some coffee.

Cleo gladly takes it. "It was okay."

"And?"

Why is her mother so great at this? Thea always knows when something is wrong. "And there were only four, well, five in the cinema, including *Direk* Gary."

"Oh, come here." Thea pulls Cleo in for a hug.

"I don't know why *Ma*." Cleo wants to cry, but she holds back her tears. She's a big girl. She's gone through the worst, so why is this making her cry? "It's okay. I'll do something else. It's not like I'm going jobless. You don't have to worry."

"Are you crazy? I care about everything you do." Thea smiles at Cleo.

"Thank you." Cleo sniffs. "I think I'll do things differently this time. I'm not giving up, *Ma*. I'm exploring. Is that okay? I mean, I know I'm already twenty-four years old, and most of my friends have achieved their dreams already—"

"Do not ever compare yourself to others, Cleo," Thea's loving black eyes are firm and solid. "You're still young, and the reason why you're you is that you don't know when to give up. If I were to tell you to give it up now, would you?"

Cleo shakes her head. She says hurtful things to herself, sometimes, but her actions and everything about her refuse to give in to those words. It's like the more she voices her doubts, the more her body rebels. It's weird how her body and head can be so out of sync with each other. She has to work on building up her confidence, though. And she'll start tomorrow.

"Cleo Walter, the actress, is signing off," Cleo informs Thea. "Does *Direk* Cleo sounds good to your ears, *Ma*?"

They laugh, and Cleo sees how beautiful her mother is when she's so relaxed. Not a sign of gray in her hair yet. Only dazzling smiles and pure love—that's what this house is.

"Yes, it does. Let's have dinner, okay?"

The day may have been sad, but it ends sweetly. Cleo can't wait for tomorrow to come. She feels good. Strong. Even after dinner. Even when she's lying on her bed, daydreaming and unable to fall asleep. Before she closes her eyes, she sends a text to wish Owen luck on his second day of exams.

Finally, Cleo's mind quiets down. This is the moment she's been waiting for: the beginning of something new. As cliché as it sounds, it lulls her to sleep, and for once, she doesn't want to dream. She wants to wake up in this reality.

🌿 🌿 🌿

"Something's up," Anne says, arms crossed. "You're always up and running in the morning. How come you're not buzzing around?"

True, Cleo's not rushing like usual. She doesn't have anywhere to go, and she plans to call her agency later in the afternoon to check on other projects. She plans to email a few directors and producers here and there and ask if she might intern under them. Chances are, they won't notice her, but if any of those directors or producers reply, that's a jackpot. All it takes is one "yes."

"No taping today." Cleo eats her favorite breakfast of *tosilog*, chewing slowly on the vinegar-dipped sweet fried pork of the *tocino* occasionally scooping up a little of the garlic rice of the *sinangag*. She'll eat the egg last. It's a hearty breakfast for a full day ahead.

"Okay, good luck, Leo. I'm off," Anne says, picking up her bag and a bunch of papers. Her job's pretty good. She gets to spend half a day at the school, so their mom has someone to keep her company for at least part of the day while Cleo works long hours on this or that set, some days.

"Say 'hi' to Billie for me!"

Anne sighs at the mention of Billie, the four-year-old kid who causes mayhem everywhere he goes. He's a big problem at school, but Anne's not giving up on him. She believes he'll settle down if she's patient enough.

After breakfast, Cleo starts on the dishes. Her mom ate earlier so she could take care of the laundry. She's such a trooper.

Cleo's phone rings on the countertop. She dries her hands with the dish towel and looks over at the phone. Her agency. It looks like she's going to have another project. That's fine. She has time.

"Hello?"

Ms. Aika is downright giddy. She only sounds that elated when she's scored a huge coup. "Who's the world's best fairy godmother? You won't believe it, but I just got you Selene Montenegro's role!"

Cleo's jaw drops.

"What did you say?" Cleo's not sure she heard her agent right. "Are you serious? Is this for real?!"

Cleo's heart is somersaulting and drumming. She wants to jump up and shriek.,

"For real!" Ms. Aika affirms with a laugh.

Cleo's still catching her breath but she manages to ask, "Who's directing the movie?"

And now she's holding her breath again.

"*Direk* Gary," Ms. Aika replies. "He's looking forward to working with you. So, what do you think?"

Oh. *Direk* Gary. Not *Direk* Everett. What did Cleo expect?

It's an opportunity of a lifetime, no question. But there's something Cleo has to know. "Thank you so much, Ms. Aika! Can I call you back in a few minutes or so? I just have to make a quick call."

"Sure! But don't keep me waiting too long."

"Thank you!" Cleo says and then speed dials *Direk* Gary. She has to know now: *why her?*

CHAPTER 6

Selene Who?
It's Cleo Walter Now

"Gary speaking."

Direk Gary's tone is formal. Cleo not being in his circle, she's an "unknown caller" on his phone screen. Amazing, really, that he took the call at all.

"Hi! It's Cleo," Cleo says.

"Oh, Cleo! To what do I owe the honor?"

Cleo prepares her black coffee as she talks. She's restless and doubts that coffee is the best cure for it, but it's her comfort drink. She needs to do something ordinary as she listens to whatever *Direk* Gary is going to say. "You're replacing Selene, and I'm taking over her role?"

"Yes! We'll start taping next week, so you have this coming weekend to—"

Cleo interrupts *Direk* Gary. "Why me?"

"Because why not?" *Direk* Gary fires back. "It's Jake's idea."

Cleo goes back to eighteen years ago or so. She could barely remember six-year-old-ish Jake, who used to play jackstones with her. Even as a little boy he was charming, but she'd never had any special closeness with him. They just played around, the way kids play in the playground, where image and status in life don't matter.

It was a long time ago, and they hadn't been in much contact since. He knew plenty of other actresses, so Cleo found it hard to believe that this was his idea.

Cleo doesn't believe *Direk* Gary, and she's a little amused by what she's sure is a lie, but she's going to run with it anyway. People can theorize as much as they want about how she got that role, and why. But she's a free woman who can do as she chooses as long as she's hurting no one. She's not stealing a role. She's taking over for someone who can no longer fill it. The only person who's allowed to come at her is herself. And since she's been dreaming of the spotlight for ages, what's wrong with taking a given chance to make it to the top?

"Oh." Cleo tries to sound pleased yet cool and calm. She wants to act like this isn't the best thing that's ever happened to her, but she can feel her smile stretching from ear to ear. "Please pass along my thanks. I really appreciate this."

Cleo crosses her legs, already imagining her mall shows. She stands and begins gliding side to side, lost in her little world.

"My assistant will email you everything you'll need," *Direk* Gary says.

"Great! I look forward to it! And thank you!" Cleo says, aware that her pitch is going up in her excitement. She coughs, trying to contain her excitement. She hangs up and picks Candy up in her arms. Candy's tongue is sticking out. She barks at Cleo.

"Ah, yes, my number one furry fan!" Cleo says to Candy, putting her down and giving her belly rubs. "Candy, can you believe it? I'll be a starlet soon! So, what's on your wish list?"

Candy barks again at Cleo as if she can understand her.

"Extra treats for you, of course." Cleo leans into Candy. "Ah, right. You've always wanted a friend. Maybe we can adopt from the shelter, and then I'll get you both a better house."

"What are you doing to Candy?" Anne asks, dropping her bag on the couch and heaving a sigh. While she loves kids, they also give her a migraine. "Oh, poor baby, forced to listen to Leo's day-dreams again."

"Hey!" Cleo protests, laughing in sheer joy. "She likes me."

Anne pets Candy and smiles. "Care to explain why Candy's acting like the number one fanatic again?"

"I am the new Selene Montenegro," Cleo says, brushing off her hair on one side and winking at Anne. "Did that have a dazzling effect?"

"Leo, just spill it."

"You have no patience at all." Cleo wags her index finger, shushing her sister. "Listen to this call."

Intrigued, Anne pulls up a chair for both of them. Sitting comfortably, Cleo puts her phone on the table and rings Ms. Aika. For a few seconds, she and Anne share a look, and on the fifth ring, Ms. Aika finally answers her phone.

"So, my little Cinderella, are you ready to slip into your glass slippers and dance the night away as you replace Selene Montenegro?"

Anne gasps, covering her mouth. Cleo shushes her. "Wave that wand! Not even the stroke of midnight can stop me."

"That's great to hear! . . . You know, I knew you could do it!"

No, Ms. Aika didn't. Cleo knows the woman's just doing her job and is sick of getting in touch with people. She wants to be promoted and focus on one actor. It'll also help if that actor is part of the celebrity A-list. But that chance just didn't come. Until today.

Cleo wagers Ms. Aika has already talked to *Direk* Gary about it, so she won't be surprised if she gets to be Cleo's road manager the next day.

"Leo . . . you're going to be the next . . . Selene?"

That sounds about right. Anne pulls Cleo into their room as if they're secretly hiding something.

"Wait—let me open my email and get the script." Cleo opens her laptop as Anne looks over her shoulder.

There are lots of attachments in Cleo's emails. That alone is new and exciting. The first sign, however tiny, that things are changing. If others see her as a wannabe model and actress, then that's even better. She's a wannabe turned into what everyone wants to be. She'll make a good story for interviews: a nobody turned somebody. She can't wait for the social media comments. She's sure there'll be mixed reactions, but it's the kind of reactions she's been waiting for.

Carefully, Cleo reads through the email threads. The movie is called *The Boyfriend Switch*. She checks out the synopsis first. She wants a sense of the overall story, and since this as was originally written for Selene, she knows she'll need to adjust.

SYNOPSIS

Two struggling-in-life best friends, Nina and Lara, are given a chance to participate in a reality game show. In this show, they have to trade boyfriends—whoever earns more scores and popularity points every week by getting to know the boyfriend of the other contestant wins the show. But then Nina begins to actually fall in love with Lara's boyfriend and finds out behind the cameras that her boyfriend and best friend may not be her boyfriend and best friend at all.

"That sounds interesting," Anne has been following along. "It's very much like Selene."

But Cleo's not aiming to be Selene, and she wants bring Cleo to the role, and to come out of it as Cleo. She has to fit the role, yes, but in her own way. She can blaze her own trail and do more for the part at the same time. It's not going to be easy, but it's not every day she gets an opportunity like this.

"Hmm . . . I don't like how these people talk about you."

Shaking off her thoughts, Cleo turns to Anne. "What do you mean?"

Anne hands Cleo her phone. Cleo's name is all over the articles on her timeline and newsfeed. The headlines all essentially say one thing: Who is this Cleo Walter?

On all the social media sites, netizens say Cleo's the daughter of *Direk* Everett, as always. It's nothing new. She's an actress, but only by name. Her photos are everywhere, and people are making a feast out of it. They tell their friends that she's pretty. And she is. There's no point pushing that under the rug—if she didn't have beauty, no one would be talking about her at all. It's what they all come for. But it makes things worse, somehow, because a lot of her beauty genes came from her American father, and everybody loves half-someone.

Cleo rolls her eyes at the photos of her and her father. She scrolls further down, hoping that someone out there is looking forward to seeing her on the big screen. And someone is. Life isn't so cruel to her, after all.

@jokinglyyourss: @CleoWalter is a breath of fresh air among other Selenes!

But someone is bashing *@jokinglyyourss* for supporting Cleo instead of Selene. Typical. Selene can't play the role now, anyway, but the fans don't even consider that angle. They're a cult of A-list worshippers.

@josterly: @jokinglyyourss, no one can replace Selene!!! Wth are you talking about?

And then something hits Cleo: *Owen*. They're supposed to have a weekend getaway, but Cleo's already said yes to the movie.

Cleo stands up, and hands the phone back to Ann, who manages to keep reading through the exchange. She grabs her own phone can calls Owen.

"Hey, babe," Owen greets, his voice soothing her jittery nerves.

Cleo bites her lower lip in anticipation, suppressing the urge to spill everything out in one go. "Hi. How're your exams?"

"They're okay." Owen sounds tired. "Sorry, we can't have dinner tonight. We have the entire weekend ahead of us anyway."

Cleo cringes at the mention of the weekend. It should have been their escape from reality, but it's also going to be her life-changing weekend. "Um, so . . ."

"What is it?" Owen almost always knows when something's up.

Cleo hesitates. "This amazing thing has come up, and now I have a real dilemma. I don't know what to do. We're supposed to go to Hong Kong this weekend, and one of the biggest directors in the country asked me to be in a film."

Cleo's quiet, and for a while, neither speaks until Owen finally says, "Hong Kong isn't going anywhere. No big deal, of course, you have to do it!"

Smiling, Cleo breathes out a sigh of relief. He genuinely sounds okay with the idea of it too. It's a win-win for both of them. He gets to rest while she gets to prepare over the weekend. A year that's starting out dark turns out to be a classic blue.

❧   ❧   ❧

Owen's been looking at his food app for hours now, scrolling through different restaurants and cafes, but he still can't find the perfect meal or snack for Cleo. She's been holed up in her room the entire day, preparing for this huge role. Kind of like being glued to your class materials to pass a board exam. Owen knows what that's like. He's sitting on his computer chair, tapping his pen mindlessly on the table. He glances back to his chatbox with Cleo on his Lookbook social media account, checking to see if she's replied. She hasn't. And so he texts her again. It's his fifth text in an hour.

"Sir?" Jenny, the maid, comes into Owen's room, bringing the coffee he asked for.

"Thanks," Owen says curtly, taking the coffee from the maid.

Jenny stands there and looks at him as if trying to solve the same puzzle he's working on. "Cleo again?"

Owen nods, closing the food app and opening multiple tabs on his computer's browser. He opens a shopping website in one tab, scrolling through a collection of flowers and clothes, but none of it catches his attention. Nothing too good for his girlfriend. It has to be something he hasn't given her before. That makes it even more difficult.

"*Ang Ganda ng* necklace *na binigay mo sa Kanya*, sir," Jenny says, looking over Owen's shoulder.

Jenny was the one who helped Owen pick the necklace he gave Cleo before. It's lovely, of course. He buys only the best for Cleo, but if he's given the best, what else can he give? She's someone who doesn't ask for anything, and it drives him crazy sometimes.

"*Pero* the gift must come from the heart."

Owen turns around and faces Jenny. She looks tired but also happy in her blue maid uniform. The wrinkles under her eyes turn up as she smiles. She's a fifty-something woman who's been part of the household for over ten years, and he thinks of her as family. He listens to her because she treats him like he's her son. Her motherly ways have helped him a lot during times when he didn't know what to make of his relationship with Cleo.

"You're right. Thank you." Owen sighs. "And don't call me 'sir'. Just call me by my name."

Jenny does call Owen by his name, when his family and friends are not around. Once in a while, she forgets.

"Okay, Owen." Jenny smiles at him before leaving the room.

With Jenny's words in Owen's mind, he stands up, stretches his arms, and checks his watch. It's only 5 p.m. The night is still ahead, and the possibilities are endless. Determined to lighten the stress on Cleo as much as he can, he goes down to their garage and hops on his motorcycle. He puts on his helmet and is about to speed away when his brother suddenly stops him.

Mark stands in front of Owen in his full black suit. He's looking at him in all seriousness. He's just like their father—stone cold. "You're not joining us for dinner?"

"No. I have somewhere to be."

"Is it a meeting? A trip to the office? A consultation with your professor?" Mark hurls one question after another. He interrogates Owen like he's caught him red-handed at something.

Owen shrugs, refusing to answer. Instead, he revs his engine and drives away, out of his sight and into the open space. He drives faster, slipping through the rush hour traffic jams. Jeepney and bus drivers honk at him as he glides in between them. He comes to a complete halt at a red light. Glancing to the side, he sees another man on a motorcycle. The man grins at him, his crooked teeth decaying.

The traffic light turns yellow. And then green. Owen smiles as he drives in a rush, and when he gets to his destination, he grins.

Cleo hears the sound of his motorcycle and runs out. "Babe!" she cries as she bolts down to the gate. It squeals on its rusty hinges as she throws it open and practically jumps into Owen's arms. "You're all sweaty. What happened to you?"

"I wanted to see you." Owen smiles at her. As always, she looks naturally beautiful, even in her white shirt and shorts. The long locks of her hair are tied in braids, her lips pursed as if she's telling him a secret that only she and the universe know. Her beauty never fails to astound him. She's ethereally angelic, but her aura defies what she looks like—an enchanter, a siren, and an apple from the forbidden tree.

"I'm sorry—" Cleo begins fumbling over the words.

Owen kisses Cleo's cheek. "Hey, it's okay."

"Thank you! I feel so much better now that you're here! I've been reading the script for hours, and it's just frustrating me, you know?" Cleo grumbles, leaning into Owen. "I'm all over the internet, and they're waiting for me to fail."

Owen doesn't know about that. He's barely on social media.

He's only there for Cleo, where he gets tagged in memes and romantic posts. He ignores them because he doesn't see the point in commenting when he can say what he thinks of it directly to her.

Owen pulls a folder out of his bag and smiles at her. "How about we read lines?"

Surprised, Cleo takes the folder from Owen and finds the printed script inside.

"It's a date. You and me, on the rooftop, reading lines. How does that sound to you?" Owen asks.

And in a flash, all the strain goes out of Cleo's face. They don't waste a minute. They lounge on the rooftop, facing each other as they read the lines. As she listens to him read, he sees a smile play upon her lips every now and then. They don't have time for cuddling tonight, but that's fine. Owen goes off graciously, as always.

Next day, Cleo's even busier. Owen knows she's under a lot of pressure. Phoning her won't cheer her up. He's lucky if he gets five minutes of her time. He sends her food, and she says thank you, and the conversation ends there. The shoot hasn't started yet, but it feels like he's already headed for the sideline. He keeps his patience. He knows she needs this after her series of disappointments. He knows what disappointment feels like.

That Sunday evening, Owen and Cleo are on the rooftop, rereading lines. This is the only time he can have her to himself. He's willing to take any time she has available. If that means reading lines, then he's happy to do that all night long, if she wants.

"Okay, you should try acting a bit cocky," Cleo comments after Owen has finished reading. "The character is a cocky man, and Jake is a—"

"Jake is your leading man?" Owen interrupts Cleo, curious. He doesn't know much about the guy, but he knows Jake is a big name.

"Yeah. I told you about Jake before. Remember him?"

"Your childhood friend," Owen mutters, flipping through the pages of the script and reading a lot of I love you's and kissing scenes. He's been so busy trying to read lines with her it has only just hit him that she's about to get all sweet with her childhood friend.

"Yeah. He thought of me for the role, too. This was his idea," Cleo adds, staring at Owen. "You're fine with it, right? This won't be the first time I'll be having an on-screen partner."

True, it isn't, but this is the first time Cleo gets to be with someone she knows. Owen simply smiles at her. "Why wouldn't I be?"

"You're the best boyfriend ever!" Cleo squeals, putting her arms around Owen. "After the shoot, I promise you, we're free to go to Hong Kong!"

Owen can't wait for the shoot to be over with already.

The Fortune of Luck and Hard Work

It's the first day of Cleo's shoot on the set, and she's still inside the tent, eating her sunny-side-up breakfast. She had a van service with the production team to get to their location at Bonifacio Global City, a commercial center filled with glitzy shopping areas. It's where all the rich people live and work. It's basically Manila's Silver City.

Cleo looks at herself in the mirror. She's dolled up like Selene— killer red lipstick and scanty sheer dress with a sultry expression on her face. She tries out a smile, but it appears too forced. She frowns and then smiles again. And again. Until she perfects it enough to fool anyone who sees her. Actors are magicians; nobody knows what's really inside the hat but them. They can pull a rabbit out of the hat and call it a dove, and everyone will see a dove.

Cleo needs to pull herself out of the hat and identify herself as Selene. Not that Selene is a dove or a rabbit—she's more of a snake.

Selene is a beautiful snake that sheds skin for her career.

"I'm not a snake," Cleo says to herself, not wanting to imagine her tongue hissing like a snake's. That'll be too cryptic and weird. "I'm a Leo. I'm a Lion."

"And they're gonna hear you roar? Are you a fan of Katy Perry?" Kristel, the production assistant, chimes in. She's got a lapel in her right hand and the script on the other. She puts the script on the table and takes the brush, combing Cleo's hair to untangle the slight mess.

Cleo smiles wryly. "Just thinking out loud."

"Do you need anything else? Water?" Kristel asks, checking her phone for text messages.

"Water's good. Thanks."

Kristel nods and turns away. The back of her gray t-shirt reads *Production Assistant*, but sometimes she seems like a director herself. She's tiny but also loud. Cleo's guess is it's one of the requirements for being a PA.

"Oh, and Jake's outside looking for you." Kristel glances meaningfully at Cleo. She doesn't need to tell Cleo to go outside. The tone of her voice is enough to make Cleo leave her vanity table and look for Jake.

The searing heat of the sun greets Cleo's skin, it's only 8:00 a.m., and the sun's all high and mighty. But what she sees in front of her soothes her, lightens her anxiety. It's a mural of pastel pink, purple, and blue doors, the doors of imagination. Life in this city may be extravagant, but what brings it to life is the mural art painting in surprising places.

"Have you ever gone mural hunting here?"

Cleo doesn't need to turn toward the voice to know it for Jake's. "I haven't had the time, but looking at it now, I think I'd like to give it a try."

"Perfect."

Cleo turns to look at Jake and finds him staring at the mural in front of them. He's in a casual black t-shirt and dark gray sweatpants as if he just came from a run and casually dropped by the set for the shoot. Now she envies him for wearing something so comfortable.

"Why me?" Cleo asks as the wind blows her hair.

Jake shrugs, fixing the gel on his hair. "You're *Direk* Everett's daughter, aren't you? You're publicity."

"You mean I'm publicity more than I'm a performer?"

"Selene got into an accident. If another random actress fills in, it'll fail because—"

"Because everyone has love teams already, except for me," Cleo concludes for Jake. "And because of my last name."

"But you're here, right? It doesn't matter. You get to be in a lead role." Jake winks at Cleo.

If Cleo were Selene, she'd have the guts to produce an award-winning dramatic slap scene with Jake right now, but she reminds herself she's not Selene. What he's saying about her is also true, so she smiles at him instead. If she can get a peso every time somebody says she's famous because of her last name, she'd be rich enough by now to change her last name.

"Oh, I am," Cleo says daringly. "I'm your leading lady. While Selene's gone, you're stuck with me, and I'm gonna give you hell for it."

"What a hell-raiser! We'll see about that, Walter." Jake smirks, leaving Cleo alone as he goes back to the production crew.

Cleo storms back inside her tent and again looks at herself in the mirror. She pulls out her phone and stalks Selene's social media accounts. She checks Selene's photos, trying to imitate how she smiles, frowns, laughs, and flirts. Selene is pretty much the definition of a lead role, so Cleo spends a few minutes watching her scenes from *teleseryes*. Just as she's playing with the expressions on her face, Kristel comes back again.

"We're rolling in five minutes," Kristel tells Cleo. "Are you good?"

Cleo makes a determined face in the mirror, replying to Kristel's reflection with "Better."

"Okay, Cleo. This is a daring role, a scandalous one. This is the place where you, as Nina, find out about your boyfriend and best friend's secret relationship. You saw them together here on the weekend, when your boyfriend told you we was sick. Got it?" *Direk* Gary stares at Cleo, who's nodding like a good girl.

"Got it," Cleo responds.

"Jake, well, you know what to do," *Direk* Gary says as a matter of fact. "Okay, on your places."

Everyone rushes to their places, including Cleo and Jake. While the director goes back to the tent complex, the assistant director double-checks everything on the set. The gaffer checks the placement and condition of the overhead equipment and lighting.

"QUIET ON THE SET!" the assistant director bellows. "Rolling in five, four, three, two . . .

ACTION!"

PROD. The Boyfriend Switch
ROLL 3. SCENE 18. TAKE 1.
DIRECTOR: Gary Hillaro

Nina pushes her sunglasses up onto her head and goes from one store to another. Life had suddenly gotten better when she got on the reality TV show. The expensive clothes she couldn't buy before are just a peso to her now. What's even better is that she and her best friend Lara get to enjoy all kinds of perks. They've been best friends for as long as she can remember, so nothing on God's green earth can come between them, not even this competition, not even when she's finding herself kind of into Lara's boyfriend, Martin.

As if on cue, Nina gets a text from Martin. He wants to meet up with her to talk about "their feelings," but she disregards it.

She puts her phone back in her bag and rolls her eyes. She'll always be chicks before dicks. There are a lot of Martins in the world, but only one Lara. And she and Lara are, like, all for one and one for all. It's a pact they made way back when they were kids.

Nina's almost tempted to reply, though. She likes Martin, but if it weren't for the boyfriend switch reality TV show, they wouldn't like each other. They've just been put together in circumstances that can make people's feel sort of jumpy, and she's not a believer in a love produced on the screen.

"Miss?" the cashier calls for Nina's attention.

Nina hands her credit card to the cashier and smiles at her. "Sorry."

Speaking of boyfriend switch, Nina wonders how her boyfriend, Ryan, is doing. He barely has time for her now, so Martin has been taking up more space in her head. It's crazy, and she's guilty of thinking about another guy instead of her boyfriend. Oh, the goddess of love must be so stressed right now for only giving her one heart that can dream of two guys.

"Thanks!" Nina says cheerily, leaving the store and strolling around the streets of BGC. The hot sun is making her throat all achy, so she ends up in Heartstrings, brewers of the best coffee in the world.

Inside the cafe, Nina inhales the smell of fresh coffee. It hits her nose like a breath of fresh air, a taste of what it feels like to be alive in a sometimes-monotonous world. A good day gets even better when she sees Lara sitting comfortably on one of the couches, a sweet smile on her face. Excited, she's about to call out to her when a man—no, not just a man, but her boyfriend, Ryan, sits down by Lara.

"What the hell?" Nina murmurs to herself, observing the two from a safe distance. She quickly slips on her sunglasses and watches them.

Yes, Nina's boyfriend and Lara are indeed holding hands. Nina clenches her fists and grits her teeth. So, after all this time, they're going behind her back? Okay, she and Martin like each other, but they didn't go as far as this.

Nina strides over to Ryan and Lara's table, her heart lurching forward, and full of fury. She crosses her arms and looks at them, dropping her shopping bags on the floor.

"Hello, love," Nina greets Ryan sarcastically.

Ryan and Lara both look guilty. Ryan stands up, trying to pacify Nina, but Nina's hand greets his face.

"AND CUT!"

Direk Gary comes out of the tent system and claps his hands. "Well done! Let's do another take and then keep on rolling, yes?"

Cleo breathes out a sigh of relief before smiling to herself. She looks at the crew and then at Jake, who is giving her a nod of approval. This once-in-a-lifetime may have been meant as a joke on her, on the part of Jake or whoever, but this joke can't be joked with. She can't help but laugh.

"Baliw ka na ba?" Kristel comes up behind Cleo, looking warily at her as if she's really gone *loca*.

Cleo shakes her head and returns to her original post, ready for the next take. If these people think they can play her around, then they've got it all wrong. She's played the game too many times to lose this time around.

"Your phone, Cleo," Kristel reprimands Cleo. "We can hear it loud and clear in your tent."

"Oh, wait. Let me turn it off." Cleo goes back to her tent and finds Owen calling her. She rejects his call and starts to type that she's busy and will call back soon, but when she hears *Direk* Gary's ready signal, she turns off her phone without finishing the text. Back in position, she stands ready for the next take.

"Rolling in five, four, three, two . . . ACTION!"

And so, for the next three days of taping, Cleo spends her entire time preparing for the upcoming scenes. She can flaunt herself out there and be Selene for now while she works on her own image. Accepting this role has been the best decision she's ever made. Owen's being an extra boyfriend too. He's been sending snacks and waits for her to finish the shoot, even if it lasts until 4 a.m.

"So." Owen scratches the back of his head when they reach the gates of Cleo's house. It's almost five in the morning, and they've both gotten barely any sleep.

Cleo kisses his cheeks, grateful for his efforts. "Thank you, babe. You're amazing. The shoot's amazing. Everything is amazing, and I'm so tired."

Cleo doesn't feel tired on the set, but on the way home she feels her energy draining. Thankfully Owen's there for her every step of the way. He makes sure she has everything she needs before she sleeps and after she wakes up in the morning. She doesn't know what she'd do without her boyfriend.

Owen gives her a little smile, his eyes locked onto hers. "Dinner tomorrow?"

Cleo can barely keep track of her schedule, but they haven't been anywhere for almost a week now. "Sure. I think call time is at ten in the morning, and we'd have an early pack up. The scenes tomorrow are—I think—easy for someone like me."

"Someone like you?" Owen raises an eyebrow at her, doubtful. "You take everything as a challenge, babe. Nothing is ever too easy for you. I love you."

Cleo yawns and grins at him. "I love you too."

🐿️   🐿️   🐿️

Owen hardly slept a wink. The dark circles under his eyes tell him it's not a great idea to run this morning, but he still changes his clothes, plugs his air pods in his ears, and goes for a run outside. He runs like his life depends on it, and somehow, he believes it does. So, he runs to compete against his racing thoughts.

The neighborhood Owen lives in has never been very lively. It's quiet, and he can hear the soft humming of the birds perched on the trees, but it's the last place in the world ever wants to be. While it's leisurely peaceful with different modern house designs, it all looks the same to him. Each house has some extravagant feature or other—floor-to-ceiling windows, Picasso-worthy artwork on the walls, crystal chandeliers. It's garage after garage with their sleek black Jaguar cars. And as he passes by these houses, he sees the colorful outfits of maids cleaning the front yards.

It seems like the only people seen outside these houses are the house staff. Meanwhile, the masters are riding home in luxury. It's crazy how alike they all are to Owen. He's gotten used to being at the same parties and events as these people, but he still can't enjoy it. He's tired of seeing these people over and over, at places he doesn't want to be.

"Good morning, sir!" Jerry, the security guard, smiles a gap-toothed smile at Owen when he comes to a complete stop at the guard's house—if one can call it that. It's just a tiny little box with a small electric fan, chair, and a radio. Yet, the guard seems content and happy for someone who can't possibly have very much. And maybe that's why he looks happy—none of this stuff is part of his life when the working day is over.

"Good morning," Owen returns, sweat trickling down his face.

"Today is the day, *hindi ba*, sir?"

Yes. Today's the day Owen gets the results of his ALE—his architect licensure exams. He's almost sure it's already posted on the news portal on the university's website. But he hasn't gone online yet. He's not one to dig around in social media. There's nothing there that interests him.

But Owen somehow feels light, like the weight he's been carrying for so long has been finally taken off his shoulders.

"Yeah. You remembered," Owen points out, smiling at that.

"Of course! You've been working so hard for it. *Alam mo na ba* results?" Jerry asks, drinking his mug of coffee that has probably gone cold.

"I haven't checked yet."

Jerry nods. "You should. Share *mo* results *sa'kin ah!*"

"Yeah, of course. I'll let you know," Owen assures Jerry.

"I'm your number one fan, sir!"

Owen doubts that, but it's fun to know he has Jerry as his fan. "I'll head home then. Thanks, Jerry, and enjoy your morning!"

Jerry gives Owen a thumbs up.

Owen shakes his head, smiling on the way home. Back in the family house, he showers and puts down a hearty breakfast. His favorite bacon and eggs as always, surrounded by empty chairs. There's nobody to keep him company. He eats his morning meal quietly. Everyone in his family is busy making money, and he can only guess what their friends say about him. He must be the weak link in the family, lounging around and enjoying the food without working for the family company.

That doesn't matter now. Owen's ready for this day to turn his life around. Money is not all there is in the world. No amount of money can ever satisfy a person. It just keeps everyone wanting more.

Owen opens his browser on the phone and types in the website of the professional directive board. Over a thousand people passed the exams. Owen skims through the list, looking for the last names that start with V. There are quite a few Velazcos, and it's kind of hard to track since the letters blur together. But as his eyes follow from one Velazco to another, he realizes there's no Owen there. The closest to Owen is Olivia. He checks the names one by one, thinking they must have mixed up his name with somebody else, but after almost an hour of scanning through the names, he realizes there's nothing wrong with the list. It's just that his name isn't on it.

CHAPTER 8

Get a Tissue,
This One's a Tearjerker

Cleo's body hums in anticipation as she waits for her mocha frappuccino. The barista, whose nametag reads "Reese," doesn't ask for her name. He smiles charmingly at her before uncapping his marker and writing her name on the cup. She waits at the other side of the counter, and after a few minutes, she finally gets her frap. She turns her cup around only to discover that the barista has written "Cloe."

That's fine. Cleo thinks she's just getting started, so people tend to misspell her name. At least Cloe is close to Cleo. She'll give the barista a B+ for the effort. It's late afternoon already, so maybe he's tired too, writing name after name on cups.

Cleo leaves the coffee shop, drained after a long day. They'd been shooting scenes for days now, and it feels like she can take a break, but on this shoot she takes nothing for granted. In front of her, the grip trucks are parked in a long straight line, an imposing presence reminding her that this is a massive project and she can't afford to fail.

"Let's pack up, people! Get some rest, and we'll continue tomorrow!" *Direk* Gary suddenly announces, looking at the script. "Call time's at 6 a.m."

Everyone moves quickly, putting the equipment back in the trucks while the catering prepares the afternoon snacks. Cleo's told to eat before she leaves, but she refuses. She has a dinner date with Owen tonight, so she's planned to starve herself so she can feast later on. She always eats much more when she's with her boyfriend.

Cleo hasn't even waited five minutes at the convenience store when Owen comes speeding in on his motorcycle. He's earlier than usual. Usually, it'll take him half an hour to be there with this kind of rush hour. It's the clocking-out madness, and everyone's dying to go home, but they end up getting home late at night because of the traffic jam. It also explains why Owen prefers they take their dinner outside and wait for traffic congestion to lighten up.

"You're dressed nice," Cleo observes. Owen's linen button-down shirt and chinos look so classy on him she's not sure he should wear them while driving his motorcycle.

Owen smiles back at Cleo. "You're not so bad yourself."

Cleo feels pretty close to "bad." She's in the most basic t-shirt and pants, and her hair is all over the place. She didn't get to have the time to fix herself.

"Don't worry about it. It's going to get messed up anyway." Owen hands over another helmet to Cleo. "Hop on, babe."

Cleo blows Owen a kiss. "A pleasure."

Cleo straddles the motorcycle and wraps her arms around Owen's waist. The wind whips her hair around, and it frees her. It's a good thing she didn't comb her hair. Otherwise, she'll end up combing it over and over again. At 6 p.m., EDSA has become a man-and-car-eater-road, sucking everything on wheels, except for the motorbikes. Motorcycles are thunderbolts and lightning. Even at this speed, it took them almost an hour to get to their destination. Driving is always more fun in the Philippines . . . .

Owen has decided they should have dinner in Intramuros, a historical district of Manila. Inside the walled city, Cleo feels like she's back in the Spanish colonial era, when the city served as the seat of the Spanish occupation. It used to house the elite citizens of colonial Manila, and no natives were allowed to live inside. as the place served as a tactical fortification to protect the city from foreign invasion. The hard-stoned walls are weathered. They've withstood many devastating natural and man-made disasters. You can't come here and not think and wonder about the past. The place has such a rich heritage. It's always been here, but Cleo has never bothered to tour around it. She thinks it'll always be there. It's so easy to take for granted the things and people around you, not realizing that one day, all of it can disappear without warning, and you may never know why.

"Wow," Cleo says, awestruck by the Manila Cathedral in front of them.

"It's not our anniversary, is it?"

Owen shakes his head, falling quiet.

Cleo doesn't want to think about it, but the thought comes unbidden: is Owen going to propose to her? She shouldn't get ahead of herself, but he's been too unlike himself lately. Is he nervous? Because she is too. She's not even sure how she's going to respond to it. She loves him, but are they getting engaged now? She still has so much going on.

"Just dinner," Owen says, holding Cleo's hand and leading her to a café next to the cathedral.

The server takes them up on the roof deck with two reservations. The yellow light bulbs above them give them a soft glow to the evening. Above, Cleo can almost see the faraway buildings twinkling in the night. They sit at the side at a safe distance from other couples. Now, she's starting to get the jitters. Owen's such a private person she can feel this is something serious.

There is candlelight between Cleo and Owen. Hanging garlands and lanterns create a romantic mood while the cathedral shines, capturing the eyes of everyone. It's old and beautiful, a classic Owen move.

"How's your day?" Owen asks, browsing through the menu.

The breaking of silence is enough to make Cleo gush about how her day went, and it's easy to keep going. Lately, life has been favoring her. And she's had so little time to talk to him these past days—hardly any at all.

"Oh, and you won't believe what happened today! The barista didn't ask for my name! He almost had it—he spelled it as Cloe, but close enough, right?" Cleo shares. "Anyway, so Jake and I have had this romantic scene, and boom, I gave him beautiful eyes, and he thought I was Selene."

Cleo's pretty proud of herself for coaxing Jake to do that romantic scene. He can be indifferent to her, but now he can't deny she did great in that intimate scene. All this talk makes her hungry, so she looks at the menu and orders beef steak and salad.

"On the second day of the shooting, love team JerLie swung by the set! They're pretty good as a couple. I think they're getting back together, and then they watched me for a while. They told me I could even top Selene's acting. Can you imagine that?" Cleo adds, swooning at the memory of it.

Owen nods as he listens to Cleo, and she's barely getting started. There's so much she has to say to him. She hasn't told him about the sexy scene because she's been too tired to tell him stories. Now that they have the time to be together, she has this need to fill in the blanks and spaces.

"Cleo . . . I," Owen cuts Cleo off.

Cleo stops short. He's not going to ask her now, is he? "Yeah?"

"Nothing. What is it about that scene?"

Oh, thank God. Cleo's heart is thumping hard against her ribcage. Doesn't want to think about marriage, even though she can already hear wedding bells from the cathedral. It's a good thing he asks about the scenes because they're safe territory and she's got tons to tell him. It's exciting her more than ever. If this ever becomes a hit, a wedding and marriage will move further down her priority list, so she tells him all about what went on for the last three days. He nods now and then to acknowledge what she's say-ing, but he seems lost in his own thoughts, kind of like she's white noise. When the food comes, he just eats his steak. Meanwhile, Cleo orders more carbonara.

"I love their food," Cleo salivates. "Thank you for this, babe. Am I talking too much? Sorry, it's just—it's been an amazing day. I can't see anything going wrong now. I'm, you know, so energized, and everything's finally falling into place. You're right, and this year is good for both of us."

"For sure," Owen agrees, staring at Cleo.

"This is the best day ever! We even got to have a date! I told you I'd make time for you. And the way I acted the scene, superb. *Direk* Gary even said it's a perfect take and . . . ."

"Let's break up."

Cleo's not sure that came from Owen. She must be hearing things, but it sure caught her attention—and knocked the wind out of her. Her mind's racing, firing questions she doesn't have answers to,

"Did you say something?" Cleo asks, putting her fork down and finally listening. "I wasn't paying attention so—"

"Exactly. I said, let's break up," Owen says. His eyes are gravely serious, and more intense than she's ever seen them.

"I—I thought you were gonna p-propose," Cleo stutters, laugh-ing nervously. The exact opposite of a breakup. She's not ready for a breakup. "Then what is with this romantic setup? I just . . .why?"

"Why? I don't know, Cleo, you tell me."

Owen's never been like this with Cleo before. This boyfriend or ex-boyfriend of hers seems determined. He's firm in his decision, but she can't understand why he wants to do this. They're having a great evening together, so what makes him think of breaking up? Why bring her here where the mood suggests the exact opposite?

"I'm not a mind reader," Cleo replies. The idea of more food makes her sick now.

"You don't need to be a mind reader to get what I'm saying," Owen counters, sighing. "We're not working out."

Cleo's baffled. Not working out?? They've been working out so well! If Owen had been unhappy all this time, why didn't he communicate that to her? Why spring it so suddenly, and so cruelly, out of the blue? Cleo's at a loss for words. This can't happen now, when her dreams are actually showing the promise of becoming reality. There are places to go and red carpets to walk down, and in all her dreams of these things, Owen is by her side. Now he's saying he wants to break up.

"Let's end this," Owen says firmly, as if the decision had been made long ago, he's already past it, and Cleo's not allowed to react.

Cleo's too shocked even to register the tears welling up in her eyes.

"Help me understand, please. I don't know where I went wrong. We've been good these past few weeks. My schedule is just hectic as always. We're eating a freaking nice dinner, so why?"

"See? You can't think of a reason why. So, what does that make you, Cleo?"

Cleo wracks her brain. "Um, clueless because you won't explain a single thing about what's happening right now? Is this because I don't want to get married yet? I know that the subject has come up a good bit, but as you can see . . . ."

"It's not that. It's never been about that, and you know it. You're just too busy for your good." Owen looks away from her, then back again. "You in your little bubble, Cleo. It's always you, you, you. Cleo this, Cleo that. I'm tired of it."

"You're saying you're tired of me." Cleo's voice breaks, but she tries to keep it from shattering.

Owen's exasperated; Cleo can see that. He's been weary before, but not like this. They always make things work until one of them eventually gives up. And he's done.

"I guess I am."

Four little words, but they clang like a bell in Cleo's ears. She doesn't have anything else left to say. She can't think straight on this beautiful and dreamy dinner date. She can't stop him from breaking up with her. It's his decision, and she respects it, no matter how much it breaks her heart. She loves him, but sometimes love isn't enough to keep people around.

So, when Owen finally takes Cleo home, she doesn't know what to say. Is she supposed to say some last words to her ex? She guesses not. So, she keeps her last words to herself. The only thing that's making this ending real for her is the "I love you" left unsaid. They part without a word or a wave goodbye, which makes it worse than it already is.

🌿　🌿　🌿

Cleo's back on the set, and she doesn't even know what she's doing there. There's no room for her to breathe or to think. She's trying to get herself back in the role, but her mind keeps flashing back to last night. This morning there were no calls or texts from Owen. The fact that there is no change in his heart is agony to hers.

"Be ready in five," Kristel says to Cleo, who's staring at the obelisk monument of Dr. Jose Rizal, the national hero of the Philippines.

Cleo's day four shoot takes place in Rizal Park, also known as Luneta Park in Manila. It's a historical urban park bearing many footprints from the past. In front of her is the bronze sculpture of Jose Rizal, dignified and indomitable. He holds a book representing his novels *Noli Me Tangere* and *El Filibusterismo*. Cleo, like everyone else, learned it all in high school—the cancerous Spanish colonization, and Rizal's passionate writing exposing the brutal truths surrounding that occupation. And for this, the Spanish executed him.

"Chop, chop, Cleo! Do you want to replace Rizal over there?" *Direk* Gary suddenly asks, giving her the script. "I'd have you executed already if you weren't my lead female."

Cleo shakes her head. She looks at the statue and the Marine Corps and security guards continually circling the perimeter to guard the monument, not necessarily because the monument needs guarding, but as an act of utmost respect. Even in death, Rizal's being protected and honored because of his legacy. Cleo wants to be like him, but she certainly doesn't want to be executed by *Direk* Gary.

Historical places are historical for a reason. Maybe Cleo should name Intramuros the City of Heartbreak. She certainly doesn't want to walk on its brick roads ever again, no matter how beautiful it is. But there's time to think about heartbreak. She's still an actress. She'd do well today to not think of Owen.

But behind Cleo, minutes before they start rolling again, the couple who just went off the *kalesa* poses at the side of the two-wheeled horse-drawn carriage, and then the man kneels on one knee, holding out the ring. Cleo can't see if it's diamond, but she's sure the girl's already crying, and everyone applauds. She feels like stabbing her heart and letting it bleed throughout the day, but she doesn't have the time to process her feelings. All too soon, they're rolling again.

"ACTION!" the assistant director bellows.

PROD. The Boyfriend Switch
ROLL 1. SCENE 3. TAKE 1.
DIRECTOR: Gary Hillaro

Nina looks at Ryan, her boyfriend. She smiles sweetly at him as he cups her cheeks. And then she sees Owen's serious face, eyebrows drawn in distaste at her. Owen's frown and low voice. Owen's decision the night before. Owen not saying a word as he drops her off. Suddenly, tears stream down her face, counter to the emotion she's supposed to express in this scene. Love hurts. Love isn't sweet as candy; it's the bitter taste of stewed coffee in the morning and of one too many drinks at night.

"CUT!" *Direk* Gary yells. "Why are you crying?"
Jake sighs, shaking his head at her.

Cleo wipes her tears away. Kristel hands her some tissues, and she's grateful for that. She's been holding back her emotions for so long, suppressing the pain that's only gotten worse since her last evening with Owen. She's been trying to focus on her work. Trying to act gaga over Jake is just too much.

"I'm sorry, I don't know what came over me, I—"

"Let's try this again! Take two!" *Direk* Gary orders.

The scene's taking up the entire shoot, and Cleo still can't fake being foolishly in love with Jake. Everyone's tired and hungry, and the required emotion isn't going to surface anytime soon. She's considering replacing Rizal on his monument because she's sure even the national hero couldn't do what she's being asked to do.

"AGAIN!" *Direk* Gary fumes.

The entire production crew sighs, and Cleo can feel their glares fixed on her back. She wants to save them from this suffering. It's like a thriller movie where the lead's dumb enough to yell out an invitation to the killer, and that lead is her. She realizes everyone's depending on her, and she can't do it, after all. She tried to run before she learned how to walk. She's not ready for this, and she doesn't want to be in a movie directed by her father's associate. Giving up isn't a weakness; it's knowing what she can and can't do. What she does after that is what marks her as her.

Cleo stops and says, "I'm sorry. I can't do it. Thank you so much for everything."

Direk Gary comes out of his tent, frowning at her. "What'd you just say?"

Cleo walks out of the scene, fearful and heartbroken. The not-so-fresh air wraps around her like the comfort of an embrace. The spectators are waiting for her near the main road, and everyone's trying to get a picture of the shoot. They'll probably make a story out of this, and everyone will love it. After all, the girl who took the place of Selene is walking out on her own accord. She can already imagine the headlines: *Cleo Walter Walks Out of a Golden Opportunity*. Or the best one yet, *Cleo Walter—the Audacity?*

Cleo can barely see where she's going. All she knows is that she has to get out of there. Fast. But she's being swarmed by people asking her all sorts of questions. What's happening with the shoot? Is working with Jake steamy? Where is she going? What's happening in the scene?

And Cleo doesn't care. This isn't her calling. She's fighting a war that isn't her war. She's fighting for somebody else's kingdom, and it's plain crazy. Maybe she's not meant to be an actor. Before that phone call from Ms. Aika, she'd been contemplating working behind the scenes. Perhaps that's what she's meant to do, be a director or a producer. What's clear to Cleo now is that she has to re-direct herself to the right path. This isn't her. She's tried, and she's done. This is just the ending of an old beginning.

Cleo lifts her face, letting people take pictures of her. Reporters quickly have their mics ready, but she answers none of them, and then, as if by some miracle, Owen's out there, smiling at her with an extra helmet in hand. He looks like he hasn't showered, and somehow, she knows he's not okay.

Cleo runs to him, wrapping her arms around his waist.

Owen says, "I smell bad."

Cleo sniffs and cries into his shirt. She doesn't want the rest of the world to see her crying, so this will do for now. "I'm sorry I'm turning you into my tissue."

Owen laughs but keeps Cleo safe in his arms, and the rest of the world falls away. "Why don't you drive?"

Cleo takes the helmet and grins. "Are you sure?"

"Yes. Go, before I change my mind. You're scaring me already," Owen jokes, and just like that, they're okay again.

Cleo has no regrets about leaving the set. She straps her helmet on her head before hopping onto the motorcycle. Cameras flash, but she doesn't mind. For the first time in many years, she doesn't care how she looks.

"Cleo, where are you going?"

"Why are you leaving the set?"

"Did you have a row with *Direk* Gary?"

"Are you more like your father or your mother?"

Cleo hears all these questions, but she's got one thing on her mind right now: home.

Take a Trip Down Memory Lane and Try Not to Cry

B ack at home, Cleo has never felt safer. No cameras, no reporters—just her and the man she loves. After days of shooting, she can finally rest easy. She doesn't need to worry about what other people will think of her, and it's such a relief to stop chasing something that's never really hers in the first place.

"I'll come to pick you up tomorrow. Get some rest for now," Owen says, tucking a strand of Cleo's hair behind her ear.

Cleo's grateful to hear those words. They're not breaking up; they're making up. She can only hug Owen and kiss his cheek. They know there's the elephant in the room, but they also know now's not the right time to talk about it.

"Thank you. Really," Cleo murmurs, oddly calm and satisfied. Owen gives her a little smile and a peck on the lips. He's about to leave when Thea suddenly comes down the stairs, holding a mop and catching sight of them on the doorstep. She'd have been cleaning the second floor. She always keeps the house spotless.

"Is that Owen? Come inside! Have dinner." Thea waves at Owen, looking back and forth between him and Cleo, and understanding dawns on her face. "Oh, I'm sorry. Am I interrupting something?"

Typical of Cleo's mother. Thea likes to tease, and she doesn't want to miss out on anything going on in her daughters' lives and loves. She's cheeky like that.

"It's okay, *Tita*. My family and I have a dinner date," Owen replies, raising an eyebrow at Thea.

Thea winks at Owen as if there's a secret just between them, but Cleo can already guess it's because her mother knows what his family is really like. It's all pretense, but they're still his family, and he needs to make an appearance.

"If you say so." Thea smiles at them before calling out to Anne to help prepare the dinner.

"Tomorrow?" Owen asks, his voice calm, and it soothes Cleo. He's looking at her softly, and she feels she could break and crumble at any moment, but she's not doing that. If anything, she feels she's turned into someone else—a better version of herself.

Cleo bites her lower lip, wanting to say what she's feeling, but she can't find words for them just now. She doesn't want to let him down anymore. "Rain check for tomorrow? But if I don't have anything, let's go somewhere far."

"Hey, I'm sorry." Owen's eyes are cast down, looking at their interlocked hands. "And sure. We'll take things slow."

Exhausted, Cleo leans into him, dropping her head on his shoulder and whispering, "Thank you. I'm sorry, too. I'll see you then."

Five minutes later, Cleo pulls away and says her goodbyes. With longing eyes, she watches Owen leave. He closes their metal gate on his way out and starts his motorcycle. He gives her one last look before speeding off onto the road.

Dinner's quiet. Usually, Cleo does most of the talking, but this evening she barely says a word. She doesn't know how to tell her family what happened on the set. She's chewing the *kaldereta's* potato and pork, but she can barely savor it. It's mildly spicy, so at least she can still identify what she's eating.

Anne and Thea probably think Cleo doesn't notice the way they share knowing looks, but she does. She's hyperaware of what's going on around her whenever she falls silent. It's very Sherlock-y of her, and it's a skill that that's been very useful to her. This exchange of looks between her mother and sister isn't new to her. It's their code for Cleo-has-something-to-say-but-she-needs-time-to-say-it. Maybe she should surprise them, see how they react.

"I'm saying it now. I walked off the set," Cleo bursts out, eating like there's no tomorrow.

"We're not, you know, asking you about it. Right, *Ma*?" Anne says, pretending not to be dying of curiosity. Cleo knows she and Thea are thinking the same thing—something happened to Cleo today-and they're just waiting for her to spill the tea.

Thea quickly masks her face with a look of astonishment. She's pretending she doesn't know what's bothering Cleo, but of course, 'it's on the internet and TV. "Right, right!" Thea says. "Oh, my. I'm so sorry, *anak*."

Stuffed already, Cleo pats her stomach and says, "I want to be a director."

Anne chokes on her food. Cleo quicky gives her a bottle of water while Thea thumps her back. Anne drinks her water and stares blankly at Cleo. "Sorry. I—you want to be like you-know-who?"

Thea taps Anne's back lightly as if to scold her, understanding in her eyes. She's always been so considerate of what Cleo wants in life, and she never has once stopped believing in her daughters.

"You'll do great, Cleo," Thea says with conviction, sweet and firm. Cleo sometimes wonders if her mom had been a life coach in her previous life. Thea's great at talking and cheering people up. Cleo was convinced that if Thea were to run for president, she'd win by a landslide.

"I don't want to be like him," Cleo clarifies to Anne, finishing her dinner and cleaning up their table. "I feel like I'm meant to be something else. I've been trying to be an actor a long time now. I didn't even stop to think about what else might be in store for me.

I boxed myself in and made myself a prisoner."

"We'll always support you. These people on social media and wherever else—they can only talk about what they see on the surface. You know how they all love gossip. But there's much depth in you." Thea helps Cleo wash the dishes, smiling genuinely at her. "You're more than just an actor."

"Sorry, Leo, I just . . . don't want you to be like him, so I got a little panicky when you said you want to direct, that's all," Anne adds, filling the pitchers with water and putting them in the refrigerator. "But I'm not gonna stop you from reaching your dreams, so you better top him, *Direk* Cleo!"

Cleo grinned at Anne and thought about what had happened today. She's lost the most promising role ever, but she's also gained a valuable insight: it's not all about playing lead roles because these roles can't come to life without the people behind the scenes. She wants to try to be a director and see how it goes. The next time she goes out in the public eye, she'll make sure she can answer their questions. Speaking of questions, one question from today has been bothering her.

When Anne leaves to fold her newly washed clothes, Cleo follows. She knows Anne must know something. "Anne, I've only just thought about this—do you know what mom used to do in her early years?"

Anne freezes for a single beat, then resumes her fold. She doesn't turn around to face Cleo. "Why?"

"Before I left the set, a reporter said, are you more like your father or your mother?" Cleo air quotes. "What do you think that's about?"

"It's probably nothing."

Cleo knows it's something, and Anne's not going to say what. She thought she was observant enough to form a theory, but she could never gather enough clues. Giving up on her sister, she joins Thea in the living room. Her mother's watching an action *teleserye* about a great policeman who manages to stay alive no matter how many bullets he takes. The show's been going on for almost four years already, and people still enjoy it. It's kind of like a nightly ritual.

"*Ma*?" Cleo starts, watching the *teleserye* too. "I want to ask you something, but I don't want you to feel like I'm cornering you—even though it's exactly what I'm doing."

"You've always been very direct." Thea laughs heartily, enjoying her play on the word. "You know you can ask me anything."

Cleo's wondering why it has only ever occurred to her today to ask about it. "There's this reporter who asked me if I'm more like, er, dad or you. Why?"

Thea stalls, the way Anne did, so Cleo quickly apologizes, wishing she hadn't brought up what might be a sensitive subject. "I'm sorry, *Ma*. Forget I asked."

But Thea just looked at her for a long moment. Cleo couldn't read her face. Finally, "I knew this day would come," Thea said, "And I always said that when it did, I wouldn't hide anything. How about we go over to the rooftop and talk?"

🌿　🌿　🌿

The photo albums Thea carried with her could be considered antique. They're covered in dust as if they had been buried in a time capsule that's not supposed to open until the end of time. There's an ominous vibe coming from them, the kind of nervousness a person feels when they step into a house of horrors. All Cleo knows is that these albums are heavy with revelations. The floral design on the covers looks cheerful; Cleo can tell the books contain nothing of the sort.

But they're here, on the edge of their seats with just the company of the moon and stars. The table between Cleo and Thea seems to vibrate with tension with each passing moment. It feels like it's getting smaller, and soon, the story will be laid out for Cleo like a deck of cards.

"You deserve to hear this story." Thea's taking deep breaths, and

Cleo recognizes this as a sign of apprehension. She and her mother are not so different, after all. "Honestly, I don't know where to begin . . ."

Unexpectedly, Anne has also joined them, carrying three bottles of beer. When Thea sees this, she laughs in surprise but ends up opening s bottle for herself. Now that's something Cleo hasn't seen her mother ever do before, which makes her curious.

"I thought we might need these," Anne comments, smiling mischievously at Cleo and Thea. "Beer is a great source of moral support."

Cleo also takes a bottle, taking a big gulp out of it. Anne's right. They need the beer for this story because whatever comes out of these photo albums will surely help her decide what she's going to do from this point on.

Thea clears her throat and then opens the photo albums, spreading the photos on the glass table. They're pictures of her when she was young. She's a breathtaking earth goddess with her short hair and chocolate brown skin. Her deep-set eyes are naturally hypnotizing, drawing everyone in with just a look. With the kind of angular face she has, there's no doubt she can be called the most beautiful girl in the world.

"On the beautiful island of Siquijor in 1995, I lived an ordinary life with my family and grandparents . . . and it had been my home for a good nineteen years or so. It's filled with the best that nature has to offer, and life was simple then. We didn't have electricity, so we did everything manually. And maybe that's why I'm such a neat freak." Thea laughs, smiling fondly at the memory of it. "The sun rises, and the sun sets, and everything we'll ever need is on the island. Not a speck of worry in our minds. I used to have my hammock when I was little, and I remember *tatay's* happy face whenever he came home with a bucket of fish."

This is the first time Cleo's heard this story, and now she's wondering why she's only just hearing it now. Siquijor sounds like a fantasy dream island, and she's itching to go there and have her mother tell the story in the house where she once lived. But despite the beauty of the story's beginning, Cleo can already sense it will end in disaster.

Thea flips the page of the photo album, and a photo of Thea in her late teens looks out from the page. She still looks young, but her jawline's much more pronounced, and there's a hint of mischievousness in her eyes. A flower crown rests on her head, and at her side are three boys whom Cleo can only guess are her suitors.

"They were my playmates back then. We used to do everything under the sun, and then eventually we moved on from the friendship state into a more, hmm . . . how do you say it now? A dating one? They wanted to be my *jowa*."

"Oh, mom, don't say *jowa*. Just say lover or boyfriend or something else," Anne groans.

Thea sighs. "Okay, okay. Anyway, I never liked any of them in any way other than as friends. They were just . . . my friends. I was their favorite, you know? I was their island girl. They used to call me *Diwata*, the goddess of Siquijor."

Cleo can see why. Her mother exudes nature. Everything about her seems so naturally inviting, and with her serene smile, she looks as if her purpose is to bring peace to this chaotic earth.

"What is it like? Being an island girl?" Cleo asks, trying to picture what Thea's life was like.

Thea recalls her past.

In the town of Maria in Siquijor, Thea had spent her days watching the incredible rise and fall of the sea waves. The whitewashed sands and crystal-clear waters of Salagdoong Beach were always a sight to behold. She didn't know any life other than this, and she had no hankering to see what was on the other side, whatever it may be. At night, she'd lie on the soft, warm brown earth as a myriad of fireflies set the island alight like Christmas lights.

"The Spaniards called Siquijor an *Isla de Fuegos*, an island of fires," Thea adds. "We're also known for our folk healing, and some might even say we bewitch people. Some people still think it's an island of magic and sorcery, but it's all just traditional healing practices. With all the herbs, barks, and woods over there, you can concoct a love potion, you know."

"A love potion?" Cleo echoes, amused. She doesn't believe in that kind of thing, but looking back now, when they didn't have much money then, her mom turned to herbal medicine. It wasn't the most practical solution sometimes, but it turned out that the skill she got from her hometown was what helped ease their financial burden.

Thea had once tried making a love potion, out of genuine curiosity. One day, she came out of their Nipa hut house and went around the island, gathering whatever herbs she could find. She took a small rock and smashed her improvised ingredients in one go. Later that afternoon, she splashed the scent around her clothes and looked for Andres, the boy she'd been spending a lot of time with these days. When she found Andres, she gave him a huge, gleeful smile.

"Why are you so happy to see me?" Andres asked. Even in his sando and shorts, he looked good.

Thea shrugged. "Aren't you happy to see me?"

Thea told Andres that she was wearing a special potion just for him. Andres laughed and told her she didn't need a potion—he liked her already. But Thea knew it was the love potion because, in the days that followed, other boys on the island started professing their love for her. They told her she was the goddess of their life. She respectfully told them she would always care for them as friends.

"*Ma*, it's not the love potion. It's your beauty," Anne remarks, drinking her beer. "You didn't need to do that. They'll follow you anywhere you go."

"Wow!" Cleo exclaims.

Thea winks at her children, laughing out loud in a way that was classy and regal as well as amused. It's like she doesn't have the ability to look silly or awkward. "I know that now. I didn't know it then, okay? I—"

"You're oblivious to your beauty, *Ma*!" Cleo cuts Thea short.

Thea puts down her beer and breathes in and out again. "But beauty can be deceiving. Being the island girl, everyone thought they loved and adored me. They made me the goddess of beauty and love, but I couldn't love any of them. They didn't realize it, but the thing they really loved wasn't me—it was my face."

Cleo knows how deceiving and tricky beauty can be all too well. Yet, it was her face that had made her able to keep food on the table and aim for other things. She owed her success to it.

"And then the islanders wanted to see Siquijor's beautiful women all together. They wanted a contest to decide who was fairest of them all," Thea continues her story.

With Thea's rising fame, the locals wanted to celebrate their island's beauty, making a competition out of it. They invited young girls to this contest and made them walk, smile, and run. Thea excelled at everything without fail, and she won the title of the most beautiful girl in Siquijor. Because it made everyone happy, she did everything they asked her to do.

"Thea, our diwata," the locals cried out.

Thea didn't mind. She had a lot of friends, and the days were always filled with fun. People got to dress her however they liked while she smiled on. These were Thea's people, and she was contented with that.

"So, you're Miss Congeniality?" Cleo butts in.

"Try Miss Naïve," Thea counters. "And then he came—the dashing American boy with blue eyes and blonde hair."

Cleo knows that when there's a boy involved, the story usually heads toward disaster, and she's not wrong.

Mirror, Mirror on the Wall, Who's the Fairest of Them All?

*T*hea's world fell apart when the American boy came crashing into her life. He stood at least six feet tall with baby blue eyes, and he came to the island on the day she participated in the local pageant. This was her first official beauty pageant, and he came right on time.

Thea found out the American was part of a PR piece covering Siquijor's local pageant. Slowly, their island was being promoted to people in faraway places. Their local government said the publicity would boost tourism. The island wasn't cursed, but blessed with magical gifts—the enchanting beauty of Siquijor. And Thea was their muse.

"Who is he?" Thea asked her friend Nena. He was talking to the local officials, and the look on his face was stony. He seemed like a determined man, someone who would push until he got what he wanted.

"Everett, I heard," Nena replies, pulling the petals off the flower one by one, playing the old game. He loves me; he loves me not. "He's dreamy, isn't he?"

Everett was dreamy, and Thea was lovestruck. When he caught her staring, she quickly looked away, blushing. She felt conscious of how she looked. It didn't matter if people called her goddess—she only needed one person to tell her that, and he wouldn't spare her even a look. He was not like the rest of the young boys on the island. He looked so deep and mysterious.

Thea realized she had to make an impression. She wasn't just beautiful; she was also intelligent. She wasn't going to make people love her; she was going to make them respect her.

Thea took a photo from the other album and showed it to Cleo. It was a photo of her with a crown made of flowers and her sash made out of leaves, and she had a winning smile.

"We weren't exactly the most developed province, so we tried to make do with what we have," Thea explains, leaving the photo in Cleo's hands. "I was crowned Lady Siquijor, and everyone believed I was going to put Siquijor on the map."

"For tourism," Anne says. "With Island Girl being Miss Beautiful and Nice on the most enchanting island, everyone will go gaga over it. You'll have the tourists rushing to come to visit Siquijor."

Thea nods, pausing for a while.

"Did it work?" Cleo probes, unable to sleep without knowing the entire story.

The island pageant was working really well. It just so happened that the locals wanted more. When news got around about the national pageant in Manila, they came to Thea's door day and night, pushing her to go further. Her parents refused, saying Manila was a dangerous city and would ruin their simple life.

Thea always believed her parents, never questioned them. To do that would be disrespectful. From what she could tell about Manila, it was a city of sin. Her grandparents, neighbors, and friends all told her so. Whenever someone chose to go to Manila, they always ended up living a miserable life. She didn't want that. She wanted to stay on the island where she was safe and familiar with everyone.

On one sunny day, Thea was collecting seashells, just as she usually did, and then she suddenly got an unexpected visitor. It was Everett in a white shirt and tattered pants. He was offering her the shells he had collected himself. She took them and wondered what he was doing there. For a while, they just shared the moment of collecting seashells until he spoke.

"People should come here on your island."

Thea looked beyond the horizon and thought of it. "I hope they don't."

"Why?"

"Because it wouldn't feel homely then. This is my safe space."

Everett sat next to Thea on the sand. "You can't stay here forever. You have to stretch your wings, reach greater heights. With your face, you can do a lot more."

"Just the face?" Thea teased; a bit disappointed. That's the only thing he noticed.

"Would you give me some of your time today so I can get to know you, and maybe then I can say something that's not just about your face?"

"That was the start of a good romance, and some people would never understand it, but your father has been good to me. He made me want to dream bigger," Thea says with bittersweet fondness. "So, when the registration for the national pageant opened, he convinced me to go to Manila. He was about to leave the country, anyway. I was heartbroken, of course. I'd never met a man who was that persistent to win in life. It made me feel like I should try to live at the same level. Everybody on the island looked up to him because he was fair-skinned and good-looking, but deep inside, he was just as lost as I was—probably still is. We spent an hour or two together every day. We didn't want to give people something to talk about. Your grandparents would have been mad if they found out I was spending so much time with a foreigner, so we were careful, and it was fine with me. I liked my private moments with him. Eventually, he did convince me to come to Manila, and that was because he'd be staying in the country, after all, as part of the nationals."

"*Para sa pag-ibig*," Cleo remarks, getting a picture now, of the sweet love her parents once shared.

Thea nods in agreement. "Yes, all in the name of love."

Going to Manila scared Thea, but losing Everett was unimaginable. If they could both achieve their goals, they could have a great future together. Thea's parents took a lot of convincing They were adamant she wasn't going anywhere. She was their youngest daughter, so naturally, they were very protective of her. It was their neighbors who managed to convince them. They told her parents that they would help with the sponsorship and that the local government had talked to some brand partnerships in the city. It meant extra income for them, and all would be paid for. All they needed to do was to send her to the city.

Thea's parents finally saw what a big opportunity it was, so they agreed. Everett went on ahead as they had a schedule to follow, so she went on her own, afraid and all alone. But the minute she stepped onto the ground in Manila it seemed, news about her had already gotten around. She was instantly famous. She was Island Lady Siquijor. She was a fresh candidate who had not the slightest touch of the crazy metropolitan.

The sponsors and brand advertisers came. They overwhelmed Thea with their offers and deals, and being someone who didn't know anything at all about this world, she said yes because it meant going forward with her goals. It involved money, and it would help her family.

Thea did things she'd never done before—she was interviewed in front of the camera, got the chance to stay in a hotel or condo, all provided by sponsors, and had to dress nicely every day. Her clothes would be so nice she didn't want to change out of them, but each new dress or outfit would turn out to be better than the last.

"Manila's hectic. I never thought I'd make it here, but I did, and I just felt so proud. I was Lady Siquijor, and everyone was cheering for me. It didn't matter that I came from an unknown island. I felt loved. I felt like I was bringing something to the city, as the people here had never met anyone like me before."

Thea spreads out the photos taken of her when she got to Manila.

Cleo stares at them and realizes how her mother hasn't changed. She's still as beautiful as ever, and her presence is naturally soothing to the soul.

"How was Manila then, *Ma*? Did it drive you nuts?" Cleo prompts, knowing this is something her mother hasn't looked back on for years.

Thea stands up and gazes at the night sky. "It did, but the good thing was that I made a friend there."

Thea had no idea what was waiting for her there, but she certainly didn't think it was going to be a woman who, in another life, might have been driving slaves forward with a whip. This thirty-something woman clad in a blouse and pencil skirt was inspecting Thea from head to toe. She made sure nothing ever escaped her eagle eye, which made the other candidates afraid of her. In terms of height, she was shorter than most of the candidates, but she was tough as a drill sergeant and completely confident in the way she stood in front of them and talked to them.

"I'm Elle, the talent coordinator for the nationals. You are all my responsibility, and failure to comply with my schedule will get you nowhere. Is that understood?" Elle asks, hands on her hips.

The other ten candidates were whispering to each other. They were talking about Elle's face.

"Is her hair really that slick? It looks like a man's."

"She's got thin lips, and they're cracked in all the wrong places. And her pimples?"

"We're not gonna be bullied by her."

Elle must have picked up what they were saying because she immediately turned to them. "Why don't you try me?"

Thea loved Elle right then and there. She wasn't afraid of her.

Elle turned to Thea and snapped. "And you, why do you think you're here?"

"I don't know yet, but I'm willing to learn."

Elle smiled at Thea. "So long as you follow everything I say, then I've got a good feeling we'll get along."

"And we did. Elle didn't have the beauty that the candidates possessed, but she had the ability to turn these faces into something more. The other candidates didn't see that," Thea elaborates, sitting back again. "She was my mentor and friend. She never gave me any special treatment. She could make others cry, but not me. I could never get mad at her. She taught me the ropes of pageantry and gave me tips in the screening process. It's especially hard for a provincial girl like me, but I was able to catch up to the other candidates over time. Everett was right. I can do better in the city."

The screening for the nationals was laborious. A lot of walking, a lot of smiling, a lot of questions and answers. For someone with limited exposure like Thea, some of the questions were hard, so most of the time, she'd come to Elle and ask her about certain topics and issues in the world. It gave her confidence in the question-and-answer portion, and she always answered with hope, sincerity and compassion.

Thea was officially a Lady Siquijor in the national pageantry as the competition progressed. There were forty out of eighty who passed the elimination. And Thea's name was the battle cry of the people from Luzon to Mindanao. The locals in her hometown were celebrating her success. Finally, they got to have a Lady Siquijor after so many attempts.

With Thea's position in the pageantry, she also got to rekindle and restart her romance with Everett. They were both pretty proud of each other, and she was thankful for him. In the coming days, life had just gotten better for her. People started making posters and banners to cheer for her and Siquijor was treating the coronation night like a holiday. Some were even saving up to come to Manila and watch in person Siquijor's proudest moment.

Thea was favored to win, and she didn't mind it at all. If it made everyone around her happy, then so was she. It was a beautiful, glimmering world of beauties, and she was more than ready for the crown.

"You're a former beauty queen!" Cleo exclaims at the revelation. "Why didn't you tell us, *Ma*?"

Anne gives Cleo a sidelong glance before taking another gulp out of her beer. "It never really came up in the conversation, Leo."

This just made Cleo feel bad. Why did she never think to ask?

"I thought I'd left it all behind, but since it's come to this . . ." Thea trails off, showing Cleo some more pictures. "Well, I withdrew from the competition."

Cleo's jaw almost drops. "You *withdrew*? Why? *Ma*, you were going to be the Lady Pearl of the Philippines! Wha—"

But Thea's smiling at Cleo, and it's so sweet and full of understanding. She radiates love and kindness. And it hits Cleo why her mother never told her.

Cleo. It was *her*.

Cleo blinks tears away. She looks up at Anne, trying to confirm that she's read the situation right. When Anne smiles back, she knows it is real. Anne pulls her chair closer to Cleo and stares at her.

"I'm sorry I didn't tell you, Leo," Anne whispers, looking worriedly at Cleo. "I didn't know how. Are you mad at me?"

Cleo can't believe Anne's asking her that. "Why would I get mad at you? You were here for *Ma* when I couldn't be. I'm so sorry."

It killed Cleo to know that her mother withdrew from the competition because of her—the product of love between Thea and Everett. She was the reason Thea had stepped out of her limelight when she was at the peak of the most significant break of her life. She, Cleo, had killed her mother's career, and there was no changing that.

Cleo can't help but cry out of frustration. "*Ma*, I'm so sorry!"

"*Anak*, why are you crying?" Thea brushes Cleo's tears away, wrapping her arms around her two daughters. "It's okay. I don't regret any of it. Even your father. You're the best blessings that ever came into my life."

"B-but how did you survive all that?" Cleo wants to go back to the past and make her mother choose differently, but life doesn't work out that way. It devastates her.

Thea was throwing up a week before the coronation night, and Everett had just left the country. The pageant found out about their relationship, so he was fired. She wanted to ask the other girls about pregnancy, but she knew they'd have different opinions. They'd either tell her to keep the baby or to abort it. Or she could do whatever she wanted since it was her body.

But Thea wasn't even sure about the baby yet. What if she was just sick? So, she kept it to herself and mindlessly went through the swimsuit competition. It felt slightly different walking in two-piece thinking about the growing baby inside her womb. As she walked, she could feel the dizzy spells brought about by the changes in her body. After a few more days, she was sure she was pregnant. She was petrified.

Three days before the coronation night, Thea had decided to talk to Elle. It was terrible for her because she knew how this would disappoint Elle. She believed Elle was rooting for her, which made it worse.

"Well, then, you don't have a choice. You understand I have to tell the officials," Elle said, point-blank. No sugar coating.

Thea sighed, apologizing for everything. She was going to disappoint everyone by getting pregnant, but she wasn't going to let this baby go.

"Or wait—let's not do that. You voluntarily withdraw from the pageant. It's the lesser of two evils. You don't need to tell the officials. Just write a letter to the management that you're withdrawing from the competition for personal reasons. I'll take the letter to them while you get packed and be gone. I'm going to get you a taxi at the back entrance of the hotel because I assume you don't want the public to know about this?"

Everything Elle had said was perfect. Thea agreed, but she had a thousand more problems. "I appreciate your help, but I don't know where I'll go."

"You can stay at my friend's house. Take some time to think things through."

Thea was moved and amazed that Elle was continuing to help her despite what Thea had done. She would forever be indebted to Elle. So that's what she did. She stayed with Elle's friends and thought things through. She sent a letter to her family and apologized. Her family was disappointed in her, but they were still her family, so they sent her money to get started.

Soon, Thea left, not wanting to impose any more than she already had. She rented a cheap room in Caloocan City, cut her hair, and sold afternoon snacks to make some money. After that, she was all on her own.

And then, one Saturday afternoon, as Thea was in her snack stand selling banana cues, those well-loved golden brown sugar-coated caramelized bananas, she was surprised to find a man calling her name. It was Everett.

"Your father figured it out and came back because it was the right thing to do. We got married out of a sense of responsibility and at your grandparents' request. I know this is too much to digest tonight, and I'm sorry, Cleo." Thea bows her head, tears freely falling, and this hurts Cleo so much that she drops down on her knees and pulls her mother's head against her chest.

"No. I'm sorry," Cleo says, her heart constricting at the crack of her mother's voice. "I'm sorry. I'm sorry, I'm sorry."

🌿   🌿   🌿

Cleo jolts awake in the early hours of the morning. She checks her phone and sees it's only 5 a.m. Her first thought is Owen's board exams. She hasn't asked him about it, but then again, he didn't say anything about it either, which could only mean he failed.

Cleo sits up on her bed and closes her eyes. She realizes she's been so self-absorbed she didn't even think to ask Owen about his results. She didn't even ask her mother about her life—didn't know anything about her mother's past until now. She gets up, washes her face, and takes a bottle of water from the refrigerator. Then, she goes back up to the rooftop where they talked last night and sits on the folding chair.

Taking deep breaths, Cleo gazes at the sky. The sun's just coming up, and it will soon cover the world in its light once again. She's thinking about her life, remembering her childhood, and reflecting. She's taking stock of everything—, actions, plans, and dreams. She's taking stock of who she had been until now and who she's becoming. It's quiet, so she has all her thoughts to herself as she looks over the tops of houses that are almost all the same color and height. The rooftop also gives her cleaner air, and she figures it's because of her mother's plants. Thea probably misses her hometown. She brought Siquijor here.

In Cleo's mind, she's asking herself: *why am I trying to be a star for the sake of being a star? Just to make it big? To prove something to my father, who has never really been part of our lives?*

And then Cleo tries her best to remember everything she did during her early years. At eleven years old, she'd been modeling to earn money for the family. Her father sent them money, but not very consistently. It was something, but it was never going to support them. Cleo didn't make huge money. It was just enough to support the house and her mother. Meanwhile, she showed up on time for the modeling jobs. She was perfect for catalog shoots and local runways as she was tall and slender. She became a sought-after respected model.

Cleo was in a print and TV ad for skateboards at age sixteen. She was "the girl" in the skateboard commercial, and her job was to sit and look pretty while the boy skateboarded because they were selling the skateboards to the boys. The message was that if the boy could skateboard well, girls would like him. What happened was that the gorgeous boy was a terrible skateboarder, and the crew was getting frustrated. He couldn't do it, but Cleo could—in fact, she was brilliant.

That video of Cleo wound up on UsTube, and it went viral on social media sites. Many viewers loved it, but plenty of others said she looked like a buffoon. They accused her of stealing the commercial from the boy. She seemed arrogant instead of confident. And then came the postings on the comments section, branding her as, the girl who got the job because she was *Direk* Everett's daughter. They thought her skateboarding was faked when it had been a hundred percent genuine, all her.

So that early bit of fame hadn't even been pleasant. And now she was asking, what did fame really mean to her? What was she supposed to do with it?

In this quiet, private moment, she makes a plan, and this time, she's going to be different. There's a sure promise in her, a feeling of determination and power. Trouble is written all over her face, but this troublemaker isn't going to lose.

CHAPTER 11

The Long Day Ahead

"Coffee?"

The sun's up, and so is Cleo. She stretches her arms upwards before facing her mother, who's looking at her with concern. But Thea doesn't need to worry. Cleo's got it all planned out in her head, and there's no losing it this time.

"Thanks, but Owen and I will catch breakfast outside," Cleo says, strangely rejuvenized. She's never been this awake her whole life. Her mind is made up, and her heart is ready for the adrenaline rush.

Thea stares at Cleo in curious wonder. "I know that look."

Cleo turns to the golden-lit skies. Her eyes burn with purpose, a vow made in the heavens. Once the sun sets again, all will be in place. And when the first stars of the night appear, the moon will bear witness to her promise, a haunting memory to keep her going. She swears she'll never let others run her life. She's not going to be chased by another wrong decision—she'll be the one to do the chasing, and whether it comes out as good or bad, the most important thing this was a choice she willingly made.

Cleo smiles as if to dare life to come up against her. Well, if it does, she'll be one step ahead of it. "I'll see you later, *Ma*!"

"You're worrying me," Thea replies, leaning against the wall with her arms crossed. "Are you sure you're okay?"

"Never better," Cleo says genuinely, grinning at Thea.

Thea shakes her head and smiles at Cleo, knowing all too well there's no stopping her once she puts her mind to something. "Take care."

So, Cleo goes through her morning ritual:

Apply skincare products to her face.

Take a shower.

Apply light makeup.

Find something comfortable to wear for the day.

It's a mundane routine, but today it seems different—everything she does counts and matters. There's no time to stay still now. She needs to chase the lead of the story she's tracking.

Cleo straps on her sandals, puts on a blouse and skinny pants, steps outside the house, and books a cab on her phone. Five minutes later, the taxi arrives, and she gets inside like it's a carriage taking her to the battlefield. But before she starts the long day's campaign, she takes a detour first to a certain someone to whom she owes a ton.

❧   ❧   ❧

Owen just gets out of the shower when his brother Mark strolls into his room like some highbrow philosopher. Mark likes to play Aristotle, thinking no one has his kind of brain. Owen doesn't question that, but sometimes it makes him look downright ridiculous.

"Anything you need?" Owen asks Mark. For a moment there, the thought of his exam results runs through his head.

"Corporate dinner later at the Larila Shang Hotel. Be there at 7 p.m. sharp," Mark says, glancing over at Owen's choice of clothes waiting on the rack. "It's a black-tie event."

When isn't it?

"Sure," Owen says instead. If attending socialite events means the family will leave him alone, then he can spare an hour or two enduring snippy and mindless conversation over dinner. If he were going to be brutally honest, it's not even a conversation, but a talk show that goes on and on about how rich they all are. Wealth is how they measure everything. Having it gives them a reason to pile on the pride and ego.

"I'll see you then." Mark leaves the room, shutting the door behind him.

Staring at his linen shirt and chino shorts, Owen has to laugh. Mark could never wear something as casual as this. Mark can have all the suit and tie ensembles in the world, but Owen doubts his brother breathes very well. His everyday attire is as tight as his attitude.

Owen gets dressed, takes his breakfast, and leaves the house. Ignoring the sleek black and red cars in their garage, he hops onto his motorcycle and drives away. Cars don't win in traffic jams; motorcycles do. He's speeding through the streets until he sees someone waving at him. He stops at the guardhouse, squints his eyes to get a better look at . . . .

"Babe!" Cleo calls out, waving her arms in front of Owen and smiling her megawatt smile that can light up the whole city. "Slept well?"

Owen's not sure if he's dreaming or if he's seeing his girlfriend in the best mood she's been in weeks. "I thought I was supposed to pick you up."

"I'm picking you up this time." Cleo winks at Owen flirtatiously. "Good morning, love of my life."

"Now, there's a smooth pick-up line," Owen notes, dazzled by the new Cleo in front of him.

"Did it work?"

Owen leans in and whispers, "Maybe. But you have to convince me a bit more."

"Mind if I take you somewhere for a breakfast date?" Cleo acts coy, smiling cheekily at Owen.

"But I already had breakfast."

Cleo laughs it off. "Then have again, silly!"

Owen thinks he's just fallen in love all over again.

*   *   *

Cleo has led Owen to Maginhawa Street, Diliman, Quezon City. As Owen drives the motorcycle, she enjoys the fresh air. The residential neighborhood where the country's national university sits is one of Cleo's haunts, mostly because the trees have been left untouched. While the university has structures—research facilities, lecture halls, and centers of all kinds—it has left most areas in a forested state. The scholars can study in peace and live in dorms sheltered from the chaotic city noise. Cleo had wanted to attend university, but she failed the entrance exams, so now she visits it whenever she can hoping to the knowledge it contains will rub off, and maybe teach her what to do in life.

Cleo thought she was dumb for not passing the exams then, but her mother said way by no means dumb. People have multiple intelligences, and she was going through something at that time. She didn't know what she wanted in life, which was okay. She took many entrance exams back then, and ended up in a private university for rich kids. It turned out she only needed motivation and the affirmation she got from her mother. In the end, she earned a full-ride scholarship and it was there she met Owen.

Looking around the go-to food market in the metro, Cleo sees the tarpaulin that reads *ALING NENA'S KARINDIRYA*. She tugs at Owen's sleeve shirt to pull him to a stop. The carinderia's usual silver steel food trays filled with affordable viands are on display as tricycle and jeepney drivers take their pick of a breakfast meal. Nothing beats a *lutong bahay* to start their day right.

"Who can say no to a home-cooked breakfast?" Owen muses as they get off the motorcycle.

Cleo knows Owen appreciates a good home-cooked meal because while the family maids make breakfast for him, the food is missing that special homely ingredient.

"How does *tapsilog* sounds to you?" Cleo asks, famished.

"Perfect."

So, Cleo orders *tapsilog* for both of them. They find a small table at the side, enjoying this calm, quiet morning. It's not a five-star restaurant, but it's a place where they can be just themselves. They don't need to please anyone. They can act like they're working a regular job and live a regular middle-class life. The jeepneys pass by them, and it takes them back to their college years, when everything was much simpler.

It also feels like a first date out of so many dates, and it gives Cleo the jitters. She remembers this is Owen—the guy who became so important to her then and has been there for her through the years. Comforted by his presence, she eats to her heart's delight; the combination of beef, garlic rice, and egg seems to being her taste buds to new heights. Or maybe she's really just plain hungry.

Owen's about to say something when Cleo cuts him off. "No, let me. How are you, babe?"

"I'm good. Why?" Owen's staring at Cleo curiously. It's not every day she asks him how he is, and she knows how negligent she's been.

"I'm sorry."

Owen looks confused.

"I'm so sorry for forgetting about your exam results. I've been so absorbed in my own life I've barely paid attention to yours," Cleo says, looking seriously at Owen.

"No, don't worry about it," Owen assures Cleo, holding her hand. He gives her a little smile, and she hates it. "You were shooting the movie. I appreciate your saying that, but it's not a big deal."

Cleo shakes her head, grasping Owen's hand. "Thank you, but it is a big deal because it's a symptom of a much more serious problem. I've been so single-minded for reasons I can't understand. I'd tell people I want to impress my father, and in some bizarre way, I've been trying to get revenge on him, and it's made me oblivious to the people I care about. I'm so obsessed with these people in my life who aren't even in my life. I don't want to be that. So, I'm going to be this other thing."

"That's cool," Owen says. "I'd love you either way, but yeah, that's great."

Cleo gazes outside and sees how calm life can be. The passersby cross the street, laughing lighthearted as chat talk about whatever it is that's funny to them at the moment. One man who's on the run stops by the side of a tree and wipes the sweat from his face. He peeks at the skies, smiles, and sprints off like he just saw his inspiration to keep going.

"When I became that one-track-mind-obsessed-person who's only thinking about my flip-flops commercial, you're the one to remind me to wake up," Cleo explains, drinking her water.

"You're an actress. I think it's part of the job package to think about yourself."

Cleo leans in and says, "Yeah, I'm not going to be an actress anymore. It's not me. I'm ending that."

Owen loosens his hold on Cleo, surprised and shaken. He pulls away and tilts his head to the side. "Woah, alright?"

"I've already decided what I'm going to do in life, and it's not that."

"What are you going to do?" Owen asks.

Cleo beams. "You'll find out soon enough. How about you?"

Owen nods his head, respecting Cleo's decision. He looks down at his unfinished food, so she knows it's still bothering him. He's not the type of man to leave a meal unfinished. If there's food left on his plate, it only means he's thinking.

Finally, Owen finishes his food and says, "I'm not going to give up on being an architect. I'll retake the exam next year."

"That's great." Cleo smiles at Owen. "I can't wait to see that day to come. I'll be the first in line to congratulate you."

Owen laughs at that. "We good?"

Cleo nods, feeling that the weight of the world just fell off her back.

"So, where would you like to go today?"

Cleo stares at Owen, a playful expression on her face. "It's okay. I'm going somewhere."

Owen's about to say something but probably thought better of it because he stops himself before he can say as much as a word. Cleo knows he gets it, so instead, they clean up their table, and she pays for their meal.

"I'll see you later, maybe?" Cleo asks.

"Anytime you're ready, babe. You got this."

Cleo hails a cab outside and kisses Owen's cheek, whispering, "No, we got this. Love you."

And off they went on their separate ways. On the way to wherever Cleo is going, she prepares for whatever is coming. She knows her mind now, and she'll be unstoppable. She's done playing by their rules; it's time she makes her own. She's on a roll, with no time to waste.

Half an hour later, Cleo stands in front of the entertainment and news company's yellow and blue lady silhouette.

"It's showtime," she mutters under her breath, smirking and sliding her hand through her hair before approaching the security at the entrance.

"May I help you, ma'am?"

Cleo may be done with acting, but she's not going to forget what she's learned, or how to use it. Quickly, puts on a distressed expression. "Okay, so, there's this reporter who told me to meet her here should I ever want to be interviewed."

The security guard looks at her from head to toe. "What's the name of the reporter?"

"I didn't get her name because at that time I was such an emotional mess, you know? I was supposed to replace Selene and my story—"

"Selene?" The security guard asks. "Oh, you're that Walter! The one who walked out. My daughters are going on and on about it. Come in, come in! Let me have your I.D., please."

Cleo smiles sweetly at the security guard and hands him a government-issued I.D. "Thank you so much."

Selene's such a VIP name. And now, it's linked with Cleo's. She goes inside the building and waits in the lobby where people already staring. If there's one thing people want from her, it's *chismis*. They are all naturally drawn to rumors, and with her a few meters away from them, they'll be inclined to come to her.

"Isn't that Cleo Walter?"

"What is she doing here? Looking for a job?"

"She's all over the tabloids, but maybe she's here to get her story out. Wouldn't that be something!"

Cleo crosses her arms and smiles at everyone who catches her eye. She's pretending she doesn't know what's happening the more oblivious she acts, the more attention she gets.

"Hi!" a boy in his late teens with his glasses skewed greets Cleo, awkwardly offering his hand to her. By the looks of it, he's an intern and would like nothing more than to impress his bosses. And Cleo's more than willing to give him a hand.

Cleo takes the young man's hands and smiles at him. "Hello, Mr. . . . um?"

The teenager perks up at the salutation. "Arjay. I've followed your story for quite a bit, Ms. Walter, and I'm impressed with that walkout. Not that, you know, it's a good thing, but phew! Nobody does that to any movie. I swear it was legendary."

"Thank you, but you know what would make it even better?" Cleo winks at Arjay.

"A story!"

Cleo claps her hands, grinning at Arjay. "Yes! Exactly. You have a curious mind!"

Arjay blushes.

"An intern like you deserves recognition," Cleo adds. "Do you think you can help me get my story out?"

Arjay nods, bringing out his pen and notebook. "Anything."

"Perfect! Um, but you'll need help. So, I'm looking for this apple-red bobbed reporter. Do you know her?"

"The only person I know with that kind of hairdo is my immediate boss, Ms. Aira. I'm sort of her underling, you know?" Arjay stops and thinks. "I think she's at her desk now. Should I call her up?"

"Why don't I come with you?" Cleo suggests and then adds: "Just so Ms. Aira can see how committed you are to the job. It'll give you some initiative points."

Arjay looks up at Cleo with hopeful eyes. "You think so?"

"Yes!" Cleo assures Arjay. "How about as we go to wherever Aira is, you shoot some questions, I answer them, and you jot it down?"

Arjay's a good kid. He takes Cleo to the elevator, and she answers his questions just like she promised. He's pretty good at asking questions. If she were Aira, she'd promote him.

"And we're here."

They've come up to the bustling seventh floor. Everyone's running off in different directions, calling people from every device imaginable and drinking mugs of coffee like it's the new tequila. It's a typical whirlwind newsroom, and it's where Cleo gets to find the person who will tell her story.

Cleo quickly finds her target: an apple-red bobbed reporter talking to someone Cleo can only guess is her managing editor. Arjay leads the way and Cleo follows. When apple-red bob sees Arjay and Cleo, she frowns.

"May I help you?" apple-red bob asks. She turns to Arjay and says, "You know what a crazy time this is, right? Where did you run off to?"

Arjay holds his hands together as if in prayer. "Wait, wait. Listen to me. I found our story! Ms. Walter's walkout scene is a—"

"Arjay, can you just check these papers for corrections while I talk to Ms. Walter?"

"But you have to listen to me. This is—"

Cleo claps Arjay's back. "It's okay, Arjay. I won't forget your name."

Arjay gives Cleo a crooked smile and takes the stack of papers from apple-red, leaving the two women alone to talk.

"I want you to be my reporter," Cleo says bluntly, not wasting a bit of time.

"Don't you even want to know my name first?"

Cleo shrugs. "What's your name?"

"Aira," apple-red answers, shaking her head. "What exactly do you want, Ms. Walter?"

"Okay, Aira. I'm offering you the opportunity of a lifetime. I want you to cover my story."

Aira laughs at Cleo. "The walkout stories? I'm sorry, but you're not . . ."

"Not that story." Cleo doesn't even bat an eye. She's as serious as the pandemic. "This is something you don't want to miss."

"You? The biggest story of the year?" Aira snorts, clicking her tongue and rolling her eyes. "Are you kidding me?"

"No. Maybe my story isn't a one-time thing."

"Then what is it?" Aira challenges.

"You'll find out soon enough. So, what do you say?" Cleo pulls out an office chair and sits on it, looking up at Aira as she waits for the reporter's answer. She's not going to take no for an answer. But if apple-red refuses, well, she has her ways.

Aira sighs. "How do I know you're not going to be a waste of time?"

With the right words, anyone can manipulate people into saying yes.

"Because I want you to take me where Elle is."

She Is the Elle

"**E**lle's going to be in Manila's Fashion Runway tonight at the Grand Ballroom Hotel. Only people with connections can get in, which means fashion designers and models alike," Aira explains, pulling out a poster from her desk drawer and showing it to Cleo.

The poster looks like an invitation to the palace of the king and queens of fairytales, and it certainly does not entertain commoners. Underneath the fashion runway title, Elle's name is in bold and italics, a name that brings people to their knees. Cleo turns it over in her head and focuses on ways to get there without making people overthink it. The more she stares at the poster, the more she sees the silhouette of outfits. Through this eye-catching silhouette, she hatches a plan.

"And reporters. They need someone to cover the event," Cleo says. "You're going to be that reporter."

"And how will that get you inside? Also, I can't get in without an invitation, myself."

Cleo smirks. "*Wala ka bang tiwala sa'kin?*"

Aira looks at Cleo as if to say, are you really asking me that? "And are you going to tell me *why* I should trust you?"

"O, ye of little faith," Cleo remarks, crossing her arms. "Get yourself ready after lunch. We'll be heading over where Elle is."

Aira glances off to the side and back at Cleo. She doesn't say anything, but Cleo knows she has her yes. Apple red leaves the table, and Cleo proceeds to the next steps. She calls her talent agency and asks for the number of the marketing manager of her flip-flops commercial.

"Oh, Cleo, Cleo, Cleo," Ms. Aika, chants. "I doubt they'd give you any project right now after what you did."

Suddenly, Ms. Aika isn't so much of a fairy godmother now. She's the wicked stepmother who's not giving Cleo an ounce of inheritance because she's probably found two other girls she can dote on. That's probably just as well. But this conversation isn't about that.

Cleo rests her arms on the table and says, "You don't have to worry. That's not why I'd be calling them."

"No. The reason I'm an agent is that I connect people. I don't help people go direct."

"Oh, why do you have to be so difficult?" Cleo whispers under her breath, losing patience and trying not to mess things up. She's had enough of people telling her no. She's going to get all their yesses today; Ms. Aika's is just one of the many she's going to get.

"I'm sorry?"

Cleo smiles sweetly. "Nothing. I just wanted to help."

"Help how?"

Cleo keeps her tone casual. "Well, I heard from this reporter that there's going to be a fashion runway tonight at the Grand Ballroom Hotel, and the biggest names in the fashion industry will be there, and I thought the flip flops can get a boost in promotion, you know?"

Ms. Aika gasps. "Oh! That's great news! I'll give them a call right now!"

"Um . . ." Cleo trails off. "But I doubt they'd get a spot with a grand event like that. I mean, it's pretty huge. I can help them—that is, if I could walk their brand, then I could talk to a friend who happens to be a part of the runway's marketing team."

"Please do tell your friend you'll walk the flip-flops brand." Ms. Aika finally gives in.

"I surely will do."

Cleo hangs up and grabs lunch. To move on to phase two, she posts about the flip-flops and the runway on her social media. After about ten minutes so she receives a text message from Aira.

Apple-Red Bob (12:55 p.m.)
Thanks to you, I'm now covering the fashion
runway. My boss wants to cover you to see how you're
managing after the whole ordeal with the movie.

"Yes!" Cleo tells herself. She's looped in the reporter, got the brand, and she's one step away from finding Elle. She needs one more yes to get Elle's attention, and that will be the end of a great day's work. She gets up and meets Aira in the hotel's lobby. She's jumping from one place to another, and so far, she's doing great.

Aria's regret seems genuine when she says, "I don't have a plus one. You have to work this out on your own."

"Don't worry." Cleo spies the event staff sitting on the couch and preparing the list of brand attendees. "Just play along, okay?"

"Play along with what?"

"Pretend to be my paparazzi. Cause a commotion," Cleo whispers. Aira's eyes widened. "What?"

"Oh, yes, I've talked to Selene!" Cleo says loud enough that the entire lobby can hear her. "I know I shouldn't have walked out on a perfect movie, but it's Selene's movie. She's a superstar and nobody can say she doesn't deserve it. So, if you want to get my side of the story, I don't think we should do this right here."

"What are you doing?" Aira mouths at Cleo.

"Play along," Cleo murmurs. Out loud, her facial expression between a smile and a scowl, she says, "I can't do this right now."

"Please do let me know when you're free. Thank you so much, Ms. Walter!" Aira plays along, and Cleo sighs, trying to appear stressed. Everyone's staring at them, gossiping, and spreading rumors, just as she has predicted.

Slowly, Cleo elegantly walks over to the event staff and takes a casual glance at the brand list. "You know what would make this fashion show better?"

A man in a ponytail raises an eyebrow at Cleo. "Oh, Ms. Walter. A pleasure to meet you."

They shake hands, and Cleo continues without pausing to ask his name. "You've got a lot of international brands, but have you ever thought of including something national?"

"Well, no we haven't, and we'll keep it in mind for the future, but tonight's lineup's fixed. We can't do last-minute calls with the brands. They'd kill me. And then they'd fire me," The man laughs.

"What if there's a brand that can handle that one-minute call?"

"We're too busy even to make that call so—"

"What if I told you the *TsineLast* flip-flops, a rising national brand, has given me their approval to walk their brand on the runway in any fashion show of my choosing?" Cleo counters, getting the paper out of the man's hand, frowning when she sees the list of brands. She sneaks a glance at Aira, signaling her to act like the crazy journalist.

"Ms. Walter!" Aira screams, pulling out her pen and notebook. "Please, can't we talk? Five minutes? *Everyone's* dying to know what happened there!"

The man in ponytail stands up, alarmed by Aira's presence. "The interviews will be after the event. Ms. Walter needs to prepare for her walk."

Cleo winks at Aira before turning her attention to the ponytail man. "Thank you. I'll let them know."

"We'll just put you last."

And just like that, Cleo gets their yes. She only needs to walk on the runway and get Elle's attention. To get Elle's interest, though, she needs to be extraordinary. Based on Thea's story, Elle has a keen eye and a good gut feeling for talent and beauty, so Cleo's hoping she can emanate her mother's vibes, or something even stronger than that.

Cleo changes into a white summer kimono cardigan open front bikini cover-up in the dressing room. It's long, stylish, and edgy. With the aquamarine flip-flops she's wearing, she's a sight you can't miss. If Elle doesn't notice her—no, Elle *will* see her. She'll get everybody's eyes once she's out there walking. She may not be the best actress out there, but she is in the spotlight when she's on the runway.

After what feels like hours of waiting, Cleo finally gets called. She's shaking, but she calms herself. She's nervous not because she's walking out there in front of the most fashionable people in the country, but because she's afraid she might not impress Elle.

Get out there, Cleo Walter. Go big or go home. Cleo berates herself.

Cleo pushes herself out there for everyone to see. The blinding lights, the snaps and the flashes remind her this isn't her first time doing this. So she walks the runway, gracefully sliding one foot in front of the other, staring straight in front of her, unflappable.

"And the rising national flip-flops brand, *TsineLast*, flip-flops that last!" the emcee informs the guests. "Perfect for a summer getaway."

Cleo's almost tempted to search for Elle while she's walking, but she's a model. She needs to get the job done.

After her turn, she looks for Aira and talks backstage?

"Have you seen Elle?" Cleo sounding calmer than she feels. "We haven't even checked if she's coming to the show."

Aira smiles at Cleo. "Look behind you."

Cleo looks behind her and finds herself fixated on a woman in her fifties with black hair curled Marilyn Monroe style. She's fair-skinned and has a mole on her right cheek, making her look even more like the actress and model who had been the all-time quintessential bombshell. The only difference is that her makeup is subtle. The pair of golden hoops in her ears accentuate her face and hair perfectly. She stands elegantly in her pump heels and sleek blue long-sleeved, ruffled dress. She's classy from head to toe and her presence is practically regal. Even the woman's scent, which gives off the luxuriant fragrance of Italian spring gardens. Her poise and aura scream designer clothes, expensive diamonds, impeccable beauty, and undeniable influence.

"I've been looking for you," Elle says, smiling at Cleo.

Cleo has a hard time reconciling Elle's physical appearance with her mom's recounting of the story.

"You're Elle?" is all she can think of to say.

Aira elbows Cleo.

"Sorry, just double-checking," Cleo adds quickly.

Aira checks her phone and says, "I gotta go. I'll see you around, Ms. Walter."

With Aira gone, Cleo and Elle are left all alone. Cleo readies herself and is about to launch into a whole narrative when Elle steps in.

"I've been watching you for quite some time now. I knew you would eventually quit your father's path. I was just waiting, and I figured it was time." Elle speaks like an oracle, and Cleo feels like this woman is drawing patterns on her hand. "I couldn't save your mom before, so now I'm saving you."

Cleo doesn't need saving, but she does need someone like Elle. "You . . . were looking for me?"

"Yes. Thea deserves better. I wasn't in the position to make her the queen that she should've been, but things are different now. I can make you a queen. For her."

In a blink of an eye, Cleo leaps. She doesn't hesitate, not even for a second. "Count me in. What do I do?"

"You are not a star," Elle confirms, smiling slyly at Cleo.

Elle's words strike Cleo. "What do you mean?"

"Have you ever thought that maybe you were born for something else?"

Cleo grins at Elle. There's a newfound excitement welling in her, and it's making her blood run faster, a thrill she hasn't felt in a long time. She knows this woman is the only person she can trust no matter what happens. She is the only one who helped her mother when Thea needed it most. And Cleo's not going to let her down.

"I'm all yours," Cleo says, bold and sure.

"I thought so. It's about time I welcome you to Reign of Queens beauty camp."

Cleo's not sure if she heard it right. "Beauty camp?"

"Come, I'll escort you to your dreams. For free." Elle has a knowing smile on her face like she's been through this scene before, and Cleo has no choice but to follow.

🐝　　🐝　　🐝

The beauty camp is like nothing Cleo has ever seen before. For one thing, the room she's in is warm and inviting in hues of pink, beige, and peach. Standing at the center of the room, she's surrounded by floor-length mirrors and mannequins that are clad in wonderfully unique dresses and gowns. Each mannequin is poised on an elevated platform, but arranged to evoke the look and feel of the catwalk. To Cleo, it's already kind of dazzling, like stars behind her eyes have burst into thousands of twinkling diamonds. The setup rivets her and fuels her drive to reach the heights she's been envisioning for herself.

"Like what you see?" Elle asks, coming through the glass doors with her usual classy look. She's changed into a vintage navy swing dress, and her hair in those Marilyn Monroe curls is like a signature. Her neat, self-assured stride is captivating, a thing to imitate.

"It's lovely," Cleo observes, trying to place her dark-washed jeans and white blouse in this room. "Who designed it?"

"We had an architect and interior designer, but I must say my beauty queens and I quite pitched in quite a few ideas for it," Elle says proudly, satisfied with the results of her collaboration with her queens.

"Oh, wow," Cleo coughs. She spent most of her time working so hard during her taping days she barely had time to sleep. Her sore throat has only just begun to catch up with her.

Elle frowns, rummaging through her bag and pulling out a spray bottle with green liquid in it. "Here. This will soothe your throat."

"Wha-what?"

"It's Pharcep, an anti-inflammatory throat spray. My doctor put me onto it, and so far, it's never let me down. As long as you're in my camp, you don't have to worry about a thing. Health is wealth, as the saying goes."

Following Elle's tip on how to use it, Cleo aims the long nozzle at the sore area. Elle's right. One spritz eases the pain. Elle really does accept—and work with—only the best.

"Thank you," Cleo says, genuinely grateful to Elle. "And not just for the spray. For welcoming me. For helping my mom."

Elle drops her designer sling bag on the velvet couch. "Can I take that as your yes? Yes, as in you're willing to put your entire career in my hands?"

"I wouldn't be here otherwise," Cleo affirms.

Elle stares at Cleo, her eyes sharp and attentive, but Cleo does not back down. "You've got nothing else to lose?"

"Not exactly, but when you get through what you think is the worst, then why not aim for something greater?"

"I like the way you think," Elle remarks, gesturing for Cleo to follow her into the enormous walk-in closet. It's a dream come true for young girls dreaming of becoming a princess. The wardrobes and racks hold a stash of dress, bag, and pump heels collections. "I've already registered your name in the national pageantry."

"The *Binibining Perlas ng Pilipinas*? That's fast. I've only just, you know, arrived." Cleo gapes at the outfits, all custom-made for beauty queens. Her head is spinning. She can't believe she's really stepping onto this path.

Elle's eyes glint with genuine passion. "The Lady Pearl of the Philippines, yes. No time is too soon for something like this. I have my ways. Besides, today's the last day of registration, and there's going to be a dinner party for all hopeful candidates."

Cleo awkwardly sits down on a silver feathered chair, fidgeting. "You mean, like, I'm gonna be judged tonight? I don't know the first thing about pageantry. I mean, I model . . . . Doing *this* only came into my head yesterday."

"You're not getting any younger, Cleo," Elle calls Cleo out, making it clear that she's on the old side to be joining pageantry. "If you don't do it now, there won't be time to try again."

Cleo casts her eyes downwards. While some part of the pageantry still confuses her, she's willing to be trained. She just feels somewhat overwhelmed by the thought of crowns and beauty camp. As in, beauty camps *exist*, and she's suddenly in the most elite camp of them all.

"Tonight's going to be a part of the national pageantry's screening, so give it your very best shot and don't be intimidated," Elle says solemnly. "Let's see how you'll steal the title from the reigning Lady Quezon City."

Cleo's heart flutters in this race against time she's found herself in. She started on this path in time to register for a major title. Now it's time to up her game. "What do I have to do?"

The corner of Elle's mouth quirked up. "Dominique will help you. He'll be your stylist. Dom?"

A man is inspecting the fabrics of the garments on the racks. When he turns around, Cleo's hit with a jolt of astonishment. He's sharp and neat, and his hair is neatly combed at the side. His black leather toecap shoes gleam, clearly newly shined. His eyes quickly register Cleo's observant gaze. He says nothing for a while then suddenly fetches a double rolling clothes rack.

"She's all yours. Get her size, check whatever style fits her, and we'll see each other tonight," Elle says before leaving them to their own devices.

"Hi," Cleo begins. "I'm—"

"Shh, honey. I know who you are. The question is, do you know who I am?"

Step Out of the Way, Please. Cleo Walter Coming Through

I t terrifies Cleo when people ask her that question, like she should know who they are. As an actor, she practiced familiarization, and that was for self-defense. It would be crushingly embarrassing to work with someone known to just about everyone but her.

But Cleo's pretty sure she should have known who this guy is. Kim, one of the famous reality show hosts, has the same aura as Dominique, but the latter seems much more intense, like the teacher she hated in fifth grade, the one with the *Miss Minchin* classroom management style. He looks like someone who'll chop her to pieces if she ever gets one thing wrong, so she racks her brain and tries to remember his face.

She thinks he may have been a former contestant in Kim's reality show Stylize—a show for aspiring fashion designers whose contestants are primarily gay. But after getting a lot of criticism for hand-picking contestants and not being inclusive and egalitarian enough, Kim started to welcome other members of the LGBTQIA-plus community and straight allies in the later seasons. If Cleo's memory served her right, two fashion designers were neck and neck in the final round. The dispute between the two contestants came when Kim fell in love with one of them—Ron. Ron ended up as the champion, even though the other contestant was better.

"You were that other contestant," Cleo concludes. "You were supposed to win the final round, and the votes favored you, but when Kim admitted he was in love with Ron, the public got caught up in their love story."

"That's right. I'm Dom, your stylist."

"Dominic, the best contender on *Stylize* last year," Cleo relates, remembering his title as she stands up from the chair to face him.

Dom glances at his golden wristwatch and pulls Cleo to the side. "No, honey. It's Dom, and the full name is Dominique with a Q. Get my name right, and we'll get along just fine. Also, if you support Kim, just be aware he doesn't represent the entire LGBTQIA-plus community just because he's the most famous gay on TV."

"I didn't say anything about being a fan."

Dom wrinkles his nose. "Everyone looks up to Kim. He fronts the whole *Stylize* as a show that features gay stylists, but the brutal truth is he wants to promote himself as some kind of paragon of gayness, which is disappointing."

"But Kim has declared gay stylists as winners before," Cleo rebuts.

Dominique takes a chair and pushes Cleo back on her seat, making her land with an *oof.* He touches her face like he's testing the quality of her it. He frowns when he feels the texture, rubbing his thumb and pointer fingers together.

"Oh, he did, but where are they right now? *Stylize* promises fame and projects, but instead, they ended up opening their micro-salons. When I say micro, I mean micro. Micro to the point you could barely feel they exist. And where is Ron right now?" Dominique dares ask, scowling.

"Tailor-fitting clothes for A-list celebrities," Cleo answers quickly, now getting where Dom's getting at.

"Exactly, honey. Ron isn't even in love with Kim. He's straight as a bamboo stick and is homophobic."

"Not all straight people are ho—"

But Dominique is on a roll now. "I'm not generalizing, honey. I'm saying who Ron truly is. Did you know that I was still a closeted gay during the competition? And then suddenly, Ron exposed my orientation, saying he embraces me as his gay competition."

Dominique steps back from Cleo and sighs.

"The public supported you, but they supported Ron even more for embracing you as an equal."

"Funny how they can turn things around, *hm*? Never mind that. I hope you won't be like them, by which I mean phony. I purposely chose you because I know what fame can do to people, and I'm here to keep you grounded. Oh, and I hate complainers and mismatchers of outfits unless you can own up to it." Dom grimaces when he sees Cleo's blouse. "But we need to spice some things up."

This is how Dominique officially begins his work as Cleo's stylist. He inspects her from head to toe, taking her measurements in the process. Cleo and Dominique skim through the wardrobe, and she ends up trying almost every piece. He wants to get an idea of how certain outfits will look on her. From smart casual to a sheath dress, she walks around the room like it's part of her. He makes her feel confident, and if a certain style doesn't fit her, he'll mix and match things around, making her utterly fabulous.

"What you wear represents your personality," Dominique teaches Cleo, brushing his hands on her fine, woolen, black pants suit, which features a slim-fit tailored design. The front jacket has a low popped collar with one large button featuring stylish vents at the sides to highlight the top. It's elegant, smart, and sleek. "No lapels."

"This is such a sharp kind of look."

"It is. You're sharp, aren't you?"

"I believe we're all sharp in our own ways. We have different kinds of intelligence," Cleo replies, recalling what her mom used to say to her.

"That's good," Dom quips. "Think of it this way: You're not a corporate woman, and it's just plain stereotypical of others when they jump on certain fashions to define who you are and what you do for a living. But that's how it is. It defines your status in this society. If you're rich and living in a *Titanic* setting, silhouette corsets and intrinsic details of flowing, trained skirts with ruffles and lace would be the trend. But if you're Jack, your wardrobe would consist of corduroy pants and cotton suspenders. See? Fashion is a double-edged sword. Take a look at yourself."

Cleo stands proud and tall in front of a long mirror with Dominique behind her. She sees herself dressed in a chic yet neat look. Then, she pictures herself as the CEO of some company.

Dominique continues, "You can make people believe you're a smart, high-powered corporate woman, even if it's just camouflage. In any case, fashion is a powerful armor. So, shall we choose your dress?"

"For tonight's dinner?" Cleo sighs. "Wish me luck."

Dominique cocks his head. "First, we need a trip to some of the best clinics in town."

And so, Cleo and Dominique leave the camp in a private car provided by Elle, headed for a dental clinic. The beauty camp is right in the business district, pretty much close to anything they'll ever need. The day's turning into a whirlwind of the pursuit of fame and beauty—elegant clothes, designer bags, and whatever else Dom has in store for her. Cleo thought it only happened on TV—rising stars being dolled up from head to toe, glamorized through a process of making their bodies and faces flawless, but she's finding that all that stuff on screen has a basis in a pretty intense reality.

Arriving at their first stop, Cleo's welcomed by the warm light of the clinic. Embossed on the walls are the letters IPD painted in gold—Institute for Progressive Dentistry. As in everything else, Elle doesn't settle for anything but the top.

Nothing in this clinic is ordinary. The lobby looks like it belongs in a posh hotel. And like that sort of hotel, this clinic might have a five-star rating, as its clients are the wealthiest people in the city. IPD is behind every beauty queen, celebrity, and influencer's blinding smile. Now, Cleo has the chance to be a part of its branding.

"Oh, wow," Cleo muses, a bit shy to show a smile now, seeing the perfect pearly white teeth of the dentist in front of her. "I've got great teeth. I only have one or two chipped ones, but they're not rotting. I'm not going to be difficult."

Cleo laughs uneasily, rambling on and on about her teeth.

"Smile, Cleo," the dentist politely asks, and because of his welcoming demeanor, Cleo does as she's asked. "Veneers will do the trick. No worries, you're in safe hands. You'll be smiling those pearly whites in no time."

The dentist is right. Cleo can't stop smiling after he's done with her. She keeps smiling from one beauty treatment to the next.

She starts to realize that this kind of beauty takes a lot of time and expert handling. There's a dazzling array of everything from artful natural enhancement to cosmetic surgery. And if someone is happy and content with what nature gave them, that's fine too. Basically, everyone should tend to themselves in whatever way they wish.

Next stop, the skin. "Ah, let me see that face." The aesthetician inspects Cleo's face, tipping her chin up. "Hmm . . . maybe just a few photofacials to improve the pores. Oh, that's a pretty face, indeed, and when we're done here, it'll be more than pretty. You'll glow like a goddess."

Cleo laughs at that thought. "That's too much but okay. I'm an ordinary person trying to be an extraordinary one."

"Well, at SpaMed we customize everything we do for our clients and that goes for both face and body. We aim for the best kind of different," the aesthetician elaborates, putting on her gloves.

"I don't want to change too much," Cleo admits, pursing her lips and then laughing at what she's saying. "Sorry, just ignore me and proceed."

The aesthetician smiles at Cleo. "It's only natural to feel that way. You're still you no matter what you change. Think of this as preventive maintenance. You're keeping your face and body in good shape so you'll look great even in your fifties.

🐞   🐞   🐞

There's something special about stepping out into the light again after being prisoner by your thoughts. It's breaking free from despondency to allow a ray of sunshine to peek inside. That's how it feels to Cleo as she steps her right leg out of the limousine and the flash of hundreds of cameras bombards her. Then, entirely putting herself out there, she flashes them a killer smile.

"Cleo, Cleo, look here!"

"Hi, Cleo! Give me a smile here!"

"Please turn around here!"

It's nice to hear these photographers say something that isn't "Cleo, why did you walk off the movie set?". They aren't particularly interested in her issues. They just want to get a photo of her, and right now, that's a breath of fresh air after holding on for so long and trying not to be smothered.

On the stairs to the hotel entrance, Cleo's fellow candidates in their shimmery long gowns and dresses in bright and dark colors are smiling at the cameras too. Unlike the single spotlight vibe of actors and models at the red carpet premiere, where the crowd has its own expectations of you, whether those expectations are grounded in reality or not, beauty queens have a kind of serene poise about them. The way Cleo sees it, they don't need to pretend to be somebody else, and it makes her feel wrapped in a blanket of security.

"And we have Cleo Walter in her strapless mermaid feather bottom ivory evening gown," the reporter announces.

Elle arrives after Cleo, like the others, and she's dressed for the occasion. She comes out to the flashing lights with a graceful walk, her flutter sleeve maxi dress leaving the photographers gawking at her.

Cleo waits for Elle, and they step through the doors together, leaving the snapping shutters behind them. Passing into the pavilion, they make an entrance at the grand ballroom with its hanging greenery, strings of long flowers, soft lighting, and the lovely warm ambiance all it creates. On each table is an elegant flower arrangement of tall orchids, hydrangeas, roses, and peonies with cascading vines.. The floral scent of the pavilion envelops them in its jasmine-like fragrance. It's a sight to behold.

Elle leads Cleo to a table near the front of the elevated platform. Soon, the pavilion's bustling with chitchat between these beautiful young ladies.

"There are a lot of us," Cleo comments, taking a sip of her water.

Elle smiles. "Of course, there are. An estimate of around seventy-one hopeful beauty queens for the screening tonight."

Cleo isn't ready for the first round of screening, and she thought this would be a meet-and-greet dinner with the other girls.

"Don't worry," Elle whispers, reading the panicked look on Cleo's face.

"What do I have to do?" Cleo takes a sip of her water again, hoping to calm her nerves.

"Cleo, stop worrying. First lesson: confidence. Stop fidgeting. I can see your legs shaking," Elle observes keeping her eyes on the platform, watching everything. "You're not a dog, are you?"

Cleo shakes her head, following Elle's focus on the front.

"Get to know the other hopeful candidates. Remember, this is just a meet and greet."

Cleo narrows her eyes. "How is the meet and greet part of the screening? Do we get up on the stage and introduce ourselves like it's the first day of classes?"

"Yes."

"Oh."

Cleo shuts up after that.

Elle gives Cleo a sideways glance, a glass of wine in her hand. "You're also being watched while you're just sitting here."

Cleo has never stood up that fast in her entire life. "Be back soon!"

Cleo roams around and mingles with the other candidates, just as Elle advised. So far, they all seem friendly and nice. Some of them, she learns, are here because winning the crown of Lady Pearl of the Philippines has been a lifelong dream. Wanting to be honored and looked up to is something Cleo can understand.

"You're Lady Caloocan City?" Cleo hears one hopeful in a yellow Belle gown ask, smiling as she corners Lady Caloocan. "I heard there were a lot of shooting incidents and robberies in your area. How would you promote your city?"

Lady Caloocan City awkwardly shifts her weight from one foot to another, visibly uncomfortable with the question, but she answers it anyway. "This is why I'm joining the pageant. I want to clear up all these misconceptions about my hometown. Crime can happen anywhere. Criminals are made, not born; they're created through their difficult lives, insurmountable situations. So, we have to improve people's lives to help these desperate people change for the better."

"Even if it's rape?" the yellow Belle gown challenges. "I can't see how you managed to be named Lady Caloocan City. Best of luck, though. Other beauty queens here are also from Caloocan."

"And you're not the only Lady Quezon City here," Lady Caloocan City counters, baring her leg in her thigh-high slit.

Cleo plants herself next to them and speaks up. "I think she's referring to the delinquents who need better guidance and those who haven't been given due process. Unfortunately, the poor are often caught in the crossfire between the wealthy individuals controlling things and the police force. I think the people and the government should work hand-in-hand through laws and a justice system that apply to everybody and make sure everyone's rights are protected."

"How long have you practiced that? And where are you from?" Lady Quezon City thrusts out her chin, leery of Cleo's answer.

Cleo smiles. "Quezon City."

Like a Thief in the Night

Lady Quezon City flushes red, not so much of a yellow Belle after all. Her once glamorous face turns sour when she sees Cleo's satisfied one. She taps her foot and says, "Oh, don't be so full of yourself! I won my title as Lady Quezon City legitimately."

"I never said you didn't," Cleo assures Lady Quezon City, smiling her nude lipstick.

"How political," a candidate with pinned curls hairstyle quips. "Aren't you afraid of all the bashing from social media"

Cleo shrugs. "We're not just beauty queens because of our faces, right? We're meant to represent our beliefs. So, we can't just dodge political issues. We're going to be asked about the problems this country is facing. If we stay apolitical, then we're ignoring all those problems."

"I agree!" Lady Caloocan chimes.

Pinned curls nods her head then offers her hand to Cleo. "I'm Lady Pangasinan. Nice to meet you, Quezon City."

"Call me Cleo. I haven't proven anything yet," Cleo responds, taking Lady Pangasinan's hand.

"Cleo, is it?" Quezon City confirms. "You're new to this pageant. Your answer isn't crown-worthy. You have to tone it down and be soft about it. Keep to the middle ground."

Lady Pangasinan comments, "Maybe that's why you get bashed a lot. You speak too much."

Unbelievable. And they're supposed to compete in the pageant with an attitude like that?

Just as Cleo's about to respond, the host calls for attention and asks them all to relax as they welcome the beauty queens vying to be the official candidates for Lady Pearl of the Philippines.

"It's nice meeting you all," Cleo says instead, not wanting to cause too much fuss. She makes her way back to Elle and sits comfortably next to her.

Being in the pageant is almost like being in the world of celebrities. They all have different reasons for being here, but at the end of the day, no matter how friendly they can be, they'll still end up competing against each other.

"How was it?" Elle asks, her eyes glinting.

Cleo presses her lips together. "Some were nice."

"And the others?"

Cleo scoffs, staring at the other beauty queens who just came in. "Not so much, but . . ."

"Daring, aren't they?" Elle implores, placing a napkin on her lap. "Who did you meet so far, and how did your conversation go?"

"Lady Caloocan's nice. Lady Pangasinan and Lady Quezon City, not so much," Cleo replies, her eyes following the three beauty queens making their way to their seats. Lady Pangasinan and Lady Quezon City are murmuring together, laughing cattily as they point at Lady Caloocan City.

"Don't trust anyone but your beauty camp. You don't know how many beauty queens I've encountered who were the best of friends until the competition reached its climax and they turned against one other. Enjoy yourself and have fun, but always remember this Cleo: everything you learn and everyone you befriend has to help you win the crown."

Cleo sighs, wondering how her mother got through this screening alive without wanting to pull anyone's hair out.

"Good evening, ladies and gentlemen," the host begins. "The Lady Pearl of the Philippines is pleased to welcome you all here. All seventy-one of you who registered in this competition will be screening for five days—"

"Excuse me." A beauty queen from table six raises her hand. "So, does that mean it begins tomorrow?"

The host sardonically smiles at the beauty queen. "It's already begun. Now, if you would be so kind as not to interrupt me, I'll p."

The beauty queen backs down, sheepishly lowering her head and avoiding everyone's dagger stares. At the table next to Cleo's, she can hear them wondering how they're being screened tonight. They find it unfair they weren't given any heads-up or instructions.

"Elle, how did you—"

All it takes is one austere stare from Elle for Cleo to keep her mouth shut.

"Only forty of you will officially be candidates. So, let's begin, shall we?" the host continues, his voice loud, lively, and polished. "If your name is called, please come up on the platform and take the limelight. You have thirty seconds to introduce yourself."

Silence reigns in the room and the lights dim as the host in a bow tie and black suit began to announce the names. The first woman to come on stage is Lady Laguna. She graces the floor in her V-neck skirt dress with a navy powder blue overlay silk. She brightly smiles at the audience on the platform, conscious of her walk. Cleo notices the way Lady Laguna's smile faltered for a second after glancing at her legs.

Lady Laguna gets to the mic and introduces herself, "*Magandang gabi sa inyong lahat*! I am Monique Lopez, Lady Laguna!"

Everyone gives Lady Laguna a round of applause. She keeps it together, even with her trembling smile, then exits.

This goes on for an hour as ladies from different cities and provinces take center stage. With their fierce eyes, dazzling smiles, and beautiful attire, they all seem to blur together in a kaleidoscope of colors. But not everyone can maintain their smile for so long. It's tough to keep up a natural and genuine smile, but it's a challenge that a beauty queen must overcome. Throughout the evening, Cleo notices the wavering smiles of those on stage. They've decided to keep a neutral face while they wait for their turn, saving their "beaming smile" energy for when their names are called.

Cleo takes out her compact mirror and plays with her facial expressions. She smiles and then slowly turns it upside down. She feels like she's being eaten alive by these monstrous, beautiful faces. She's overwhelmed watching the walk to the microphone and back. To some people, the walks and the poses are all just that—walking and standing. But the way Cleo sees it, it's an art form. The way the women pose seems to her not so different from the stance of statues of historical and artistic significance. The artistry applies to every strut and sway of a beauty queen.

"Watch them closely, Cleo," Elle urges Cleo. "It's not just the introduction they judge, but also the walk—the discipline of power in softness. Because when a woman walks, it should be as delicate and subtle."

Cleo stares straight ahead. "Do you believe that? That we're delicate and subtle?"

"Do you?"

"I . . ." Unsure, Cleo bites her lower lip. "I don't know enough to make a stand about it. I'm sorry if that seems like a boring and neutral answer."

Elle fleetingly smiles.

"Great. I'm not dumb. I'm just, you know?" Cleo blabbers. "I want to make a stand, too. Just not now when I don't know anything. I mean, what I know at this point . . . it isn't enough."

"Have you ever considered working in a comedy bar?" Elle poses, amused at Cleo's unfiltered speech.

"The thought didn't cross my mind until now."

"You're a bit funny sometimes, but you're doing great," Elle reassures Cleo. "I don't have a true and false, Cleo Walter. I only have perspectives. What may be true for you may not be true for me and vice versa. Feel free to speak your mind."

Cleo wants the ground to swallow her whole, but she's got a screening to win. When her name is called, she saunters over the stage with ease. Hours of standing still during photo shoots have honed her legs to follow her desired movement.

With the mic in front of her, Cleo speaks animatedly with a loud and clear voice. "An actor and a model-turned-beauty queen, Cleo Walter from Quezon City! As a beauty queen, I've come to realize one thing: beauty is only as good as what you do with it. Thank you!"

And a round of applause. Cleo goes back to her seat and hears Elle's whisper of "well done."

Moments later, dinner came. Cleo gets an oven-roasted salmon with a half tablespoon of olive oil to coat the fillet. It's irresistible and savory, and this is also where her cheat meal days must come to an end.

"Stay hydrated," Elle reminds.

Cleo drinks her water in response. Their water must have come from Mt. Fuji to taste this good. She doesn't know what's in the water, but it's not what she's used to.

Dinner is uneventful. Thick tension rises in the air, and everyone's quiet, unlike hours ago. The beauty queens from Quezon City and Pangasinan have also stopped talking. Meanwhile, Cleo makes small talk with the other beauty queens at her table. They're pleasant and friendly enough, but the general silence in the room is deafening her.

Thankfully, the host has called them on for photo shoots. Cleo can see a few who have heaved out a sigh and are smiling now after hours of trying to act picture-perfect to please whoever the panelists are.

"Go. Have your picture taken," Elle tells Cleo, already preparing to leave. "I'll wait for you in the car."

Cleo and the rest of the beauty queens lined up at the side of the stage according to their table number to get their group. Individual photos were also taken. Says a silent prayer of thanks that she's not at the same table as the beauty queen version of mean girls. Lady Pangasinan and Lady Quezon City are still making snide remarks, as if their real reason for coming was to ruin everyone's evening. Not her evening, though.

"Are you going to keep looking around, or do you think you might smile for the camera?" a deep voice asks, interrupting Cleo's thoughts.

Startled, Cleo looks up to see a photographer with curly hair and dark eyes. His chiseled jaw and thick eyebrows make her wonder if he's half something too. He's lean and tall and could pass for a model with those features, except for the crooked nose and the scar on his lip. He could even be a boy band member, but the question there is, can he sing?

"Sorry," Cleo apologizes, finally smiling at the camera. "By the way, do you sing?"

"No."

"You look like Harr—"

"It's my hair that looks like him. I don't sing. Smile," he commands, snapping photos of her.

Cleo does as she's asked. The backdrop is a wall of vines and flowers, lovely and natural-looking.

Ever since this evening got started, the people in charge of it have been sort of grumpy and disagreeable, and while she understands that this is a competition, it's no excuse for rudeness.

"Smile."

Also, how can Cleo smile when the photographer is emitting dark vibes? He seems indifferent and blasé. He strikes her as someone who couldn't care less about the event and the beauty queens. It's almost like they'd just as soon burn their photographs after the shoot.

"Are you on your period, Mr. Photographer?" Cleo dares, smiling slyly at his camera. "I'm Cleo, by the way."

The man doesn't even acknowledge Cleo's presence. She can only hope he's taken good photos of her.

"Next," he calls out.

Cleo exits, but not before calling him the name of a famous singer who used to be in a boy band.

"Don't call me that. My name's Erik, not Harr—"

Cleo pretends she doesn't hear anything. "What's that? Okay, bye!"

As Cleo's leaving the pavilion, she stops in her tracks and looks behind her, giving the other beauty queens one last sweep of a glance.

Seeing this opulent and alluring world, she sets her eyes on the platform where Lady Quezon City takes her photo.

"Five days. In five days, I'll come and steal that title from you," Cleo swears under her breath, grinning wickedly at the sight before her.

Hi! Nice to Meet You All . . . Or Not?

"Well, some of you may know her. She's a model and an actor, and so we're taking her in."

Nobody questions Elle, but Cleo can feel everyone's glares. In this room full of mirrors, the ten other girls in the national pageant seem to multiply into hundreds They're not like the other beauty queens she met last night. Half of them, she can tell, are half-something. With that leg-up, it's probably worth the investment in becoming a client of Elle's.

The thing that stands out most is that they're all poised, and even without any makeup at all, they look so stunning. Even Cleo envies their unique and natural good looks. They wear their high heels like they are fuzzy slippers, and by the looks of it, they could even go for a run with ease. They're not the type to be intimidated, either. They're the ones who dominate and could, without a doubt, be their own defense in a criminal case.

"Cleo? Come," Elle orders, compelling Cleo to present herself in front of these ladies who have already decided to hate her. She's not blind. Their faces are all hostility and disdain. Not a smile from any of them.

"Welcome, Cleo Walter," the tallest one of them greets in a

monotone, like Cleo's just one of the many who will soon quit.

Cleo slows down when she passes her and utters, low enough that only the tall one can hear, "Thank you. I'm not quitting."

The tall one smirks and the rest of them narrow their eyes at Cleo.

"I'm Cleo Walter. Nice to meet you all," Cleo politely introduces herself, smiling at the wolves around her. She pictures their eyes blazing red, bursting into volcanic eruptions. She won't let them trouble her.

"Show Cleo the basics of our training and what beauty pageantry is like. I have some calls to make." Elle graciously walks out on them, leaving Cleo and her fellow beauty queens standing there, waiting for someone to break the ice.

"I'm Nadia," the tallest one says.

Cleo stares at Nadia and her high ponytail. "Oh, you have a name."

"We all do. And do you know what else we have?" a doe-eyed girl interjects, stretching her arms upwards.

Cleo doesn't answer. She's wondering if she can get out of this day alive. She's grateful to Elle, but these girls are hell-bent on making her quit, and she hasn't even done anything—not yet.

"Titles," doe-eyes goes on "And you're Miss Nowhere."

Nadia snorts. "Not even a lady. You're Miss Unknown. Tell us, just for curiosity's sake, how did you get Elle's approval to be here? I mean, you don't look so bad. But being a beauty queen is not just about the face. Right, Julia?"

"I can never really understand Elle sometimes. Honestly, a charity case?" Julia lounges in the plush chair, checking her toenails and bringing out her green nail polish. She throws her head back and stares at the ceiling.

Cleo looks at herself in the mirror. And what she sees is not just a body. It's the little girl in pigtails dreaming to become an actor someday. It's the teenager who did a good job as a model. It's the Cleo with a slim and fit body and a pretty face. She's like them, but different. She's Miss Nowhere, the underdog of pageantry.

Cleo sits next to Julia, taking a peek at her nail polish. "I might be a charity case, but this charity case isn't backing down. Also, ruby would look much better."

Someone behind Julia laughs out loud. Her hair has big, loose curls and spirals, glossy and perfectly s-shaped. It's beautiful.

"What's so funny, Chezka?" Julia challenges Chezka, sitting upright and glowering at her. "Always acting like the president of this beauty camp."

Chezka grins at Julia. "She just got here. What's your problem?"

Julia's about to say something when Nadia stops her. "Give it up, Jules. Let Chezka, the Lady Pasig, handle the rookie because we're sure not gonna play friends with her. We don't have the time for it. Not when we're competing in the nationals."

"Come on, Cleo!" Chezka waits by the door, and Cleo follows. They proceed to the back of the house, where the pool is. The pool has LED lighting, creating a separate world of beautiful colors. Underneath the dark skies and the silver moon, the iridescent glow of the swimming pool invites them to take a swim.

The beauty camp has everything they'll ever need and more. Elle has the amenities, skills, and talents to make a woman the queen that she can be. So, it's also not surprising that the others prey on Cleo because she didn't pay anything to be here.

Cleo dips her feet in the pool. "So this beauty camp's kind of like something that came straight out of a reality show?"

"This one, yeah." Chezka winks, likewise dipping her feet into the pool. "They're not all like this."

"A luxurious house in BGC, Taguig. This place screams rich."

"That's Reign of Queens beauty camp for you." Chezka leans back on her hands and adds, "If you're here, it means Elle sees your potential. You're a threat to us, Cleo."

Chezka's a blunt person, and Cleo likes that. She doesn't need sugarcoated words to make her feel better.

"Actually, we're all a threat to each other. We compete, but that doesn't stop me from making friends. If I lose, at least I got to know people. So anyway, I'll give you an idea about how this all works. But first, I need to ask you this: do you have a boyfriend?" Chezka probes, narrowing her eyes at Cleo.

Cleo wants to tell Chezka it's none of her business, but she also knows this girl isn't taking a non-answer. "Yes. It's not against the rules, is it?"

"Nope, it isn't." Chezka pauses. "But boyfriends can be very distracting. Anyway! You have to be here every day from 5 p.m. onwards. Some of us have other jobs, so it can't always be full-time training, except on weekends, maybe. It all depends on everyone's availability. The good thing about it is Elle's going to be here for a full five days for the screening."

"The closed-door screenings. Is there a schedule for it?"

Chezka gives Cleo a thumbs up. "Yes, Elle has it."

"How does it work?" Cleo's not sure if what she's doing so far is right.

"It's mostly just the panel trying to get to know you. Usual pageantry stuff. Don't worry, being in Elle's camp is an advantage. She'll teach us well."

Cleo bites the inside of her cheek. "Thanks."

"And Nadia and the rest? Don't mind them. I liked the way you handled them. It's the first step to becoming a true beauty queen." Chezka chuckles.

"Handling them?"

"No. Speaking your mind."

Cleo and Chezka exchange knowing looks, freely laughing and snorting at the thought of Nadia and Julia.

"Well, well, you two are getting along so well."

The two hastily scramble to their feet and face Elle, who's staring at them like they're some rebellious teenagers high on sadness and searching for the meaning of life.

"We, um, just dipped our feet in the pool. I—" Cleo starts.

Elle interrupts Cleo. "Not a word, Cleo. Chezka, you all should be getting sleep by now. Wrinkles are a no-no."

"Yes, sorry. I got carried away. I'll be going home then." Chezka turns to Cleo and waves her goodbye, apologizing again to Elle and promising to be back tomorrow on time.

"What did you learn from Chezka today?" Elle's looking fixedly at Cleo.

Cleo suddenly feels like this is an interrogation or a quiz on what she's learned in the short amount of time she's spent with Chezka. "That I should speak my mind."

"Aside from that. What did you learn from her?"

Jeez, I don't study human behavior, Cleo thinks to herself, not wanting to speak that one out loud. "She's bubbly?"

"Rules can be bent," Elle answers for Cleo, watching her reaction. Cleo's stupefied, honestly. She's gawking at Elle like she can't believe *the* Elle just said that. "Rules are created for a fair system, correct?"

Cleo can only nod.

"But if the rule isn't fair for you, you bend the rule. Ideally, rules are fair, but what happens when a rule suddenly becomes unjust? Sometimes, you bend the rule for your benefit. Otherwise, the rule will end up bending you."

Cleo smiles. "Isn't that just being selfish?"

"Everyone is selfish, Cleo." Elle opens her phone and takes her time scrolling through her messages. After a while, she finally talks again. "The local government unit has asked me to take in Lady Quezon City too in the beauty camp. They're willing to support and sponsor her."

"Oh, what did you say?"

"I said yes."

Minutes before Cleo leaves the house for training. She corners her mother in the living room. Thea's watching an afternoon TV drama and Cleo has no idea how to open up the topic about her inclusion in the pageant.

"*Ma*?" Cleo calls out, sitting down next to Thea.

Thea smiles indulgently. "What's on your mind, *anak*?"

Cleo's quiet, trying to get a feel for her mother's frame of mind. Thea's in a good mood, and she's always been so gentle with people, but does she really need to know right now that her daughter has registered in the national competition? Should she know yet?

"Nothing." Cleo leans her head on her mother's shoulder. "How do you always know when there's something in our minds?"

Cleo has decided the time's not quite right. She needs to be an official candidate before she can tell her mother. She needs to prove that she's not just playing around—she's serious about it. When the time does come—when she's an established candidate—then she'll give it to her mother to decide whether she continues it or not. This time, she'll give her mother the decision she didn't get to make for herself.

Thea caresses Cleo's arm. Her touch is calming. "You're my daughter. How can I not know when something's up?"

Cleo wants to stay in her mother's arms forever. Here, she's safe. Here, no one gets to judge her. Here, her mother will fight for her, which is why she can't stay still. She can't let her mother fight her fights.

In the middle of thinking about what she's been doing, Cleo's phone interrupts her reverie. It's Owen, her escape and solace in this tough time. Usually, she'd have spilled everything to him by now, seeking his comfort, but now that's all changed. She needs to help herself—be independent of her emotions and not always pour out everything to her boyfriend, who has struggles of his own.

"Hey, babe," Cleo says, propping herself up by putting a pillow at her side.

"Just checking on you. Do you need to be anywhere today?"

Cleo hasn't told anyone yet about her registration, not even Owen. She wants it to be a surprise. She doesn't want to keep talking; she wants to keep doing. She wants the news to break it out for them, not her.

"I'm good. Just trying to find a job," Cleo assures Owen, knowing all too well he'll worry.

"I have a friend—"

Cleo knows Owen has a lot of friends who can offer her a job. "Babe, it's okay. Really. I can do this."

"Okay, call me if you need anything. We'll eat wherever you want." Owen's voice sounds hoarse, like he hasn't been sleeping. That's not the Owen she knows.

"How are you, babe?"

"Better now that you've asked," Owen replies, his tone a bit lighter now, less dreary. "Thank you for asking."

Cleo blushes at that, twirling a lock of her hair. "I promised you I'd stop being so self-centered, right?? Keep me in the loop, okay?"

"Will surely do. I'm going to go catch up on some sleep now. Love you, babe."

"Love you, too."

Thea smiles at Cleo.

"*Ma*, stop it!" Cleo giggles, not wanting her mom to see how *kilig, how mushy, she's feeling right now.* "Yes, he still gives me butterflies in my stomach."

Thea delicately holds Cleo's hands. "I know you're doing something crazy again. I don't know what it is, but Owen, Anne, and I are here for you. Always."

Good Lord, what have I done to deserve them?

"Thank you!" Cleo feels giddy, ready to face another hectic day. She kisses her mom's cheeks and leaves the house. Whatever happens from here, she'll take responsibility. One step at a time. She needs to come out as the Lady Quezon City.

Cleo can put Nadia and Julia on the back burner for now. She's got a position to steal, and it's not theirs. She calls this plan *prioritizing the enemies.*

CHAPTER 16

The Prioritizing My Enemies Plan

"Well, we have to make the game fair. Girls, meet Gladys, Lady Quezon City."

If there's one thing that makes Gladys stand out among the crowd, it's her full bangs and voluminous shoulder-length hair. It's sleek and trendy, an appropriate ideal picture of her personality. But she deserves to be called Lady Quezon City by all means. Cleo doesn't doubt that, not even a tiny bit.

"Thank you." Gladys cocks her head to one side, the corner of her mouth twitching into a half-smile. "I'm honored to be here today. Being in Elle's beauty camp is already a dream come true."

Nadia steps into the living room wrapped in a towel, dripping wet. Her footsteps have left watermarks on the floor that she didn't bother to clean up. "Elle called me to come right away, so I came as I am. Oh, who do we have here?"

"I'm Gladys, Lady Quezon City." Gladys's angelic smile is arresting. It's the kind of smile that hypnotizes people into doing their bidding.

"Nadia, Lady Cebu City." Nadia indicates Julia, who's only just woken up from her afternoon nap and is not in the mood to talk yet. "Julia's Lady Bulacan."

Cleo does not mind them too much, though. She's there, but she's not listening. She's looking at the new welcoming room for candidates, and it's a flashy feast in the eyes of someone who hasn't had anything come remotely close to it. The décor and furniture are way luxurious. From the velvet couches to the Persian carpets, she's dying to caress it all, feel it under her hands.

Several vintage pieces include lamps and a cocktail glass table to accentuate classic antiques from different Asian countries. Anything in this room that isn't vintage comes from a designer brand, so the throw pillow against Cleo's back is possibly around two hundred thousand pesos. And that's just an estimate. She still hasn't considered the table napkins, which, she guesses, are in the same range as the throw pillow.

"Cleo."

Cleo almost falls to the floor, stopping her hand from reaching toward the carpet and seeing everyone staring at her apparently bizarre behavior. She claps her hands instead, exclaiming,

"Welcome, Gladys. It's nice to finally meet you by name."

"Thank you, Cleo." Gladys bats her eyelashes as if they were natural. "Lady Quezon City is also part of my name."

In a silver botong pants suit, Elle comes in and stands between Cleo and Gladys, facing the other girls. "Since Cleo and Gladys are here, I need to see how well they'll fare with the Q and A. I'll give them both five minutes to freshen up. But let's make this exciting for everyone. The rest of you can ask questions and take sides. It's a healthy competition. Whoever gets the bigger score wins a free relaxing spa."

The room buzzes with excitement. Then, suddenly, everyone rakes eagle eyes over Cleo and Gladys's chances, scrutinizing the candidates, taking guesses at which will fare better with the Q and A.

"Of course, it'll go to the lady with a title. Not some Lady Nowhere," Nadia remarks, already picking her side. Julia and the rest of the girls clearly agree, except for Chezka, who wraps her arms around Cleo.

Chezka pouts. "What's wrong with being Lady Nowhere?"

"Everything, apparently," Cleo supplies, moving ahead of the game by going to the bathroom and washing her face. She changes into a cotton shirt and shorts, relaxed and cozy enough to absorb her sweat if she ever gets nervous.

Behind her, Chezka's brought out her makeup kit. With one hand on her brush, she cajoles Cleo into letting her do her makeup. "Let me color your face. I swear I won't mess it up, and you'll be the highlight of this round."

"Why are you helping me?" Cleo holds Chezka's brush away from her. She's not sure she's ready to trust someone she just met, excluding Elle, of course. "I mean, what will you get from it? You're the only one who wants to be on my side."

Chezka looks away, putting her brush down. Cleo can see her darting glances at the wall clock. They only have three minutes left.

"Can you keep a secret, Cleo?"

Cleo takes the brush and gives it to Chezka. "I'm sorry, you don't have to tell me—"

And then Chezka utters her secret softly and quietly, like a murmured prayer at a funeral she's not a part of. A prayer for someone she knows but can't expose. It's the side of her that no one can ever know because rich and pretty girls like her should be just that.

"I'm . . . I don't know what to say." Cleo can only look into Chezka's eyes; the dark orbs are hauntingly beautiful. Vulnerability has never looked this strong. "But thank you for sharing that with me. I'm not going to tell anyone."

A tear escapes Chezka's eye, but she quickly wipes it away with a tissue. "I grew up thinking it's wrong to love . . . my own kind."

"What is it that draws you to Nadia?" To be honest, Cleo doesn't like Nadia. She has no idea how someone as good as Chezka can fall in love with someone so spiteful.

"We join a lot of pageants. I'm joining this one because I want to be with her. I want to have fun, Cleo. But trust me, Nadia wasn't always like this. I just want her to have fun, too."

Cleo is in awe. "Let's have fun. And in case you ever need a reminder, there's nothing wrong with what you're feeling. Your heart is big enough to accommodate all the kinds of love this world has to offer."

Chezka becomes her upbeat self again, powdering Cleo's face with foundation and enjoying the moment. Cleo lets her face be used. If nothing else, it'll give Chezka a chance to practice her makeup skills.

No, Elle, Cleo thinks. *Chezka's taught me that we can be whoever we want to be and love whoever we want. Our minds can be confused by what we're told is right, but what our hearts feel can never be wrong.*

"Time's up!" Elle announces, sitting on a plush red throne-like chair. She keeps her knees and legs together, slightly slanting her legs to the side. She looks queenlier than all the other women in the room combined.

Cleo and Gladys stand in front of Elle with their five-inch heels as the girls surround them in a semi-circle. Both of them are unwavering, not a shake of leg in sight. Elle does not smile, but her eyes seem to smile for her.

"Who wants to answer first?"

Gladys swiftly raises her hand, leaving Cleo to cross her fingers behind her. Chezka inserts the air pods in Cleo's ears, blasting rock music while Gladys answers whatever question Elle has posed. After twenty seconds, Cleo gets her turn to answer the question.

"You've got thirty seconds to answer the question," Elle reminds Cleo. "What is the biggest challenge to young people today?"

"The biggest challenge to young people today is the idea of a perfect life they get from social media. When we think about it, nobody posts about the grueling hustle, the sad times. Nobody wants that negativity. But I believe that when we embrace the down times as much as the happy times, we can all slow down and take our time to get to where we want to be. Thank you."

Chezka's the only one who gives a round of applause, which is fine by Cleo. She doesn't need fake applause from people who are just waiting for her to make a mistake.

"Thank you, Cleo. It's around twenty-five seconds. That's safe, but it can be shorter. Remember brevity. Make the point larger than the scale of the problem," Elle advises, receiving a folder from Julia. Cleo guesses it's their score sheet. "Second round of screenings will be at 5 p.m. Make an impression on the panelists. Nice job, Gladys," she adds.

"Thank you, Elle," Gladys bows her head. "I appreciate that."

"You only have yourself to thank." Elle snaps her fingers. "Everyone, change your outfit. Your stylists will help you. Let's meet outside once you're done."

Cleo sits down for a breather. She hears Gladys telling everyone how she came up with her answer, and they're all praising her for how on point that is.

"Cheer up, Cleo. Elle is our mentor, not the panelist," Chezka says, offering a hand to her.

For someone who's not a panelist, Elle sure can feel as intimidating as one.

Cleo takes Chezka's hand and stands, and off they go to their respective stylists. Dom with a Q meets Cleo in the walk-in closet. He tips her chin up like he always does, feeling her face before he can get the inspiration to dress her.

"How's the Q and A?" Dom inquires, glancing back and forth between Cleo and the collection of outfits.

"Brevity."

"Ah, Elle's favorite!" Dom exclaims.

Cleo waits for Dom to say something else.

"What are you standing there for? I'm not going to comfort you, honey. Come, use your eyes and take a pick. Just because I'm your stylist doesn't mean I'll hand everything to you."

Cleo grumbles, stomping her way toward Dom with a Q, who's the stylist version of Elle.

Dom puts his hands on his waist, watching Cleo take every dress she sets her eyes on. "Are you complaining?"

"I'm not," Cleo says through gritted teeth, not wanting to come off as angry, but people are testing her patience today. She's got the panel to worry about, and Dom isn't helping her at all. Too drained to even think about her attire, she picks a yellow sundress and changes into it. When she comes out of the dressing room, Dom has the nerve to laugh.

"Oh, honey."

Cleo glowers at Dom. "It's a dress."

"Exactly. You're required to wear a white shirt and high waist skinny jeans."

Cleo clenches her fists and forces a smile. She changes into a white shirt and highwaist skinny jeans, just as Dom has advised.

"Patience, Cleo. You'll learn patience from me, and you do not complain and throw a tantrum. Beauty queens should work well under pressure. No scowling. Smile naturally." Dom takes away the clothes Cleo has so effortlessly thrown around the floor. "Even if you have a menstrual period."

"In my next life, I want to be a man."

Dom points to his mouth, and Cleo pulls off a smile. "Maybe we can arrange that. You can be Dom, and I can be Cleo."

"Works for me. Let's go."

⚜   ⚜   ⚜

There are twelve panelists in suits and ties and elegant dresses. They're seated at a long table, and Cleo stands alone in the middle of what seems to be their activity center. She's got the entire space to herself, and somehow this makes the situation more real for her.

"Introduce yourself," a panelist with bits of gray hair initiates.

Cleo gleefully flashes her winning smile, one leg in front of the other. "You might have heard of the name Cleo Walter before."

One of them says, "I have. *Direk* Everett, right?"

"Yes. When your father is a famous director, everyone expects you walk in his footsteps. It's either you measure up to him, or you become a better version of him."

"And which one are you?" the one with a blue tie demands.

"Neither. I'm not him. I don't want to be known as the director's daughter. I want to be known as Cleo Walter. I want people to see me as someone who can do more than ride a parent's coattails. And that's what I'm here for: I want to learn how to be truly me." Cleo looks at each one of them. "I want young girls and boys to be who they want to be. No dream is ever too big for any person to pursue. Being in the pageant, while I'm still new at it, I realize it's not just 'mirror, mirror on the wall who's the fairest of them all'. It's tapping into what's on the inside, so the best version of ourselves can grow and make us the person we've always wanted to be."

"Should you become an official candidate, how will it change your life?" the woman in a pencil skirt locks her eyes on Cleo.

Cleo keeps her gaze focused on the panelists. She holds still and then opens her mouth to speak her mind. "Every aspect of my life will change, and I'll make sure that this change will cause a domino effect in the life of others. When one good act touches another, the results can be amazing. I don't want to inspire people. I want to be with them as they express their thoughts and discover their dreams."

"And what do you feel right now?"

"A little bit of everything, but overall, I'm thrilled to be here," Cleo answers, laughing with pure bliss. "I've never introduced myself this way to anybody else, so this is a first . . . out of many."

The panelists thank Cleo, smiling at her as she finally exits.

When Cleo sights Elle waiting for her, she clasps her hands together and says, "I know I'm lagging, but I promise you I did my best there."

"I know," Elle replies, looking after the next beauty queen who's coming up next. "Take some rest."

Cleo breathes out a sigh of relief, leaving Elle with the rest of the beauty queens. Once outside the building, she gets a text from Owen.

Owen Velazco (5:55 p.m.)
I'll come to pick you up. Let's have our movie night date.

Cleo silently sends up a prayer. This day feels like one of the best days ever, and she hopes it continues to be that way.

CHAPTER 17

Snap, Snap, Lookin' Good! Great Click Bait

Cleo's days have been nothing but training and exercise. As the coronation day draws near, the screening focuses increasingly on exposing who the candidates are until their souls feel practically naked. The panelists are all interested in their backgrounds, so everyone goes through another round of interviews where they share their history, no matter how good or bad it is.

But opening up to a group of people Cleo doesn't know is proving to be difficult. At the beauty camp, Elle has started talking to them privately, one-on-one, to help them bring out their most genuine side. Elle invites Cleo for a coffee break on the fourth day of screening. Finally, everyone is getting a break from being grilled by the panel like they're on trial which, in a sense, they are.

Elle's office is a proud exhibit of mementos. Photos, paintings, and posters of beauty queens she trained over the years hang on the beige-painted walls. Glam magazines with different starlets on the front cover obnoxiously taunt Cleo from the glass desk. But, of course, Cleo's image doesn't appear in that collection. Elle's own screening process seems to involve scouting for celebrities of a certain kind. Celebrities who have the aptitude to be a beauty queen.

"Take a seat," Elle tells Cleo as she slides her reading glasses up to the bridge of her nose and settles herself comfortably in her cushioned chair.

Cleo obeys, sitting upright on the loveseat where she can see the mannequins draped with sashes of previous runners-up of the world and international pageantry at the side. The sashes are pristine and new-looking. Cleo can also smell the expensive perfume emanating from them.

"Like the sashes? I make sure they're as well cared for as the crowns are. A crown may be the winning glory, but the sash identifies the beauty queen," Elle explains, drinking from her coffee cup and looking at the sashes tending so carefully. "The sash reminds me of their origin, of how hard these queens have worked to be where they are right now."

Cleo loves the smell of the coffee. It keeps her feeling awake throughout the day, and she definitely needs it now, after being given the pep talk she didn't know she needed.

"This screening . . ." Cleo jumps right into the topic. "It's more of a personality and discipline test."

"It's already a given that you are all beautiful. The smiles and walks can be practiced. However, the attitude and personality of the beauty queen must be unique enough to the panelists that they can single her out."

Cleo folds her hands on her lap, unsure. "Do you think I stand a chance? I mean, I've been raging on and on about doing this and that, but maybe I'm just convincing myself."

"And are you convinced?" Elle questions, brows pulled together.

"I like to believe I am."

Elle's eyeglasses slide down her nose a bit, and she eyes Cleo from over their top. "Then there's your answer. As long as you believe in yourself, the rest of the world doesn't really matter."

"Do you think I'm as good as my mom back in her day?" The

coffee's making her say things—it's like her shot of vodka, loosening her tongue.

"How can I compare two different people? You can choose to be like her, or you can be better than her. The problem with you, Cleo, is that you always keep comparing yourself to others. You move at your own pace. You have your own journey. Own up to it, and you'll get there, no matter how many detours you take."

Cleo chuckles, staring at her soon-to-empty cup. "I don't mean to compare myself to others. But when you grow up with a father who keeps comparing you to almost every star on TV, then you tend to do it to yourself."

"Have a little faith in yourself, Cleo Walter. They don't get to decide how you live your life." Elle pulls out a black and white photograph from her drawer and gives it to Cleo. "The reason why I was rooting for Thea was that she has a pure soul. She's only known kindness all her whole life."

It's a picture of Elle and Thea during the press presentation of the official candidates of the Lady Pearl of the Philippines. Thea's face is vibrant, pulsing with energy that can wake everyone up in the morning without feeling the slightest bit crabby. Beside her, Elle is as elegant as ever. They both look proud of themselves. The photograph tugs Cleo's heartstrings.

"It's yours if you want it," Elle adds.

Cleo sniffles. "I'll keep it. Thank you. I'll make sure I won't fall behind."

"You better not. Now, get out there and join them."

"Copy that!" Cleo exults, giving Elle the finger heart. "You are the best."

Elle sips her coffee. "I am only *the* Elle."

Cleo doesn't finish her coffee. Instead, she rushes out of Elle's office and pours it down the pantry sink. When the rest of the girls catch her return, they give her the stink eye. She ignores it, lacing up her feet in the five-inch heels and joining their game of a trip to

Jerusalem. They circle the chair as the hot and sensational music plays in the background.

"Why are we playing this?" Cleo playfully asks Chezka, who's circling the monoblock chairs.

"It exercises the legs and the muscles for sitting down and standing up again." And then Chezka whispers something in Cleo's ears. "It's kind of fun until one of them gives the chair a little push, if you know what I mean."

Elle has an odd way of training them, but it works, because within half an hour everyone's having their own best version of fun. Though when some of the girls don't land a seat, they either roll their eyes or say the game is boring. Not very good sports.

With one chair left, Cleo and Gladys are the only ones left, and with the ongoing heat of a battle between them, the girls who were once bored are back on their feet, cheering for them. But, unfortunately, the only person who's on team Cleo is Chezka.

As the music plays, Gladys rambles on about Cleo's mysterious sponsor. "So, Cleo, come on, share it with us. We won't tell anyone. Who's your secret sponsor? You can't be at an *elite* beauty camp and not pay for anything."

Nadia's sneering at Cleo, whispering whatever Gladys told her to another girl. Cleo doesn't answer. She doesn't owe them anything.

"Sugar daddy?"

Cleo huffs out, blowing tendrils of her hair away from her face. "Oh, please. If I had a sugar daddy, I wouldn't be here right now."

"I know!" Nadia yells, amused by the banters. "You're a nude model!"

"I'm not. But even if I was, there's nothing wrong with being a nude model. It's an art form, and the only reason we're conscious of our naked bodies is because of that stupid snake in the garden of Eden," Cleo protests, and then Julia stops the music, which takes her by surprise so obviously, Gladys grabs the chair.

Chezka eyes Nadia. "Nads, really?"

"Trying to be a superhero, Chezka?" Nadia fires back. "It doesn't suit you. You're just a creepy friend who won't leave me alone because you think we'll happily be best friends forever and ever until the end of time."

"Hey, Nadia—" Cleo seethes. "That's below the belt."

Julia gets in the middle and closes her eyes. "Girls, girls! I think it's about time we meditate. Relax our minds, you know? It's only just the beginning, and we're all supposed to come out as official candidates. Why don't we just save the fighting until after we get that spot, huh?"

"You've only ever cared about the crown, Julia," chides one of the girls at the back.

"You're clinging to Nadia because you can't do it alone."

"Shut up, you little bi—"

"Enough!"

They all line up in front of Elle, whose expression is unreadable. She's as cold as ice, and that makes her scarier.

"I didn't take you all here under my wing just so you can freely trash another person. You are all beauty queens. I don't see any beauty. Julia, watch your words." Elle frigidly stares at Julia and then turns to the rest of them. "Since you all want to talk so much, let's do another round of Q and A. Ten seconds to answer. All of you will participate, and your names will be randomly called. There'll be a different question for each of you, and I'll score you based on my standard. Whoever gets the lowest score between now and tomorrow will be released from the beauty camp."

Total silence reigns.

One by one, their names are being called.

"Yasmin, if you could change one thing in your life right now, what would it be?"

"Nothing, because everything I have right now is the result of the choices I made in life," Yasmin answers without fail.

"Nadia, what would you tell your 10-year-old self?"

"I'd tell her just to take her time, and everything will be all right."

"Gladys, are you in favor of marijuana?"

"If it's for medicinal use, then I'm all for it, but if it's not, then it has to be taken moderately for recreational use."

"Cleo, if you can have one superpower, what would it be?"

"The power to carry another person's emotional burden so they can rest."

And the odd Q and A goes on for some seven more girls. After a few minutes of enduring Elle's endless questions, they all make it out alive. Eventually, Elle walks out on them, and they're left feeling drained. Tired, they all flop down on the carpeted floor, taking big gulps of water from their mugs and bottles.

"Remind me to never get on Elle's bad side," Cleo says to Chezka, trying to calm her fast-beating heart. "I think I need to recharge my brain."

Chezka groans, lying down on the carpet. "I think I need to sell mine."

Cleo worries her lower lip. She has no idea how she scored in that quick quiz. She can never really tell what's going on inside Elle's mind. Even with her history with Elle, she doubts the woman will give her a free pass at this, and that's good. She doesn't want to win because she's the daughter of a former beauty queen. Anyway, the only notable thing Elle has done for her is to welcome her without pay. The queenmaker knows how to get on everyone's nerves.

As they're all dismissed, they pick up their bags and leave without a word. Across the street, Elle's on her phone, halting Cleo in her tracks by raising her index finger to indicate she wants a moment of her time.

Cleo waits for five minutes before crossing the street and engaging with Elle. Awkwardly, she puts her hands in the back pocket of her jeans.

Elle's expression doesn't give anything away. "That's your strength."

Cleo has no idea what she means.

"Flash bursts of questions. Spontaneity. You answer much better when it's out in the air, and you don't have a chance to think twice."

"I was *panicking*," Cleo clarifies.

"Not all who panic can get a good answer out of it. Good job earlier. Improve on clearing your mind, and don't be afraid to answer. What else is your brain for?" Elle commends, switching off her phone. "Tomorrow's the last day of screening. Get a good night's sleep. Ciao."

♣   ♣   ♣

Gladys takes a picture of Cleo and Elle across the street. She isn't dumb. She can tell when someone's being favored. The two seem to be having a good conversation, especially since tomorrow's the last day of the screening, where the official candidates will also be announced. It ticks her off that someone so small could pick up a title just like that.

Little Lady Nowhere will remain Nowhere—Gladys promises herself that. Before she goes home, she calls the local government unit that sponsored her to be in Elle's beauty camp. She worked hard to be Lady Quezon City. She's not going to let anybody else take it away from her.

The PR officer comes on the line. "Good evening. What can I do for you, Ms. Gladys?"

"Elle engages in favoritism," Gladys says in a deadpan voice. "How could you not have noticed that?"

The PR officer scoffs at this. "No disrespect, ma'am, but this is Elle we're talking about. *The* Elle. And, ultimately, we can't do anything about it."

"Elle is being unfair! How can you put up with an injustice like that?" Gladys almost screams, wanting to pull her hair out in frustration.

"I can't publicize something like that without any basis. We'll be tarnishing the name of our city, and the mayor won't like it. That, I can assure you."

"Hold the line. I'll send you a photo of their secret meet-up." Gladys scrolls through her phone's photos and finds multiple takes of it. There are some good zoomed ones, and she's pretty sure anyone can tell who these two women are. She emails them to the PR officer.

"How sure are you that this is a secret meet-up?"

Gladys wants to strangle the man for being so slow. "There's a reason why I'm Lady Quezon City. I have a strong feeling that Elle isn't who she says she is. I don't know what's behind the story of Little Miss Nowhere, but it feels like I'm missing something here. What I am sure of is that Elle wants this Cleo to win."

"Elle is a mentor. She can't just give beauty queens a crown. They work hard for it," PR man volleys back.

"Believe what you want, but I've got a bad feeling about this."

"Okay, Ms. Gladys. I'll let the mayor know. I'm not going to be the one to put this out there."

"Or you can lose your job," Gladys snidely remarks. "I got you that job, PR man. If it weren't for me, you'd still be living in the slums. I want those pictures out tomorrow. Post it anonymously, use another account. I honestly don't care. The mayor will believe me if somebody else who isn't us posts that. Catch my drift?"

PR man sighs heavily. "Fine. I'll make my way around it, Lady Quezon City."

"As I always will be."

This is your stop, Cleo Walter, Gladys thinks to herself, grinning from ear to ear. *Nobody can just waltz in and take the sash. This is as far as you go, Little Miss Nowhere.*

I Didn't Mean For That to Happen, Honestly

"Leo, I'm thinking about us starting our own business."

A rooftop Saturday morning session with Anne consists of iced coffee, Spanish bread, and a lifestyle magazine on the glass table. As they flip through the magazine's pages, the homely and healthy life of young entrepreneurs and influencers make them green with envy. These personalities have traveled all over the world to feature the culture of the country they're visiting, and they get paid for it.

Cleo dangles her legs over the arm of the wooden chair she's lounging on, pushing the magazine away from her. "What kind of business?"

The only reason Cleo likes to wake up early is because of the gentle breeze in the air. The temperature's not so hot either, and it's the only time of the day when she doesn't have to sweat so much. Living in a tropical country makes her want to travel to some cold place. Winter sounds good to people who have only ever known summer their whole lives.

"Cookies? *Ma's* been baking for a few weeks now." Anne yawns, tears forming in the corner of her eyes. "I think we can sell it. Lately, she's been trying to find a hobby that sells, so what do you think?"

"If it's for *Ma*, you know I'm all for it."

Anne taps her pen on the table, thinking. "Online selling of cookies."

"I can help with the materials and ingredients," Cleo pitches in, logging in to her online banking account on her phone. "Wait, let me check how much I've saved up this month . . ."

"Speaking of savings. How are you earning after the whole movie with *Direk* Gary?" Anne inquires. Cleo can understand why her sister's curious as to where she's getting the money, but the truth is she's been using her savings for about a month now.

What Anne just said reminds Cleo that she needs to find a regular job or do modeling again. It can be distracting to the competition, but she can't just stop working. There are no set times and dates for the training, either. She can tell Elle she'll be a bit busier than usual. That way, she can still do both pageantry and modeling.

Cleo closes her online banking account and smiles sheepishly. "Don't worry. I've got savings."

"Leo." Anne slams her hands on the table, startling Cleo. "Let me take over for now as you look for jobs. I have a salary, too."

"I'm the eldest, I'm—"

"Oh, stop it with that I'm-the-eldest-so-I-should-be-the-breadwinner thing. Anyone in the family can win bread, you know Just because you're the firstborn doesn't mean you need to carry all the family's burdens. Besides, you've already done so much for us. It's my turn to help." Anne's eyes flashed with determination, pleading. "I'm not discrediting all your hard work, but at least let me help. What are sisters for?"

Cleo places a hand over her heart. "You just squeezed my heart. Okay, okay. Thank you."

Anne closes her eyes and clasps her hands together in prayer. "Oh, dear Lord, I wish Leo only the best in life from now on. Please give her the courage to ask for help when she needs it."

"Hey!" Cleo says, tears welling in her eyes even as she laughs.

Anne peeks at Cleo and raises an eyebrow at her. "That a good enough prayer?"

"So good the prayer didn't pass through the angels. Went straight to the good Lord."

Anne mutters her countless thanks, already finding something else to do as she jots down the ingredients she and their mom will need for baking. In between searching on the web for quality baking tools and comparing the prices of chocolates to use, she looks up at the skies, and it lights up her whole face.

How could I not be willing to work hard when I've got a sister like her? Cleo thought to herself.

When Cleo's phone alarm rings, she quickly remembers what today is—judgment day. Leaving in a rush, she finishes her iced coffee and waves goodbye to Anne. She takes her backpack and finds a white van sitting outside their house. Not caring whose van that is, she books a cab on her phone until she gets a text from an unknown number.

+63 91X XXX XXXXX (9:31 a.m.)
A white van will be waiting for you. Be on time.

Cleo doesn't even need to know whose number is that. Approaching the white van, the door slides open, and Chezka's painted face pops out, screaming out her name. "Cleo! You're late! Run!"

Once inside the van, the girls are staring at Cleo as if she committed a murder. They're in their best dress with their faces and hairstyles so put together. She's the only one who still hasn't done a thing to herself.

"I thought we'll meet at the camp, so I didn't—"

Nadia sizes Cleo up. "I honestly don't know what to do with you. Final screening means final. What part of that did you not understand?"

"Elle will meet us there, and she can't see you like that," Chezka stresses, pulling out a long, black slit maxi dress from the back of the van. "Come here and wear this."

"Oh God, oh God, oh God, Elle will execute me," Cleo squeaks, following Chezka to the back and trying to change clothes.

Chezka pulls out the newspapers underneath the seats to cover up the windows. She's also put a fabric between the driver and the back seats so Cleo can have her privacy. While Cleo changes clothes, Chezka takes her phone and makes a call.

"*Kuya*, can we stop at the next traffic light? We'll just be picking up one more person," Chezka directs the driver.

Shaken, Cleo almost hits the window when the driver hits the brakes. She's trying to fix her dress, find out where the holes are, and neatly smooth it out afterward. It's safe to say she isn't properly dressed yet. Thankfully, her savior comes right in when the van comes to a complete stop. Dom steps inside the van and makes his way to her.

"Honey, what the hell are you doing?" Grimacing, Dom pulls out the dress and helps Cleo with it. "Do this again and next time you'll be wearing nothing."

"Drive ahead, *Kuya*. We can't afford to be late," Chezka prompts the driver, going from one girl to another to ask for help. "Do you have your makeup kit with you? Or lipstick? Blush?"

"Why would we help Cleo?" Gladys rebukes, her sinister stare locked on Cleo.

Chezka shakes her head, disbelieving. "We're in the same camp, Gladys. If you don't want to help, fine."

Cleo takes the makeup kits Chezka passes to her, profusely apologizing and thanking her for her help. Then, with Dom's help, Cleo applies the primer on her face, using the concealer to hide the dark circles under her eyes.

"Foundation," Dom demands, holding out his hand to Chezka, who's passing him the makeup essentials.

Cleo chuckles at what they're doing. It's as if she's having surgery and Dom is the surgeon. And while she's silently screaming on the inside, her heart warms at the thought that they're still willing to help her despite her stupidity.

"Smile!"

Cleo smiles the best she can as Dom paints the apples of her cheeks with a rosy flush. With the overall face done, they move on to her eyebrows, even harder to do in a moving vehicle. It's one bump after another, and when the driver's app tells them they're ten minutes away from their destination in Makati, she almost cries but holds back to keep her mascara intact.

Dom then proceeds to Cleo's hair, messing it up slightly to make it seem more naturally loose. He keeps her hair stylish but straightforward with a half-bun.

"Oh God, oh God, oh God," Cleo jabbers.

Chezka attempts to calm Cleo, offering her a water bottle. "Breathe in, breathe out. You're looking good."

Cleo takes one big gulp out of it, soothing her voice.

"Who's beautiful?" Dom raises the question out loud. When Cleo doesn't answer, he reprimands her. "I didn't do all this stuff for nothing."

"I am."

"Claim it."

"I am!"

"Why are you whispering?"

"I AM!" Cleo screams at the top of her voice.

Cleo gets a compact mirror from Chezka and sees how beautiful she is. It doesn't look like messy work. It's perfection. With the nude and gold eyeshadows, she's got the touch of Midas.

"We're here," the driver announces.

The beauty queens are dazzling. They're heavenly beautiful with their long gowns and impeccably-chosen makeup palettes. In earth tones and icy blues, they blend exceptionally well with nature's hues. They keep one leg over another whenever they pose, resting their weight on the front foot. It punctuates the solid, imposing presence each of them projects A small wave here and there. The world is theirs to conquer.

Staring at the other contestants, Cleo doesn't even notice she's the only one left in the van. Dom's just sitting there, arms folded and waiting for her to get herself out there.

"How long are you going to stay here?" Dom crosses his legs.

Cleo beams. "Thank you so much."

Out of the van, a curly-haired photographer snaps a photo of Cleo. He's a mix of formal and casual in a white polo shirt paired with a black suit. He doesn't seem like the type to wear full-out formal attire. He has to throw in something a bit irreverent and unexpected.

"Hi, Harry Sty—"

"The name's Erik," Mr. Photographer drawls out, lazily taking a picture of Cleo. "Nice hair."

"I've been through hell. My hair should be the least of your concerns. It's good as it is." Cleo smiles at him, turning to her side with one leg forward as she slightly arches her back.

Erik watches Cleo touch her hair. "So, are you going to stand there and defend your good-as-it-is hair?"

"If I don't, then who's going to convince you to take a picture of me and my good hair?"

The corner of Erik's mouth curves into a half-smile. "Touché."

After mussing her hair up a bit more, Cleo genuinely smiles for the camera. The day is far from over, but she can already feel her lips getting numb from smiling all the time.

Done with the photo session, Erik finally leaves Cleo alone. She bides her time, hoping to calm her erratic heart. And then she begins her walk to her soon-to-be-future, praying silently and wishing in the deepest crevices of her heart that today will be the start of good beginnings.

In the lobby of the building, Elle's being hounded by reporters, and it does not look great. At all.

"Is it true that there's favoritism?"

"We've seen photos of you meeting one of your trainees in secret. Who is this trainee?"

"How did your girls react to this issue?"

If there's anything that's way too familiar to Cleo, it's the word *issue*. Everyone makes an issue out of everything. While she's not surprised that Elle has an issue or two, she didn't expect it would be about favoritism. In the amount of time she's spent with Elle, she's become sure that her mentor is the last person on earth who'd ever have favorites. If these reporters only had the time to visit the beauty camp during one of the training sessions, they'd see that Elle is not someone who is easily swayed.

And although Cleo's mother has a history with Elle, Elle is as strict with her as she is with the others. No special treatment. She supports all the girls equally. Whoever is spreading this "issue" is desperate for attention.

The rest of Elle's girls stand behind Cleo, whispering amongst themselves, doubting Elle.

Cleo faces them. "You guys seriously believe these reporters?"

Even after everything Elle's done for them, these girls are still acting high and mighty.

Unbelievable.

"You have faith in Elle because she took you in for *free*," Nadia comments. "The only way you can save her from this black cloud is if you tell them who's sponsoring a newbie and Lady Nowhere like you."

But then, before an argument can erupt between Cleo and Nadia, Elle's voice echoes loud and true. "I don't have favorites. I make sure they are all worthy of the crown."

"Ms. Elle, Lady Quezon City has given a statement minutes ago. She claims it's only right that she keep her title as Lady Quezon City. She maintains that it's not fair for you to have favorites, especially if that favorite is from the same city as herself."

Elle shrugs it off. "No candidate deserves a title just by thinking she deserves it. It's the people who should decide who's deserving. And no candidate should act paranoid during this time. Being a beauty queen means grace under pressure, and I don't see Lady

Quezon City achieving that."

After that answer, Cleo and the rest of the girls huddle in the lobby, talking about what just happened. Gladys swoops as the conversation is ending, but by now, everyone is quiet.

"What did Elle say?" Gladys is trembling, clenching and unclenching her fists. Nobody answers, so she repeats her question.

Silence.

"Gladys Tiangco." Elle arrives like a devil in her best shawl. "You are no longer with us."

Elle ended Gladys's dream just like that.

Elle turns to the beauty queens who are still part of her camp. "Be grateful for Gladys. Because of her, the scores I made internally are invalidated. Everyone is saved. Let's go, girls."

No one says a thing. Not even those who once sided with Gladys. They stick to Elle's decision and do not spare Gladys a glance.

On their way to the final screenings room, Cleo stops in her tracks, takes a tissue from one of the tables, and runs back to where Gladys is. She's on the floor, crying.

"We might not have seen eye to eye, but you'll always be one of my worthiest rivals." Cleo leaves the tissue on Gladys's lap and goes back to her team.

Waiting is, as usual, torture to every one of the beauty queens. Out of seventy-one, only half of them will proceed to the nationals. Cleo's prayed every prayer there is, and all she needs to do now is to believe in herself.

"Come on in, Cleo Walter," the receptionist invites Cleo, and she enters.

Again, Cleo faces the panelists. They so their usual thorough checks as she goes through all the paces: wearing swimsuits and gowns, walking with high heels, and showing real and candid facial expressions. She executes these requirements well. If she didn't have any confidence before, she exudes it now.

"One last thing before we wrap up. What makes you different from the rest of your fellow beauty queens?" This is the question Cleo's been thinking about for days.

"I'm different not just from each of my fellow beauty queens, but from everyone else in the world. No human being is the same as any other. As Cleo Walter, I have my own set of flaws, but they only me more reason to love who I am at this moment and who I am becoming."

🌿 🌿 🌿

The final screenings have ended, and they're told to make themselves comfortable inside the theater, where everyone else is also taking a break. They're given refreshments, and finally, after what seems like a lifetime's worth of anticipation, one of the panelists enters the stage with a mic and paper in hand.

Cleo's on the edge of her seat, her hands gripping the hem of her dress. Nadia and the others aren't a bit fazed. Oh, what she'd give to have Nadia's confidence.

"There's a thin line between confidence and complacency," Chezka whispers under her breath, winking at her.

Cleo smiles timidly, watching the panelist take the stage.

"May I now call forward the top forty candidates for the Lady Pearl of the Philippines. Once your name is called, please come on the stage so we can officially welcome you to the national pageantry competition."

Forty names is a lot. Cleo's counting off in her head, and so far, most of the names that are being called are from Elle's camp. Chezka's name comes out of the panelist's mouth on the twentieth slot. Cleo congratulates her because she deserves it. Time ticks by until there are only three beauty queens left in Elle's camp, waiting for their names to be called. What gives her hope is that there is no Lady Quezon City yet.

"Cleo, Cleo, Cleo," Cleo repeats to herself, crossing her fingers and lowering her head.

"Cleo. Cleo. Cleo."

Let me be Lady Quezon City.

"Cleo Walter, Lady Quezon City!"

CHAPTER 19

The Cost of Being an Official Candidate

earing the title attached to her name gives Cleo a sense of pride and satisfaction. She walks at her own pace, slowing down when she reaches the stage. She giggles like a teenager who finds out that her crush likes her back.

Striding on the stage, Cleo lines up next to the last candidate called. She keeps up her smiling face during the entire hour of deliberation. She doesn't hear the names of the others. In her head, *Cleo Walter, Lady Quezon City*, keeps on repeating like a broken record. She searches for Elle and finds her mentor's first smile of pride.

"Congrats," Elle mouths the words, and Cleo is on cloud nine.

Once the forty have been called, the candidates get their first official group photo. The panelists congratulate them, saying they're looking forward to seeing more of them in the next two months. Cleo doesn't digest any of this, not even until they're released, and they're back in the white van. This time, Elle rides with them.

"Eight of you from this camp get to be official candidates. Congratulations," Elle says, looking at each and every one of them, but she pauses on the other two. "To the two who didn't make it, I congratulate you as well. You did your best, and I'm proud of you.

Rest assured, you will still be welcomed next year. Thank you for all your hard work."

Chezka begins to clap, and then it gets louder and louder, and suddenly they're all clapping—a mutual round of applause. For the first time since Cleo's arrival, Nadia doesn't have a catty remark or sour expression.

While the group celebrates, Cleo's phone beeps its familiar notifications tune. She doesn't need to open it to know it's her social media on a blast.

"Take a look at what people have been saying to you," Chezka suggests.

Cleo shakes her head, planning to save the drama and cheesy gossip news for later. She's fed up with people who make assumptions about everything in her life.

"Cleo, just look at it."

Cleo opens her social media accounts and finds the news about her.

Just In: Cleo Walter is An Official Candidate for the Lady Pearl of the Philippines!

The actress-turned-beauty queen, Cleo Walter, has not run out of luck just yet. She keeps everyone on their toes with every little thing she does and is quite a strong, brave woman for championing herself into a national pageant.

Meanwhile, the founder of elite beauty camp Reign of Queens, Elle, has confirmed that she has admitted Cleo into her camp.

Click here to check the list of the top forty official candidates for the Lady Pearl of the Philippines.

As for the comments and reactions of people on the social media platform Chirp:

@tellaaachin: woah! That's some big career change @CleoWalter

@triciavv01: gURRRL LOOK AT THOSE LEGS!!! SHE'S GOT 'EM GOOD LEGS and could probably slay the RUN-WAY!

@adrienneyen: looking at it now, she actually fits the beauty queen role.

@veniceerz: not really a fan of hers, but her history took me here. my personal favorite is
Lady QC. can't wait to see them compete internationally!

@OnAnna: unbelievable!! this lady ain't done with TV yet????
whatever floats ur boat
@CleoWalter

"You did great!" Chezka assures Cleo, her eyes obviously looking for Nadia.

Cleo pats Chezka's back and whispers, "Go check on her. She seems to be in a festive mood. I'll be fine."

Chezka grins and sits at the back where Nadia is.

Cleo props her head on the window side, momentarily closing her eyes and taking a break. She wonders how her family and boyfriend will react to the news. Unbidden, a smile plays on her lips. She can't wait to get home.

🐝   🐝   🐝

"OH MY GOD, WHY DIDN'T YOU TELL US?"

Cleo shies away from Anne, covering her ears, unable to stand her sister's screeching voice. When she got home, Anne was waiting for her in the living room, switching all the lights on like she's some sort of criminal caught in the act.

"Because I wanted to be sure it would happen. I'm sorry, Anne," Cleo laughs cheekily at her sister. Anne throws a pillow at her, and she easily dodges it.

Candy struts over to Cleo, wagging her tail and picking up the pillow on the floor. She barks incessantly, joining Anne in her protest. She stretches downward, her tongue lolling out. In her little dog way, she fixes her angry but cute eyes on Cleo, almost as if she's been betrayed too.

Cleo picks up Candy and babies her. "Aw, little cutie! I'm so sorry."

"*Ma!* Leo's not listening!" Anne complains, burying her head in the pillow. "I can't believe I didn't wish you good luck earlier!"

Cleo puts Candy down and goes to find her mom in the kitchen. Thea's baking cookies, just as Anne said she'd be doing. "I'm an official candidate for the Lady Pearl of the Philippines, and I don't know if this is good. I know it is kind of too late to say this, but I want to consult you, *Ma.* My name's on social media again, and it's going to be in the tabloids tomorrow, but I can still make it disappear."

"How do you feel about their comments?" Thea removes her over gloves and washes her hands.

"In an odd way, I feel kind of okay. It doesn't bother me as much as it did before. There are more positive ones now than negative."

Thea faces Cleo, offering her the first batch of fresh, yummy dark chocolate chip cookies. "And this is what you want?"

"Yes."

Thea doesn't reply right away. She keeps her focus on the cookies she's been preparing. Unable to withstand the silence, Cleo helps her mom personalize the message for each cookie box.

"I'm sorry, *Ma*," Cleo says apologetically, taking a bite of the cookies. "I should have asked you first. At this point, though, n one's that interested in me. But if by some miracle I get the crown in two months, then somewhere along the way, the story about you will come up. How do you feel about that?"

Thea's tears fall down her cheeks, and Cleo begins to apologize for even asking.

"No, it's not that, *anak*." Thea wipes her tears away. "I'm just proud of you."

"If this makes you feel uncomfortable . . ." Cleo trails off, unsettled.

Thea's sweet aura turns ferocious. As Cleo gazes into her mother's eyes, she sees a reflection of Thea's past and of herself. She feels like she's two people in one body somehow.

"Go ahead and do it. You win it, and you win it for me. You'll complete what I couldn't finish. You sure are not the naïve girl that I was," Thea says firmly, but another intrusive thought makes her waver a bit. "But then what about your father?"

"Exactly," Cleo confirms. Thea's decision to support her has made her want to go further than she's ever been. If she can get the crown for her mother, she can get a reaction from her cowardly father. She understands that what she's asking of her mom isn't easy. But this is her mom, who should have won the nationals all those years ago, willing to make that heroic sacrifice.

"I'll always support you, Cleo." Thea offers her arms for an embrace, and Cleo gladly goes into them. "It's been a long day for you, so get some rest."

"I will."

Relieved to have her mother's blessing, and exhausted from the day, Cleo flops down on the bed and pulls the blanket over her. Then, just as she's about to close her eyes, she gets a call from Owen. Half-asleep, she answers his call.

"Hey, babe. I'm so sorry I didn't tell you anything about it. Too tired today," Cleo explains, yawning.

"Congratulations. Sorry I called right away. Go sleep, babe. I'll just let them know you're too tired to—"

"Who will you let know?"

"My parents want to invite you to the Golden Polo Club tomorrow, but it's okay, you're too tired, and you need rest," Owen says softly.

Cleo jolts awake. "Your parents? As in *your* parents?"

"Yeah."

"I'll be there with you!" Cleo implores Owen. She'll do anything to be close to his parents, and it's not because of money. She just wants them to acknowledge her as their son's girlfriend. "This is a great chance for me to get to know them."

Owen replies something incoherently.

"What?"

"It's nothing. I'll see you tomorrow, then. Have a good night, babe."

Drowsy, Cleo pulls her pillow close to her. "Good night, Owen. Love you."

🐿️   🐿️   🐿️

Out in the open green windy field of the Golden Polo Club with his girlfriend in a lace-embroidered jumpsuit, Owen knows he's with Lady Quezon City. They've only been here for five minutes or so, and his family's elite friends are already crowding them.

"Owen, won't you introduce your girlfriend to us?" Vina, their family's closest friend, asks, her sunglasses uneven on her crooked nose.

Owen wraps an arm around Cleo's waist, politely introducing Vina. "This is Cleo, my girlfriend of seven years."

"Wow, seven years, and you've only just introduced her now? How can you not introduce a beauty like her?" Vina turns to Cleo, who's smiling radiantly. "So, how's the training? I didn't think you'd be able to come, with your busy schedule."

Cleo tucks a strand of her hair behind her ear. "This is my only free day. Tomorrow it's back to training. Elle is—"

"Right, right! You're in Elle's beauty camp. What's she like?"

While Cleo and Vina converse about Elle and fancy clothes, Owen's watching his brother, Mark, and father, Luis, play a practice polo match game. Riding their respective horses, they make a good prince and king. Armed with a long, flexible mallet handle in his right hand, Mark swings the mallet, hurling the wooden ball into the goalpost.

Mark has always been the main offensive weapon of the team anyway, while their father plays the role of the tactical leader, who controls the play. They make a good team, only because they always agree on everything. Mark chooses who gets to be his other two members most of the time, and he knows who plays well. And it's not Owen.

"Hey, O!" Owen's cousin, Jeremiah, huffs out, removing his helmet. "Want to be number two?"

"I'm with my girlfriend," Owen calls back, pulling Cleo much closer to him even though she's busy entertaining Vina.

"Even more reason to join us! Come on. It's just four Chukkas."

Owen knows it won't be four Chukkas. Seeing Mark on the field, it'll be around six to eight, depending on the team's play.

Jeremiah snorts, the name of his ex-girlfriend tattooed on his right arm like a heavy weight that's been pulling him down. He turns his attention to Cleo and listens to her talk about pageantry and crowns. As soon as Cleo stops, he takes this opportunity to butt in.

Owen forces a smile and introduces the two of them.

"So, beautiful Lady Quezon City, would you like to see Owen play the polo game?"

Jeremiah charms Cleo with his smooth words, even going as far as to kiss her hand as if they were living in the age of chivalry.

Cleo flushes red, looking up at Owen. "Babe, do you play?"

Just when Owen thinks it can't get any worse, his mother, Reyna, swoops in to take Cleo in hand. "Nice to finally meet you, Cleo! Or am I supposed to call you Lady Quezon City?"

"Cleo's fine, Mrs. Velazco," Cleo says courteously. She and Owen both know Reyna hasn't warmed up to her the tiniest bit in the years they've been together. "Thank you for inviting me to your game."

Reyna waves it off and grasps Cleo's arm, clinging to her as if she'd never said anything hurtful or refused to accept her as Owen's girlfriend. "I apologize if I haven't been much of a *tita* to you. But surely, we can leave the past behind, yes?"

Owen catches how Cleo brightens up at the thought of that. She's not her usual crazy self. If she were, she'd be nodding frantically by now. Today, though, she's subdued, a compressed version of herself that he never thought he'd see. It doesn't suit her.

"Owen, we'll stay over at the tent area. Why don't you play with your brother? Cleo will be cheering for you on the sidelines," Reyna says. A suggestion, firmly given.

Everyone else knows better than to try to gainsay Reyna. But Owen's not like everyone else. He looks placidly at his mother and says, "No. I don't feel like playing today."

Reyna's eyes darken, smoldering, but Owen's not bothered by it. He's spent his whole life going against his mother's wishes. How is today any different?

"Cleo, don't you want to see Owen play?"

Of course, Reyna will turn to Cleo. She knows perfectly that Cleo is the only person who can make Owen do what she wants.

Owen's unmoving. He waits for his girlfriend's answer. Cleo seems to be thinking it through. She's biting the inside of her cheek like she does when she's unsure of something or feels stuck between two very conflicting decisions. Owen stares at her, willing her to read his mind. They've known each other so long they can finish each other's sentences. He's sure she gets the message: he doesn't want to play.

"Babe, why don't you just give it a try?"

Hell. Owen can't believe what he's hearing. He clenches his fist and takes the helmet from his cousin, joining his team and playing the game because his girlfriend told him to—oh, she suggested. Same thing . . . .

As Owen mounts his horse, Cleo blows him a kiss. "Good luck, babe!"

Owen refuses to look at Cleo. Instead, he looks down at the number two on his polo shirt. He hates this number. He's always assigned as the number two who scores but is directly behind number one. He's just an extra player to complete the four-member team.

Trying not to let it get to him, Owen focuses on the game, swinging his mallet before hitting the ball. He rides his horse well, but Mark, who is on the opposing team, is in a better position to target the goalpost. Through sweat and the exhilarating rush of the game, he releases his pent-up anger by taking over the ball that's passed to him. Usually, this kind of energy expenditure would cure him of his anger before the game is half over. But this time is different.

Owen's holding back. To make matters worse, he's been crossing the line of the ball, causing foul after foul. This fiasco goes on for about an hour until Mark's team wins.

Mark's team wins every damned time, Owen thinks, finally back on foot and letting his helmet and mallet fall carelessly on the ground.

Owen comes back to Cleo's side and takes her hand, grasping it tightly. He leans in and whispers, "Let's go home. Please."

"We can't. Your mom's not done introducing me to the rest of these people," Cleo replies lowly, smiling at whoever passes by her.

"Come on, babe. You don't like this. Hell, they didn't even like you."

Cleo keeps her composure, schooling her face with a cool expression. "Didn't. Past tense, Owen. And no, I like meeting people. You're the one who doesn't like this."

Owen keeps himself from saying things he might be sorry for. He doesn't want to cause a scene here, so he endures Cleo's too-pleasing personality.

"Ah! Mark's team wins!" Reyna exclaims, gushing over Mark and his mallet. "I know! Why doesn't Cleo, as Lady Quezon City, award the medal?"

Owen stares at Cleo, waiting for her next move.

"It would be my pleasure," Cleo generously accepts the offer, leaving Owen behind as she makes merry with his family. She stands there in all her radiant glory, flashing her pearly white teeth in a dazzling smile, a medal in her hands, while Owen watches from afar.

It's Mark's twentieth medal of the year. Cleo, Owen's girlfriend, is presenting it.

After a happy little post-presentation moment, Owen pulls Cleo to the side and says three words that burst her bubble. Suddenly, he's had enough.

"Let's break up."

Cleo's flabbergasted. "We can't just make up and then break up again. This is insane."

"No, we're not going to do that again," Owen replies icily. "There's no making up this time."

"Why? You know this is what being Lady Quezon City means. This is the job, Owen."

"I just want to be an architect, Cleo. You don't need me in your life. You've done great without me. I'll never be a star." Owen glances askance. "I never liked this world I've been stuck with."

Cleo's face is serious, sincere. "That's not what I want, anyway. Not Owen the star. I want Owen, the happy architect."

"But the other stuff you want—fame, stardom, and getting the public's attention—they don't interest me. I'm not good at this stuff. We're just different." Owen admits, rubbing the back of his neck, feeling totally exhausted from all of it.

"We've always been different," Cleo whispers softly, looking at Owen with the most beautiful eyes he's ever seen—the last time he'll ever see them in person.

Owen smiles sadly at Cleo. "Not different like this."

Elle's Killer Duo of Commanders

Cleo's been staring blankly into an empty space, not listening at all to the commotion that's been going on for over an hour. Her heart is out in the open, ripped apart and suspended in time. But still pumping, keeping her alive and moving, no matter how shattered she is now.

Love used to occupy that space, and maybe there is still love in there, but anger and sadness are taking up a lot of space right now. And that's okay. Cleo reminds herself that the heart contains a multitude of emotions. It's the fragments of memories that make it worse. They're there when she wakes up in the morning and gets no text from him. They're there when she sees a restaurant where they used to spend their Friday nights. They're there when she hears familiar music on the radio, and she's got no one to sing the lyrics with. They're there at the end of the day, and there's no one to hold her and keep her heart warm.

"Earth to Cleo."

Cleo blinks and finds Chezka snapping her fingers. "Yeah?"

"Are you okay?" Chezka furrows her eyebrows, placing the back of her hand on Cleo's forehead to check her temperature.

"Do you feel sick? Need time off? You know you can always tell Elle about it."

Cleo pulls away and languidly stretches her legs on the floor, sliding half of her body in the armchair. "It's nothing."

Chezka acts surprised. "As if."

"I'm okay."

"Wait here." Chezka rushes into the kitchen and runs back with two teacups on a silver tray.

The moment Cleo lifts the cup, she smells its sweet, light and floral scent, a meadow in the guise of a drink.

"Chamomile tea," Chezka confirms, holding her teacup like she's a duchess. "Perfect for today's teatime, you know, *chismis*."

"There's nothing to share."

Chezka sits cross-legged beside Cleo, taking her tea. "I don't believe that."

"My boyfriend and I broke up," Cleo relents, putting down her cup on the coffee table. There's no use hiding it from someone as persistent as Chezka. Unexpectedly saying it out loud has somehow given her more room to breathe.

"Oh. Do you want a piece of advice, or do you want me just to listen?"

Cleo's lips trembled. Her face turns red and blotchy, but she holds back the tears, pressing her fingers into her palms. She wants to answer, but a lump in her throat stops her. Chezka notices this, giving her a pillow to hold onto.

"It's okay to cry, Cleo." Chezka embraces Cleo. "I don't know if you picked up this bit of news yet, but from now on, Elle's two other trainers will be the ones to handle us. The two of them, Guinevere and Deborah, have scheduled meetings with us individually so they can get to know us. Do you want me to re-schedule yours?"

Cleo retreats, putting up a smile. "No. This isn't going to be like what happened before with him. I'm not going to suffer. I am *not* going to let heartbreak squash my elation at getting to where I am at this moment."

Chezka holds up her hands in endorsement, even admiration.

"I'm a strong, independent woman," Cleo proclaims, rising and shifting back into her Lady Quezon City persona, chin up and head held high. "If a man can only handle me at my worst because it makes him feel better, then he doesn't deserve me at my best when my success has nothing to do with him."

"That's right! Long live women!" Chezka's eyes flicker with excitement and solidarity

Julia passes by with a water bottle in hand. She gives them a judging stare, murmuring, "Weird. Too weird."

Cleo and Chezka share a look, laughing at themselves.

"Cleo Walter. You go first," Nadia presses, gesturing towards the welcoming room and calling out another candidate. "Lady Iloilo, you're next after Cleo."

Nadia doesn't want to address me as a Lady Quezon City, Cleo thinks and then shrugs it off. It doesn't matter whether she's Lady Nowhere or Lady Somewhere. But being in this new world of hers proves to be a challenge. She has to prepare herself physically, mentally, emotionally, and spiritually for two months. She has this seedling of hope that people can see her as worthy, and she doesn't want to kill that.

Waiting for Elle's two beauty queen commanders, Cleo checks them out on the internet. She doesn't need to look at Guinevere, but she still searches her name on the web out of curiosity. Guinevere was her childhood friend and Jake's twin, so she has an idea of what she's like. From what Cleo can remember, Guinevere supported the best cause, pushing to help farmers and save their land. She was an advocate for these hard workers who didn't have the advantage of understanding how business works. Long after the competition, she continued to visit rural areas, talk with the farmers, speak out on their behalf.

Cleo also liked Guinevere's answer in the Q and A portion, which brought her to the second runner-up position in the international competition. She's honestly amazed at the woman Guinevere has become. Guinevere hated the loamy soil and would always rather live in the city, but her joining the pageant changed all that. More than a lot of pretty faces competing with each other, the pageant is a thought-provoking and mind-changing event for these women.

Now Cleo is looking up Deborah, the beauty queen who topped as the first runner-up in the Queen of the Universe competition four years ago. Deborah's known for being quirky, the type who always mixes different styles and colors to make her even more different from the others. She's the daughter of a rich man, heir to a big conglomerate company, but she has chosen to work closely with non-government organizations in helping children cancer patients.

Clicking on "images." Cleo finds a photo of the two beauty queens. Guinevere's the female version of Jake, all deep black hair and toned legs. Deborah, on the other hand, has bronze highlights in her shoulder-length hair and a prominent duchess nose. It's incredible how the two of them have come together to serve as trainers in Elle's beauty camp. Elle wastes no woman in her camp.

"Hello, Cleo."

Cleo looks up and finds Guinevere in the same white t-shirt and pants as herself. "Hi, Guin. We meet again."

Guinevere chuckles, and then another woman, whom Cleo can assume is Deborah, walks into the room. Deborah smiles appreciatively at Cleo.

"Hi!" Deborah leans in to Cleo, greeting her through *beso-beso* in a cheek-to-cheek kiss. Like Cleo and Guinevere, Deborah is also in a plain white t-shirt and pants.

"Nice to meet you," Cleo says. She feels genuinely grateful for this team. "I can't wait to get started on the next phase."

Deborah laughs. "Believe me, once we officially start, you'll regret saying that."

"I won't give up," Cleo promises, eating her heartbreak like it's dessert.

Deborah gives Cleo a list of acceptable meals. Cleo finds the menu a bit of a surprise.

Hydration:
8 glasses of water

Breakfast:
Coffee with a splash of cream, 1½ cups of Greek yogurt with 3 diced strawberries, a handful of blueberries, a tablespoon of honey, and mangoes.

Lunch:
Grilled-chicken Caesar salad with diced cherry tomatoes, 2 tablespoons of dressing, and ⅓ cup of low-fat Parmesan cheese

Snack:
2 handfuls of roasted almonds (no salt), dried mango with a side of cottage cheese

Dinner:
Oven-roasted salmon with ½ tablespoon of olive oil to coat fillet, 1 cup of spinach topped with feta, 1 cup of steamed broccoli with fresh lemon juice, olive oil, and garlic, 2 red bliss potatoes, sliced, with olive oil and fresh rosemary

Dessert:
2 small scoops of low-fat chocolate caramel ice cream

Cleo re-reads the list again because it seems to be really simple and, at the same time, sophisticated. There's so much intricacy in the way every aspect of her life is being planned. She's never been super-set in her ways, but this list is one of the many things she'll have to get used to.

"Oh, wow," is Cleo's initial reaction. "This is nice."

Guinevere and Deborah proceed to the shoe racks, striding off in their seven-inch heels. When they're done, they walk back to Cleo with so much presence and energy she can almost see the static in the air. They are absorbing to watch. The way they carry themselves is pride and poise personified.

"Come here," Guinevere invites Cleo to hold her weight like them in a standing position.

Slowly, Cleo also slips on seven-inch heels, facing them with the same fervor and determination. They're great, but she aims to surpass them. Heartbreak is a vitamin that keeps her strong, and she'll prove that in the following days.

Cleo can already imagine herself waving at millions of people as they welcome her with her head up in the clouds. The entire crowd will chant her name, stomping their feet on the ground while they raise their hands in the air to show their support. It's what she's always loved about being a Filipino. Their unity is solid like no other nation's. Together, they're one, and she firmly believes in that, leans on it, rests in it.

"Good," Deborah says, tilting Cleo's chin up. "You'll be joining the rest of the girls today in the studio."

"But I thought you wanted to talk to each one of us?"

"We're rescheduling," Deborah answers, checking her phone for her calendar of activities.

"Don't disappoint me, Cleo," Guinevere warns playfully before leading Cleo to the studio where the other candidates are already waiting. They're standing there like some sort of military regiment that will quickly snap and answer whenever asked. Since Cleo's new, she has no idea what to do, so she follows the others.

"All right, ladies, we do head-to-toe exercises. We'll just be exercising the whole day. Got it?" Deborah instructs, leading the day's training.

The exercises are gruesome. They do a lot of stretching, neck rotations, squats, and waist movements to shape their waists better. It's a full-body workout. Anyone who complains is reprimanded by either Deborah or Guinevere. And so that they can see their every movement, they are surrounded by mirrors. Most of the women constantly check the mirror to see if they're in sync with the others, while Nadia's just being her overconfident self.

Training the whole day, the candidates are covered in sweat, and whenever they're given breaks, they don't even have the energy left to chat among themselves. Sometimes, Cleo can hear the other girls badmouthing Deborah. Like Cleo, they're grateful to be a part of Elle's beauty camp, but it's proving to be a difficult task. Wanting to get along with the other girls and not be someone like Nadia, Cleo offers them water bottles.

"Oh, thanks. I'm Mariel, Lady Masbate," one of the candidates gratefully accepts the water bottle, introducing herself in the process.

Cleo smiles her megaton smile. "Cleo, Lady Quezon City."

Cleo wants to start fresh, so she wants to make friends. On the practical side, the women might hesitate to badmouth someone who was a friend to them during beauty camp. She also doesn't want to revert to the old Cleo. Old Cleo didn't have many friends in the industry, and she was always desperate. Starting today, she's going to be the girl that everybody loves.

Unfortunately, no matter how nice Cleo is, she can still hear whispers: "That's all just for show."

Cleo sighs.

"The competition's getting heated." Chezka comes up behind Cleo, all sweaty and tired. "They all hate you for dethroning former Lady Quezon City."

"I'm just trying to make friends."

Chezka leers. "No, you're trying to find allies."

Chezka's bluntness reveals a certain sharpness, and Cleo knows that while they're somehow friends, the competition is still a competition. Chezka said it before, Cleo is a threat to them, and maybe she's not doing enough to be considered a candidate. She's still a sketchy person in their minds.

"Break over—back to work, ladies!" Guinevere announces, so the candidates all return to stretching and swaying their hips in between their long strides.

Cleo finds the exercise session funny. They look like ducks who got lost on the way to the pond. But it does help stretch out their bodies—bodies that have been insufficiently challenged for too long. Hours later, her legs burn the strain. In her mind's eye she sees herself trying to crawl her way back to where she'd been sitting. After training, Guinevere calls for their attention and delivers some motivational speech to boost their spirits.

"Tomorrow, same white shirt and pants. Bring extra clothes. But I want you all to come here looking like you're going to attend the most glamorous party the world has ever seen," Deborah adds. "You were all chosen by Elle because she saw your potential. Many have decided to quit in the last few years. They let themselves and the rest of us down I hope you won't do the same because this is a grand opportunity to showcase who you truly are. This competition isn't just about the crown—it's about finding your true self."

Day one of training for the national competition most definitely feels like day one hundred. Exhausted, Cleo lies down on the matting of the studio, hands over her eyes. Deborah and Guinevere left, and she and the rest of the candidates are still here, too drained to get up and go home.

"Isn't it unfair that some of us get to sleep here and wake up on time?" one candidate raises the question. "I mean, obviously, they'll have good makeup on."

"How is that a problem, Lady Valenzuela?" Cleo recognizes Lady Masbate's high-pitched voice. "I came all the way from Masbate just to be here. Elle offers rooms to candidates who have come from faraway provinces."

"Oh, so you're the island girl now?" Lady Valenzuela taunts.

Cleo's ears are thrumming from the sniping. She just wants to rest for a few minutes before she goes home, but with their screeching voices, she finds it hard to take a break. At her breaking point, she bursts out, "At least you don't have to commute."

"Right, right! Be sensitive to Cleo because she doesn't have a car," Nadia pipes in, always so ready to stroll in whenever Cleo's involved. "Boohoo."

Cleo clenches her jaw and turns to her side.

"Sorry. Just tired," Cleo replies because she honestly doesn't mean to explode like that. So much for trying to make friends.

"Whatever, Cleo," Nadia retorts.

Between the bickering and the outright nastiness, Cleo's had enough. Unable to stand another minute in the same room with them, she walks out without another word and commutes back home.

CHAPTER 21

Beauty in All of My Haggardness

<u>Day 1 of Commuting While Still Looking Gorgeous</u>

The public transportation assistant, also known as the barker, yells out the locations and number of seats available to the passengers who are waiting. With Cleo and Anne next in line, the barker shouts, "*Apat pa!*"

In Cleo's experience, barkers are always wrong, sometimes by a little, sometimes by a lot. *Apat pa*—four more—could mean one two more. Or one. More often than not, barkers tell commuters that there are plenty of seats available when in truth, there's only one or two left, just like now.

A twelve-seater jeepney painted in colorful artwork is waiting to fill up, but because it's rush hour and the traffic jam envelopes the city, Cleo and Anne have no choice but to squeeze themselves inside. Since there's only one seat available, Cleo gives it to Anne while she sits on the center floor. She feels lucky compared to the men who are at the jeepney's bar at the rear, hanging onto the railings and blocking egress on and off.

"*Sabit*, boss," one man says, paying his fare to the barker as he tightly grips the railing. It's dangerous, but they'll do anything to get to their jobs on time.

Cleo's supposed to book a ride on the way to BGC, but it looks like all drivers are busy. She can't get hold of one, so this is the next best option. Taking the jeepney means squeezing her butt inside and absorbing the sweat of the other commuters in their long sleeves and black pants. Sitting in the middle, she's finding it hard to breathe, and even if she can get some air, the heat and odors will probably suffocate her She honestly doesn't know if her makeup will survive the trip. She can feel a light layer of sweat forming., She decides to tie her hair in a bun.

Anne takes a notebook out of her bag, handing it over to Cleo as a fan substitute. Cleo waves the notebook at the side of her neck, hoping to get some air on her skin. She can't stand the stench emanating from her t-shirt. It feels like she didn't shower at all.

"Leo, are you okay?" Anne asks, almost falling from her seat with the way people are squeezing around them like canned sardines.

Cleo wants to laugh and cry. She doesn't want to dwell on the pageantry or obsess about the pageant and her breakup with Owen. But she knows she needs to keep up with the other candidates. She's already lost love; she can't afford to lose her career, too.

"Sometimes, Anne, I just want to be a kindergarten teacher like you," Cleo muses, gazing at the coloring books Anne has in her clear plastic envelope. "It must be nice to see all these little bits of happiness."

A vendor sells bottled water at the roadside. Anne buys one and gives it to Cleo.

"One day at a time, Leo. But know I'll always be here for you, okay? And happiness starts within you."

Cleo drinks the water, not wanting to reveal more than she already has. It's also kind of embarrassing to have an emotional breakdown moment with twelve people inside the jeepney. In a moment when some are busy on their phones and others are sleeping, Cleo tries to use the time to regroup and reach the beauty camp with a much more organized mind.

Unfortunately, Cleo gets to the beauty camp half an hour later than their call time. Deborah's waiting for her in the living room, staring down at her and inspecting her face and body.

Cleo's hair has gone astray, melting alongside all those other warm bodies has ruined her makeup. She's not looking so great, but she tried her best. Deborah's not impressed with how she presented herself, though. And she's not in an understanding frame of mind.

"Sweat. Smeared makeup." Deborah circles around Cleo. "Unkept hair. High heels covered with dirt and . . . is that bubble-gum I, see?"

"I'm so sorry. Traffic is—"

"Wake up earlier. It's not my fault we don't have a good road mapping system."

Cleo sighs. "Got it. It won't happen again."

<u>Day 2 of Commuting While Still Looking Gorgeous</u>
If there's a day Cleo hates more than Monday, it's Saturday. She only hates it at times like this. The Saturday morning traffic is hell. Coming from a subdivision in Quezon City going to the commercial hub in the high streets of Taguig, Cleo knows she'll spend at least two hours in transit. If there's anything she hates in this country aside from its handful of corrupt politicians is the infuriating traffic. Since it's a Saturday and everyone wants to be out somewhere, the roads are filling up with six-wheeler trucks, twelve-to-thirteen-seater jeepneys, cars, motorcycle ride-sharing services, and the FX express van she's currently on. Even more problematic are drivers who won't follow the traffic lights, so they all somehow end up squeezed together in the middle, completely stationary.

Tap. Tap.

A woman in tattered clothes, carrying a sleeping baby in her arms, taps the driver's window. As usual, the driver taps the window back as a sign of refusal. Along with the traffic are the beggars, street vendors, and street dwellers. Traffic for them is a blessing because it means they have a better chance of a handout or a sale.

Cleo sees the motorcycle taxis and almost wishes Owen were with her. If he were here, he could get her to the beauty camp in no time, but she has to do this on her own. Part of her problem before was that she used to rely on Owen to get her anywhere. She knows he'd never leave her alone without any help. This time, she needs to make her own way.

From jeepney to FX rides, Cleo's sort of getting the hang of commuting from one side to another. If there's no FX available, she takes the jeepney and vice versa. She's living by a rule that the first public transportation she sees, she grabs. Even if it's not a direct drop-off point, if she waits any longer than five minutes, she'll be late. It's already a blessing that she gets to be in the FX.

The most important part thing is for the jeepney or the FX to get her to the Triangle Mall so she can get to the train station on Quezon Avenue in time to catch her train. From there, it should be smooth sailing, but the lines for rail transportation take almost three hours or more on a bad day.

Thankfully, Cleo's arrives only fifteen minutes after the set call time.

"It's 9:15. Late. Again," Guinevere chides Cleo, shaking her head in disapproval.

"I'm sorry. I'll try to be here earlier."

Day 6 of Oh, Wait, I Lost Count
Trying to get out of the train car, Cleo pushes her way out of the crowd, carrying her high heels in one hand, and just when she's about to finally free herself from the pack of people shoving and pushing her to the other side, the train's door closes.

Cleo silently mouths a curse word. She has no choice but to wait for the next station, which is Buendia. She holds onto the train's safety handrails and hopes her high heels will still be in one piece by the time she gets out of there. Already, her head's aching from spending so much time commuting.

As soon as Cleo hears the announcement that they're approaching Buendia she gears up and readies herself. She stares hard at the door, lifting her precious high heels first and hoping that everyone knows better than to cross a woman who has her high heels in hand. The instant the doors open, she runs out of the train car like her life depends on it.

"Phew," Cleo mutters under her breath, hands on her knees. She tries to catch her breath, and when she does, she taps her card on the station's turnstile and dashes down the stairs. She books a car, hops on it and flops down on the seat. She re-applies her makeup and fixes her hair on the way to the destination, ensuring that not a single strand strays into her face. She smoothes out her white t-shirt and goes into beauty queen mode, stretching her smile.

Minutes later, Cleo reaches the beauty camp, wondering who'll be meeting her this time to tell her she's late. But day by day, her late time gets shorter, so she's expecting that today will be better than the previous ones.

"Lady Quezon City!" Deborah exclaims, tilting her head to one side and checking Cleo from head to toe like always.

"How many minutes this time?" Cleo worriedly asks.

Deborah smiles. "On minute."

"Really?" Excitement flashes through Cleo's eyes, her face brightening up at the thought of being on time. "Oh, thank God!"

"Tired?"

"Yes."

"Great. We're going for a run in a forest park in Ermita, Manila. The van's waiting."

🐝   🐝   🐝

"Chezka, I just don't understand why I was still asked to come to the camp when I can go directly here?"

Cleo and Chezka stand in running attire, doing warmup stretches. "I'm telling you, those two are crazy."

"Listen up!" Guinevere calls the candidates' attention. "Go for a relaxing run, and then we'll spice things up later. I don't want to see any of you here at the entrance on Debbie's whistle. Got it?"

"Yes!" the candidates agree in unison.

As Deborah blows the whistle, the candidates sprint towards the trails, which are lush with greenery, and Cleo instantly feels the warm breeze. Distracted, she takes in the beauty of nature. This forest park of Ermita, Manila, is the only nature park in the city. It's home to thousands of tree varieties, like the *macopa*, mango and *santol*. The thick bushes and fruit-bearing trees are a sight to behold. It's paradise in the midst of chaos, and the tranquility it offers slowly seeps into Cleo and feels like a long-lost friend. Alongside the forest is a river where the sunlight casts its golden rays on the dark waters.

Cleo's so enamored with the picturesque view she didn't catch what Guinevere was saying. She slows down and accidentally collides with another candidate who's opening the bottle cap of her energy drink.

"Oh, so sorry!" the candidate exclaims, worrying over Cleo's stained sports bra.

"It's okay." Cleo smiles after finally getting a fresh breath of air. "Let's just run."

The candidate presses her hands to her flushed cheeks. "I can feel my cheeks getting red from the heat. Look, I want to make it up to you, so why don't you sit over there, and I get you something?"

"No, it's really okay, Lady ..."

"Rizal. And please," Lady Rizal insists. "I'll get you a water. If I can't help you with the stain, then the least I can do is get you a drink."

Seeing as there's no use arguing with her, a breathless Cleo sits on a bench. She smiles at Lady Rizal and tries to breathe her pounding heart back to its regular rhythm.

"Wait for me," Lady Rizal says. The two moles on her right cheek stretch when she grins.

"Okay."

And so Cleo waits, humming a lullaby to herself The park has been closed down for their visit, so it's nice to be alone for a while. Quiet. Still. She almost laughs at herself for remembering the word *still*. She's far different from being still now.

As Cleo contemplates, she hears a shout from Deborah. "What are you doing? It's a race, Cleo! Keep up!"

Deborah breezes past Cleo, who's taken aback. It only just hit her that she's the only one left lagging behind. No, she isn't going to wait for the mineral water. And besides, it doesn't look like Lady Rizal's coming back. This entire situation yells sabotage. Great, just great. After finally getting to the camp on time, she ends up being tricked by a candidate.

This competition isn't for good-natured safe-playing people. What looks like a simple race is a game of faces, tactics, and manipulation skills; in other words, the game of outwitting opponents. She's being targeted, just as Chezka said.

Cleo darts ahead with all her strength, applying enough pressure to the heels of her feet to keep up. She's panting and running out of breath, but she doesn't care. She isn't going to let Lady Rizal rattle her.

"Look here."

Snap.

Of all the times Erik could choose Cleo's photo, he just has to pick a time when she's sweat-drenched to capture an epic failure of face. Just like the rest of them, he's also in his running gear, and he looks good in it. As he runs with her, the other girls glance over their shoulders so they can ogle him.

"Looks like you got yourself some fans," Cleo observes, slowing down to catch her breath.

"Why do you seem so surprised? Because you don't have any?"

Cleo stops and leans her hands on her knees, trying to calm her rapid breathing. "Are you crazy? I'm *maganda* kaya, and I'm going to be the Lady Pearl of the Philippines."

Erik snaps a photo of her again, laidback and unconcerned. "See? Confidence isn't so hard, is it? And you are, Cleo."

"I am what?"

"*Maganda*." Erik winks, leaving her struggling on her own as he takes photos of the other girls.

Cleo believes that. She is beautiful. She feels beautiful. And no matter how much other candidates sabotage her, she'll always be the beauty queen she is.

Cleo runs again and catches sight of the finish line. Since no one else is around, figures she's winning. The thought gives her a rush that spikes her adrenaline, so she tears through the ground as she's never done before. She stops distracting herself, focusing solely on the finish line.

When Cleo sees the old mailbox, the marker of their finish line, she dashes past it and broadly grins, happy that she got here first. Drained, she collapses on the ground, stretching her legs in between wheezes.

"Last place."

Cleo looks up and finds Guinevere offering her bottled water— the cause of her delay. "What?"

"You're the last one to finish," Guinevere comments, disappointment on her face.

Cleo takes big gulps from the bottle and wipes her mouth with her hand. No matter how much she tries to downplay the sabotage that held her back, it's just not working out. Oh, Lady Rizal has just declared war.

Let the Battle Commence!

A few days later, they're given the schedule of pre-pageant events and activities. There's the talent night and fashion show on Valentine's Day, the national costume photo shoot in the second week of March, press presentation on the following week of the photo shoot, a national costume fashion show and parade in April, and the grand coronation night in the last week of April. In between, they still have charity houses to visit.

With the schedule of events posted on the camp walls, Cleo and the candidates work hard at their workout exercises and walks. Every day they get better, but improvement isn't what the commanding duo requires. They want perfection, and so far, nobody has achieved that just yet. And Cleo wants to be the first one to get it right.

During mid-break, Guinevere announces they'll be heading to in orphanage tomorrow, so they have to come up with a plan to make the children happy. It is, again, a training ground for them. After all, they are symbols of hope and empowerment, and those two things call for sweet smiles. So, while Cleo is facing the mirrors, she gets a light-bulb moment She takes a pen from her table and places it in between her lips, biting on it as if her life depended on it.

Looking at herself in the mirror, Cleo thinks it's brilliant. She's smiling like a silly girl, and it amazes her. She would totally be in love with this smile if she were a kid.

"What's up with that silly smile?"

Erik's standing by the door with his camera again, taking a snap of Cleo's bizarre smiling face.

Cleo takes the pen from her teeth and says, "Making fun of me doesn't start until late afternoon, Erik."

"You know what they say, no rest for the wicked." He smirks, taking a pen out of the pocket of his dark jeans and biting on it as Cleo did. She laughs at him in response, making a face when he pulls it out and offers it to her.

"Ew. Throw it away," Cleo complains.

Then Erik's surrounded by the other girls, asking him for the pen trick. Cleo's actually quite offended because it's her idea, and he's making it about him. But then he says, "Go and ask Cleo. She'll teach you how to smile."

Well, what do you know? Erik has his good side.

The candidates follow Erik's advice, approaching Cleo and asking her how to smile better. And for a moment there, she doesn't think about how mean they can be. On the contrary, it's actually nice to be in their company.

Snap.

"You all look beautiful when you're having fun," Erik notes, staring at Cleo, his eyes lighter than usual like he isn't sure what to make of her. "Good luck, ladies."

Erik leaves, leaving Cleo stunned with the realization that he's referring to her—she's having fun and not stressing about what they all think of her. She's focusing on winning. She forgot to have fun, and it's only now that she has the chance to mingle and get to know the other candidates.

Erik has a point, but he also forgot this is a competition. In the end, they'll just compete against one another. Still, she appreciates what he did.

"Settle down," Deborah announces, her diamond-studded earrings catching the eyes of the candidates. "I need ideas for tomorrow's visit to the orphanage. Anyone?"

Bubbling with enthusiasm, Cleo suggests they come in wearing heroes' costumes. It'll be fun for the children to see their favorite superheroes.

"What if it's too scary for them? And, anyway, we barely have the time to design our costumes," Lady Rizal argues. "I think we should just take them to a park and play with them."

"The logistics will take time. It'll also be a hassle for the children," Cleo counters, while the other candidates turn their attention between Cleo and Lady Rizal, interested not just in knowing what they'll end up doing for the children, but wanting to see who will win this battle.

"Majority wins. Raise your hand for superhero costumes," Deborah settles, slamming her hand on the desk table.

Everyone raises their hands except for Lady Rizal and two other candidates. Cleo knows that as much as Nadia hates her, she wants to dress up in her best costume.

"Looks like there's no need for the second option." Deborah then begins to write their names on the whiteboard. "Give me the superhero you want to be tomorrow."

Lady Rizal raises her hand. "Cat woman."

Another candidate, Lady Masbate, has raised her hand out of concern. "Could we also dress up as Superman?"

"No." Lady Rizal shuts her down. "There's a reason why he's called Super and Man, and you're neither of them."

"There's always Supergirl," Nadia remarks, making a popping sound by opening and closing her mouth to check her new matte lipstick.

Cleo supports Lady Masbate's idea. "she said Superman, not Supergirl. Do you see any man here? No? I don't think so. I think it's a great idea, Lady Masbate."

"We're super ladies because we can take up any role. Supergirl or Superman, either way, you're all free to dress up as whomever you like," Deborah interjects, her striking eyes daring anyone to go against her. Since nobody argues, the request to dress up as male superheroes is been approved.

"Or a cat," Cleo mumbles under her breath before smiling at Lady Rizal, who only grimaces at her.

This game between them is far from over. And Cleo wants to see what Lady Rizal has in store for her. Thankfully, Deborah has released them so they can meet with their stylists. Before leaving their so-called classroom, the candidates write the superhero they want to be on the board. Cleo chooses to be Wonder Woman.

Cleo calls on Dominique to help her with her costume. They grab a private room, and with a few pieces of fabric they're able to get a solid start. Cleo runs her hand over a sleek pair of armbands.

"I just need to transform these with a little paint," Cleo notes, taking blue and red spray paint from Dom's eco bag. Painting the armbands, she focuses on what she's doing, partly to shut out thoughts of Owen that keep popping up. With so many things happening in the pageantry, including sabotage, the feeling that she has no one to share things with, like she did before, makes her feel empty.

"You don't seem okay, but you're doing great." Dom helps Cleo with the spray paints and doesn't ask any questions. It's one of the things she likes about Dom—he doesn't hover unless it's about her wardrobe. She can't afford to spill her heart out when they have so much to do.

Cleo and Dom spend another three hours or so on the costume. It looks strong and beautiful, like the armor has a life of its own with its ripping edges and piercing shiny breastplate. Cleo is happy with it—she doesn't want it to appear princess-y. She wants to look free and strong, an image of pure strength and bravery. The costume is iconic Wonder Woman—tiara, bracelets, and lasso. The costume prides itself in swatches of red, blue, and gold, the shades of war and peace.

Cleo puts on the metallic knee-high battle, iron-strapped boots.

"Badass!" she shrieks in delight. Out of habit, she takes a close-up selfie-and full-body mirror selfie wearing the costume, then laments that she has no one to send it to. Dispelling Owen from her thoughts again, she sends it to Anne and Thea instead.

"You broke up with Owen," Dominique perceives. "Correction, it fell *apart*."

Cleo shrugs, acting like it's no big deal. She refuses to think about what was said between them that day. Besides, she's making her way to the crown, and it's far from over.

      🦋   🦋   🦋

The candidates reach the orphanage in their best superhero costumes. Lady Rizal is in her all-black cat woman costume. She's some modifications to her costume. Her costume has turned into something much sexier, exposing her top with the zipper down, so her chest is on display. As for the other candidates, their costumes range from the most colorful to the darkest ones they can come up with.

As the candidates are given the freedom to choose any international or local superhero, they cover a big list: Superman, *Darna*, Flash, and *Lastikman*. It's turned out to be pretty amazing. They pulled it off like it's their second skin.

"Welcome to the Youth Care Shelter for Abandoned Children," an older woman wearing thick glasses greets the candidates.

The candidates smile warmly ather and introduce themselves. Cleo has no idea why, but the elderly have always had an emotional pull on her. So caught up in her dreams and worries, she realizes how comforting it would feel to be in the presence of a tender older person. Like a bit of peace during a long war.

"I'm Africa. Please follow me." Africa leads the way as the candidates follow her. Their procession is both languid and steadfast. Through corridors, Cleo sees rooms filled with double-bunk beds and ABCs posters on the walls. Africa informs them that those are the children's bedrooms. She has gathered them in a much bigger room so they can all meet.

Africa pauses as soon as they've reached the common room. She goes in, gesturing for the candidates to come inside too. The candidates wave at the children sitting on the cushions and happily gazing up at them. Cleo doesn't just smile; she grins broadly at them, her most radiant beam. She loves seeing the smiles of the children.

The candidates pose in the middle to highlight who they are. When it's Cleo's turn, she pulls out her lasso, and a certain someone "*accidentally*" steps on it, which makes her lose her balance, but then a boy around six years old takes the end of the lasso and holds it up to her, pointing at Lady Rizal.

"The girl stepped on your weapon," the boy says innocently, blinking up at Cleo.

Putting aside any irritation with Lady Rizal, Cleo pinches his cheek, smiling. "Do you want me to catch the bad guy who stepped on my lasso?"

The boy's eyes widen in surprise, and he nods eagerly. So to give the boy some real action, Cleo mimics Wonder Woman, bringing up her lasso at the side and facing Catwoman.

"Come and fight me! I shall avenge the wrong done to my lasso!" Cleo cries, posing in a battle stance to challenge Catwoman.

Deborah and Guinevere are at the side, observing Cleo and Lady Rizal, so Catwoman, has no choice but to play along and be done with it. It's not like they'll physically hurt each other. They're just acting for the children, and acting is something Cleo's familiar with.

"I accept your challenge, Wonder Woman!" Lady Rizal yells back, posing in a cat stance, putting up her paw-like hands.

Cleo and Lady Rizal circle each other, figuring out who'll strike first. Cleo turns around and makes a fake lasso whipping at Lady Rizal's side. Lady Rizal screeches in response, baring her teeth at Cleo. Cleo tries to hide her laughter and just acts with her. With the comic relief, everyone begins to jeer and stomp their feet, cheering for their favorite superhero.

"Wonder Woman for justice! Wonder Woman for justice!" Erik loudly cheers, prompting the others to cheer for their superhero. His cheer has inspired Cleo to smile and lunge at Lady Rizal wickedly. Because of this, any Catwoman fans are switching sides.

"Who would you like to win?" Erik adds, adding fuel to the fire.

"Wonder Woman!" the children cry out altogether, laughing as Catwoman is being fake-defeated by Cleo.

Erik snaps a photo of Cleo and Lady Rizal, repeating his question, "Who would you like to win?"

"Wonder Woman!"

"Louder!" Erik commands like he's Peter Pan and the children are his lost boys.

The children scream at the top of their lungs, yelling, "WONDER WOMAN!"

Lady Rizal has to follow the children's wishes, so she stumbles around and falls on the floor, admitting defeat. The crowd erupts into cheers, and Africa smiles at them, thankful for what they've done. Meanwhile, one of Africa's co-workers has brought trays of sandwiches and refreshments for the children. Cleo and the others help distribute them to the hungry kids.

Cleo approaches the little boy, giving him the snack. He leans into her and whispers, "I like you, Wonder Woman."

Cleo chuckles at him, whispering in his year, "I like you too, Wonder Boy."

Blushing, the little boy goes back to his seat, murmuring to his friends about Cleo. Later on, the candidates get the chance to talk to the children. During their little sharing, Cleo discovers that most of them have been abandoned in churches. Her heart constricts painfully at the thought of it. Being left alone is one of the most terrifying feelings of all—that sense of abandonment that can make anyone question their own existence; Cleo doesn't want any child to know that feeling.

"You know, one day you'll find a family of your own, one you'll call home. You will be their greatest blessing, okay?" Cleo assures a pair of twins and Wonder Boy. "My name's Cleo, and you are?"

One of the five-year old twin girls hugs Cleo, and her heart feels a sweet tug.

"I'm Alexandra," the girl in pigtails says shyly.

Her sister, in ice-cream-designed pajamas, babbles, " I'm Alessandra."

"You're gonna be wonder girls in the future, Alex and Ales," Cleo kisses their cheeks as the little boy retreats, shying away from her.

Cleo turns to him, patting his head. "Don't be shy. You'll do great things one day. What's your name?"

"J-John," he stutters, blushing in embarrassment again.

Cleo smiles at him and holds out her hand to him. "Let's be friends, okay?"

"Okay!"

And just like that, Cleo has a friend.

Team Cleo, Assemble!

"We would like to congratulate everyone for bringing happiness to the children in the orphanage. Your kindness hasn't gone unnoticed. Now we want you to prepare for the next step in becoming a true beauty queen—giving advocacy," Guinevere says, calling the candidates' attention to the board. "I need to know tomorrow what causes you want to advocate for, so spend the rest of the day learning more about what you would want to focus on."

Most of the girls have left the classroom, wandering on their own. Thinking about it, Cleo doesn't want to choose a topic she has no idea of. As if by fate, her eyes fall on Eric's open bag, and, nestling just inside is a book called *The Little Prince*. She looks at the book, just to see where he might have gotten it. She figures he might have borrowed it from a library. She thinks it's odd because he doesn't strike her as the bookish type. He seems more of the get-a-book-because-the-class-requires-it type, but again, she doesn't want to make any more assumptions.

"Stealing books now?" Erik asks, appearing with his camera and leaning against the door frame. Seeing his height made Cleo realize he's taller than she is, and that's saying something because she's always been the tallest one in any group.

"You're a shadow person, you know," Cleo observes. "You're

there, and everyone notices you, and then you retreat into your dark recesses."

"I'd rather see the dark before the light," Erik says casually, pulling his bag away from her.

An idea pops into Cleo's head. "Where'd you get that?"

"Bookstore, obviously."

"I know, I just—do you know any libraries around here?" Cleo checks her phone, scrolling for nearby libraries she could use for the day.

"I know a very nice one."

"Where is it?"

"I'll take you there with Dominique," Erik offers, his eyes trailing over Dom, who's smoking outside.

Cleo doesn't even argue, and Dom just says yes to almost everything, so half an hour later, Erik has given them a ride to a heritage library. The library instantly hits Cleo with the woodsy scent of years and years' worth of paper—old books, new books.

"Wow," Cleo utters in awe, stunned by the massive bookcases lined up in rows. "How'd you find this place?"

"I look around," Erik mentions, putting his *The Little Prince* book back where it belongs—behind the glass door of the bookcase.

Dom glances at Erik, mystified and cautious.

Erik sighs. "My adoptive parents donated some money to this library. And yes, they're rich."

"So you're Mr. Grey?" Dom fires, ever the doubtful one. "Loads of money and spending your time with women?"

"I don't put people through abuse, Dom. I mean, just because *your* name screams DOM . . . ."

Dom ignores Erik's witty remark, focusing instead on checking out the titles of the books. Neither man is what Cleo would call a friend, but they know what they want, and somehow it makes her feel secure. They're decisive, and Cleo's natural when it comes to deciding.

But oh, look, Cleo can't decide where to start first.

"What would you like to tell the world?" Erik shrugs off his hoodie jacket, whistling as he pulls out random books.

What do I want to tell the world, aside from not giving up on achieving your dreams? World peace? That's too generic.

Cleo walks around the shelves, her hands caressing the spines of the books. The books speak of different stories presented in different skins—paperbacks to hardcovers and leather bounds. Just then, her eyes catch the front cover of a history book. She thought it would be like any of the history books she used in school. Still, this one is prominently dedicated to Gabriela Silang, the revolutionary Filipina who led an uprising against a foreign power. There've been a lot of movies and books about male national heroes, and yet there's this woman, brave yet not so loudly sung.

"The power of a woman," Cleo muses, turning to Erik. "When I was still new in the film and TV industry, I was offered this role to be the sexy chick that always says yes to every man's demands. I said yes because I wanted to be famous., But I didn't stick with it, because it was hollow. Empty. What I needed was to find and work with people who believed in me."

Erik doesn't say anything. He looks at her and listens.

"My dad didn't believe in my mom. I'm not sure he believes in anybody, but I think he still expected me to follow in his footsteps. If that was really what he wanted . . . it didn't happen. I tried his path, and it didn't work out too well. So, I went to my mom's path, and it felt like a sigh of relief. Pageantry celebrates the power, strength, and beauty of a woman," Cleo concludes, glad that she's said it out loud to someone else. "And I want to be part of that."

"That's a good choice. And, anyway, only you can decide how to get where you want to be," Erik comments, comfortably lying down on a couch with long legs extending over the end of it. "I'll think I'll take a nap."

"I don't think you should sleep in a—"

But Erik's already closed his eyes, not a care in the world. Cleo wants to be like him sometimes, laidback and doing whatever he wants.

Cleo leaves him in peace, going through some more books. She re-reads the fairy tales she used to love and realizes that the women are almost always waiting for someone to come along to rescue them. The original *Grimms' Fairy Tales* may prove better than the sugarcoated retellings even though they're as grim as their name, because they express a certain truth about life: it's not always rainbows and unicorns.

Cleo turns her attention to history, reading about discrimination against women. The books she skims through cover unequal treatment, employment, and in some countries, forced marriage. It's all kinds of wrong. She isn't going to let anyone dictate what she should want, can have, or can achieve just because she's a woman and therefore too emotional for the demands and challenges of the world. Besides, there's a lot of power in emotion, and in the ability to empathize. The feelings, thoughts and actions of women are every bit as great as those of men.

But to empower women, society must also enable men. Men should not be expected to deny their emotions Men can cry, and women can "man up." People are people, and some needs are basic to all, regardless of the culture or beliefs in which they are raised

Cleo wants to point out that we can't fully empower one gender without empowering the other. Equality must mean equality for all. Freedom must mean freedom for all. On every level and in every way.

So, the next day, Cleo knows what she wants to advocate for. In the practice interview with the duo of commanders, a candidate has to stand in front and share her thoughts about her cause. The rest of the candidates will then pose a question, so the one in front will have the chance to clarify and, if necessary, defend what she believes in.

Nadia goes first. "Education for the underprivileged. I believe education should be a right and not a privilege. There are thousands of children in the *esteros* who dream of being in the class-room, learning, instead of living their days crushed by poverty."

Cleo raises her hand to question her. "As Lady Cebu City, how will you bridge education to the underprivileged?"

"As Lady Cebu City, I'll reach out to NGOs and be their part-ner in providing the needed materials," Nadia responds, smiling at Cleo and almost daring her to keep going with her questions.

Cleo doesn't. With the coronation night drawing near, she needs to save energy for the right battles. Eventually, she takes the spotlight.

"Women and men empowerment—"

Lady Rizal laughs at Cleo. "You're trying to be different or something?"

Cleo ignores Lady Rizal's remark and continues.

"Women and men empowerment. Women can "man up," and men can cry and wear pink. Women can be soldiers in the mili-tary, and men can clean the house and do the laundry. Women's and men's rights should be recognized as interchangeable. What men can do must also be applicable to women and vice versa," Cleo speaks out loud in a clear voice, fiercely challenging anyone to ques-tion her. "What a person can do does not come from what they've been told, or what their background is. The value of a person comes from what good they have done today."

Then came a round of applause. Cleo has no idea that there are reporters out there. At the end of the practice panel, the candidates are approached by these reporters who are asking them about the preparation they've done so far. Unfortunately, no one's that inter-ested in her. Whatever questions do come to her focus on her father and her breakup with Owen.

"Why are they going on about my breakup with Owen?" Cleo looks at the other candidates happily being interviewed. She wants to be like them, not this girl whose whole life revolves around her father and her love life and any other people she doesn't want to care about at this moment.

Dom appears next to Cleo, scrolling on his phone and then giving it to Cleo. "Take a look at this."

Cleo Walter and Boyfriend Owen Velazco Officially Broken Up
Months into Cleo Walter's journey to the Lady Pearl of the Philippines' crown, she gets caught in a personal setback, breaking up with her longtime boyfriend, Owen Velazco It's only a few days before the coronation night, and she's still far from winning the hearts of the people.

Now, the growing fans and critics of Cleo ask: has fame gone to her head? Or is she trying to outdo her father, Direk Everett?

"For months, I've stopped myself from using my social media, and I still get this kind of spin?" Cleo snaps. "I'm not going to let them speak for me."

"What are you going to do?"

"Wait here." Cleo avoids the cameras and looks for the reporter she enlisted at the start of this venture. Thankfully, she quickly spots Aira in the crowd. She takes her mic, smiling at her as if to remind her of their deal. "Care to interview me?"

"You're something else, Cleo," Aira comments. "We had a deal, so fine."

"Can we go somewhere in private?"

Cleo takes Aira and Dom into another room. If no one's going to ask her the right questions, then she might as well form her own team of creatives for her social media. It's not like Deborah and Guinevere can help her with it. Elle is even less likely. It's one thing that only she can control. If talk about her is running loose, the camp can't do anything about it, but she can.

Dom suspiciously eyes Aira. "You're sketchy."

"As are you," Aira retorts, sitting on the beanbag chair and taking out her pen and notebook. "What do you want me to do?"

"Wait, wait. You invited this reporter?" Dom interjects, glancing at the notes in Aria's notebook.

Cleo holds her hands up. "Yes. Just listen. The questions these reporters have for me will never change unless I do something about it. I've been answering the same set of questions for years, and I want to move on from that. It's about time I make my side of things heard."

"Oops, wrong room."

Cleo, Dom, and Aira turn to look at Erik, who's trying to close the door quietly, but Cleo quickly runs to him, pulling him inside. "You're not going anywhere."

"What?" Erik tilts his head to one side, genuinely curious.

For some reason, Cleo trusts Erik. If she has a reporter, a stylist, and a photographer on her team, then it's the perfect combination to build up her image on different social media platforms. It's one of the only ways she can differentiate herself from other candidates. She's doing her best in the training and pre-pageantry, but she's missing one thing: the crowd.

"Cleo 2.0," Cleo explains, pushing Erik and Dom to sit on the beanies too. "I want to re-write my story. I want people to get to know who I am, and I can only do that with your help."

"What makes you think I'm willing to help you?" Erik rebuts, opening his DSLR and inspecting the photos he got earlier.

"You'll see once you get to know who I am. I know it's too much to ask, and I might be putting your job in danger since you're the official pageantry photographer, but has there never been a time in your life where you just wanted people to understand what you see behind the lens of the camera?"

Erik turns off his camera, glances at Dom and Aira, and then looks at Cleo. "Then you have to give me your most genuine self."

"Woah, flirty much?" Aira comments, scrunching her eyebrows at Erik.

"Amen!" Dom agrees. "The tension in the air is so palpable—"

Erik stares hard at Dom.

"Sorry, sorry, just trying to lighten up the mood." Dom shifts in his seat, turning his attention to Cleo.

"This is not a love story, Dom."

"I know, honey. I know," Dom says pitifully, like he knows something Cleo doesn't. "The eyes never lie, though."

Aira makes a gagging sound at the back of her throat. "So, are we going to hear her plans, or do I just write a scandalous story about this? It'll be perfect next to the Owen fiasco."

"Okay, so I'm trusting Erik to take my photos in my most natural self. Dom styles me up like usual, and Aira writes my story. Slowly, I want to take over the tabloids' story about me. That stuff is outdated, and it's not worth talking about. Today, I just want to be interviewed exclusively by Aira. The headlines will be something like Cleo Walter: the Unknown Story.' How does that sound?" Cleo asks, worried she might be rambling on about inane things. "Tell me if my idea sounds stupid."

"It's perfect, honey," Dom agrees with Cleo.

Erik snaps a photo of Cleo. "Here's one."

"Then let's start the interview," Aira says, switching her voice recorder on. "Who is Cleo Walter?"

And the Lady Pearl of the Philippines is . . . Drumroll, Please!

he Untold Story of Cleo Walter

T*People see her as Director Everett's daughter, the try-ing-hard actor, the extra, the talent, the wannabe model, and the wild heartbreaker. But she is Cleo Walter, an actor-turned-beauty queen.*

Cleo has kept her silence amidst her issues with her father and her supposed biggest movie break. Now, she's breaking her silence and speaking up: "I walked away from something that's never been mine, to begin with."

Cleo Walter has admitted she wants to prove to her father that she can be as good as he is. She refuses to acknowledge that her roles are because of her father. In fact, she's stated that they've never really been on good terms. When she got the lead role in the movie The Boyfriend Switch, *she knew it was about time she got a spotlight of her own, but days into shooting the film, she realized it was not for her. She'd been so caught up in the idea of working alongside Direk Everett that she never really considered what she wanted inside or outside her acting career.*

Cleo planned to resign from the cameras and the big and small screens but when she found out about pageantry, she told herself she'd give the spotlight one last shot. In Reign of Queens beauty camp, she's learned tremendously about the true essence of being a beauty queen. And it's not just walking on the stage with her beautiful smile; it's standing up in front of millions of people and representing the place's history, culture, tradition, and lifestyle. Being a beauty queen means carrying that knowledge within her.

The national pageantry season is set for tomorrow, April 25, and Cleo's ready to take the crown.

🌿　🌿　🌿

The stage is set, the candidates are behind the grand opening of the curtains like they're in a play. They're wearing a traditional *Filipiniana* dress backstage, but with a twist. Elle has raised her concerns that their opening act be done according to the idea she suggested—a Gabriela Silang-themed-style costume.

Their Gabriela Silang outfit has a chiffon ruffle, flared long-sleeved loose top and a flowing skirt. They each wear a head tie. While others have their hair in a braid or ponytail, Cleo's head tie is in a twisted halo, her mermaid hair is loosely curled. She recounts last night's dinner with her family as she and the other candidates prepare for their entrance.

Over dinner, Cleo told them about the competition tomorrow. Anne was unusually quiet, which made her worry, so she had to ask her what was wrong

"There's nothing wrong, Leo. It's . . ."

"Be honest. What is it?" Cleo asked Anne.

Thea held her hand and answered for Anne, "She's concerned about you. We don't want you to be disappointed again. I don't think we can bear to watch you crumble."

Oh. They were afraid she wasn't going to win. They were terrified of how she would react if she lost the competition. But they didn't

need to worry too much. She did everything that she could do to sur-
vive this one.

"Just trust me, I'll own this," Cleo told them as she went on enjoy-
ing her dinner.

"Sorry, Leo, I just don't want you to be sad again."

Cleo smiled at Anne. "I'll do my best, okay? Kaya ko' to!"

"I know you can." Anne smiled happily for Cleo.

When they finished dinner, Thea talked to Cleo, wrapping her in
an embrace and assuring her she could do this.

"I'm proud of you, Cleo," Thea said sweetly. "I wish your dad were
here to see you."

Cleo hoped he would see her, because she was about to prove him
wrong. She was going to make him regret leaving them.

Now, taking a peek at the audience, Cleo sees the crowd in the
coliseum, cheering for their respective bets. The overall design of
the stage had been altered. It's morphed to look more like an island
and a tropical beach. The lighting is in shades of orange, red, and
yellow. Sand fills the bottom side of the stage, glinting against the
golden glow of the mock-up sun, illuminating the platform with
its bedazzling sparkles. Only then is she hit by the realization that
there's no going back now. She has to take a step and make her way
out in total confidence.

When the competition begins, there's no stopping it.

As soon as Sia's *Titanium* plays, the VTR rolls on the wide LED
screens, giving the audience a glance at every candidate's twirl and
walk. Moments later, they come out from backstage, engulfed by
blinding lights and loud cheers from the crowd. The national flag is
raised in the middle, and the candidates surround it in a semi-circle,
saluting before presenting their opening number. Side to side, they
sway their hips, embodying a true Filipina with beauty and grace.

Walking across the stage, the candidates strut around to present
themselves, waving and smiling. They turn around, raising one
hand in the air and then swiftly bringing it back down to their
thighs. Giving it her all, Cleo projects a beauty beyond the physical

look. Once the dancing has ended, they revert to their usual pose with their hands placed on their hips. One by one, they introduce themselves. When Cleo turns around, she finds out that her bandanna has gone missing. Still, she introduces herself without missing a beat.

Facing thousands of people, Cleo musters the courage to speak her name aloud. "Cleo Walter, twenty-four, Quezon City!"

The audience bursts into loud cheers.

In the competition, Gaby and Kim, famous hosts of big events, enter the stage in matching black and white outfits with Gaby's lips painted in candy apple red. They welcome this year's national pageant theme "Bold, Brave, and Beautiful" through anecdotes of the courage it takes for a candidate to get there. Momentarily, the top twenty-five finalists are announced, and Cleo's the first one to be called. She sees Elle smiling at her from the VIP section, pleased that she got in.

Where has she been all this time? Cleo thought.

"As the list goes on, the stakes and tension are high for these hopeful ladies. Who do you think will be the next one, Kim?" Gaby turns to Kim.

"We won't know until we read the names, so let's find out."

All eight of Elle's beauty camp candidates are called names and are still part of the top twenty-five.

"Congratulations to the top twenty-five ladies!" Gaby announces, thrilled with the results. "But this contest is far from over. The swimsuit round is up next to add more spice under the sizzling heated battle."

On cue, the candidates instantly wave and smile at the camera. After a while, they proceed backstage to change into their swimsuits. While changing, Cleo keeps hearing Lady Rizal fishing for compliments.

"Does the swimsuit look good on me? I really can't wait for this night to be over and be crowned!" Lady Rizal cries out loud for everyone to hear.

"Don't be so sure." Cleo winks at Lady Rizal, flaunting her butt. "We're not done yet."

In response, Lady Rizal simply flashes Cleo a smile, saying, "Try not to lose your bandanna next time. That was very irresponsible of you."

Cleo's sure she had the bandanna with her. She has no idea who took it, but she has a good hunch that Lady Rizal had something to do with it. It doesn't matter. She'll do great even without it.

After the panel of judges is introduced, the candidates stroll out again and give their very best, exposing their sensuality. As Cleo has wonderfully toned legs, she strolls in great strides, strutting in a smooth rhythm. She twirls around, flirtatiously giving the audience a heated look. Caught up in the lively, upbeat music, she's learned to enjoy the intensity of the competition.

And as the competition drags on, the long gown competition ensues. It's the loveliest time of the evening, and the candidates are brilliantly dressed in multicolored gowns, sparkling in splendid designs from Filipino designers.

Do, for one, designed Cleo's gorgeous off-the-shoulder tulle long-sleeved pearl pink dress. Proud of her gown, Cleo takes her time on the stage as she walks, captivating the many curious eyes of the spectators and judges. Not much later, the candidates have been reduced to fifteen, and she's still in the competition. And then the awaited Question and Answer session rolls around.

The candidates will be called randomly by the eight judges; five men and three women from entertainment, pageantry, modeling agencies, government, and corporate business. While the names are shuffled, Cleo's heart beats loudly, crashing against her chest. Her mind's running with hundreds of questions she's heard from the camp.

As Cleo's trying to calm her nerves, her name is called. She moves forward and gracefully smiles at the judges, greeting none other than Selene Montenegro. Despite the jolt, Cleo keeps her smile, already imagining a thousand scenarios.

"If you could go back to the past and meet your fifteen-year-old self, what would you say to her?" Selene asks.

Cleo doesn't even need to think of this one, so she answers right away. "If I could go back to the past and meet my fifteen-year-old self, I would tell her that there's more to life than just living a dream come true. It's putting that dream to good use because, in the end, what matters is that we are able to face ourselves because of what we've done for others. Thank you."

The crowd applauds, impressed by what Cleo has just said. They understand her. She feels unstoppable.

Finally, the Q and A comes to an end, and the hosts call on the candidates for the special awards. Cleo wins as Best in Long Gown, Best in Swimwear, and Lady Photogenic. Thankfully, most of the top fifteen are from Elle's camp.

Nearing the end, last year's set of queens, Lady International, Lady Global, Lady Intercontinental, and Lady Pearl of the Philippines, have begun to walk their final walks.

"And now it's time to place a crown to the new rightful heirs," Gaby proclaims. "Are you ready for it, Kim?"

Kim smiles at Gaby. "As ready as this crowd!" A roar comes up from the seats.

"Well, then, without further ado, we shall present the four queens starting with the Second Runner Up." Gaby reads the envelope and then announces the results. "Lady Caloocan City!"

Cleo's genuinely happy for Lady Caloocan City. As the candidates take the crowns, she's still waiting and hoping for her name to be called last. Nadia is named the first runner-up, while the rest of the candidates in their beauty camp are still hoping to be the next Lady Pearl of the Philippines.

"And the next lady to be crowned will carry with her a big responsibility . . ." Kim trails off, further building up anticipation. "Representing the Philippines is . . ."

This is the moment that terrifies Cleo out of her wits. She has done everything and then some to come this far. She isn't going to let herself down, win or lose. She knows deep within her that she has done her best to walk the stage, to smile sincerely and answer honestly.

LADY QUEZON CITY, CLEO WALTER!

Stunned, Cleo gasps, in awe of what she has just won. Astonished, speechless, even breathless. She realizes she's crying. Her heart is full to overflowing. She's forever grateful to have won the crown. And God, that crown feels good on her head.

Oh, You Think You're Done? It's Only the Beginning of a Brand-New World

Cleo's attended a lot of after-parties before, but this after-party? She owns it. Not just the staircase she's standing on with her black studded ankle strap stilettos, but every surface her feet meet.

Beneath the posh chandelier, guests and beauty queens fill the room, murmuring among themselves about their plans. They might not have won the crown, but they know pretty well they're still going to places—and this is especially true of those who came from the same camp as Cleo. Elle has assured them all that it's not the end of everything.

Meanwhile, Cleo gets her congratulations. Reporters and journalists alike take her side of the story, and once she's begun talking, there is no stopping her from spilling out how she's worked hard to get the crown. She's squashed any doubts and rumors the people might have about her. No one is going to ruin this day for her. They're going to listen to her story, and if it still doesn't convince them, then it doesn't matter. She's already won.

"Enjoying the crowd?" Elle appears next to Cleo in her cape-let sheath dress. She's got nude lipstick on and an award-winning smile, greeting the guests in her best regal form as always. There's no one like her, and she knows it.

Cleo looks down below, the billowing, colorful gowns of the dancers sweep the floor, and looking at all those beautiful faces, she knows she's finally stepped up her game. Once upon a time, she would have been terrified at the very idea of being in the same room as these people. Not anymore. She's made a place for herself here, and it's apparently a very big one.

"Maybe," Cleo teases, chuckling before turning to Elle. "Thank you for this, Elle. Really. I can't wait to be back home."

"It's all you, Cleo."

"Where have you been all this time, by the way?" Cleo hasn't seen Elle for what seems like forever. She was hoping Elle would be the one to guide her all the way through as she had been for Thea, but the training has always come from Guinevere and Deborah.

Elle looks hard at Cleo, which makes Cleo remember the no-questions-allowed rule. "I've been busy, if you're so curious about it."

"Oh. I just thought you'd—"

"Train you personally?" Elle finishes for Cleo.

Cleo presses her lips together.

"I will," Elle informs Cleo, watching the others down below make connections. "You think this is the end? It's only just the beginning."

Cleo furrows her eyebrows. "But I've won already."

"In the nationals, yes, you did. But you have to go further and be bolder than ever. You've caught the hearts of the Filipinos, but how about the world?"

"I haven't thought of that yet," Cleo admits, smiling at the guest who passed by and offered his congratulations. "Thank you."

"Cleo, you are going to be representing the Philippines. You will carry the red, white, and blue flag emblazoned with stars and golden sun."

Cleo smiles at the vivid imagery, but then anxiety gnaws at her. "I already have a crown. What if I'm asking too much and end up being a disappointment?"

"A Lady Pearl of the Philippines who stops short of the next title," Elle pauses and then continues, "is just admitting you're an actress who became a beauty queen. You won't know until you try."

Elle leaves Cleo after that, approaching the men in suits, smiling, and making small talk. Cleo's mentor's good at that—knowing exactly what to say in every situation managing to keep the men on her leash. She's not just a queenmaker; she's a kingmaker. In a crowd of men, she knows how to stand out.

Cleo's decided to mingle with the others. She steps out at the center of the ballroom and gets her photos taken. Chezka, Nadia, and Julia have joined her in the photo as they're all from the same beauty camp.

"I guess congratulations are in order," Nadia says casually, posing in front of the camera.

Cleo smiles at the camera. "Thank you."

"Not that you deserve it."

"Nadia!" Chezka scolds Nadia, pinching her arm.

"Fine." Nadia gives out, leaning in close to Cleo for the picture. "Just to make things clear, this doesn't mean we're friends. Congratulations."

Cleo smiles at that. Julia says the same thing to her, but she's much freer now as if she's glad the national pageantry is over. In between photos, Dom slides into their group, a bouquet of roses in his arms.

Cleo puts her hand over her heart, touched. "Aw, thank you, Dom, this is so sweet of you and—"

"Shush. This isn't from me." Dom quickly transfers the bouquet of roses to Cleo's arms.

The bouquet is beautiful and classic. The aroma fills Cleo's nose, a perfect honey meadow kind of perfume. It reminds her of a love once shared in sweet stolen moments. And then she finds a card between its blooms. She rips open the card and reads the message.

"Congratulations, and good luck in all your future endeavors."

Cleo doesn't need to know who the roses are from. Even after the relationship ended, Owen is still the same man she knew. And though they themselves might change over time, the history they shared is theirs forever. This gift is a breath of fresh air after going through so much for days, weeks, months. She didn't have the time to sulk or mourn, and Owen knows that. He knows she's not going to stop, and these roses are his message that though they may not be as they were before, she'll always be in his heart. They're better together, but they're at their best when they grow on their own.

"He's a really great guy, huh?" Chezka glances at Cleo's roses.

A tear escapes Cleo's eye. She smiles her best in front of the camer, and says, "He truly is."

🌹　　🌹　　🌹

Dinner proceeds without a hitch. The slightly formal after-event party has turned into a full-blast party after everyone's had their fill. The music shifts into a wild party song, and Chezka, being such a wild beauty queen, rips the fabric of her dress.

"Chezka," Cleo calls out, and while she attempts to make it sound like a scolding, she ends up laughing the entire time. "Elle's going to kill us!"

"Go on."

Cleo and Chezka turn to Elle, gawking at her command. Elle's smiling at them, and this is probably one of the almost-never times they'll get to see her like this.

"Enjoy this time. You deserve it." Elle winks at them.

Cleo's stupefied. "Who are you, and what have you done to Elle?"

"Come on, before she changes her mind!" Chezka pulls Cleo onto the platform, where Nadia invited a live band to perform.

"Let's all show them we're not just princesses with tiaras. We can also rock!"

As soon as everyone hears that, the grace and etiquette that have ruled these ladies are thrown out of the window. They started tearing the fabrics of their dresses and messing up their hair, jumping up and down along with the beat of the band. It's a crazy party, and Cleo loves it. Just for tonight, she can let loose, and for once there's no hostility in the room: no judging stares nor glares.

This is how it should be between women—no catfights, no sabotage, just women having fun and enjoying the night.

"NO LIEEE!" they scream.

Suddenly, Sean Paul's *No Lie* is blasting through the speakers, and everyone's serious about making it the best night of their lives. Cleo sings along with Chezka, swaying their hips from side to side. As they dance, they are caught on camera, and from the corner of her eyes, Cleo sees Erik going around the room to snap those photos—no filters, just their raw and beautiful faces.

Cleo drops down on the floor—quite gracefully—and latches onto Erik's arm. "Tell me you'll also dance."

"I don't dance." Erik pulls away from Cleo. "Enjoy your party, Lady Pearl of the Philippines."

"Don't you know how to have fun?" Cleo teases.

Erik puts his camera back into his bag and places it on the table. He smirks at her. The dimple on his right cheek makes him look sly and cunning. He rubs his hands together and then jumps into the crowd, creating a space for himself. Getting everyone's attention, he breakdances, giving the audience a spectacular view of his power moves. His footwork is astounding.

"God, he's spinning his head," Chezka tells Cleo, already cheering for Erik. "Was he a dancer in his past life?"

"I have no idea!"

"He's a heartbreaker, isn't he? He'll not only spin your head, but your heart, too," Chezka sighs dreamily.

Cleo stares at Chezka, amused.

"What?" Chezka demands.

"I thought you liked Nadia."

Chezka shrugs unapologetically. "I'm just appreciating the view. You should, too."

"You mad woman!" Cleo laughs out loud as they watch Erik from the sides. And when he finishes his moves, every girl in the room swoons.

Erik stands up and offers his hand to Cleo. "Shouldn't the Lady Pearl show off some moves too?"

"I don't—"

Too late. Chezka has pushed Cleo to Erik. Balancing herself on her feet, she smiles wryly at Erik.

"Just follow my lead," he says "Dance however you want."

Then Erik lets loose with his dance moves, again, spellbinding to watch. Cleo thinks it's crazy, but she dances anyway. She's just shaking her hips and spinning round and round, getting herself dizzy. Thankfully, he's there to steady her. She's not a good dancer, but she's having fun. Eventually, everyone joins again, the party floor is filled with giggles and laughter.

The electrified rush pushes Cleo to move her body to the rhythm of the music. Her sweat doesn't even stop her. She's tired, but she keeps going. She can be a jellified version of herself, and she'll still be dancing just because she wants to. The hours pass by, and the drinks just keep coming. Lady Rizal's drunk and slurring her words, but Cleo figures they mean "congratulations." The other girls are still in high spirits, eating desserts and holding their friend's hand, who seems to be sobbing. They're all a little drunk, and some are full-on drunk, but it's their secret after-after-party of a lifetime.

"Honey." Dom taps Cleo's back. "Hate to be the one to ruin your party, but someone wants to see you at the garden."

"Who?"

Dom stares at Cleo and then drops his head on her shoulder.

"You're drunk, Dom." Cleo almost loses her footing. "C'mon, sit down for a minute."

"Let me help," Erik offers, already placing Dom's arm around his neck.

"I have to go somewhere. Can you take care of him for a while?"

Erik lifts Dom like he weighs practically nothing. "What do you think?"

"Thanks!" Cleo smiles at Erik before running off to the back, where the garden is. Her instinct says the person waiting for her is someone special, and maybe her heart does a little *thump, thump*. It's not that she's still expecting things to work out with that person, but perhaps this will be the final closure on . . . .

Cleo stops in her tracks. The man in the pavilion garden has his back on her, but she can guess who it is, and she doesn't like the fear that comes with seeing him. And then she remembers who she is right now—she's the Lady Pearl of the Philippines. No one's allowed to doubt her today. She's proven herself more than enough.

Slowly, Cleo walks over to where the man is. "Nice to see you here, *Direk* Everett."

Direk Everett turns to Cleo, and he's still as charming as ever in his black suit. He has a few graying hairs, but his blonde hair and icy blue eyes never fail to intimidate whoever comes his way. He's someone who knows what he wants and will clearly do anything to get it, so whatever he's coming here for, he's hoping to get it from her. But for the moment she's willing to give him the benefit of the doubt.

"Congratulations," *Direk* Everett says, straightening his tie as if he's been practicing saying that word for days now.

Cleo comes close to *Direk* Everett and locks eyes with him. "That's not what I need to hear from you."

"You're not going to make it easy for me, are you?"

Cleo stares at *Direk* Everett.

Direk Everett sighs. "How can you wear the crown that's rightfully your mother's and be so different from her?"

"Maybe because she's my mom . . . and you're my dad," Cleo fills. He's still her father, even though he hasn't been her dad for a long time now. It's not her fault she can't be like the other actor kids he'd wanted her to be like in the past. When she was young, he'd always liked Guinevere and Jake, but ultimately, he realized that she could never be like them.

Something in *Direk* Everett's face changes. He's not so intimidating now, and Cleo senses he's let his guard down. "Cleo, I didn't leave the family. I tried my best to play the part."

"Just like acting?"

Direk Everett shakes his head and continues, "I didn't leave because of you. Your mother sent me away because I wanted other things in life. I couldn't make a career with a family slowing me down. I admit I wasn't ready to be a husband and a father. That's not what I wanted in life. I became restless, always jumping from one place to another for weeks and then months. Eventually it was as if I was never at home at all. I didn't want to compete with Gary and his children. They're great, and you and I, at that time, were just nobodies."

Oh, the audacity of this man.

"You didn't want to be with a nobody?" Cleo's clenching and unclenching her fists. The party she was enjoying a while ago just turned sour. This breakup with her dad is far worse than her breakup with Owen.

"I was selfish, yes, but I'm still a father, Cleo. I did my best to make a future for you. I have watched you ever since I left. Every reel, *teleserye*, movie, anywhere you were. Even as an extra. A talent. I watched over you because you're my daughter," *Direk* Everett explains, defeated.

It all clicks in Cleo's head. Behind the scenes, her father, *Direk* Everett, tried to fix things for her. He probably pestered talent agencies and managers to take her in. He made the movie with *Direk* Gary possible. It wasn't *Direk* Gary's idea. Not even Jake's. It was her father. He was, in a way, rigging success for her to atone for what her mother was deprived of. She's baffled. All this time, everyone's been right about her—she only got all those roles because of her father.

"I wanted you to follow in my footsteps, Cleo. I did. I didn't want you to be Lady Somewhere."

"Why?" Cleo says through gritted teeth, daring her father to come up with a good reason.

Direk Everett just smiles and says, "Because I'm still protecting your mother's dignity. The pageant season is a nightmare. It's my hell loop, so when I saw you become the Lady Pearl of the Philippines, I knew trouble was around the corner. I can only influence so many people, Cleo. Pageantry is different from acting. I just want to let you know that I can't help you from here."

Cleo laughs mockingly at *Direk* Everett.

"There's nothing funny about it, Cleo."

"I already talked to Mom about it. Of course, you don't know that. You're not here. Do you think I'm just going to go withdraw and go back the same way Mom did? No. I don't recall asking for your help, either. Acting didn't work out because you kept meddling, but you have no clue as to what I want in life. You don't know me. I won't let myself get in a hell loop. Good luck with life, *Dad*," Cleo says, leaving him alone to his thoughts.

Elle's right. Cleo needs to win the Queen of the Universe crown. This is her territory, and her dad can watch her take the crown. She doesn't need him, and she certainly doesn't want to be like him because as much as he's proclaimed himself to be successful, he's all alone.

Cleo's not alone in this. She has a good team, and she only needs to believe in herself. She won't let her father take this away from her too.

Queenmaker

"You're right."

Elle gestures for Cleo to take a seat. Her office, as usual, screams power and confidence. The only time Cleo visits her mentor's office is when they have serious matters to discuss.

"I'm always right about a lot of things, but which is it this time?" Elle asks, inspecting the folders and envelopes on her table.

"I have to be Queen of the Universe. My father thinks I can't do it." Cleo laughs derisively. "He's wrong."

Elle uncaps her pen and scribbles something on the stack of papers that have been in her "in" tray for weeks now. She pulls a photo out of a drawer and slides it over to Cleo when she's finished.

"Oh, you will. Trust me, I'm a queenmaker," Elle points out.

Cleo glances at the black and white photo. A beautiful woman with her black hair pinned up high seems to be staring at someone from a distance. She wears a butterfly necklace and a pair of stunning earrings. Although she's smiling, her aura is almost the same as Elle's, but hers is more of a warning. She's someone who can hide her true intentions, play everyone and everything to her advantage without ever getting her own hands dirty, and everyone will believe her.

"The Lady Manila who went on to become First Lady. This woman is crazy," Cleo comments, giving the photo back to Elle.

"It's straight out of children's books, but we all know it's more of a horror story than some book you read to your daughter before she goes to bed."

"Actually, it is a bedtime story, Cleo. Written to educate the children while they're still young. The main point being that she's a kingmaker. The woman is cunning, and she's not alone. She's like everyone who gets a taste of power. Give a man a sword, and he'll think he's the greatest man in the world. Wrong. The woman who gave him that sword can survive him. The people will hate him, and rightly so. Soon, they'll want to oust him, but what happens to the woman? She lives long enough to create more kings she can use to her advantage."

"That woman is just as bad as the king," Cleo notes, leaning back in her chair. "I won't be that woman, Elle. A title and a crown won't show the world who I am. What I *do* with the crown and title will do that."

Elle smiles quizzically at Cleo. "Always such a good person, Cleo. I'm just trying to say that sometimes, you have to think like that mad kingmaker. If you can't beat them, then join them. Anyhow, I'll handle your training from now on. I want you to stay in the camp and do as I ask."

"Anything you say, Elle," Cleo promises, smiling back at Elle. She knows she can win if Elle is behind her.

"Anything at all?"

Cleo stares at Elle, even more, determined than ever. "Anything."

"Let's hit training, then. Oh, and tell your family you'll be staying with me from now on. Every day and every night. Allowance included."

🪶   🪶   🪶

Cleo slays the full-on training program Elle devised for her. She's told Thea and Anne about her decision, and they understand. They're happy with what she has achieved so far, and Anne tells her to keep her posted at all times. Meanwhile, her mom couldn't be any prouder. They'll wait for her to come home with a crown on her head.

Given that Cleo has basically submitted herself to Elle, she's free from distractions and can perfectly walk her catwalk. The Q and A sessions with Elle are much trickier and harsher, and most of the time it feels like there's no correct answer.

"If you feel like there's no right answer, it's because there isn't," Elle explains while Cleo sits across from her in the classroom. It's the same classroom they used before. The only difference between then and now is that she's the only student left.

"I mean, really, what am I supposed to say to a foreigner who comes to our country? *Mabuhay*! Everyone will love you here because we love foreigners and their dollars?" Cleo asks, twirling her pen and wondering what she's supposed to do if the question is about foreigners.

Elle chuckles at that. "Are you sure you don't want to be a comedian? And I doubt they have dollars."

Cleo holds up her hands, thinking about foreigners and dollars. "Foreign dollars then. We love anything foreign, and we'll probably find foreign dollars to be far superior to US dollars."

"They are funny questions, and maybe your funny answer can win you that round."

"For real?"

Elle shrugs. "Who knows?"

Cleo gives Elle a thumbs up.

Elle then stands up and takes Cleo's pen from her. "Sell me this pen."

"Are you seriously going Leonardo on me?"

Elle twirls Cleo's pen, cocking her head to the side to listen. "Aren't I the Wolf of Wall Street? It's a brain teaser. Go on."

Cleo takes the pen back and says, "Do you need a pen?"

"No."

"Not at this moment, no, but when's the last time you bought a pen?"

Elle smiles. "I don't buy my pens. I have my assistant to do that."

"Then I'd love to talk to your assistant. Your assistant can get great discounts from me."

And then the charade stops. Elle goes back to her seat and says, "That'll be great, *if* the judge will respond to you, but Q and A's are most often one-liners. Give me a liner."

"Pens are the key to unlocking that new home, business, security, and leisure, and it all begins with writing a single letter," Cleo fires off. "How's that for an answer?"

This goes on for quite a while. Cleo's enjoying it so much, she doesn't even mind if they do it the whole day. There are bizarre questions that are fun to answer and serious ones she's still thinking about, but what matters to Elle is that they can run through any topic and Cleo doesn't blank out.

Cleo's finally getting the focus and attention she needs. At the rate she and Elle are going, the crown is an arm's reach away. She feels sure she can win because she's doing her best, and her faith and trust in Elle are unparalleled. Eventually, they take a break. Out of habit, she checks her social media accounts. After all, it's one of the few things she can control on her own. Elle's not tech-savvy but that's fine. Cleo has Dom, Erik, and Aira. But what she sees on the internet hits her in the gut.

The Lady Pearl of the Philippines is the Daughter of a Former Lady Siquijor

Cleo Walter is not just the daughter of the renowned Direk Everett. She's also the daughter of a former beauty queen and Lady Siquijor, Thea Walter. In the—

Cleo doesn't need to read the entire article. She knows the story, and now everyone else knows the story. She had expected this, but she didn't expect it to come so soon. Worried, she quickly calls her mother.

"Hi sweetheart, what's wrong?" Thea asks.

"You've seen the news?"

Thea chuckles. "Yes. Sweetheart, I'm okay. I did what I had to do then, and I was able to give you a good life. That's all that matters. Aren't you busy?"

"I am, but," Cleo pauses, catching a glimpse of Dom, who just came in through the door of the beauty camp carrying fabrics and props. "I'm just worried for you, that's all. I know you don't like to be in the spotlight, and it's exactly where I've put you. I'm sorry I di—"

"Shh. Don't worry about me. Just keep giving it your all, okay? No matter how persistent these reporters are, hold on. I'm getting a lot of calls . . . .

"*Ma*! I knew it," Cleo says. She knows her mother's getting a lot of calls. They want her side of the story.

"Don't worry about me, okay?" Thea repeats. "I'll call you later, sweetheart. Love you!"

Thea hangs up, leaving Cleo powerless to do anything about this. There's no deleting anything already posted on the web. This is a risk that she'd accepted early on. Sighing, she turns off her phone and presses her fingers to her temples. This is giving her a headache.

Dom swoops in and grabs Cleo's shoulders. "So, honey, did you see the dress for the charity gala?"

"Yes, I saw it, but it needs to be more than that." Cleo doesn't want anything less. She has to have a dress that'll be striking. She has to be better than the other foreign candidates because if she's not, then she's just wasting her mom's trust in her, and she'll only be proving her father right. She can't make any mistakes.

"More?"

"Yes, more!"

"All right, honey, calm down. We have enough time," Dom soothes. "I know you're pressured, but you've got to trust us."

"I know, um, can you just ask Elle about the dress? She knows better," Cleo tells Dom, trying to think about her next social media plan.

"But Elle's not you. She's not going to be the one to wear the dress."

"I KNOW, DOM!" Cleo bursts out, biting her lip and then rubbing her temples. "Sorry."

And as if Dom isn't enough, Erik strolls into the room, taking pictures of Cleo. He smiles at her, enjoying her little show. He takes an apple from the table and bites it, following her every movement.

"You on your red sea?" Erik asks.

Cleo ignores him while Dom presents the national costume he's designed for her. She takes the design and inspects it. It's an eagle-themed costume with overbearingly large feather-like wings and a fearsome full mask.

"My face can't be seen if I'm in a full mask," Cleo points out, giving the sketchpad back to Dom.

Dom touches Cleo's face, sliding her hair to one side. "In the parade, you'll eventually pull it off, exposing a dark makeup that resembles a half-mask. Am I a genius or what?"

"Dom, it doesn't have a wow factor."

Dom gasps, insulted. "Excuse me? Am I or am I not the stylist here?"

"You asked for my opinion," Cleo groans, not wanting to have a row with Dom. "Can we talk about this some other day?"

"I don't like the way you are right now, honey."

Cleo feels like she wants to explode. "You don't have to like me to do your job."

"Okay. Have it your way, *Lady Pearl*," Dom stresses Cleo's title, relaxing his arms and leaving the sketchpad on the table. He shakes his head, glances at Erik, who's watching their heated little exchange, and then walks out.

"I didn't mean it that way—" Cleo takes the sketchbook and writes notes about what she wants to happen with her national costume. "I just wanted to take this matter into my own hands. I'm trying to win here, and people are taking it the wrong way."

"You know what you need, Cleo?" Erik butts in.

Cleo doesn't even bother responding. She's busy making adjustments to Dom's ideas. Besides, if she says something, Erik might walk out too. She can't afford to rift with them at a crucial time like this. She'll just handle Dom and the issue with her mom later on.

But Erik can be very persistent. "Come with me."

"Can't you see I'm busy?" Cleo snaps.

"I can see that, but I can see you're also stressed," Erik responds, calm and undisturbed. "Catch you later then."

Just as Erik's about to leave, Cleo changes her mind. She draws in a deep, calming breath. "I'm coming with you."

For some reason, Cleo's thrilled at the thought of an impulsive decision. She just wants to get away somewhere far from here, away from the pressure, and he's her ticket to nowhere.

"Wait."

Cleo goes back to her room, slips out of her high heels, and wears her running shoes. Since she's been staying full-time in the camp, Elle's given her a private room, and it's great. She ties her hair in a bun, rushing outside in fear he might have gone off. But he's there, waiting by his car.

Erik stares at her, amused. "Come on."

Cleo sits on the passenger side with the car window open. Erik makes sure she isn't going to forget about this mini-adventure because he quickly speeds off into the highway. Around them, the city lights twinkle like tiny little stars. It's a lovely scene to take in as they race to the unknown destination and it gives her adrenaline a fresh boost. Only now does she realize that, maybe for the only time she can recall amidst all this pageantry intensity, she's actually living in the moment, free of outside expectations—just her and her soul reaching toward her dreams.

But she's loving this space between all that pressure and the end goal. She wants this ride to go on and on. She feels free after a long period of striving and setbacks and obstacles tossed in her way, and freedom has never felt this good.

Just for tonight, Cleo doesn't need to worry. She's Cleo tonight.

No Walter, no Lady, no anything; just a girl in a car trying to map out her life, but knowing she can loosen up every once in a while.

"Amazing, right?"

Cleo grins gratefully at Erik. "Thank you for this."

"Anytime," Erik smiles at Cleo.

Erik is reminding her what it's like to soar—it's free-falling, jumping out in a parachute thinking she can die any time, but also realizing it's only then that she can truly enjoy the best part of the life she has because life has no second takes. Just through having a little time with the wind in her face and no knowledge of where she's going, Cleo feels braver and bolder. But rides like this one don't last long. They come to a plaza full of dancing people. Erik parks at the side of the fence and waits for her to get out.

"Is this even safe?" It looks like *Little Tondo*, one of the poorest areas in Manila. The streets filled with *batang hamog*, children from broken families, and living under the open sky. They're known to rule every corner and highway, growing up to be thieves and gangsters.

Erik smiles warmly. "A revel of some sort."

Getting out of the car, Cleo comes close to the plaza and finds several teenagers and children dancing around the dimming lamppost. Their oversized shirts and tattered shorts are obviously from the dumpsters, but their grinning faces invite her to join them. Even though they're dirty on the outside and probably hungry on the inside, they're happy. Genuinely and truly happy doing what they're doing.

As soon as they see Erik, they run to him, saying, "You came!"

"Of course, I did. Why wouldn't I?" Erik says, smiling as Cleo has never seen him smile before. "How are you?"

One of the little kids pointed at Cleo and said, "You brought a girl with you!"

"Hi," Cleo greets, finding it hard to connect the children standing before her with the children who are forced to wander around and sleep on the streets.

"She's prettyyy!!!" the little girl holding a torn teddy bear chimes in, pulling Cleo with her.

"They're my foster brothers and sisters," Erik begins, ruffling the hair of the little boy. "We used to live together with our adoptive parents They weren't anything close to having real parents, but my mother has been a mother, one way or another. We had a strictly enforced set of chores—housework for the girls and heavier work for the boys My little brother, that guy with a fake mustache, was always sickly and would always get slapped around by our father. Being the eldest, I would always take the beating while my mother shielded us from my father. She had never once cringed in front of him, but then she died in an accident, and my father left, leaving us on the streets."

"And your now adopted family found you. Took you in," Cleo concludes, afraid that talking about this might be hard for him. "I'm sorry, Erik."

Erik stares at his foster brother. "It doesn't matter. Later on, I found them again here, living with an old grandmother who took them in, and I give what I can."

"But you've never known your real parents?" Cleo asks him, sitting on the fountain's marble stone.

Erik shakes his head, pulling his little brother in for a hug. He pulls a *Jack and the Beanstalk* book from his bag, and gives it to the little boy. "Here, read this, okay? I'll come back tomorrow for some snacks."

Cleo's at a loss for words. The children are harmless. They don't even know why they are here on the streets. And here she is, wondering if the area is safe and startled by the news that Erik comes from this. And here's Erik, full of love for his foster siblings and sharing his good fortune with them. There's nothing greater than a heart that loves hugely without expecting anything in return.

Cleo glances at Erik, and it hits her how different he is when he's with them in the competition. It's these beautiful ragged children, not the flashy world of beauty queens, that fills her heart with light.

He's a beautiful person, after all.

"Tell me if you want me to take you back already," Erik reminds Cleo, his eyes set on his other siblings.

With all the love Cleo's seeing before her now, she doubts she wants to ever go back. This is just beautiful. The children remind her of Anne, who's always there for her, someone important to her but who barely gets any of her time now. Suddenly, she feels guilty for being so caught up in the whirlwind of the competition. She takes a mental note to check on Anne soon.

"Why don't you dance?" Erik's little brother insists. " I'm Jasper. Nice to meet you, pretty lady!

"I'm Cleo," Cleo replies, surprised at how easily she can get along with them.

Jasper takes Cleo's hand and places it on Erik's. "Dance for us, please."

Cleo pulls her hand back, lowers herself to Jasper, and whispers, "Why don't you show me how to dance first?"

Erik opens his phone and plays a song for everyone to set off an example. Jasper grabs a partner and begins to dance like crazy. While everyone's having fun, she just watches them, enchanted to witness their pure joy. The cool breeze linger sin the air, but the tapping feet and crazy dancing made them all sweaty. One of them pulls Cleo out of her seat and tries to twirl her around. She taps her shoes in a whimsical rhythm, genuinely happy. This is the kind of world she has been dreaming of—surrounded by people who are genuinely happy.

CHAPTER 27

Elle Knows Best

I t's past midnight when Cleo gets back to beauty camp. She sneaks into the living room, hoping not to wake anyone. Chezka, Nadia, and Julia are still residing at the camp. The three of them have been chosen to be part of the Filipino delegates sent to Japan to establish friendship and cultural understanding between two Asian countries. It's an excellent opportunity for them, and Elle made it happen.

Just as Cleo's off to her room, the lamp near the sofa lights up, revealing Elle sitting with her usual poise—legs slightly slanted at the side. "It's past your bedtime, Cinderella."

"I—I just went out to get some a-air," Cleo stutters, flailing over the words. "The story about my mom has been . . ."

"Revealed, yes, I know. So you're throwing a tantrum?"

"It's not a tantrum, okay? It's personal." Cleo drops her head, too tired to argue. She knows there's no winning against Elle anyway.

Elle pats the space next to her, and Cleo sits. "All the more reason to win the crown. Let them talk about it. It's all they can do. Ignore, Cleo. You should be more than focused by now. You also know that getting to bed late isn't healthy."

"I know, I'm sorry. I just . . ."

Cleo wants to tell Elle that she's just trying to get a little space from all the pressure. She's planning and strategizing how to counter-attack that big reveal. She doesn't want people to think badly of her mother, so she's got to do something on her social media account. But that one isn't Elle's territory.

"Are you still with me on this?" Elle questions, her hands on her lap.

"Yes."

Elle smiles at that. She then hands a picture to Cleo. It's a man in his mid-fifties and looks decent enough. "Have dinner with this man. Just be your charming self and talk to him."

"I don't think that's a good idea. What's that got to do with me?" Cleo trusts her gut instincts, and it's giving her all the red flags. But she's wavering, and the only reason for that is that the request is coming from Elle.

"Goody Two Shoes wins Lady Siquijor but goes no further. You won the national pageant for Thea. But you've done that! Now you're going to win for you."

"Why?"

"No questions, Cleo."

Cleo laughs at Elle. "I know that. Why?"

"You want to do this now?" Elle dares, and when she sees Cleo's serious face, she continues, "You want to win? This is how you win. You acquire power if you have influence. Don't waste my influence, Cleo. This is politics in every way, unless you want to let Thea's sacrifice go to waste?"

Cleo's getting headaches again. She squeezes the pillow at her side and closes her eyes for a moment. She's come so far; she can't ruin this for herself and her mother.

"Of course not. When do I meet this man?"

"Tomorrow night. It'll be at the Elite Hotel. VIPs only," Elle elaborates. "Get some sleep, my little Cinderella, and wear your best evening dress with your charming smile."

🐿️   🐿️   🐿️

"Okay, do I look good in the picture?"

"For the nth time, yes," Erik replies, giving his camera to Cleo. "What's all this about again?"

Aira, who's been sitting so quietly on the couch, has suddenly decided to speak up. "A counter-narrative for the Thea story. She's going to make herself the hero of the crown or something close to that. Where is that honey boy of yours anyway?"

Right, Dom.

Cleo had texted Dom hours earlier about their secret meeting, but he hasn't replied to her. In a book café—hidden from most of the public eye—with a good lounge, it's a good secret HQ for building what she's started, and Dom would have loved the place. But unfortunately, the little argument they had yesterday has pushed him away.

"They fought," Erik answers for Cleo.

Aira scoffs. "Then just apologize."

"I did. Many times. I texted him, but nothing." Cleo rechecks her phone, hoping Dom's answered at least one of her messages. She calls him, and thankfully, he answers. "I know you hate me, but please hear me out first. Don't hang up. I'm really, really sorry, Dom with a Q. I'm not Lady Pearl of the Philippines without you. Please marry my dress."

Seconds turn into minutes until Dom has finally answers. "I've married a lot of dresses. I don't need another one, but I know you won't survive without me."

"Really? So, we're good?" Cleo sweet-talks Dom.

"Acting cute doesn't suit you, but okay. I'll be there in half an hour."

Cleo grins, pumping her fist up in the air, and Erik bumps his against hers. She looks at him warily, and then he says, "I thought you might need it."

"Dom's on his way!" Cleo announces, going back to her original position in between bookshelves. "Okay, so back to the photo shoot. By the way, do you guys think a video of me would get more audience?"

"Why not?" Aira says.

Cleo scrolls through her social media, thinking that the issue will resurface no matter what she does. If she responds to it, it'll just highlight more of her mother's past, so she thought maybe if she could share how her everyday training is progressing, she'll be shifting their attention to it.

"Change of plans. I'll give you guys my training schedule, and then late at night or on weekends, the content can be about the best places to visit in the city. What do you think?" Cleo suggests, taking a bite out of her croissant. "But for now, we can make a video of me sharing what's it like to be a beauty queen."

"Got ya," Erik tells Cleo, already positioning his camera at the side. Cleo then invites Aira to sit across from her.

"Okay, Aira, this will be like a talk show. Just ask me random questions, as in really random. Sort of like five things you didn't know about Cleo Walter, but much more fun," Cleo instructs, and Aira just nods.

And so Cleo has managed to find new content. Being a famous personality gives everyone access to her life, but it should be Cleo who gets to decide what she shares. They don't have to know everything—they just have to know enough to keep them interested. In the end, it'll still be she who gets to control it.

Once Erik has finished setting up his camera, Aira begins with the interview. "So, we know who you are, but we don't know you. If not a beauty queen or actor, what would you have been?"

"My secret dream is to be a dancer. Sadly, I can't dance to save my life, but I can be funny sometimes." Cleo chortles out a laugh at that.

"Oh, come on! Everyone has moves. Can you give us a sample?" Aira teases.

Cleo doesn't know how to dance, but she wanted this to happen, so she's decided to be bold about it. She shakes a bit of booty here and there, looking at the camera with a wink. She slides to the side and turns around, smiling and whipping her hair back and forth. And then she adds a catwalk for the final touch.

"Well, well, what do we have here?" Dom slides in the frame, watching Cleo with her moves. "Oh, are we rolling?"

Cleo's never been so happy to see Dom. She grins, wrapping her arms around him. He groans and attempts to pull her off, but she's not letting him. "You're here!"

"Of course, I am."

Cleo turns to the camera and introduces Dom. "Okay, guys, this is Dominique, as in Dom with a Q. He's my overall stylist, and he makes me magically beautiful."

"Correction: she is beautiful in her way," Dom adds. "Alexa, play pretty hurts by Beyoncé."

"Yes." Cleo stares softly at the camera. "We are our own beauty."

The video ends there. It's a snippet of what's more to come, but Cleo feels good about it. If there is at least something totally of her own, then it's this. Elle can make her do anything but this. She has her secret weapon. She just hopes tonight will not be what she thinks it is.

🔥   🔥   🔥

"Cleo Walter? Please follow me."

In an elegant short maroon dress and burgundy pumps, Cleo waltzes into the restaurant of the Elite Hotel. She doesn't need VIP access; Elle's taken care of everything she could possibly need. Thankfully she can count on one hand how many of those are there. Most of the clientele are foreigners and aren't fans, so she'll have no problem thinking about what this will look like to them.

Cleo follows the hostess until she spots a short, stocky man with a goatee. He's seated under dim lighting at the far edge of the restaurant near the skyscrapers. The booth seems to be private, and as they get closer to him, she knows this is the man she'll be talking to over dinner.

"Dinner will be served shortly. Let me know if you need anything else," the hostess says, leaving the two of them alone.

"It is a pleasure, Lady Pearl," the man greets, taking her hand and kissing it. "You look stunning as always, more so with your flawless diamond earrings."

"Hmm . . . you know your gemstones," Cleo observes, hoping to keep it professional between them. She still doesn't know what this meeting is all about, but Elle insists it's a crucial part of the plan.

"I have a sharp eye for perfection, no matter how small." The man grins at Cleo. "Is this table agreeable to you, or should we find another?"

Cleo sits down across from the man and smiles. "This is fine."

"Are you hungry?"

Cleo tilts her head to one side. "I wouldn't be having dinner with you if I weren't."

"Ah, now I see why you're Elle's favorite. Obedient, but also a spitfire." The man laughs, amused. He locks eyes with Cleo and reaches for her hand across the table. Cleo doesn't blink.

"If you were anybody else, I'm sure I'd be talking to air."

"But I'm not anybody else. I'm Cleo Walter, and I'm Lady Pearl of the Philippines, and I'd appreciate it if you'd take your hand off mine," Cleo says with conviction, taking her hand away from him.

The man backs away, his mouth curving into a smile. Cleo holds herself back, but she wants to punch the man in the face. "I'm just being friendly."

"You don't have my *consent*."

The man pops open the first button of his polo shirt, relaxing. "I apologize. I didn't mean to come off as a pervert. I wanted to see how you'd react."

To see how she'd react. Cleo forces a smile, stopping herself from getting up and leaving because has asked her to do this. If it weren't for her mother's sacrifice and her father's meddling, she wouldn't be here. She doesn't want to wait for dinner. She just wants to get this over with quickly.

"Oh, good! Here's the food. I hope you like steak," the man is enthusiastic about the approaching tray.

Feeling trapped as wonders where this is going, Cleo decides to keep him company. She eats the food on her plate and sips her wine, waiting for him to open up about whatever important thing she needs to hear.

"How's life as Lady Pearl? Elle giving you a hard time?"

Cleo doesn't even know what his name is. "Mr. . . . um, how would you like to be called?"

"Mister or Sir is fine."

As far as Cleo's concerned, not knowing the name of the man she's talking to means this meeting is shady and sketchy as hell. She shouldn't be here, and she wants to get out of this building right now, but Elle's words echo in her head. Goody Two Shoes can only take her as far, and is she willing to give it all up because she feels weirded out by this man?

"Okay, sir. Training has been excellent, and I've gathered a good following on my social media. Elle and my team are working their hardest to put my name out there. So far, I think it's working well." Cleo's confident in what she's saying because it's all true.

"And you're close to winning, aren't you?"

Cleo savors the tender, juicy steak. "I like to believe I am."

The man is looking at Cleo, and it makes her feel uncomfortable. Why can't he just eat his food like she's doing right now? She doesn't want to be rude, but she might say something she means if he continues staring.

"I think you are." The man smiles as if he knows something she doesn't. "You've got a very rich background, and everything that's happened to you has pushed you toward the crown. You're good at surviving, Cleo Walter."

"Thank you."

I want to survive this dinner, too, Cleo thought.

Their small talk lasts for almost an hour, and Cleo's still not getting anything she needs from him—whatever it is. At some point, the man hands an envelope. He tells her not to open it just yet.

"I need to talk to you about something," the man finally says, wiping his mouth with a tissue.

Cleo finishes her wine, expecting to return to the camp as soon as possible. She knows it must have something to do with this envelope she's holding. "What is it about?"

"Can we talk somewhere in private?"

Cleo stops, and it feels like time is suspended. She's endured so much of this torturous dinner already. The man's suggestion is a quick drop from a rollercoaster. Her heart's beating fast, and her leg's shaking. She wonders, what's the cost of the crown? What does she sacrifice? And does she trust Elle more than she trusts herself?

"No, thank you." Cleo stands up and smiles. "Dinner was lovely, but I have to go back. If it's about the envelope, you can have it back."

The man frowns at Cleo, disappointed. "I won't hold you back, Lady Pearl. Take the envelope as a gift from me. Let Elle know I've enjoyed the dinner anyway. Good night."

Cleo leaves the hotel and takes a cab. On the way back, she's only thinking of one person: *Elle.*

CHAPTER 28

Beauty Queen and Their Pretty Little Secrets

The following day, Cleo finds Chezka pulling her trolley bag out from her room. It turns out that today's the day Chezka and the others will be leaving for Japan. Cleo would have been one of them in an alternate reality, but that reality isn't hers to live.

"So, Japan, huh?" Cleo interrupts Chezka's preparation.

Chezka brightens up as soon as she sees Cleo. She drops her bags and bounces to her side, always so full of energy. "Cleo! You know it's funny we're living in the same camp, but we barely see each other. How's training?"

"Stressful. You know Elle."

"Totally!" Chezka laughs and then pouts. "I'm going to miss you. It's too bad I can't be there for your coronation night."

Cleo takes Chezka's trolley bag, helping her with it. "We'll see each other again soon. Have fun in Japan, okay? You deserve it. I mean, Nadia will be there, too. I didn't get to ask you this before, but have you ever . . ."

"Confessed to her?" Chezka continues, smiling. "I haven't. I know she doesn't like me that way. I'm enjoying the way things are between us—it's enough for me."

"You're a great person, Chezka. I'm sure you'll find someone who'll see you as you are and love you every day for it," Cleo assures Chezka.

"I hope so. I really, really hope so."

Once Chezka's bags are inside the van, she bids Cleo goodbye. Nadia and Julia don't say much to Cleo, but they wish her good luck for the biggest pageantry competition. They haven't been the best of friends, but they did compete in the nationals with the best intentions.

"Break a leg," Nadia tells Cleo, her signature high ponytail still in place. "We hope to see a crown when we get back."

That somehow touches Cleo. She smiles at Nadia and says, "Thanks. Enjoy your time there."

A few more words with Chezka, and then Elle comes in. The Elle. The Elle she's wanted to corner for hours now. But that can wait. They have the entire day to talk about it, and she's not going to start training without an explanation because last night was just terrible. No one should ever go through something like that.

"Make me proud," Elle reminds Chezka, Nadia, and Julia.

Julia huffs out a breath. "Of course, we will, Elle."

"Take care, girls."

Cleo and Elle stand on the sides as the van drives away. They don't move or say anything else. It's a cloudy, windy day, a perfect time to be outside and play outdoor sports, but Cleo doesn't have that luxury. She's got to keep moving and working towards the crown after receiving some truth from Elle.

"We need to talk," Cleo starts like they're two people in love, and they're on the verge of breaking up.

Elle isn't fazed. She schools her expression. One of her many talents is repressing her emotions, and it's because she has to be in control. It serves her well most of the time, but not this time.

"It seems that we do," Elle goes back inside, and Cleo trails after her. They lounge in a once lively living room that's now charged with tension. Silence hangs in the air, deafening their ears. It's louder than the ghostly chatters of the beauty queens who used to occupy this space. But aren't all silent truths deafeningly loud?

"What was with last night, Elle?" Cleo begins, shuddering at the mere thought of the man who for sure fantasized about a night with her. "I was so, so terrified. I thought it was for your business or something!"

Elle drinks her cup of tea, quiet for a few moments.

"Well?" Cleo presses Elle.

"I understand you're angry, bu—"

"I am!"

Elle raises one hand as if to calm Cleo down. She stares at Cleo, her eyes smoldering with unmasked anger and irritation. It's the first time she's showing her true face. "Grow up, Cleo. If you're serious about winning the global title for the Philippines, it's time for you to realize that this is what winning is. Winners do what it takes to win. Whatever it takes."

"So, what is this envelope for, huh?" Cleo hands the envelope over to Elle, but her mentor refuses it. Exasperated, she opens the envelope instead and brings out documents containing information that's damaging to the other candidates. Her stomach churns. She can taste bile stuck in her throat. She can't begin to understand what this all means, but it makes her feel sick.

Elle spreads out the documents on the glass table. The documents are about some of the foreign candidates who apparently have had facial surgery, a history with a notorious drug, a relationship with a sugar daddy, a secret marriage, and a woman who used to be a hostess, to name a few. Quite simply, these documents can ruin the chances of the other candidates. But whatever some of them may have done or been through, the past should not define who they are right now.

"Subtly tip off the reporters about this. Be smart, Cleo. Don't involve your name so—"

Cleo gasps. "You think I'm actually going to do it? You don't know why Lady Kenya, Lady Vietnam, Lady Bolivia, and whoever other lady is in those documents did whatever they did. I'm not judging them because of their pasts. They're running towards a better future, and I'm not going to take that away from them!"

"You're favored to win, just like your mother before you. If you stop now, you'll lose your standing and you won't be able to gain it back."

Cleo puts the paper down. With her mouth set in a hard line, she snaps at Elle. "This is not how I'm supposed to win, Elle."

"You can't win at this moment being such a good Samaritan. You gotta be dirty. You've got to be bold. Nobody wins something out of being just good, and that is the reality of life, Cleo. You can't make it to the top if you don't go beyond what you are taught, so do it," Elle insists, her voice clear and almost laced with threat.

Cleo smiles coldly at Elle. "No."

"No?" Elle repeats, tipping Cleo's chin up like she's a broken doll. "Do you think Thea would have survived without me?"

Cleo doesn't say anything, but she keeps her eyes on Elle's. She knows the answer to that question anyway.

"Thea wasn't going back to Siquijor. She had to make it to Manila. You almost certainly would have never been born," Elle declares. She recalls Thea's journey to the crown and her downfall, making Cleo's blood boil.

Cleo pulls away from Elle. "That's not fair, Elle."

"Nothing ever is. Oh, and Everett only came back in the country because he was required to support you and Thea financially, not because he's a good guy. And the money? Thea had to use most of that to pay back her sponsors from the competition. She worked hard, so she didn't have to rely on your father," Elle reveals, putting her teacup on the table. "Life is never fair, dear."

Everett.

The hard truth from Elle strikes Cleo. She didn't know her mother had had to pay many debts. And all because of her. She had to withdraw and use the money to pay her sponsors back. Cleo owes Thea more than just the crown.

With a heavy heart, Cleo can only nod at Elle's commands. She's choosing her mother because her mother chose her. Elle has been Thea's friend, and if this is how she'll secure the coveted title, then so be it.

"Good. Let's get on with the training."

🦂   🦂   🦂

Aira's bored. She's been waiting for Lady Crazy to meet her at their usual hidden café spot, and she's on her fourth coffee of the day. Work has been stressful and hectic the last few days. With the Queen of the Universe coronation night happening in their own country in just one week, she and her fellow candidates have been going from one hotel to another.

Representing the host country also means more pressure for Lady Crazy, so Aira can't blame the woman if she's in a complete and total meltdown. As to that lady, Aira's bosses have been praising her sky-high bosses for following the story of an actor-turned-beauty queen who's been criticized her whole life. Surprisingly, Cleo's immunity to the public eye makes her even more of an interesting subject.

"Sorry, I'm late! Elle's making every minute count."

Aira observes Lady Crazy as she drops her bags down under the table. Quickly, she pulls out brown envelopes and lays them on the table without so much as a hint as to what it's about. But that's who she is, always running off in every direction.

"And this is?" Aira asks, stirring her cup of coffee and adding a bit more sugar into it.

Cleo grips the chair and sits on it, catching her breath.

Aira wants to give Cleo points for rushing out in her six-inch heels. It takes a good balance to walk it the whole day. Women are superheroes.

Cleo leans in close, so Aira does the same. "This is a secret."

"Um, FYI, I'm a reporter, and I expose secrets," Aira points out, arching an eyebrow at Cleo.

"So, unless you want to keep it safe from everyone, then I'm not the person you should be meeting. Also, where are Dumb and Dumber?"

Cleo looks aghast. "Dumb and Dumber? Dom and Erik aren't dumb."

"Oh, I thought I'm the only one in this group who's thinking."

"Talking about fashion isn't dumb. Fashion is an industry of its own, and it feeds families—just like media and entertainment people feed theirs," Cleo reasons. "*Your* family."

"Okay, okay, point taken. What do you want me to do?"

Cleo purses her lips. "Before I tell you anything, how willing are you to go beyond what you know so that you can write a great story out there? I mean, on a scale of one to ten, how evil are you?"

"Satan." Aira winks at Cleo, pointing at her red bobbed hair. "Red is such a passionate color. It's hardcore love, revenge and hell."

Aira loves red. It's always been her favorite color; it burns, sets other things on fire. She grew up wanting to be a detective but decided instead to write scandalous and entertaining articles. She's always been the tattle-tale and the rumor-monger in the family, so she figured she could try the entertainment industry. She gets to be in high places, connected with the right people, but so far, no big story ever came to her until she met this Lady Crazy.

Cleo's a bit taken aback—very candid, is Aira—but she recovers pretty fast. "Okay, that's great. I knew I picked the right person to team up with. I have here, um, information I got from a concerned citizen who is an avid fan of the pageantry competition."

Aira takes the envelope and takes out the documents. She reads through it without even a flicker of emotion on her face. She knows Lady Crazy's watching her and is most likely going crazy about it. Whatever is in this document must be juicy in every way possible.

"Want me to write it?" Aira teases Lady Crazy. She can't see Cleo spreading this information to everybody else. She has an image to protect, but Aira? Her job is to write about spicy and sensational issues. People will drool over this.

"If you want to," Cleo pauses, taking a deep breath and then continuing her thought. "Yes. Hidden pasts aren't fair to candidates who are trying to represent their country honestly. I know this doesn't look good, but it'll help those who are competing honestly."

Aira slips the documents back into the envelope and grins. "You can count on me, Cleo. So, this is everything for now? No content to feature today on your social media?"

Cleo nods.

"I'll go ahead then. It looks like I have a lot to write. Maybe afterward we can have dinner. My treat." Aira takes up her bag and slides the envelope inside.

But as Aira's about to leave, Cleo touches her arm, holding her back. "Can it come from an unknown source?"

"Don't sweat it. I'm on your side." Aira smirks at Cleo. The poor girl has been sweating and shaking, but who can blame her? Having this envelope with her makes her a target for every country in the competition.

"Thank you."

With a lot more to do, Aira hails a cab and gets in. For some reason, she's thrilled to get back at the office. The rain outside is harsh, but surely her articles will make tomorrow a better day. She can't wait to be the life of the party once again.

Aira calls her boss. "Good evening, Ms. Roxanne. I've got two or three articles you might want to look at tonight."

"You're on a roll these past few weeks ever since the Cleo thing. Send them all in. And make sure it's worth my staying up late."

Aira grins. "Absolutely."

*EXCLUSIVE: Queen of the Universe Candidates
and Their Pretty Little Secrets*
This year's Queen of the Universe pageant is the best Pandora's box the world has ever seen. It looks like the screening committee hasn't flushed out everything there is to know about the

candidates. A reliable and concerned insider has come to our office in hopes of making things right for those who are truly much more deserving of the crown. The documents below contain information about some of the candidates and their pretty little secrets. It starts with Lady Vietnam, who used to have a sugar daddy, and many others with something to hide. Click on the link below to view the documents and photos.

The reading public is as judgmental as ever. The victims in Aira's article are getting all kinds of nastiness all over the internet. None of these posters know the whole story, of course. But when did that make any difference?

"Are you okay?" Lady Kenya asks, her dark, fine chocolate-brown skin richer than Cleo's. She's charming and powerful.

Cleo forces a smile. "Yes, are you?"

Cleo has found that "are you?" to be increasingly important since the dirt on these candidates came out. She's talked with some of them. Lady USA and Lady Vietnam had told her it was devastating. Lady USA had surgery on her face. It was a nose job that happened years ago, so her team is now defending her to the officials. Meanwhile, Lady Vietnam confirms that the sugar daddy story is true, but again, it was years ago when she desperately needed money. They're disappointed but not surprised. They know someone's bound to pry into their lives and dig up any detail that can be pounced on, and they can only hope that people can see them for who they are today.

Fortunately, Lady Kenya is not that bothered by what people tell her. She admits she's struggled with bulimia before and may still be struggling now, but she's promised herself she'll never be pressured again.

"I'm worried about the others. They don't deserve all the hate, especially if it's from the past," Lady Kenya admits. "You know what? I think I will tell all those reporters that they deserve a chance in the competition. Just because they're smiling doesn't mean they're okay. Beauty queens also cry."

"That'll help," Cleo assures Lady Kenya. She wants to say she'll do it too for the others, but she'll be a hypocrite. She's the cause of their misery, and attempting to play as their friend is brutal.

"All right, ladies, line up!" the photographer orders.

At Cleo's side, Lady USA is trying her best to stifle her croaks. It only makes her feel like the worst person on the planet.

🌿　🌿　🌿

Along with some of the ladies' personal photographers, Erik has been continually working for hours to capture the contestants' growing bond. They get to drink, rest on the chaise lounges, and dip in the pool.

After this competition, Erik's moving on to street photography. The luxurious, glittering photos are great, but he's had enough of that. Also, his lens doesn't capture the enormity of the grandness and luxury of it all. It captures the raw, gentle, and sometimes hard sides of the Lady Pearl of the Philippines.

Cleo holds so much potential in her, and it's a shame she doesn't know that. Erik can see every facet of her face, and it all reflects power, strength, and vulnerability. And with the way she resurfaces from the pool, hair wet and smoothed over at one side, she's nature herself. So he quickly snaps a photo of her, but she looks tense in this one. Her usual beauty queen aura is missing.

"Turn to your side," Erik orders, getting the right frame for Cleo. Surprisingly, Cleo turns.

"You're pretty compliant today."

Cleo flinches. "Is that bad?"

Erik stops, putting his camera down for a moment and walking over to Cleo. He gazes at her, and her eyes capture his. When he finds her face, it always seems like the first time he sees it. Her face is bare, free for him to read. Her thick eyebrows are scrunched together in worry, and she's biting her lip, indicators that she's not okay.

"That depends on what you're after." Erik sees Cleo worrying again. But you're you, Cleo.

Cleo brings her arms to the side of the pool, tilting her head to one side. "What if, all your life, life, you did your best to be good, but then you did something bad because you want to protect that good?"

"There's always a gray area, Cleo. It's part of human nature to protect what we think is good for us. The only question is, do you still want to be good?"

"Yes."

"You can't change what you did, but you can always make up for it. You'll be fine, trust me."

Cleo smiles at Erik. "Thank you. Really."

And for the rest of the day, Erik gets to capture one of Cleo's rarest raw moments. She doesn't have any barriers around her. She's letting him in, and he can read her every expression. Everything from what's going on in her lovely eyes to the expression on her full lips. Her slim and fit body works as if she's dancing in front of his camera, and only he can hear the soft, thrumming music. She doesn't just smile. She grins. She acts fierce too, a hint of war in her mind, but underneath it is her softness, like a comforting caress

Whatever it is that's on Cleo's mind, Erik's sure she can solve it. She's a work in progress. It may also be one of the reasons why he likes her. She doesn't run away from her problems—she heads straight into it them.

🐝　🐝　🐝

"Thank you for your concern, but I do not want to be interviewed." Thea hangs up the phone, sighing. It's the fiftieth call of the day, and it's only noontime. There's more to come later, and reporters and journalists are all waiting at their gate, hoping to get a minute of her time.

Anne takes away the books she's been reviewing on the table, following Thea over to where the phone is. "*Ma*, are you okay? Want me to tell Leo?"

"No. She's doing the best that she can with Elle." Thea's determined to do everything for Cleo. She owes her daughter that much . . . and Elle. She wants to see the Elle who helped her back then. But for now, has a lot of damage control to do right here.

"Why not just let them all ring?"

Thea ties her apron around her waist and grabs a spatula. "I did that this morning, but it's giving me headaches."

"Okay, let's plan this. How about we do rounds, *ma*? My turn on the telephone. You can have the cellphone, and then we switch every hour or so. That way, you can cook, do whatever you want," Anne suggests, giving Thea a thumbs up. "I'll take care of the noise outside."

Thea ties her hair in a bun and looks at herself in the mirror on the wall. She's got a few creases on her forehead, but she's former Lady Siquijor; her beauty doesn't pass that fast. She's aged well, and she doesn't seem to be over forty. It has been years since she's last truly seen herself, so to inspect her face seems a bit unsettling.

"No. I'll take care of them," Thea says firmly.

Anne thrusts her fist in the air. "For Leo!"

"For Cleo."

Thea walks out of the living room and plants herself near the gate. She quickly scans the crowd and finds reporters from different news outlets flocking the streets. They've got their mics and cameras ready, which brings back many memories. She didn't expect to be in the same spotlight again. What does she have? She's using the apron as her sash and her spatula as the crown, but that doesn't matter. She's a mother more than she is a former beauty queen, but that doesn't mean she's lost her touch. In fact, she might as well give them the last goodbye wave and a final walk.

"Thea, is it true that you withdrew from the national pageantry because you were pregnant?"

"As former Lady Siquijor, what do you think will happen to your daughter?"

"Miss Thea, how's your relationship with *Direk* Everett? What do you think of Cleo, who was originally taking her father's path and is now representing the country?"

"Isn't your daughter too skinny for the competition?"

"I also heard about Cleo's breakup with Owen, the son of Mr. Luis, the CEO of Sta. Isabel Land Inc. Is it because of money?"

Thea understands her daughter has it worse than she did. It's been a long time since she's done this, but it has to be done. So, she flashes them her smile, and even without a gown or a crown on her head, she knows she's still got it.

"I would like to thank each one of you for taking an interest in my daughter, Cleo," Thea speaks to them softly, making sure they understand every word. When facing the public, always thank them first. "She's a great woman, and I'm proud of her."

Everyone's stopped asking questions. They're listening to Thea, as they should be. Her warmth makes them feel welcome. There's no need for the continuous firing of questions that are sometimes, well, more often than not, out of line.

Thea stands tall, one leg in front of the other. "I apologize to the people I disappointed years ago, but the past does not define who I am today. What I do today and tomorrow will define what will become of me. And I choose to be the mother of the Lady Pearl of the Philippines."

"Wow." Anne has come out to be with Thea, clapping her hands. Soon, everyone's applauding Thea as if she's just answered a Q and A. "*Ma*, you're good at this."

"I missed that." Thea laughs at herself, and instead of getting questions, she's getting a lot of picture-taking from the reporters.

"Leo's gonna flip when she sees this on TV." Anne makes a peace sign, winking at the cameras.

Thea hopes she's helped her daughter with the crowd, at least.

※　※　※

After the press presentation, Cleo goes back to the camp to help Dom prepare the final touches on her costume. Thankfully, they've both agreed on the design. It's a long day ahead, but her mind is still stuck on the issues of the other candidates. They were good women and didn't deserve what had been done to them. When she confronted Elle about it earlier, she was told she didn't know any better—that she should let an adult, a senior like her mentor, handle how she's going to win.

It sucks for Cleo because she's being treated like someone too naïve to know anything. She's an adult too. Elle might be older, but maturity doesn't come from age, does it?

Dom has turned on the TV in the welcoming room while Cleo touches the fabrics he's brought in. She's trying her best to focus on the task, but then she hears a familiar voice from the TV.

"Dom, turn the volume up."

Cleo turns around and sees Thea and Anne on TV. Her mother's talking about how proud she is of her.

"Isn't that sweet?" Dom comments, hands on his hips as he smiles. "Looks like you don't need to defend your mother. She's freaking Lady Siquijor."

"She is," Cleo says wistfully, and she knows she can't stop now. She's doing this for the mother she loves, who gave up everything because of her. "Let's get started."

"Honey, can you get the black bag in the trunk of my car? My sketchpads are in there, and I have my hands full at the moment," Dom requests, arms loaded with fabric.

Cleo's more than happy to help Dom; she doesn't want to stay still. They've only just arrived, but they have to keep things going. They're one week away from the competition, and they still have to keep her social media content updated. She's close to winning the hearts of the people. She only needs to . . . .

Elle's office door is ajar. Cleo's about to check in with Elle to announce her arrival back at the camp, but then she spots Guinevere and Deborah off to the side. It's been a while since she's last seen these two. She wonders where they've been, so she stays for a while, listening.

🌰 🌰 🌰

Guinevere crosses her legs, wearing her former sash. She and Debbie have been busy. Very busy, apparently.

"Remember Maria? She was close to winning the crown, but you exposed her as GRO," Guinevere muses, smiling at Elle, who's been staring at the papers on her desk for a while now. "You adored that girl, right? You took her in like a lost puppy. She used to be your charity project until the most attractive offer came in from Russia."

"And Maria doesn't matter anymore, right? She's a guest relations officer—a sex worker," Debbie adds, going around Elle's office and smiling at the posters of former beauty queens.

Guinevere throws her head back, laughing at Debbie's statement. "I mean, with such a great offer like the one you got from Russia, I could probably take a three-year vacation or so! So where did you spend the money, Elle?"

"Please keep your voices down," Elle pleads, her hands shaking.

"The Elle is begging?" Guinevere taunts. "Hey, Debbie, keep your voice down."

Debbie rolls her eyes. "You're the one who's too loud."

"Are you afraid your little Cleo will hear us?" Guinevere's enjoying this. It's not every day she gets to rile up the oh-so-great Elle. For years, the woman has been untouchable because of her influence and power, but everybody's got dirt.

Elle composes herself. "It was ten years ago. I did it to save the beauty camp. I was in a bad spot. I had to accept the bribe."

Guinevere doesn't believe her.

"Aren't you the one who taught us that the world is fair because it's unfair to everyone? We're only taking advantage of that fairness to keep that balance," Debbie explains, scrunching up her nose. "Maybe it's the end of an era for you, Elle. You've always been The Elle of pageantry. If we hadn't found out about the cheating you did in the past, we would still be looking up to you, you know."

"Not this way. I'm doing what you both wanted me to do, isn't that enough? I'm making Cleo cheat, so we could expose her in the end and let Lady Russia win. But please, let it be the last," Elle's voice is hoarse as if she's been screaming as much on the outside as on the inside.

Guinevere laughs and says, "That's what you said the last time. It's too bad Cleo's favored to win. Otherwise, we wouldn't be in this situation. She's just too good, isn't she?"

"It was the first and last time I did that. After that, I promised myself I would never do it again. I was desperate."

Deborah gets behind Elle and whispers, "You still cheated. This pageant is rigged. I don't believe in you anymore, Elle. What if you did that to us too so you can earn more money? Oh, how the tables have turned. You take us in as if we're your pets, but really, you just want to control us and take all the credit. And what do you know— your favorite candidate's about to hate you too."

"And who would refuse such an offer from Russia? This year's Lady Russia is a general's daughter, so naturally, the daughter would want to bring glory to her country. So do us a favor, Elle, and make sure our little Lady Nowhere wins the crown. Make her savor it because after that comes hell to pay for the sin you committed— exposure of her massive screw-up."

The Bigger They Come, The Harder They Fall

*e*lle is doomed, and there's nothing she can do about it. One way or another, she's bound to fall from her pedestal, her empire sacked by Guinevere and Deborah. But she taught them that—how to usurp the position of someone greater than themselves. She's pretty good at teaching these beauty queens how to rise to the occasion, but this one has backfired disastrously on her.

No matter what Elle does, Cleo will hate her. Every one of them has the right to hate her. Beauty queens who have come her way are entitled to the Elle Loathing Card. But they never dared cross her because of her influence, until Guin and Debbie. Of course, they'd discover that secret. They've been with Elle for five years, and somewhere along that road, they've become who she is.

Elle hasn't eaten anything all day. It's almost dinnertime, and she should have used the day to train Cleo, but she can't look her in the face, this woman who's hoping to win the crown for her mother. Elle's not only disappointing the child. She's also letting down the mother. How terrific.

"Elle?"

Elle masks her expression and invites Dom inside her office. "Yes?"

"I know you're busy, but Cleo left over an hour ago to be with her family for one night. No worries, though. We've finished the finer details of her costume, and will you be training her tomorrow?" Dom's staring at Elle like he's never done before, or maybe she's simply being paranoid.

Elle can't dwell on this forever. She has to follow through with Tweedledee and Tweedledum's orders. As they reminded her earlier, they're the boss. They're the new Elle. They think they know all about being "The Elle," but they're wrong. Her downfall is only the beginning of all the hard work they'll have to do to reach that title. The question is, if they do reach it, how long can they keep it up? Someone out there will always come into their lives to prove that they're not the smartest people in the room. It's the unpredictable wheel of life. Unlike them, she has made her peace with it.

"Yes, we'll resume training tomorrow," Elle assures Dom, noticing how he's traded his black leather toecap for a brown one. He's also rolled the sleeves of his polo. It seems that hanging out with Cleo has made him more . . . casual.

Dom smiles, but it doesn't reach his eyes. He brings out a white envelope and hands it over to Elle. "Cleo asked me to give this to you."

An envelope. Why does this remind Elle of Thea's withdrawal letter? She can only hope that Cleo's fate doesn't go in the same way her mother's did.

"What's this about?" Elle asks calmly, but deep inside she wants to run after Cleo. She can't have her candidate running off a week from the competition. She certainly can't fail Guin and Debbie.

Dom shrugs. "I don't know. I'll head out."

Elle likes Dom because he doesn't pry. His focus is solely on the job assigned to him. He's a good man, and she knows he'll be more than successful in the future. He also knows whom to trust. And for Cleo to win his heart—now that's a feat that only she can perform.

"Thank you."

Dom nods and closes the door.

Elle wonders why Cleo has decided to send an envelope through Dom. Curious, she opens the envelope and finds a short handwritten letter.

Dearest Elle,

As a short thank you for everything you've done and are doing for me, I feel like a celebration is in order. We're one week away from coronation night, and everyone's rooting for me. I wouldn't have made it this far if it weren't for you and your beauty camp. So, it would be my honor if you could come tonight and celebrate with me on our rooftop.

Love,
Cleo

Elle isn't a fan of any gathering, even if it's only going to be Cleo. And . . . Thea will be there. She's not sure she's ready to face Thea. But she owes the two women a visit to their home, if it's what they want. So, she thinks of this as the only chance they'll have to celebrate as a team. It's too bad it's the only thing she can give them.

Elle makes up her mind to go. She takes her bag and contacts her driver. When the car arrives, she gets the back seat and steels herself to face t past and the present ties. The night was young, and she thought she should bring something to their little party.

"Where to, ma'am?" the driver asks.

"To the nearest bakeshop."

Indeed, everyone loves cake. Not that the gesture could ever make amends for what she's doing to Cleo. Guilt consumes Elle and she wishes she could push it away. All the way to Cleo's home her thoughts gnaw at her. For the first time since she became the queen of queen-makers, she's afraid. And she doesn't like being afraid.

Her biggest fear is that once she steps into the home of these two beauty queens, they'll see through her, and she can't afford to give herself away.

Elle has never been this uncomfortable, but she's determined to go through with it. Just for one last time, they can act like everything's okay and she's their superhero. That's what everyone expects her to be. No one wonders how she's handling it, and it's better if they don't know. Not many people are willing to sacrifice so much for the things they want in life.

"We're here, ma'am," the driver announces as Elle stares at the modern two-story house with a rooftop. It's not a grand mansion, but it's not so small that no one has space to move around. It's an improvement over Thea's old house. Cleo worked hard for this.

Elle inhales sharply and murmurs her thanks to the driver. "I won't be long."

Elle steps outside, so this can all be over already. She waits at the rusting gate, calling Cleo to get her attention. They may have a lovely house, but the gate's another matter entirely. And maybe they should consider added a doorbell.

No answer, but a few minutes later, Elle sees Cleo rushing out to open the gate for her. Cleo doesn't look stressed at all. She's smiling warmly at her.

"Come in," Cleo says.

Elle feels like she's invading, even though she was invited. She's not one to visit people in their homes. In the entryway, though, she switches her heels to the bunny slippers Cleo provided. Not her kind of home footwear, but it's not like she has a selection to choose from.

The living room is decent. Nothing too ostentatious. A lamp, sofa, large screen TV, carpet, and a few potted plants. It's spacious, and it's everything they need. It's also well-kept—by Thea, Elle assumes. Thea has always loved keeping rooms spotless. Cleo, on the other hand, is not her mother.

"Mom's on the rooftop already. I thought it'd be nice to reconnect you two," Cleo Says.

Elle holds on to the cake like it's her ballast. It would have been nice to see Thea again, but not under these circumstances when she's out to ruin her daughter for the sake of keeping the beauty camp and her image alive.

"Oh, that will be lovely," Elle responds, stepping slowly and carefully on the stairs. She's stalling. She knows that. But now they've reached the rooftop, and there's no turning back.

"Good evening, Elle."

Elle stares. Thea's beauty hasn't faded. She's as lovely as she was back in her glory days. Her jet-black hair is in a bun, and the loose tendrils get in the way of her face, but there's no mistaking she's still the same island girl. She will always be the Lady Siquijor who almost won the nationals and would have been the Queen of the Universe if she hadn't become pregnant.

"I thought I taught you better than that. Your hair," Elle comments, smiling. She's pleased to know that her help hadn't gone to waste. Thea has done well, thriving in a life that does not involve fame.

Cleo offers Elle a glass of wine, and she gladly accepts it.

"I know." Thea smiles back, offering Elle a chair. "But I'm not a beauty queen anymore. I'm a mom, and moms focus first on other things, so spare me the lecture for now."

Motherhood suits Thea, Elle things as she sits in the armchair. "How have you been all these years?"

On the one hand, Elle doesn't need to ask because she already knows how Thea's been. She keeps track of Cleo and Everett, so she knows what's been happening. But she hasn't seen the woman in person for years. She hasn't known the invisible part—she could only try to guess whether her old friend has been happy all these years. Except that Thea radiates contentment.

"It's a beautiful life, Elle." Thea sits next to Elle while Cleo sits across from them.

Cleo watches them with curious eyes. "Even if I let old dreams get in the way sometimes. Part of my beautiful life is my crazy daughter," Thea laughs, glancing at Cleo. "How have you been, Elle? I'm sorry I haven't looked for you."

"I found your daughter anyway. Life is what it's always been since day one—a little rough around the edges, but I keep up. I learn from my mistakes. I do what I think is best." Elle gazes into the skies. Yes, she's been trying to live a good life. Nothing good is ever free, and now she's paying for that.

Thea holds Elle's hand. "You've made a name for yourself. No matter what people say of you, you will always be the Elle I know. That's the real Elle."

"People change, Thea," Elle replies.

Thea offers a toast to Elle. "As long as the change is good, then change is nothing to fear, right?"

"Always the good one," Elle murmurs under her breath, and she's sure Cleo's heard it because Cleo looks up at her.

"Well, I only came down to check on you and as I've been cleaning the house the whole day, I'm tired. So, I'll leave you two alone," Thea says.

Elle stands up and offers her hand, but Thea wraps her arms around her, whispering, "Thank you for taking care of my daughter. It means a lot to me."

Guilt is never a good feeling.

"You deserved that crown," Elle replies, and Thea only smiles, then retreats, leaving her and Cleo alone.

Cleo drinks her wine and looks at the moon. "Just how important is the beauty camp for you, Elle?"

"It's everything to me." Elle has devoted her entire life to that beauty camp. Every bead of sweat, every rejection, and sleepless night–it was all worth it. She can't be a beauty queen, but she can *make* queens. She got this far because of herself and not because of her mother, whose whole reason for being was to see her children win in life.

"What about the beauty queens you've trained?"

Elle ponders that.

"Do you trust me, Elle?" Cleo presses, staring at her with eyes, so fierce Elle's suddenly afraid of her.

Elle doesn't trust anyone. Not her family. Not Thea. And most certainly not Cleo. She can't bring herself to answer these questions, and she has no idea why Cleo's being intrusive. They've already agreed—no questions. And yet here she is.

"My mother thinks you're her miracle. You've saved a lot of dreams, Elle, including mine. I-I trust you more than anybody else," Cleo croaks out as if she were pleading for her life. "Do you know what my mom told me when I won the nationals?"

Elle keeps quiet, drinking her wine. She's not a miracle. She's a hoax—a perfect hoax. Why would Thea think she's anything more than that?

"'Cleo, take care of Elle. She can be hard on people sometimes—she's hard on herself too—but I know you're in good hands,'" Cleo quotes Thea.

Elle's hit by the hard truth that she's not a better human being for trying to save her beauty camp and herself. But someone who has women thanking her for saving them might not be such a bad person. And Thea hasn't lost any of her belief in her. It makes her heart warm. She hasn't had that feeling in a long time.

A tear slips from the corner of Elle's eye. She grips Cleo's arm and spills everything out. No more secrets.

"Being blackmailed is scary, but I'm asking you now to put your faith and trust in me. Can you do that?" Cleo asks, and for a moment there, Elle sees a woman without a crown but with eyes that can make anyone believe what she says. "Let me help, Elle. Let's help each other."

"Okay."

"Do you want me to share with you what I'm about to do?"

"No," Elle stops Cleo. "Better if I don't know. I might end up ruining it. And Cleo?"

"Yes, Elle?"

"I'm willing to face the consequences now."

Elle isn't used to sitting in the back and letting somebody else drive the car. This will be the first time in her life that she's ever let anyone do it, and by God's grace, she hopes they don't end up crashing into anything. If they do, she's glad she gets to rest in the back seat.

🔥 🔥 🔥

"That's your great plan? Is that even a plan at all?" Dom protests. "You're just going to keep training minus the cheating as if that makes any difference?"

Cleo shushes Dom, hands on her hips. "Yes. Any problem with that?"

Cleo has told her team, mainly Dom, Erik, and Aira, about what happened between her and Elle. It involves them taking shots and screaming "Why?!". Thankfully, they understand her motives. She can't change the past, but the present and future are hers to take.

Erik pats Dom's back. "She wants to win genuinely."

"The point is, Cleo's already cheated," Aira points out.

Cleo is tired of hearing the word "cheat." She knows what she did, and now she's trying to make things right.

"As Erik has said, I want to win genuinely," Cleo explains, her heels clicking on the marbled floor of the welcoming room as she exercises her footwork. "No more consulting Elle. I'll get involved in every decision that has to be made. We'll release daily videos until coronation night, and it'll be about getting to know the other candidates."

Dom looks puzzled. "Other candidates?"

"At this point, most of the candidates will already be polishing their walks. The mini talk show between us can be Q and As. We know how they answer, but do we really know who they are?"

"But you can't talk to all of them, and aren't you giving them airtime on your social media?" Dom fires back.

"Exactly. Think of this as a get-together before the coronation night. I think it's only fair for people to truly get to know some of the candidates whose reputation I've damaged," Cleo says, forever regretting that decision. "It'll balance them out. I know you never expected me to do what I did, and I'm terribly sorry I did it. I'd understand if you guys want to back out, but can you help me one last time?"

Dom smiles at Cleo, dropping his crossed arms. "It's a good plan, I admit it. It'll really help them gain the trust of the people again, especially in their home countries."

"I didn't like what you did, but I'm all for making it right again," Erik responds, and she understands he's wary of her right now, but she'll make it up to her team after all this is over.

Aira raises both her hands and smiles like the she-devil she is. "It's a promising story, so count me in."

The Queen of the Universe

ady USA

"Hi, Lady USA! How are you holding up so far?" Cleo asks, glad that Lady USA has agreed to a mini talk show. It also helps that since they're three days away from coronation night, they've all been put into the same hotel. So now she's going door to door, hoping to get a few minutes of their time.

Lady USA smoothes her blonde hair and smiles shyly at her. "Not fantastically, to be honest. But no matter what people say about me, I'm still trying my best to be their Lady USA. What I do with my face and my body is nobody's business. My body, my rules."

"That's so true, Lady USA."

"Yes. Thank you. I believe each one of us can grow. I wasn't always Lady USA, you know? I was once a child who was bullied because of my awkward face, and I know we should always love ourselves as we are, but that's not easy, and learning to do it is a long process. Joining this beauty pageant has helped build my confidence."

Lady Kenya

One of the women Cleo most admires is Lady Kenya. Cleo would go as far as to call her a girl crush. The woman has a stout heart and a strong mind. She's beautiful inside and out. "Is it okay if I ask you about . . ."

"Bulimia. Say it because it has a name, and it's a serious eating disorder," Lady Kenya says with a smile. "When I was a kid, I was skinny. I was malnourished. And then I was adopted, and my life improved, so I ate everything I could. I didn't want ever to feel hungry again, which was why I gained weight, and it scared me. I was afraid my adoptive mother might hate me for my figure and no one would ever want me again, so I . . . I suffered. I ate too much and then purged it out."

Cleo hates herself for doing this to Lady Kenya. She's bringing up issues they have battled with for so long. "I'm so sorry. How are you today?"

"I'm much better than I was yesterday. This pageant made me see how much better I am. But the main reason I'm here is that I don't want to see any more hungry children begging for love. I've been there, and it's terrible."

Lady Vietnam

Lady Vietnam wipes her tears away with a tissue. "I once had a sugar daddy because I needed the money for my mother who had cancer. Because of that man, I was able to extend my mother's life for a year, and it was the best year of my life. I have no regrets. So, if people hate me for it, that's fine. I did what I had to do then for my mother."

"I'm sorry you had to go through that," Cleo replies, and she is. Her heart breaks for Lady Vietnam. "I'm sure your mother is proud of the woman you've become today."

Lady Vietnam smiles warmly at Cleo. "I hope so, because I am."

Lady Lebanon

"Hi, Lady Lebanon. How are you?" Cleo begins, finding it more difficult to talk to the contestants she wronged. She feels crushed by her decisions, and doing this is just a tiny part of her apology.

Lady Lebanon laughs. "I'm free of all the hectic schedule as I am out of the competition. And yes, I was once married, and I thought I could hide that fact here because this was supposed to be my way of helping my people. I was married when I was only *fourteen*. And it wasn't by choice."

Cleo wants to apologize profusely to Lady Lebanon. She doesn't deserve this outcome. "Is there anything you would like to say? I know this can be barely called a stage, but I'm sure there are people out there who are still rooting for you."

"Well, then, if you're still rooting for me, thank you. I'll do what I can back home. I want to help the children live a good life and not be forced into marriage. My journey doesn't end here, and nor does yours."

♣   ♣   ♣

The day of the Queen of the Universe coronation night has arrived, and everyone's buzzing. Everyone in the country is treating it like a holiday. Some retail businesses have decided to close for the day, while barbershops and salons are open so people can watch the live telecast with them. They're even giving discounts on haircuts. All of social media is rallying behind Cleo, and it honestly feels fantastic.

While Cleo isn't able to talk to all the candidates, she's at least covered a few ladies here and there. And right at this very moment, she only has herself to worry about as backstage has grown even more hectic. Various perfumes cloud the air, and the sweat is no joke, so it doesn't smell all that good.

"Get ready," Dom says strictly, pressured but still maintaining his composure. He's pressing fresh powder on Cleo's face while she's applying lipstick.

It's a crazy day, and the chaos isn't subsiding in the slightest. Hairstylists and makeup artists are running all over the room carrying pins and adhesive tapes—probably due to a wardrobe malfunction. It's a whole new war.

Once the VTR has ended, Cleo knows it's showtime.

"Good luck," Dom tells Cleo in all seriousness.

Cleo attempts to keep it light, keep herself composed. "Thank you."

Cleo proceeds to the stage, a bit nervous but determined to win the crown. Since they're being called by continent, she comes together with her group in the Asia Pacific. Parading again, they line up, smiling brightly and showing off their pearly white teeth. Looking around, she finds the man she met at the restaurant, and funnily enough, he turns out to be one of the judges. She ignores him and focuses on the task at hand.

Staring out at a sea of people, Cleo's in awe of the glittering lights and dazzling star-speckled walls. She knows that the entire world's watching. It's the celebration of the beauty, heart, and soul of every woman.

As the competition progresses, Cleo's home country is called. She knows from that moment on she's doing this for the Philippines. Witnessing her bare soul carved out from the physical body are the people of her country, who have had their revolutions—many of them—through pen and sword. Tonight her heart beats with all of theirs, and she feels her oneness with every Filipino.

"How are you?" the host in a bow tie asks when he calls her name as one of the top twelve.

Smiling at him, a warm, genuine smile, Cleo answers, "I'm really, really good. Thank you."

"And what can you say about the challenges and the comments aimed at you with your mother being a former beauty queen?"

Cleo doesn't even need to think about this one. She can see the Philippine flag among the crowd, her *kababayans* supporting her. "If I win this crown, it will be for my mother as well as for me."

The crowd roars its approval, and Cleo gives them a wink, silently telling them she's got this.

Cleo smiles as she delivers her opening statement with her head held high. "*Mabuhay, Pilipinas!* As a woman, I would always hear the word no, not just in my community or my country, but everywhere in the world. No, you can't do that. No, you have to stay at home. No, you can't choose who to marry or even who to love. And I say: No, we will not be dictated to. Not anymore. I believe men and women must empower each other to break old norms and rise as human beings. *Maraming Salamat po!*"

The elimination round passes by in a flash. The candidates are down to the top six, and Cleo's still in the competition. In her VTR, she shares her story of what it's like to be an actress.

"When I was a kid, I knew I was going to be an actor. My dad, who is a renowned director, has been an absentee father. And for the longest time, I have been angry with him, so I promised myself I would make him proud of me someday. I became an actor, portraying the lives of people who came from different walks of life, and there is nothing more fulfilling than having the chance to tell their stories. I might have been chasing the wrong dream for a very long time, but I'm here today because of that dream. With me, I carry love for all people. I believe in people, in the feelings we all carry deep inside us. Fragile as we may all seem, we are most connected when we share our sentiments and passions."

Hearing the words coming from her, Cleo feels overwhelmed with emotion. This is her last stand, and although she hates the terrible mistakes she's made, she's proud of herself for learning so much on this journey. Soon, the candidates are out in their colorful swimsuits, switching from one leg to another as they saunter. Cleo walks confidently, happy with the body she has. The regular exercise and balanced diet were worth it in the end.

Strutting her body, Cleo doesn't feel exploited, the way she did when she was in TV shows that required her to wear a bikini. As she sashays on the stage, she feels like there's nothing wrong with her body, and she theorizes that part of the competition's aim is to make women feel comfortable with the bodies they have. And in her yellow two-piece suit, she owns her body, and no one has the right to tell her what to do with it.

Backstage and in preparation for the evening gown competition, Dom takes care of Cleo's needs again. Staring at the exquisite emerald backless gown he has designed, she knows that this one is a winner. They took inspiration from a *diwata*, a fairy from

Mount Makiling, because she had provided well for the people. She appeared in every storm that surged, restoring nature to its original state.

"Do you like it?

"Why wouldn't I like it? We worked on it together," Cleo beams, giving Dom a small smile. "I love it. Thank you so much for everything, Dom."

Relieved, Dom smirks at Cleo, fixing her hair. "What would you ever do without me? I'm proud of you."

Cleo leans back and closes her eyes. If it takes everything she has in her, she's going to make things right.

After wearing the evening gown and re-touching her makeup, she's back on the stage again. The people on the internet have named her walk *The Maria Makiling* walk. Elegant and striking, the walk spoke of rebirth, constant growth, and the flourishing of a person who went through life's greatest storm.

"Oh, and would you look at that. She's so at ease with her gown, and she walks as if she's the goddess of nature," the commentator observes. "Watching her on the stage takes me to the beautiful forest."

The crowd went wild and their cheers came louder. They're shouting only one word: Philippines.

Cutting down the list again with the top three, Cleo hears her name again. And for the very first time, she feels that she can do it. On her own. Without any under-the-table deals. It means so much to her since she has finally learned how to trust herself. She's going to be in this competition until the very last walk.

In the long-awaited question-and-answer portion, Cleo smiles naturally. She's happy with what she's doing. Being the first one to answer, she's nervous, but she keeps her face calm.

The question given to Cleo is: "How would you empower women as 'The Queen of the Universe'?"

Cleo takes a deep breath and answers the question in a smooth, clear voice. "As The Queen of the Universe, I would immerse myself in the home, workplace, and public spaces for both men and women. Empowerment begins in the smallest part of society, and I believe that men must also be empowered to understand the status and the state that we, women, are currently in. Empowerment, for me, means recognizing the rights of a person."

Wrapping up the competition, Cleo's left with Lady Russia and Lady Kenya. They're the top three vying to be the next Queen of the Universe. Cleo's holding her breath. Until things had transpired to this point, deep down she'd been full of doubt that she'd get this far. But even with everything she went through, and what she has planned, she has no regrets about being in this Queen of the Universe competition.

The top three look out to the audience with their dazzling smiles as the announcement begins. The end of the pageant was going to be a new beginning for someone.

"And now the moment you've all been waiting for!" the host teases, holding an envelope that contains the result. "The second runner-up for Queen of the Universe is . . ."

Cleo prays silently.

"Kenya!"

Cleo cheers for Kenya, giving her a huge smile. Finally, the moment everyone has been waiting for has come. It's either Cleo or Lady Russia. Facing each other, they hold each other's hands.

"You have both been beautiful and amazing throughout your journey, but only one of you will be crowned the next Queen of the Universe," the host reminds them.

Cleo's terrified. What she longs for is to become the Queen that serves her people. She envisions a bright future not only for her country but also for the entire world. She wants to be the woman that renews and restores the spirits and hearts of others. And she'll do just that, no matter what happens, because she is no longer a pawn in this game.

"The Queen of the Universe is . . ."

Catching her breath, Cleo bows her head, humbled by the

extraordinary ladies she's gotten the chance to be with during the competition.

"PHILIPPINES!"

The home crowd erupts, all of them chanting her name: Cleo Walter, The Queen of the Universe.

Cleo's immediately enfolded in Lady Russia's arms.

"Congratulations!" Lady Russia says, smiling.

It's a beautiful moment as Cleo receives her Queen of the Universe sash. The crown. exquisitely encrusted with diamonds, comes next. It's every little girl's dream and then some. From her mother's island to Manila, she's brought home two crowns and sashes. She's given her country a public figure, a queen who embodies the true Filipina. They may be a small country, but the citizens' fighting spirit makes them bigger than any crisis.

"Take your first walk as the Queen of the Universe." The host looks at Cleo, a grin on his face.

But this is just the beginning. Cleo smiles for the audience and the cameras—and removes the crown from her head. The crowd gasps, and the host tries to help her get the crown back to her head, but then when he sees that she's doing this on purpose, he backs away, gawking at her.

"I can't accept this," Cleo announces. She looks toward Lady Russia, who smiles and takes a step forward. "The first runner-up is also not a legitimate contender."

Cleo steps to Lady Kenya's side and puts the crown on her head. "I give you the true Queen of the Universe."

Lady Kenya covers her mouth, astonished. The audience is baffled but on their feet, clapping. They don't know what's happening, but they know this deserves a standing ovation. Cleo whispers something to the host, who gives her the mic.

"I cheated to win the crown, and so did Lady Russia, and for that, I apologize from my heart to every one of you." Cleo stares at the crowd and the Philippine flag. "My countrymen, I am ashamed of what I have done. None of you deserve this. I have no excuses.

Systems aren't the only things that can be rigged. People can easily give in to temptation. I've been such a person. I've been corrupted, I may not have intended that, but I did what I did regardless, for my mother and father. I was wrong in many things, but what I do know is that this competition shouldn't be about an individual winning a title or a crown—it should be about our country."

Nobody is moving. Cleo launches into the story of how she got herself into this mess and how she's regretted all of it. She knows what she did is wrong, so she's not even going to defend herself. She's also shared what happened in the past with Elle's cheating to save the camp and how Guinevere and Deborah are blackmailing her now so Lady Russia can win once again. She hasn't filtered anything; she spills the truth because the watchers, the judges, the contestants—past and present—all deserve it.

This is what Cleo's been planning all along. She'd expose herself rather than let Guinevere and Deborah do it for her.

"What if you didn't win?" the host interrupts Cleo. "Wouldn't this plan fail?"

Cleo smiles sadly at the host. "I knew I was going to win because I cheated. Elle made sure I'd win. But I don't want to win based on a fake version of myself. I don't want to win through a lie. I'm taking off the crown so I can step up to something more—to free myself, to do important things. I've also come to realize that the power is not just in the crown—it's in the woman herself."

Suddenly, Elle arrives on the stage, pulling Cleo to her chest and murmuring her thanks. She stands on the center stage, taking the mic from Cleo. "This is not entirely her fault. If you must blame someone, here I am. I am *The* Elle, and I used Cleo Walter. I did it because I love the Filipino people. We wanted to win. I made it happen so I could sustain the beauty camp and keep on trying to make it happen. If I made mistakes along the way, I did it because I love my country and I want to do all I can to help us be seen and recognized. But while my reasons were right, my actions were wrong, and I am sorry. Nobody deserves to be used and nobody deserves less than a fair and honest pageant."

Cleo waves goodbye to everyone. She takes her final walk and goes backstage. Dom welcomes her with open arms and she bolts to him, crying.

"I'm sorry, Dom."

"Shh," Dom caresses Cleo's back. "You're not your father, Cleo. You owned up to it."

"I owned up to it."

And that's enough to make Cleo feel better.

Epilogue

The Philippines and Russia are banned from joining the Queen of the Universe pageant for three years as a penalty. Meanwhile, Elle gets to retire and quietly enjoy what remains of her camp. Guinevere and Deborah left the country for good without a letter or word of apology. For her part, Cleo has decided to immerse herself in the projects and activities of local government. She feels that she needs to understand what's happening right here before she can go on to achieve whatever might be waiting for her.

The problem with the system is that some people in high positions have never been in the trenches, so how can they serve anyone but themselves?

And yes, Cleo's getting all kinds of glares and strange looks from people, but that no longer matters to her. What is important to her is that she's actually doing something meaningful and authentic. Apologizing to her countrymen was a small start, but slowly, she's being welcomed again and not as Cleo from the TV shows. Not the Cleo who's passive. Not the Cleo who was led around by Elle. But the Cleo who's living an ordinary life for now.

Cleo might have fallen from the ranks, but she still has Dom, Aira, Erik, Chezka, and even Nadia and Julia. And her family? They're proud of her. The world has come to know her as the Queenslayer—the woman who abdicated her crown and exposed herself and the rotten icing on the cake. She's both the hero and the villain in the story, and she's made quite a name for herself, as she's all over the tabloids, news, radio, and TV. But she hasn't given a single interview. She needs that break.

After a year, Cleo received a letter of invitation to Erik's art photography studio. She's happy he's doing what he loves. As for Dom, he has pursued his dream of designing for a branded fashion line. He even gave some of his pieces to Anne, who happily accepted them. So, Erik's invitation to them—extended to Chezka, Nadia, and Julia, too—is a grand reunion for all of them.

Cleo's fallen in love with Erik's beautiful iridescent photos— images he's captured of the places he has been.

"Does he sell this?" Chezka asks.

Dom looks around and says, "Probably. Would you buy it?"

Chezka and Dom's conversation evaporates into thin air when Cleo spots Erik in a black and white suit. This isn't his usual attire, so she can't help but laugh at him on the rare occasions he dresses up.

Erik gestures for Cleo to follow him, and in the middle of all the photos is a large one of a beautiful woman. It's the only black and white photo out of all the other pieces in the studio. Written below the frame is:

The Dark Knight of the Soul.
Through light and darkness, I have loved her.

"Now, this is juicy," Nadia remarks, glancing at Cleo.

Flushing, Cleo laughs in surprise and delight. It's a picture of her practicing her smile at the camp, and she looks happy and contented. She has never felt so appreciated in her entire life. His words and photo of her have tugged at her heartstrings.

"Do you like it?"

Cleo smiles at Erik. "I love it."

And then they all look again: at the corner of Cleo's photograph is a girl in her late teens, looking up at the picture and copying Cleo's sweet smile with a pen between her lips.

"Books to Span the East and West"

Tuttle Publishing was founded in 1832 in the small New England town of Rutland, Vermont [USA]. Our core values remain as strong today as they were then—to publish best-in-class books which bring people together one page at a time. In 1948, we established a publishing outpost in Japan—and Tuttle is now a leader in publishing English-language books about the arts, languages and cultures of Asia. The world has become a much smaller place today and Asia's economic and cultural influence has grown. Yet the need for meaningful dialogue and information about this diverse region has never been greater. Over the past seven decades, Tuttle has published thousands of books on subjects ranging from martial arts and paper crafts to language learning and literature—and our talented authors, illustrators, designers and photographers have won many prestigious awards. We welcome you to explore the wealth of information available on Asia at **www.tuttlepublishing.com**.

Published by Tuttle Publishing, an imprint of Periplus Editions (HK) Ltd.

www.tuttlepublishing.com

Copyright © 2023 by Pia Alonzo Wurtzbach

Published by arrangement with ABS-CBN Books, Quezon City, Philippines

Library of Congress publication data is in progress

ISBN 978-0-8048-5695-9

Distributed by:

North America, Latin America & Europe
Tuttle Publishing
364 Innovation Drive
North Clarendon VT 05759 9436, USA
Tel: 1(802) 773 8930
Fax: 1(802) 773 6993
info@tuttlepublishing.com
www.tuttlepublishing.com

Asia Pacific
Berkeley Books Pte Ltd
3 Kallang Sector #04-01
Singapore 349278
Tel: (65) 6741 2178
Fax: (65) 6741 2179
inquiries@periplus.com.sg
www.tuttlepublishing.com

26 25 24 23
5 4 3 2 1   2307VP
Printed in Malaysia

TUTTLE PUBLISHING® is a registered trademark of Tuttle Publishing, a division of Periplus Editions (HK) Ltd.